To all of those who still have the heart of a child
— M. C.

To Ambra, Maria, and Michele
— L. M.

First Edition

ISBN 0-316-14922-5

Library of Congress Catalog Card Number 93-86640

10 9 8 7 6 5 4 3 2 1

Printed in Spain

Marianne Cockenpot   Lorenzo Mattotti

EUGENIO

Little, Brown and Company
Boston New York Toronto London

This is the beginning of a story that has been told many times and in many different ways. The lesson of the story, however, never changes. . . .

Once upon a time a beautiful baby was born to a young couple, and they named him Eugenio. The sad fact of the matter was that this couple was so poor that they often went hungry. They feared that their precious babe might starve, and they wondered how they could give him a better life.

"I hear that circus people have heart," said Eugenio's mother. "They will take care of my little one." So with heavy hearts they brought Eugenio to the circus grounds and placed him next to the most beautiful trailer there. They left a note in the baby's basket explaining their plight, and after taking one last look at their son's eyes, they turned and disappeared into the night.

Imagine his surprise when only moments later Georgio, the magician, stumbled on the sleeping babe. The baby's coos and gurgles went straight to Georgio's heart, and after he read the note, he immediately took the waif in from the cold darkness and made him his son.

Many years passed since that fateful night, and the baby, being raised in the tradition of the circus, grew up to be the one, the only, the fabulous clown, Eugenio. He was the most popular performer in the whole circus. Every night when the clowns, the elephants, and the other fantastic creatures of the circus tumbled into the big top, children would cheer most loudly when Eugenio made his appearance.

But one night when the drums rolled and the spotlight
sought him out . . . Eugenio did not appear.

The audience chanted his name, "Eugenio . . . Eugenio," but the clown never made an entrance. Finally the other clowns went to find him. They discovered him sitting alone behind the scenes, and asked him what was wrong.

"Tonight when I began to think of all those people cheering for me, I suddenly began to feel so sad," said Eugenio. "I can no longer make others smile. Something — I'm not sure what, but something — is missing from my life."

It was true. Eugenio had lost his most precious possession, his talent for joy.

"We circus people help each other," said Co-Co, another one of the clowns. "What you should do, Eugenio, is seek out the advice of the other performers. Some of them are quite wise, you know."

"Perhaps you are correct," Eugenio said with a sigh. "It can do no harm to ask the others, and maybe one of them will tell me how I might find my laugh again."

First he went to see Hush, the ventriloquist, who was practicing his new act with a huge dinosaur balloon.

Eugenio tilted back his head and called up to the ventriloquist, "Hush, I need some advice. I feel very sad. Do you know what might make me happy again?"

The dinosaur suddenly roared out, "I can tell that circus parades will not make you feel better, . . . nor cotton candy cheer you up. Many applaud and love you, but I sense that is not enough. Be still. Listen to your heart. It will tell you. . . ." And the dinosaur turned its head and stalked away.

"Wait!" cried Eugenio. "It will tell me what?"

He ran after the beast, but he tripped on its giant tail and fell headlong. When Eugenio got to his feet, Hush and the huge balloon were gone off into the night.

Next Eugenio went to see the acrobatic Flip-Flop sisters. He asked them for their advice.

"Ah, Eugenio," said Flop. "Life is a balancing act. Your sadness must be equal to your joy or else all will end poorly."

"My sister is right," cried Flip. "Only your laugh will keep you upright. Try to find it before it is too late!"

"Tell me how," begged Eugenio. "Give me a clue." But the sisters became so involved with their new trick that they didn't answer.

"You must be strong, Eugenio. Don't feel sorry for yourself," said Roko, the strongman, when the clown asked him his advice. "With strength you can overcome anything." And with that he reached out and hoisted little Fantino into the air.

"Nonsense!" exclaimed Fabuloso, the conjurer. "Once you learn that life is only a series of illusions, you will be able to laugh again. Just pick the illusion you like and keep it for your own." Fabuloso gestured grandly and summoned a huge buzzard from a paper egg. "Choose what you want, choose what you need," the buzzard called and flew up to the top of the circus tent.

"But I don't know what I need," said Eugenio sadly. "None of this advice is very helpful."

"Why, you're all twisted up," said Mash-Mish, the contortionist, descending on a trapeze. "Too many people have given you too much advice. Pay no attention to any of them. Simply go off, find a friend, and then do something that gives you both pleasure. That's sure to straighten you out."

"Thank you, Mash-Mish," said Eugenio, and he went off to find his friend Snowy, the bear.

"Eugenio," said Snowy when he heard of his friend's trouble, "music has charms that can make anyone feel happier. Come, play with me."

As his friend tapped out a remembered childhood tune, Eugenio picked up his old concertina. There was no question about it, the music did make him feel better.

Just then there came a rapping on the door.

"What is it?" Eugenio demanded. "Leave me alone. I think
I might be about to get my laugh back again."

"Eugenio, come quick!" called Fabuloso. "We have all been discussing your sad case, and we have decided we must take you to Madame Cobra, the fortune-teller who lives over the hill. We should have thought of this much earlier."

"How can that sly old snake help me?" Eugenio asked.

"Don't worry," said Mash-Mish. "She can see into everyone's future. She is sure to tell you if you will ever feel happy again."

With that, they popped Eugenio into a small wooden chair. As storm clouds and lightning danced across a fantastic horizon, they carried him off to see the scaly fortune-teller.

ATLAS OF
MESOPOTAMIA

Examine the substructure, view the brickwork.
Is the brickwork not of brick?
Did the Seven Sages not lay the foundation?

EPIC OF GILGAMESH, TABLET I, ll. 17-19

MARTIN A. BEEK

PROFESSOR OF OLD TESTAMENT EXEGESIS
UNIVERSITY OF AMSTERDAM

ATLAS
OF
MESOPOTAMIA

*A survey of the history and civilisation of Mesopotamia
from the Stone Age to the fall of Babylon*

TRANSLATED BY D. R. WELSH, M. A.

EDITED BY

H. H. ROWLEY M.A., B.LITT., D.D., LL.D., F.B.A.
EMERITUS PROFESSOR OF HEBREW LANGUAGE AND LITERATURE
UNIVERSITY OF MANCHESTER

NELSON

1962

THOMAS NELSON AND SONS LTD
LONDON AND EDINBURGH

THOMAS NELSON AND SONS
NEW YORK

THOMAS NELSON AND SONS
(CANADA) LTD
TORONTO

THOMAS NELSON AND SONS LTD
JOHANNESBURG
MELBOURNE

SOCIÉTÉ FRANÇAISE D'ÉDITIONS NELSON
PARIS

———————ELSEVIER INTERNATIONAL EDITIONS———————

The *Atlas of Mesopotamia* has been published in
English (Thomas Nelson and Sons Ltd, London and Edinburgh)
German (Gütersloher Verlagshaus Gerd Mohn, Gütersloh)
Dutch (N.V. Uitgeversmaatschappij Elsevier, Amsterdam)

N.V. UITGEVERSMAATSCHAPPIJ ELSEVIER
© 1962
THOMAS NELSON AND SONS LIMITED

ORIGINALLY PUBLISHED AS ATLAS VAN HET TWEESTROMENLAND (ELSEVIER AMSTERDAM)

Foreword

The Atlas of Mesopotamia directs our attention to a region which may justly be regarded as the cradle of European civilisation, in so far as this was influenced by Judaism and Christianity. The Bible informs us that Abraham originated from Ur of the Chaldees, a city which we may perhaps identify with the Ur in south Iraq, west of the Euphrates, excavated by Sir Leonard Woolley. The narratives about the patriarchs thereafter make mention of the connections existing with the district of Haran, which lay enclosed behind the great bend of the northerly course of the Euphrates. The historical and the prophetic books of the Old Testament alike bear witness not only to the alarm aroused throughout Palestine by the Assyrians and to the exile of Israel and Judah under the heavy yoke of a Sargon or a Nebuchadnezzar, but also to the cultural and religious influence which Nineveh and Babylon exerted there.

It is therefore not surprising that a curiosity inspired by interest in the Bible should turn towards the region where men thought that they had found again Noah's Ark, the Tower of Babel, and even traces of the Garden of Eden. To seek for such things in the land of the two great rivers proved perhaps rather disappointing for some, but for most it might be compared to the journey of Saul, who went to seek his father's asses and found a kingdom. On the banks of the Euphrates and the Tigris, of their tributaries, and of the age-old irrigation canals, a culture was found which had flourished for centuries and which could speak through both its monuments and its literature. From the time when perhaps 7,000 years ago men in the mountains of modern Kurdistan passed through one of the most momentous transitions in the history of civilisation, that from food gathering to food producing, to the fall of Babylon in 539 B.C., the culture of Mesopotamia is recognisable by its individual hallmark.

It is a somewhat unsatisfactory undertaking to compress these forty-five centuries of the history of civilisation into brief compass, all the more as the material at our disposal has grown to unmanageable bulk. This applies both to the objects exhibited in museums and to literature. It is especially the cuneiform literature recorded upon clay that gives us insight into the daily life of Mesopotamia in all its facets. To this material we are indebted for authentic texts, sometimes tens of thousands of them from a single period and from a single region. And what varieties of interest are not involved in these texts? Theology, law, economics, medicine, astronomy, philology, mathematics, history, literature — to name a number of categories at random, are all well represented, and each of them now demands a specialisation to which a scholar could devote his whole life. Thus we have become increasingly aware that foundations were laid by the Sumerians in south Mesopotamia upon which we have without knowing it continued to build; and thence it is that the great expert on Sumerian civilisation, S. N. Kramer, could give his excellent book on the subject the challenging title: *History Begins at Sumer*.

We are not conscious of our dependence on our spiritual ancestors. It would be a rewarding experience to follow the life of an educated European step by step through a whole day, and from action to action remind him of the spiritual inheritance of the ancient world, from the moment in the morning when his alarm-clock goes off and, still half-asleep, he looks to see what time it is and has recourse to the culture of the Mesopotamian scholars, to whom he owes the division of the day into hours and of the hours into minutes.

An atlas of this kind gives more to see than to read. Thus the written sources come off badly. It is however a consoling reflection that so much of these has been made readily accessible to every one by good translations. This applies especially to the masterpiece of Babylonian-Assyrian literature, the heroic epic of Gilgamesh. In addition compilations of texts of importance for their contemporary association with the Old Testament have appeared in both German and English and have long fulfilled a useful function in Biblical exegesis. To these the user of this atlas is referred if he wishes to read sources, even if only in translation. This atlas counts on the characteristic, becoming increasingly recognised in the age of television, of man as 'an animal who sees'.

In choosing the illustrations the purpose has been to communicate to the viewer something of the wonder which must fill the visitor to the Iraq Museum of Antiquities in Baghdad when he contemplates the results of creative skill from period after period displayed there. To these magnificent collections I am indebted for the enthusiasm required to bring this atlas to completion, much though it necessarily leaves unshown and unspoken. But above all I am indebted to the unforgettable journey that I was privileged to make in the winter of 1956 throughout the whole of Iraq in company with my friend Dr P. Buringh. My travelling companion, who as a soil expert in the service of the Iraqi government had learnt to know the land through and through, passed on to me valuable information and arresting insights. I will further express the hope that the co-operation of soil experts and archaeologists, which in the low-lying lands of the Netherlands has already shown itself so fruitful at the mouths of the great rivers, may be extended to Mesopotamia also. I am convinced that many striking results would emerge from this, especially in what concerns the earliest history of Mesopotamia, as to which such stubborn misconceptions are still prevalent.

In planning this atlas I asked myself carefully to whom its contents were primarily addressed. In this I was not to think overmuch of the small circle of specialists, who will certainly possess in their libraries, in books and journals, everything that they find collected here. In any case they have a much more copious and better documented compilation in the work of Svend Aage Pallis, *The Antiquity of Iraq* (Copenhagen, 1956); I must record gratefully that I have often profitably consulted its wealth of material. I have, however, in writing, in choosing the illustrations, in composing the maps, thought rather of the wide interests of the educated layman. In this I kept before my eyes as an inspiration the articles written by Dr G. Roux on Mesopotamian antiquity in the monthly *Iraq Petroleum*. It is greatly to be regretted that his series had to be cut short when the journal ceased to exist in 1959.

Although the composition of an atlas such as this can speak for itself, I will however say one more word as to my purpose. It seemed well to me first to transport the reader to the soil and climate of Mesopotamia, because in many respects they conditioned the inhabitants' conception of the world. Then I would make him share the adventure of the discoveries, both of the buried sites and of the literature in cuneiform script. The sketches and engravings of the pioneers can help us to experience afresh, as it were, their emotion and their astonishment.

In treating of the history of civilisation I have not consistently maintained chronological order, so that in this way what belongs together thematically might better be kept together. Thus I have not divided the two periods of the Sumerian culture by the domination of Agade but have placed this Semitic interlude separately at a later point in the order of events. I hope, moreover, that the division into chapters and subsections will facilitate study of the material.

I long hesitated as to whether I should include also illustrations which overstepped the bounds of the Mesopotamian civilisation, both in time and place. I finally yielded to the argument that the expression of a culture gains relief by comparison with its closest environment and its most immediate heirs. Therefore a few products of the sculpture of Asia Minor and Persia have been included.

I am conscious of having given only a fraction of the factual material that is now at our disposal. But I have endeavoured to make the most profitable use possible of my space. This means that the text, the illustrations with their letterpress, and the maps, must complement without repeating one another. I trust that taken together they may indicate the broad lines of what we know so far of our spiritual ancestors in Mesopotamia.

M. A. BEEK

Contents

The Land and Climate of Mesopotamia

THE INHABITED GROUND (see Map 5)

Mesopotamia, the 'land between the rivers', is the name given by the Greek historian Polybius (second century B.C.) and the geographer Strabo (first century A.D.) to a part of the region enclosed between the Euphrates and the Tigris. They confined the name to an area stretching from the edge of the highlands in the north, where the rivers enter the plain, to what is now Baghdad, where the Euphrates and Tigris approach each other most closely. Not until later did the name acquire a much wider significance than that intended by the two Greeks, and it came to include southern 'Chaldaea'. When we speak of Mesopotamia nowadays, we always mean the whole of the region between the great rivers, from the mountain country to the Persian Gulf.

The name Mesopotamia became known in Europe as a result of the translation of the Bible. The Old Testament (Gen. 24 : 10) mentions a district called Aram Naharaim, which literally means 'Aram of the two rivers'. The Hebrew writer probably did not mean the Euphrates and the Tigris. It is more likely that he was referring to the Euphrates and the Khabur. But when the translator of the Old Testament in Alexandria was searching for a Greek equivalent, he hit upon the name Mesopotamia, which was subsequently introduced into the cultural sphere of Christianity by way of numerous Bible translations. To readers of the Bible Mesopotamia became a familiar sound, a word full of associations, because it designated the country from which came the father of the faithful, Abraham.

For us, therefore, the term Mesopotamia covers a variety of regions between the mountains of Kurdistan in the north and the marshes of the river delta in the south, between the steppes and deserts in the west and the mountain slopes of Iran in the east. Virtually the whole of this area is now included in the Republic of Iraq. The etymology of the Arab name Iraq is uncertain. Some think it can be translated as 'cliff', suggesting that the heights facing the traveller who approaches from the southwestern steppe have given their name to the whole country on the principle of *pars pro toto*.

If we wish to conjure up clearly the form of the ancient civilisation which flourished for roughly 4,000 years, from the Stone Age to the fall of Babylon in 539 B.C., it is exceedingly important that we should know under what conditions of climate and terrain its inhabitants lived. Over the last few years most intensive investigations have been carried out in which modern methods have been applied, extensive use being made, for example, of aerial photography. These have given astonishing results and are now compelling us to revise many traditional ideas on the subject.

The climate has not changed significantly since the time when the mountain dwellers came down to the river plains and began to develop primitive agriculture there in the fifth millennium B.C. This migration to the river valleys, like that from the Sahara to Egypt, must have been the result of climatic changes. These must have taken place slowly, almost imperceptibly to human awareness, over a period of generations, although their consequences were much more drastic than those of battles lost or technical achievements. Geologists speak of pluvial and interpluvial periods in which the rainfall, the rise and fall of the sea coast, and temperature fluctuations determined the lot of humanity until relative stability was reached about 5000 B.C. From then on the inhabitants of Mesopotamia lived in climatic conditions which probably differed little from those existing at present.

The soil, however, has suffered very great changes, mainly as a result of layers of sediment deposited by the rivers, whilst aeolian formations have also contributed, though in a smaller measure. We will now examine in greater detail what these mean to the soil of Mesopotamia.

THE PROBLEM OF THE COAST-LINE

It is a well-known fact that the Euphrates and the Tigris and their tributaries bring down vast quantities of material from the mountain country and deposit it along their lower courses. The resultant sediments are on an average 16 to 23 feet thick, while in some places they even cover the original soil to a depth of 36 feet with their thick and impenetrable carpets. Calculations have shown that the Tigris sometimes removes as much as 3,000,000 tons of eroded material from the highlands in a single day. According to other computations the Euphrates and Tigris together remove 76.2×107 cubic feet of alluvium annually. It was formerly thought that all this material was conveyed to the Persian Gulf and that it caused the coast there to advance in a southerly direction. That is why on most maps drawn to illustrate the state of things in antiquity the famous city of Ur is shown to be only a few miles distant from the sea.

The reasoning behind this seemed logical enough but made no allowance for several facts which have only come to light in the last few years. It has been found, for instance, that the rivers have deposited all their sediment by the time they reach the sea. The amount conveyed thither by the Shatt el-'Arab, in which the Euphrates and Tigris converge, is practically negligible. So there is no reason to assume that the coast of the Persian Gulf has been extended southwards by successive deposits of alluvium. There are in fact geologists who believe, on the basis of research by Lees and Falcon, Dennis and Wright, that the coast originally lay farther south than it does now. Aerial photographs taken over the Persian Gulf are thought to show traces of ancient habitations which were covered by the gradual rise of the sea level. To this theory archaeologists object that hardly any traces of civilisation have ever been found farther south than Eridu. The explanation, however, might be that these traces are not to be found on the surface but deep under the layer of silt that covers the soil of Mesopotamia.

If the latest theories on this subject are carefully considered, the question arises how it is possible that the lakes and marshes have not disappeared. The enormous quantities of silt that the rivers have deposited in the course of thousands of years must surely, it is argued, have filled the lakes up. For this region is like low-lying land raised to make a building site by pumping sand and water on to it, a process that can be seen on any site reclaimed in modern times from sea or marsh. The water drains off and the sand deposit raises the level of the site. If that has not happened in Mesopotamia, it can only be because the ground there has subsided. In that case the subsidence must have kept pace with the rate at which silt was deposited. When the ground sinks in one particular area, it can be expected to rise in another. Such a rise has in fact been observed in the hills between Iraq and Persia. Aerial photographs reveal that canals here have risen approximately 20 feet since the time of the Sassanids (third to seventh centuries A.D.).

The archaeologist has to make due allowance for these facts about the change in the soil, for they place the question of the earliest human habitation of southern Mesopotamia in an entirely new light. He is

9

sometimes compelled to abandon drilling because the ground-water level has risen. It is certainly for this reason that the Babylon of Hammurabi (eighteenth century B.C.) is beyond the reach of the digger's spade. Even when the archaeologist thinks he has reached the virgin soil, he must stop to wonder whether this is not a layer of sediment and whether the remains of important early settlements, if not cities, lie buried beneath it.

For archaeologists, who possess other source material than that of the geologists and soil experts, the problem of the Persian Gulf coast-line is far from simple. They have, for instance, an inscription of King Shulgi, who reigned ca. 2000 B.C., which reads, 'Shulgi, the son of Ur-Nammu, devoted special care to the city of Eridu, which lay on the sea coast.' In the view of Lees and Falcon, published in the *Geographical Journal* of March 1952, Eridu cannot have been situated nearer the sea in ancient times than it is now. But it is also certain from the age-old traditions of the Sumerians that Eridu was associated with the sea. That is also true of Ur, where ships were a familiar sight and which possessed a reasonable harbour. The latter fact can be explained if we realise that the Euphrates was navigable and was connected to a river port by a side canal. At the same time we must ask ourselves what was meant by the 'sea coast'. Perhaps people considered the extensive area of swamps, where small settlements could maintain themselves on the islets but no city could prosper, as forming part of the sea. At any rate Ur and Eridu were considered by the ancients to be market towns with regular access to the sea by ships.

There are few texts containing accurate information about the distances from identifiable places to the coast. One such text contains a statement by the Assyrian king Sennacherib, who in 694 B.C. undertook amphibian military operations against Babylon and Elam. This action was primarily directed against Merodach-baladan, the king of Babylon, who is mentioned in 2 Kings 20 : 12-19 as sending an envoy to Hezekiah. For this purpose Sennacherib built a fleet with the assistance of shipwrights from Tyre, Sidon, and even Cyprus, with which the Assyrians, who knew it as Yadnan, had long maintained trade relations. The fleet thus built with technical assistance from abroad was stationed partly at Nineveh and partly at Til Barsip on the upper reaches of the Euphrates. The Nineveh detachment sailed downstream to the vicinity of Opis, which was probably not far from the subsequent site of Seleucia. From here the ships were transported overland to the Arakhtu canal (the Euphrates by Babylon). Then the two fleets linked up and continued together to the Persian Gulf. This arrangement suggests that the lower reaches of the Euphrates were more navigable than those of the Tigris. Sennacherib's soldiers finally arrived at a place called Bab Salimetti, which is expressly stated to be a distance of 'two double hours over land' from the 'terrifying sea'. Thus, if we had some means of knowing where Bab Salimetti was situated we would have a fixed point from which to mark off about twelve miles to the sea coast. The text also relates that the soldiers crossed the Persian Gulf in the vessels and disembarked in order to fall on Elam like swarms of locusts. In thanksgiving for his victory Sennacherib threw a small golden ship, a golden fish, and a golden crab into the sea as votive offerings to the gods who had assisted him. During the entire operation Sennacherib's headquarters had been at Bab Salimetti. It was not till afterwards that Babylon was sacked, an event which so terrified even the inhabitants of Bahrain that they hastened to offer tribute to Sennacherib.

Interesting as this text also is from the historical viewpoint, it cannot as yet be made to yield material which field archaeologists can use to combat the theories of Lees and Falcon. In the light of the

1. The bleak landscape of the Dokan region of northern Mesopotamia. Subject for centuries to a slow process of erosion, this plateau is almost entirely treeless. 2. The first stone of the Dokan dam across the Little Zab was laid in the spring of 1957. This dam will submerge an area of great interest to archaeologists but will also provide 7 million cubic metres of water to irrigate 66,500 acres of agricultural ground – a situation similar to that at the Aswan dam in Egypt.

3. Landscape near the ruins of Ashur. The photograph was taken looking northeast from the top of the tell. 4. In the marshy area not far from the confluence of the Euphrates and Tigris the scenery is characterised by numerous date palms. Even in remote antiquity this tree was an important source of food, and it is therefore a favourite motif on the reliefs of Mesopotamian sculptors. 5. The entire south is intersected by irrigation canals. The water contained much silt and the canals had to be dredged frequently; hence resulted the dikes along both banks. When these became too high a new canal was dug and the old one drained dry. The traces of countless canals can therefore still be found. 6. As it flows past the ruins of Ashur the Tigris is a wide, stately river. On the west bank can be seen not only the remains of the ancient city but also the outlines of the house used by the German expedition (see Pl. 173).

results of recent soil and geological investigations no attempt has been made in this atlas to reconstruct a coast-line other than the existing one. This applies with even more force to the coast-line which is alleged to have been discovered south of Samarra. This 'coast-line' is shown on a number of maps although no one knows exactly who came to the conclusion that the sea stretched so far into the interior of Mesopotamia thousands of years ago. A geological investigation on the spot definitely established that the transition from the second to the third river terrace had been mistaken for a coast-line.

THE PLAIN

The low-lying Mesopotamian plain, which is rightly regarded as the cradle of every civilisation that has been influenced by the ethics and religion of the Bible, is about 400 miles long from Samarra to the Persian Gulf and 125 miles across. The following areas can be distinguished from north to south.

In the vicinity of Samarra can be found the river terraces rising over 33 feet above the plain. Agriculture and cattle breeding here depended on the rains, technical knowledge being insufficiently advanced to provide irrigation at such a level. The first efforts to irrigate the area effectively appear to have been made in the time of the Sassanids (A.D. 226-636). The Nahrawan canal, traces of whose bed can be identified at numerous places, also dates from this period. This canal is the longest canal ever dug anywhere in the world, but large stretches dug later in the north were never filled with water.

To the south of the terraces begins the river plain proper, the structure of which has been determined by the behaviour of the rivers. In the months of April and August the waters of the Euphrates and the Tigris rise, covering extensive areas. In this respect there is little difference between the rivers. There is some mineralogical difference, but it is too small to have any effect on agriculture. In periods of high water the plains, which lie below the normal level of the river water, may be flooded, while life on the river banks goes on. The oldest form of irrigation consisted in regulating the quantity of water by a system of canals, dykes, and dams during the dry period. The farther south one goes, the more insufficient the rain becomes, being restricted to light falls in winter and sometimes none at all. It was always possible to convey irrigation water to areas below the level of the river beds, but it was not until a much later period that a technical improvement in equipment led to lift irrigation. In fact, a reasonably effective system of pump irrigation capable of bringing water to areas at a higher level did not come into use until the end of the twentieth century. The behaviour of the rivers is capricious. They have both changed their courses, their former beds being still distinguishable on aerial photographs. The downfall of cities with a flourishing, centuries-old civilisation can in several cases be traced back to a shift in the course of one of the rivers at a time when lack of power or technical ability made it impossible to direct the vital water back to the city. The rivers have formed meanders, then cut them off; they have followed new courses through the low-lying plains, bringing distress to the people living there. Unfavourable combinations of circumstances have caused such severe inundations that it can well be understood how the story of the Flood originated in Mesopotamia.

Because of the dryness of the climate the soil of Mesopotamia is hard and nearly impenetrable. Consequently, when heavy rainfall in the northern areas coincides with the melting of the snow in the Taurus and Zagros Mountains, the rivers wreak destruction which can only be prevented by a system of dams such as has been constructed in the last few years. The great dam at Samarra, completed in 1956, makes it possible to discharge the superfluous water to the Wadi Tharthar Depression where it forms an artificial lake. A great flood of the kind which swept away part of Baghdad as recently as 1954 need no longer be dreaded.

The catastrophic inundations which caused such a hiatus in history that men started dating events as before or after 'the Flood' formed

strata of sediment which visibly separate habitation layers from one another. Where such a stratum occurs, however, it must not be too readily ascribed to the great flood or deluge described in Genesis 7-9 or recalled in the Gilgamesh epic. A local inundation is not the same as the Flood which is supposed to have covered the entire earth. Examination of the soil in Mesopotamia has not yet succeeded in proving the historical veracity of such a flood. This negative verdict applies in particular to Ur, where Sir Leonard Woolley thought he had found traces of the Flood. The layer of sand which he found separating habitation layers was in fact not the sediment laid down by a flood but an aeolian formation, as examination of the sand grains proved.

Aeolian formations are caused by the *idyah*, the dreaded dust-storm which occurs in spring and summer and looks like a thick fog. The *idyah* comes mainly from the west, where it removes the top surface of the desert, which is not anchored by vegetation of any kind, and whirls it off towards the cultivated land. The fine dust passes through every hole and slit in even well-built houses, it catches the breath of anyone who is caught in it, and fills every nook and cranny in the deserted heaps of ruins. These dust-storms also cause the formation of dunes which can still be observed in an area stretching from east of Babylon to Nippur. It is often striking to see how mounds which were excavated only a few years ago are already filled up with the powdery sand raised by the wind. It is not hard for an expert to tell the difference between an aeolian formation and a layer of sediment. Yet although many tells have been formed in this way above former habitation sites the dust-storm has, in comparison with the rivers, changed the appearance of the Mesopotamian land to only a small degree.

On the other hand, human activities have left a definite imprint on the river plain as we observe it today. On the whole the plain is wide and bare, relieved here and there in the region south of Baghdad by luxuriant groves of date palms or citron trees. The courses of old irrigation canals can be clearly made out running straight across these often seemingly endless plains.

Although efforts were made to keep as strong a current as possible flowing in these canals, they had nevertheless to be regularly dredged, because the river water, as already observed, carried large quantities of material in suspension. The dredgings formed dykes on both sides of the canals and as time went on these dykes became too high. The canal was drained dry and a new irrigation canal was dug parallel to it. The dykes along the old canal were nevertheless allowed to stand, and today they give a peculiar character to the landscape of what the writer of Psalm 137 called 'the waters of Babylon'.

Travelling from the river plain to the delta one arrives without perceptible transition at what is, physiographically speaking, distinctly new territory. Here the rivers have kept forming new branches and changing their courses. And then one slowly approaches the region of swamps where the Sumerian was reminded of the start of the world's creation, when the inhabitable, cultivable surface of the continent began to rise from the primeval waters. There are no fixed boundaries between the land and the water here. A large proportion of the water carried down by the rivers disappears mysteriously in the swamps, by evaporation, by irrigation, by draining off into pools and lakes. It has been calculated that between Qurna and Amara the rivers lose 90 % of their water. This amount never reaches the Persian Gulf. It is also in the marshes that the rivers deposit their heavy load of silt, so that possibilities exist of reclaiming land from them. According to the latest information the earliest land reclamation began here during the Persian period in the fifth century B.C. The areas thus won proved eminently suitable for the cultivation of rice. Nowadays enough rice can be grown here to meet the needs of Iraq.

The effect of ebb and flow is felt in the area bordering on the Shatt el-'Arab, in which the Euphrates and Tigris converge after they have lost by far the greater part of their water and silt. The water level here rises and falls twice daily by an amount of about six feet. The salt sea water penetrates inland as far as Abadan. Along the coast near the river mouth some tectonic movement is perceptible. To the east of

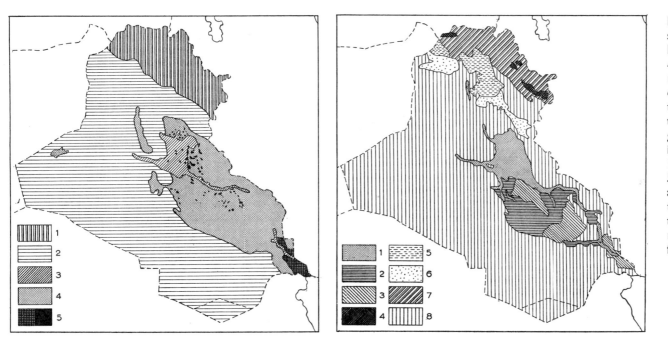

Left: Soil salinisation in Iraq. 1. no salinity; 2. deserts and soils with local salinity; 3. moderate salinity; 4. serious salinity; 5. serious salinity, accompanied by solonchak conditions. Right: Soil classification of Iraq. 1. particularly suited to irrigation; 2. suited to irrigation; 3. moderately suited to irrigation; 4. extremely suited to both irrigation and dry farming; 5. particularly suited to irrigation and also to dry farming; 6. suited to irrigation, moderately suited to dry farming; 7. suited to cattle rearing and forestry; 8. unsuitable for agriculture.

the Shatt el-'Arab, the character of the landscape is determined by the rivers which reach the low-lying plain from the Persian mountains.

The courses of the rivers in the area of the delta and marshes have changed repeatedly in the course of the centuries. Yet this does not necessarily mean that the nature of the land or the possibilities of habitation have been subject to great changes. The marshes, difficult of access, always provided a refuge for tribes who for one reason or another wished to avoid contact with their more civilised neighbours. For a whole year (1955-6) Professor Westphal-Hellbusch of Berlin studied the mode of life of the Ma'dan who live there nowadays. With her husband, and despite great hardships, she shared the lot of the marsh-dwellers, in whose customs she found many points of similarity to those of classical Mesopotamian civilisation, for example in the manufacture of reed mats or the shape of their boat, the *mahhuf*, which is so similar in type to the well-known boat from a grave at Ur (Pl. 12). As the historical sense of the marsh-dwellers is undeveloped and their traditions consequently do not stretch further back than two centuries, it is impossible to speak with any certainty of a genealogical tie with the ancient inhabitants.

If we return now to the north, what strikes us most is that the centres of Sumerian and Babylonian civilisation nowadays give us the impression of great poverty, particularly with regard to agriculture. This cannot be entirely due to the shifts of the rivers. The disappearance of agrarian prosperity from around Babylon cannot be explained by the change of course of the Euphrates, for the river is replaced here by a broad and navigable canal. Nor can the destruction wrought by the Mongols be considered wholly responsible for the impoverishment of the country. It is true that Tamerlane's proceedings at the end of the fourteenth century were of a cruelty that we can scarcely imagine and that dykes and canals were destroyed during that period. Nevertheless, the country should have been able after centuries of human activity to recover from these blows.

THE SALINISATION OF THE SOIL

The soil has been attacked by another stealthy enemy. The real cause of the disappearance of prosperity was salinisation. Traces of it can be seen on the surface by any observer, for a crust of salt covers the surface at many places and sometimes gives the impression of hoar frost. The causes of salinisation are twofold. The irrigation water from the rivers is slightly saline, and if it·has been brought over the land for century after century and evaporated, the cumulative effect can be considerable. More significant is the salt that is forced to the surface by the ground-water. Only efficient drainage could counteract the salinisation of the ground, for the rain which should wash the salt away falls in insufficient quantities, while drainage is also hampered by the hardness of the soil. Agriculture here is thus faced with a

difficult problem which even the construction of a good irrigation system would fail to solve.

The peasant who is given such ground to farm estimates its value according to its salt content. He knows that $\frac{1}{2}$ % salt means no wheat, that with 1 % salt he can expect no barley harvest, and that with 2 % salt even the date palms yield no fruit. This salinisation of the soil is the real cause of the northward shift of civilisation, which was already under way in the third century B.C. The question not unnaturally arises what proportions this soil problem had assumed in the classical period of Babylon.

It is generally thought that irrigation by canals did most to promote salinisation, for the huge dykes on either side of the irrigation canals divided the low-lying ground into small units which could not be drained. The ground-water here rose to the roots of the field crops, and in this dry climate salinisation was then inevitable. Natural irrigation, without the help of canals, was much less dangerous in this respect. But since the canals were dug at an early date salinisation is probably equally ancient. The consequences could to some extent be counteracted by surface irrigation and by growing crops which tolerate a high salt content in the soil. But its effect on wheat and barley must have been rapidly visible, so that it is important to compare ancient data concerning the yield of particular fields. If the texts recorded on clay tablets clearly reveal that harvests were deteriorating, we have our first clue. An investigation along these lines was carried out by Professor Thorkild Jacobsen in the Diyala area, and it led to surprising results.

That the salt was regarded as a dangerous enemy of the harvest could be learned from very early texts. The archives from the temple of Baba, wife of the city god Ningirsu, preserved a report on the first year of Urukagina's reign, in which it is stated that salt had made parts of the temple domain unusable for agriculture. Then, on a boundary stone of the thirteenth century B.C. can be read: 'May Adad the supreme director of irrigation in heaven and earth bring forth moist salt to destroy his fields and dry up the barley, nor let the green herbs grow.' The myth of Atrakhasis, which was found in Ashurbanipal's library, speaks in the same vein. The god Enlil cannot sleep for the noise made by mankind. To recover his peace he decides to exterminate the human race, and one of the means he devises for this purpose is salt in the soil. In a text dating from the second half of the sixth century B.C. Nabonidus reports that the temple of Ishtar has been 'burned down' with saltpetre. It is beyond all doubt that salinisation was in progress. To what extent it existed must therefore be interpreted from texts which are known with certainty to refer to the yield of fields whose surface area remained unchanged over extensive periods. At the same time allowance must be made for other factors which could have affected the yield unfavourably, such as neglect, inexpert farming, or war operations. With due regard to these com-

7. The landscape of the Mesopotamian flood plain is characterised by a wide horizon and an absence of trees. 8. The mud houses of northern Mesotamia differ little from those of the ancient inhabitants. 9. The reed hut such as this, seen being built in southern Mesopotamia, is probably very like the picture evoked by the Gilgamesh epic when it tells how Ea betrayed the secret of the Flood to the reed hut. 10. Boats on the Euphrates at Nasiriya, not far from Ur. 11. A shepherd drawing water in a leather bag. 12. This silver boat found in a tomb at Ur is of a type still seen on the Euphrates – a proof of the static nature of life in this region. 13. A still uninvestigated tell in northern Mesopotamia. 14. Draught animals have not yet been completely replaced by diesel pumps for irrigation purposes. 15. Ploughing in Kurdistan also is still done in the traditional way. 16. This solitary tree owes its preservation to a mysteriously acquired sacredness.

plications, Professor Thorkild Jacobsen published in 1958 the following information in the journal *Sumer*. The investigation was conducted in the area of the river Diyala. The written records spanned a period from ca. 2600 B.C. to A.D. 1400, that is, about 4,000 years. Analysis of the texts was combined with an actual field survey. The chronicles from ancient times revealed two main periods of salinisation. The danger of soil deterioration was very serious at Tello, where salinisation began in 2400 B.C. and spread westwards towards the Euphrates. Salinisation of a less serious kind was reported in north Babylonia between 1200 and 600 B.C.

Sufficient information was found to calculate that ca. 2400 B.C. wheat still accounted for 16 % of the total harvest of wheat and barley. Three centuries later the proportion had dropped to barely 2 %, while between 2000 and 1700 B.C. reports contain no mention of wheat. The yield of barley dropped from 28 bushels per acre in 2400 B.C. to 15 in 2100 B.C. and 10 in 1700 B.C. Professor Jacobsen was, in fact, of the opinion that the decline of Sumerian civilisation and the shift of the cultural centre to the north could be entirely accounted for by the salinisation of the soil. Yet it also became clear that the agricultural practice of the ancient inhabitants had been on a very high level. Taught by experience, which must have gone back to ca. 4200 B.C. in the Diyala area, farmers were able to extract the maximum yield from the soil. In addition, they were familiar with the most effective way of combating salinisation or at least delaying it. This is quite clear from a Sumerian agricultural manual of ca. 2100 B.C. in which we learn that only one crop per year was attempted in order to let the soil recover, and that a method of irrigation was employed which could not be much improved upon in later times.

In the more northerly areas salinisation did not assume such catastrophic proportions, because the water table was lower there and the ground-water could not reach the roots of the field crops so readily. A protective dry layer between the level of the roots and the ground-water meant that the capillary effect, which brought the salt towards the surface, was very slight. In these areas wheat formed somewhat more than 25 % of the harvest ca. 1300 B.C. and somewhat more than 18 % ca. 500 B.C. The barley yield was still quite considerable then, more than 20 bushels per acre. Though the reports of Herodotus on the fabulous yields of the harvest in Mesopotamia must not be taken as scientifically accurate, they do indicate that the problem of salinisation had been overcome. He visited Babylon in the fifth century B.C., that is, in the time of the Persians, and speaks of 200-fold to 300-fold yields. But when, upon the death of Alexander the Great, the first of the Seleucids transferred the centre of his empire northwards, and founded Seleucia there, it may be an indication that the area around Babylon had become less prosperous.

For the Persian kings Babylon was a winter residence where they could escape from the cold of their mountains. Nowadays the temperature at the site of Babylon can drop below freezing point in winter. In summer the heat is often unbearable. The normal temperature then is about 108°F in the shade and between 120° and 140° in the sun. That is why the excavation campaigns are limited to the months from November to March.

THE NORTHERN TERRITORY

Towards the north the rain falls in larger quantities and the problem of salinisation does not exist. Yet the inhabitable area is limited to strips in the vicinity of the rivers. Here, too, the land has been irrigated by canals since ancient times. We have, for instance, an inscription of Sennacherib, dating back to 694 B.C., in which he proudly details the beneficial results of a canal dug at his command. About three miles south of Bavian an aqueduct has been discovered which formed part of this irrigation system described by Sennacherib. The problems in the north, in ancient Assyria, were quite different from those in the south, if only for the reason that it was mountainous country, with a markedly continental climate. The red-brown loam deposited by the rivers makes a fertile soil, but the highlands present the picture of a

heavily-eroded plateau which is covered only in winter with a thin layer of vegetation. The systematic deforestation of the region by a population lacking fuel has promoted erosion since time immemorial and greatly diminished prosperity. In what was once Assyria the winters can be raw and cold, and the summers dry and hot. In early spring the landscape of Kurdistan is magnificent, the high peaks in the north and east being covered with snow. If only as a result of the climate and the character of the land, there must, even in ancient times, have been a great difference in mentality between the inhabitants of the northern highlands and those of the southern plain, however intensive trade and consequently cultural exchanges were along the Tigris. The total habitable area of Assyria in antiquity was probably about 5,000 sq. miles. The growing population could only be sufficiently fed if corn was imported from the south. This need explains the increasing interest displayed by the kings of Assyria in gaining control of Babylon. There was little they could offer in exchange for wheat and barley. They did, of course, possess supplies of stone, but the mania of the kings of Nineveh and Ashur for building was generally such that their own subjects had to be content with mud dwellings. Asphalt was available in large quantities because it could be mined without difficulty in the area around Kirkuk. Nor was there any shortage of timber, for in antiquity the mountains of Kurdistan were still covered with forests. On the other hand, metal needed for the manufacture of arms had to be imported. That is why caravan tracks led to the north, where iron, copper, lead, and silver could be had. As their needs grew, and particularly at a later period, the trade route became a warpath which the Assyrians followed to seize by force what they were no longer willing or able to obtain by peaceful means.

OIL

There is one aspect of modern Iraq which was wholly absent from ancient Mesopotamia; for Iraq is now one of the world's largest oil-producing countries. The oil which gushes from the ground at Kirkuk – a very ancient habitation site – and is led by pipeline to the west, was not a factor of any significance in the ancient world. The combustible nature of the oil which seeped to the surface in places was familiar. Much practical use was made of asphalt, which was chiefly found near Hit on the Euphrates. This product was mainly employed for joining bricks together and for making floors and walls watertight, and it was often incorporated in jewellery; but petroleum was of no account in economic life and consequently in political life. For modern Iraq oil is the main source of revenue, enabling the country to build roads, found industries, and improve agriculture and irrigation.

THE NEED FOR EXPANSION

The possibilities, however, remain limited, and in particular the wide steppe region between the rivers is anything but promising. In the course of thousands of years nothing in this region has changed. The nomads roam through the desert, moving with their flocks to the most suitable grazing grounds according to the season, without troubling about useless, man-made frontiers. Any relaxation by the central authority causes them to infiltrate into the cultivated areas in the neighbourhood of towns. Conversely, a population which has settled in cities and is on the increase seeks ways of expanding because its growth means a lack of *Lebensraum*. A glance at the soil map of Mesopotamia may thus help to explain a feature of ancient history. This history is full of campaigns in which the armies of the Assyrians and Babylonians burst from their frontiers and followed the road to the sea in the west. It is incorrect to explain these operations as being entirely due to desire for power and love of war. What we see are mainly attempts to extend authority in the west so that the caravan routes to the 'land flowing with milk and honey' on the shore of the Mediterranean could be kept under continuous control. That the Mesopotamians should encounter the armies of the Pharaoh on their way there was inevitable.

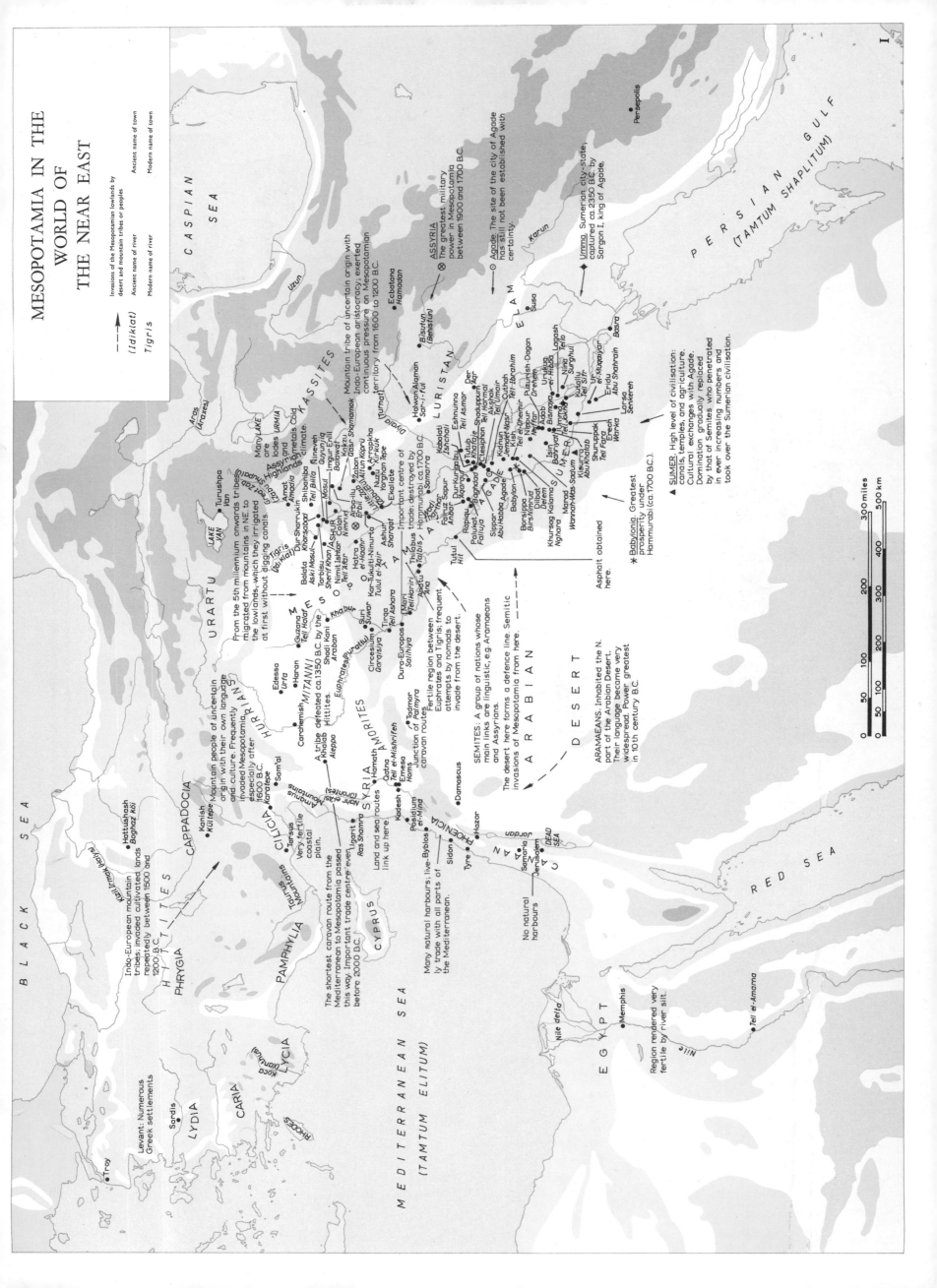

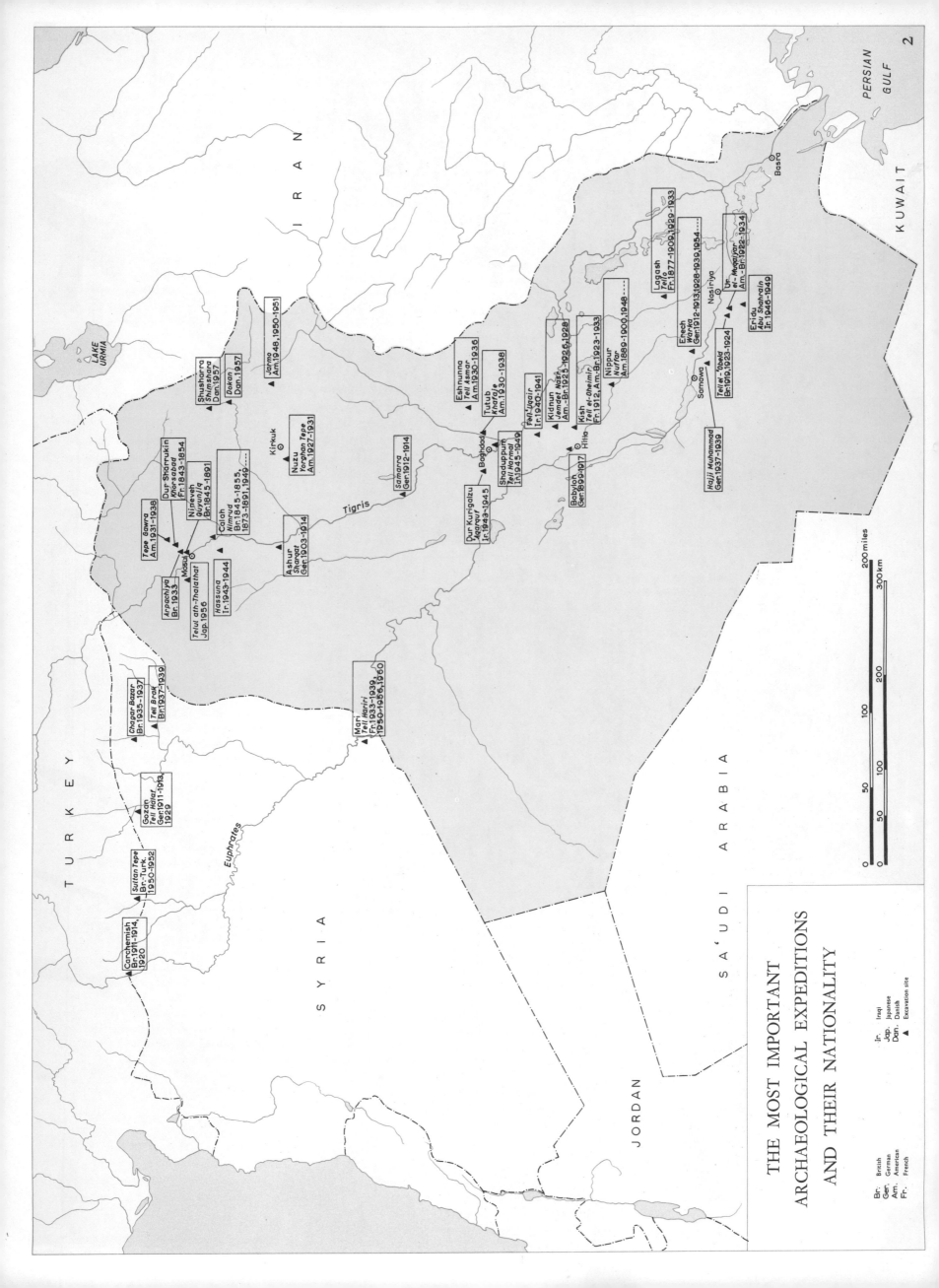

2

PERSIAN GULF

IRAN

TURKEY

SYRIA

JORDAN

SA'UDI ARABIA

KUWAIT

LAKE URMIA

Tigris

Euphrates

Basra

Carchemish
Br.:1911–1914, 1920

Sultan Tepe
Br.-Turk.: 1950–1952

Gozan
Tell Halaf
Ger.:1911–1913, 1929

Chagar Bazar
Br.:1935–1937

Tell Brak
Br.:1937–1939

Mari
Tell Hariri
Fr.:1933–1939, 1950–1956,1960

Tepe Gawra
Am.:1931–1938

Arpachiya
Br.:1933

Mosul

Telul ath-Thalathat
Jap.:1956

Hassuna
Ir.:1943–1944

Dur Sharrukin
Khorsabad
Fr.:1843–1854

Nineveh
Quyunjiq
Br.:1845–1891

Calah
Nimrud
Br.:1845–1855, 1873–1891,1949

Ashur
Sharqat
Ger.:1903–1914

Shushara
Shimshara
Dan.:1957

Dokan
Dan.:1957

Jarmo
Am.:1948,1950–1951

Kirkuk

Nuzu
Yorghan Tepe
Am.:1927–1931

Samarra
Ger.:1912–1914

Dur Kurigalzu
Aqarquf
Ir.:1943–1945

Baghdad

Eshnunna
Tell Asmar
Am.:1930–1936

Tutub
Khafaje
Am.:1930–1938

Shaduppum
Tell Harmal
Ir.:1945–1949

Tell Uqair
Ir.:1940–1941

Kidnun
Jemdet Nasr
Am.-Br.:1925–1926,1928

Kish
Tell el-Oheimir
Fr.:1912, Am.-Br.:1923–1933

Babylon
Ger.:1899–1917

Hilla

Nippur
Nuffar
Am.:1889–1900,1948

Lagash
Tello
Fr.:1877–1909,1929–1933

Nasiriya

Ur
el-Muqaiyar
Am.-Br.:1922–1934

Erech
Warka
Ger.:1912–1913,1928–1939,1954

Samawa

Tell el-'Obeid
Br.:1919,1923–1924

Hajji Muhammad
Ger.:1937–1939

Eridu
Abu Shahrain
Ir.:1946–1949

0   50   100   200 miles

0   50   100   200   300 km

THE MOST IMPORTANT
ARCHAEOLOGICAL EXPEDITIONS
AND THEIR NATIONALITY

Br.   British
Ger.   German
Am.   American
Fr.   French

Ir.   Iraqi
Jap.   Japanese
Dan.   Danish

▲   Excavation site

The Awakening of Interest and the First Excavations

TRAVELLERS AND THEIR TALES

In the year 1160 a learned Jewish merchant, Benjamin Bar Jona of Tudela, journeyed to the East. By way of Italy and Greece, Cyprus and Palestine he finally arrived in Mesopotamia and Persia. He kept a kind of diary which reveals his interest in the life of Jewish communities in the Diaspora. But the monuments of antiquity did not pass unnoticed by him, and we find in his account notes on Nineveh and Babylon. Of his visit to Mosul, for instance, he says: 'This city, the first in Persia, was very great even in olden times and lies on the Tigris, being joined by a bridge to Nineveh. The latter city was destroyed, but many inhabited villages and hamlets now stand in the area it occupied.' Travelling from Baghdad to Hilla he saw the ruins of ancient Babylon, which extend over a distance of three miles. Of the ruins of Nebuchadnezzar's palace he relates that no one dared enter them for fear of snakes and scorpions. He also states that he found the 'Tower of Babel', but it can be deduced that he meant Birs Nimrud, the ancient Borsippa. He climbed the winding stairs to the top and from there beheld a wide and flat landscape. The incinerated remains of brick walls which he found at the top, and which still make an impression of mystery on every visitor, were, he explains, caused by a stroke of lightning which destroyed the tower. Although, in medieval fashion, he uncritically retails local traditions and his descriptions contain nothing of striking importance, Benjamin of Tudela's notes should not be underestimated. His influence was at first restricted to Jewish circles, but later, as a result of the translation of his book into French and English, Nineveh and Babylon were brought to the notice of European scholars under a novel aspect. The names of the cities were familiar from the Bible or the classics; but now, it appeared, there were mounds of ruins which could actually be seen.

After Benjamin of Tudela many others visited and wrote about Mesopotamia in the course of the centuries. One of the best known of these was the Italian nobleman Pietro della Valle, who was in Babylon in 1616 on his outward journey to the East and visited the ruins of Ur in 1625 on his way home. He was the first man to send copies of the mysterious cuneiform writing from Persepolis to Europe. He also brought some bricks with inscriptions back from Babylon. Thus, in the seventeenth century, he awakened the interest of Europe in Mesopotamian culture, although it was not until the end of the eighteenth century that this interest became intense. It was then associated with the Romantic movement which evoked a longing for all that was distant in space and time. Explorers set off for unknown lands and archaeologists started digging for the remains of ancient and even primeval civilisations.

From then on dozens of travellers visited Mesopotamia and left accounts of what they saw to posterity. Within the restricted space available here we shall be able to mention only a few of them. There was the Danish scholar Carsten Niebuhr, whose account was published in Copenhagen in 1778. He is much more precise in his statements about Nineveh and Babylon than previous travellers, and much firmer in his conviction that the sites of these cities were definitely those near Mosul and Hilla. That is why he occupies an honoured place amongst the pioneers who sought for the buried civilisations of Mesopotamia. None of these early visits resulted in excavation; they were too short and too incidental for that.

The possibility of digging was not seriously considered until some learned and interested Europeans started making longer stays in Baghdad. Among them was the Abbé de Beauchamp, papal vicar-general at Baghdad from 1780 to 1790, who twice made extended visits thence to the ruins of Babylon. His accurate accounts were published in the *Journal des Savants* in 1785 and 1790 and must be regarded as important factors in creating a steadily increasing public interest in the subject. Enthusiasm was particularly great in Britain, and the East India Company in London actually instructed their agents in Basra to send bricks bearing inscriptions to England. The situation at the end of the eighteenth century was therefore as follows: descriptions of the ruins of Nineveh and Babylon were available, those of the latter being particularly detailed, and several specimens of cuneiform script were known on which the decipherers now started to try their skill.

An important episode in the story of how the ancient Mesopotamian civilisation was brought to light is Claudius James Rich's stay in Baghdad as resident of the East India Company. French by birth but entirely Anglicised by his upbringing, Rich possessed an extraordinary gift for Eastern languages and was perfectly at home in Turkish and Arabic. He died of cholera in 1821 at the age of thirty-five, but his memoirs on Babylon, Nineveh, and a number of other tells, mostly published by Mrs Rich after his death, are remarkable for the quantity and accuracy of their information. A description of Rich's short life is given in Constance Alexander's *Baghdad in Bygone Days* (London 1928). Seton Lloyd drew on this book for his vivid evocation of an Englishman's life in Baghdad at the beginning of the nineteenth century in *Foundations in the Dust*, which first appeared in 1947. Rich's house in Baghdad was a centre for others such as Buckingham, Bellino, and Robert Ker Porter, who explored the country under the extremely difficult circumstances created by unbearable heat, sandstorms, and the constant threat of nomads.

THE FIRST EXCAVATORS

In December 1842 Paul-Émile Botta, French consul at Mosul, stood on the mound at Quyunjiv, beneath which a part of the ancient city of Nineveh lay buried. When he began digging there, it was the start of the history of excavation in Mesopotamia. No one before him had ever dug for the remains of buried cities in the tells of Mesopotamia. This beginning was not a successful one, but a chance passer-by assured Botta that he knew a place where he could find everything that any one could hope for. This man turned out to be a villager from Khorsabad, and after investigations Botta transferred the site of his activities to what proved later to be the mound of Dur Sharrukin (see Pl. 19). The famous Assyrian sculptures of the eighth century B.C. were uncovered and news of the discovery reached Paris.

The way in which the first trophies of French archaeology finally found their way to Europe is typical of the difficulties which crippled pioneers in Mesopotamia about a century ago. There was a lack of skilled labour, and Botta had reason to congratulate himself when he engaged the services of some Nestorian Christians fleeing from their Kurdish persecutors. He was obstructed by the Turkish governor of the province of Mosul and had to wait for months before he obtained from the Porte at Constantinople a firman, or permit, to start excavation. The heavy objects which he dug up had to be taken on wagons, sometimes drawn by two hundred men, through the mud to the Tigris and then conveyed downstream on the kind of raft

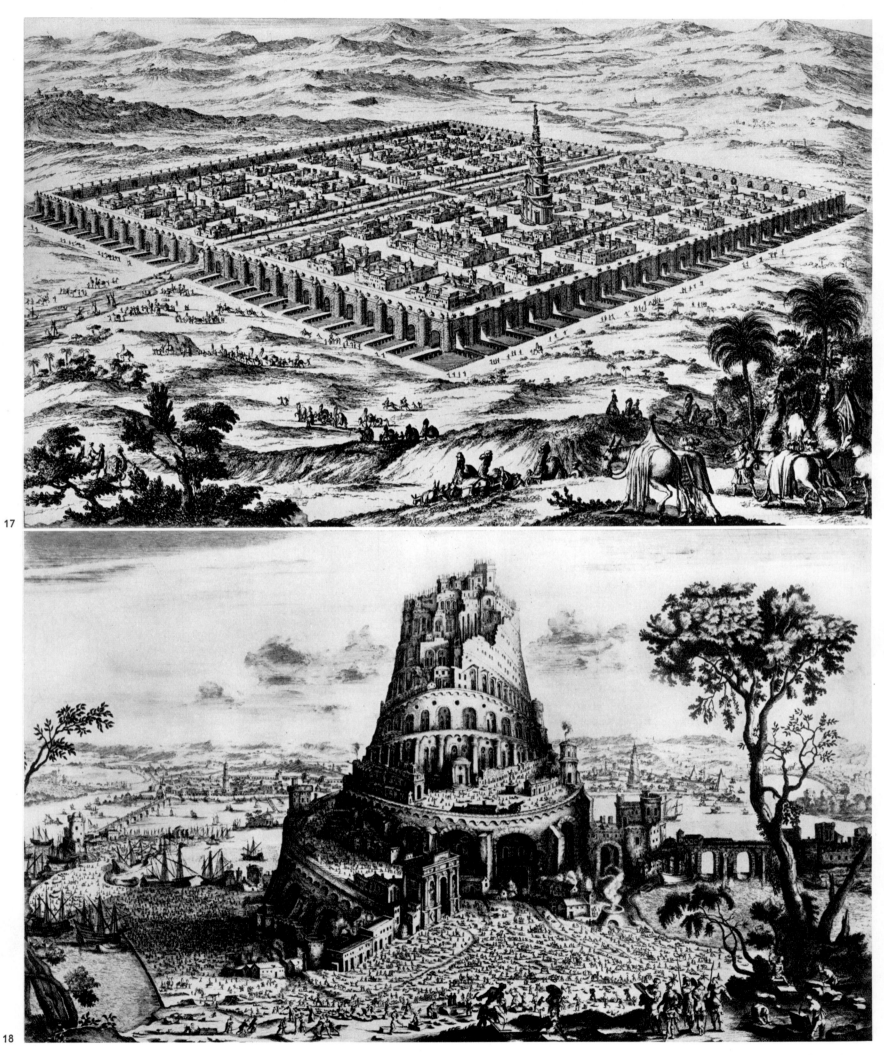

17-18. Taken from the works of Olfert Dapper (1636-89), an Amsterdam doctor who in 1680 published a volume describing, among other things, 'The Provinces of Mesopotamia'. His ideas of Babel were based partly on Biblical and classical sources and partly on travel books such as those by R. Fitsch, John Eldred, and Pietro della Valle. The illustrations are characterised by a combination of reliable information and fantasy typical of the seventeenth century. **19-21.** These pictures herald an entirely new period of interest, and the water-colours and pen-and-ink drawings of the nineteenth century conjure up the personally experienced atmosphere better than photographs could. They intimately express the feelings that gripped the artists on beholding the mounds of, respectively, Khorsabad (from P. E. Botta's *Monuments de Ninevé*, with drawings by E. Flandin), Nineveh, and Nimrud (from A. H. Layard's *The Monuments of Nineveh*, Vol. II, Pl. 70, and Vol. I, Pl. 98).

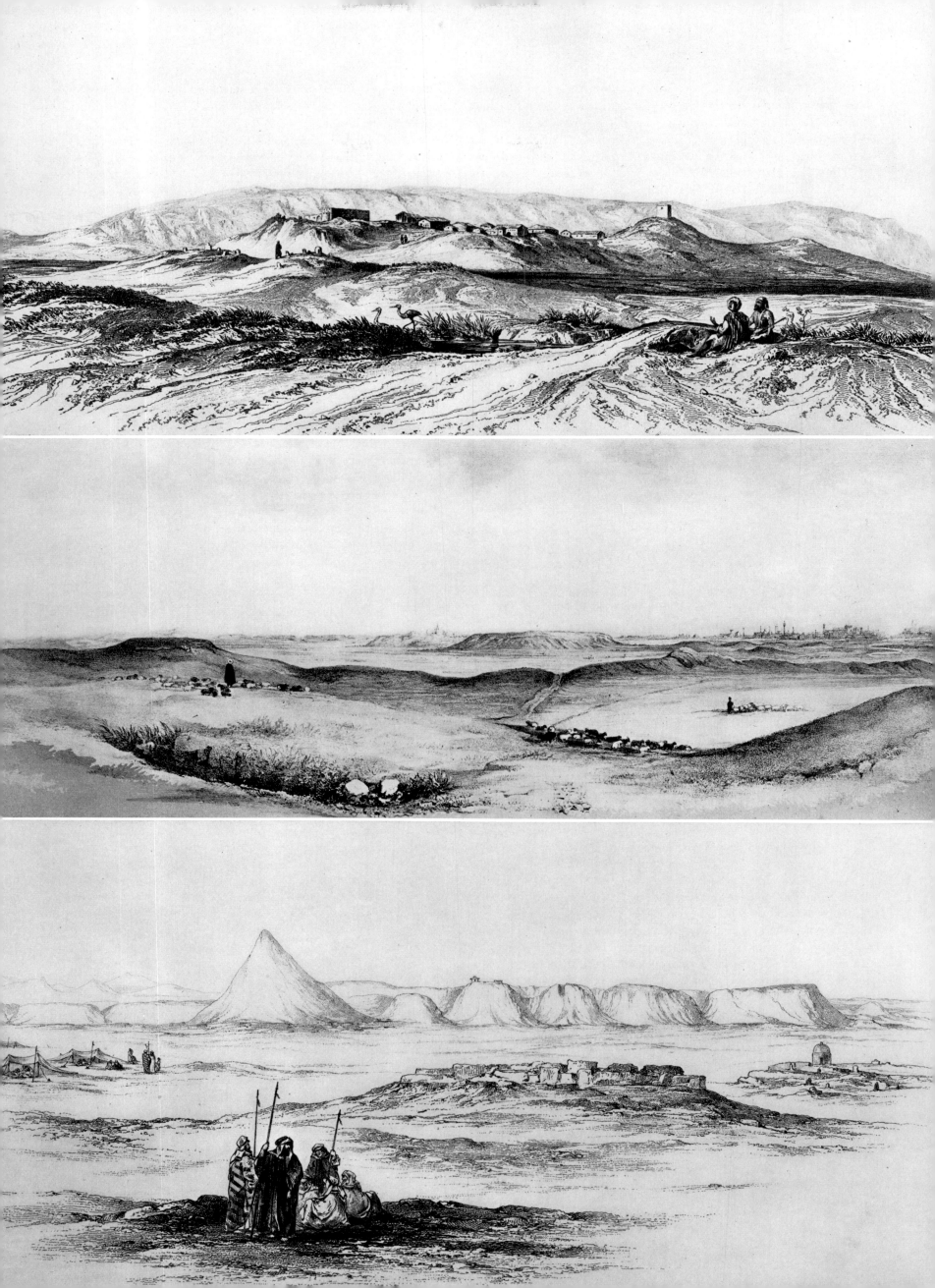

built on inflated animal skins called *kelek* (see Pl. 47) to Baghdad. How time-consuming all this was will be clear if we reflect that Botta finished excavating in October 1844, and did not receive his finds in Paris until February 1847. Even so, he could count himself fortunate that pirates had not attacked his ships and that he had returned alive.

The second man to appear on the excavation scene was an Englishman, Austen Henry Layard. He had made Botta's acquaintance in Mosul and, encouraged by the Frenchman's success, he too determined to try his luck. At the end of November 1845 we find him at work at Nimrud (see Pl. 21), the mound of a city which is called Calah in the Bible (Gen. 10 : 12) and Kalkhu in Assyrian literature. His excavations were no less successful than those of Botta. In the course of 1847 he returned laden with archaeological trophies to his native land. His finds created the same sensation in England as Botta's had caused in Paris. He was given a chance to continue his work, and from 1849 until the spring of 1851 he dug in Quyunjiv as well as in

An old engraving of the ziggurat of Ur conveys the impression made by the mound on Western visitors in the middle of the nineteenth century.

Nimrud, and explored numerous tells in the vicinity. He then retired completely from archaeology, probably on account of his incompatibility with the man who succeeded him as supervisor on behalf of Britain of all archaeology in Mesopotamia – Rawlinson, the decipherer of cuneiform. The careers of Botta and Layard, which had crossed at Mosul, both came to an end too soon. Their names remain honourably inscribed on the first page of the history of the excavations in Mesopotamia.

There was a rather unedifying sequel to this story, for possession of the mound of Nineveh was disputed by Rawlinson and his assistant Hormuzd Rassam on one hand and Botta's successor Victor Place on the other, the methods employed being definitely not in keeping with the dignity of scholars or scientists. Nevertheless, Place's work at Khorsabad (see Pl. 19) gave him considerable satisfaction. He discovered Sargon's palace, which is still regarded as the most imposing monument built by an Assyrian king. His architect assistant, Félix Thomas, recorded the beauty of the buildings in a book of drawings. But Ashurbanipal's library and this Assyrian king's hunting scenes had fallen into the hands of their English rivals.

This strange Anglo-French competition in the archaeological field was continued round Tello, the site of ancient Lagash. Ernest de Sarzec, who was French vice-consul in Basra at the time, decided, partly from commercial motives, to excavate Tello without permission from Constantinople after an antiquary of his acquaintance had drawn his attention to this gold mine of antiquities. In 1877 and 1878 he managed to acquire a large quantity of sculptures and inscriptions and even to get them safely to Paris, where he sold them to the Louvre for the then colossal sum of 130,000 francs. In de Sarzec's absence,

Rassam, also without permission, started to plunder the mound. Clandestine diggers without the slightest skill also did their share towards scattering the antiquities of Tello over the entire world. Meanwhile, in spite of everything, de Sarzec's enterprise had done science a great service: the works of the Sumerians which he had taken to the Louvre attracted the attention of art historians, and Sumerian literature was brought within the ken of Assyriologists. Until 1931 the tell remained a firm favourite of the Louvre, yet it was never completely excavated – though, for that matter, no tell ever is.

America entered the field in 1877 with an expedition under the leadership of Peters. The first undertaking ended in chaos and disaster. The objective chosen was the ancient city of Nippur, a choice which, as it turned out later, was inherently a happy one. Peters and his collaborator Hilprecht, however, did not possess the tact necessary to get on with the local Arabs. The result was that scarcely two months after work had started the Afaq Arabs drove the members of the expedition away after setting fire to the camp and plundering it. The Americans did not allow themselves to be discouraged by this disappointing beginning. They returned in 1890 and have retained their interest in Nippur until very recent times. It is to them that we owe tens of thousands of tablets – generally speaking, the finest haul from any excavation in Mesopotamia – including some 2,000 literary Sumerian texts, which have now been, or are being, edited by Samuel Noah Kramer.

So far we have given only a short survey and an impression of what happened by way of excavations in Iraq in the second half of the nineteenth century. Many excavators of merit have not been mentioned. Ernest Alfred Wallis Budge, Leonard W. King, R. Campbell Thompson, and others belong to the 'heroic' period of archaeology in Mesopotamia. Together they brought more spectacular things to light than was possible for a later generation. To them we owe the most impressive exhibits in museums in Paris, London, and Berlin. They also did much irreparable damage. And in the background we see an army of clandestine searchers and dealers. Hundreds of clay tablets were carelessly transported in bags on donkeys and arrived as dust. Others were packed in bales of raw cotton and ground in the machine before they were discovered. But at least an interested public in Europe and America knew by 1900 that a vast literature had been dug from the soil of Mesopotamia and that this raised the problem of 'Babel and the Bible'.

About the beginning of the present century the exploration of Mesopotamian antiquities entered a new phase, of which the chief characteristic is more intense concentration on a single objective. Large mounds of ruins are excavated systematically at the cost of much money, time, and man-power. The period of treasure-hunting is largely over. The field archaeologist's primary task is not the acquisition of fine museum pieces, but the systematic uncovering of a part of a city or a group of temple buildings, effected in such a way that the various layers of civilisation can be distinguished. Thus it has slowly become possible to interpret the history of a district from a single building and there are some habitation sites whose changing fortunes have been reconstructed from the fourth millennium B.C. until several centuries after the start of the Christian era.

The archaeological activities of the western countries have always depended on political conditions. It will therefore come as no surprise to learn that German excavators dominate the scene in Iraq – then still a Turkish province – in the decades preceding the First World War. They worked in an extremely competent fashion on the most imposing mounds of ruins to be found in Iraq: Babylon, Ashur, and Erech. At the same time they undertook smaller test digs in neighbouring tells such as Birs Nimrud (Borsippa) and Kar-Tukulti-Ninurta. We see them appearing once more near the famous Baghdad Railway which was then under construction, at Tell Halaf near the sources of the Khabur. All these excavations, as was to be expected, were characterised by thoroughness and method. The First World War put an abrupt end to excavations, and after the war it was only at Erech that work was resumed on a large scale.

The Decipherment of Cuneiform Writing

The first written records from Mesopotamia date back to about 3000 B.C. When inscriptions from the sphere of influence of Mesopotamian civilisation were first published in Europe in the course of the seventeenth century, they appeared to consist entirely of combinations of wedge-shaped signs. Since then this writing has been known as Assyro-Babylonian cuneiform script. For inscriptions on monuments it was engraved in hard stone, while for daily use it was written with a pointed wooden stick or reed in soft clay which was then dried in the sun. The decipherment of this script was a hard-won victory by science over a riddle to which there was at first not the slightest clue.

The success of the work of scientific detection is due to 'trilinguals' (inscriptions in three languages), left behind by the Persian kings, who, as we now know, proclaimed their fame to posterity by causing the same texts to be engraved in Old Persian, Elamitic, and Babylonian. The first investigators, however, were only able to observe that they were in the presence of three different systems of writing, probably corresponding to three different languages, and that the simplest of the three possessed not more than forty different characters and was therefore alphabetic in character.

The decipherment of this last system is due mainly to a Göttingen lecturer, Georg Friedrich Grotefend, who, on 4 September 1802, submitted to the Learned Society of Göttingen a paper in which he claimed to have deciphered thirteen of the signs. That Grotefend was able to achieve this success was due only to his great knowledge of history, his intuition, and the work of a few pioneers. The legends that have formed round Grotefend's name often unduly stress his intuition and forget that his success came anything but easily. The Danish scholar Münter had shown him that a frequently recurring group of cuneiform characters in a particular inscription must mean 'king' and 'king of kings', and also that the text must have been composed on the order of a king of the Achaemenid dynasty. To this Grotefend added the identification of the title 'great king' and then proceeded on the deduction that the title must be preceded by the sovereign's name. The word following the name and title he explained as 'son of'. He then proceeded with great perspicacity to compare two texts, of which one read: name, royal title, son of, name; and the other: name, royal title, son of, royal title, name. He identified the first name in the first text as the second name in the second text. He next reasoned as follows: We have here a grandfather, his son, and his grandson, and since the grandfather has no royal title, he must be the founder of a new dynasty. This founder could only be one of two persons – Cyrus or Hystaspes. If he was Cyrus, the son's name should begin with the same letter, for he was called Cambyses. This was not the case, so that the only possible sequence was Hystaspes, Darius, and Xerxes. By spelling the name Darius as it occurs in the Old Testament, Grotefend managed to decode the first few letters in the Old Persian script, the simplest alphabetic cuneiform. And there decipherment came temporarily to a halt. It was not until 1836 that the French scholar Burnouf and the Bonn professor Lassen succeeded in transcribing and translating Grotefend's two texts. One was found to read, 'Darius, the great king, king of kings, king of the lands, son of Hystaspes, the Achaemenid, who built this palace', and the other, 'Xerxes, the great king, king of kings, son of Darius, the king, the Achaemenid'. The second great step forward was made by Henry Rawlinson, an officer of the British Army in India, who was later detached to Kirmanshah in Persia. Not far from his temporary abode the rock of Bisutun juts out above the plain. On the face of this rock, 400 feet up, reliefs and inscriptions had been carved by order of Darius. Rawlinson copied these texts in extremely difficult circumstances and published them in 1846. The Old Persian version of these was now legible, and the Elamitic text with 111 different characters was translated in 1853 by the English scholar Norris. But the third system of writing was not so soon unravelled. Meanwhile Botta's discoveries at Khorsabad and Layard's at Nimrud had focused attention particularly on this script. As the inscriptions from these two places became known in Europe, they gave rise to the belief that they not only agreed with the third script from Bisutun but might also hold the key to an understanding of the literature of the great empires that had been founded from Babylon and Nineveh. But the task to be faced was anything but a small one: some 500 different combinations of cuneiform signs had been counted! The script could therefore not be alphabetic. The Swedish scholar Löwenstern pointed out that the words for 'king' and 'son' were represented by a single character. It was therefore possible to identify such characters without being able to pronounce them. The Irish scholar Hincks discovered in 1846 that a character represented not a consonant but a consonant plus a vowel. There were seven characters for *r* and these in fact represented *ra, ri, ru, ar, ir, er*, and *ur*. He was also the first to see that a character could also stand for two consonants with a vowel between. He further realised – and this was perhaps the most important step towards decipherment – that one character could have various values, both as to sound and as to meaning. Despite all these advances the Assyro-Babylonian cuneiform remained a fascinating riddle for scholars, and even now, retrospectively, it is still a subject for amazement that within a few years the inscriptions could be transcribed and translated. Outside their immediate circle, however, the efforts of the decipherers were regarded with some suspicion, mainly because different interpretations of a single character often caused individual transcriptions to vary greatly from one another. This distrust was ended by an experiment conducted in 1857. The Royal Asiatic Society in London submitted copies of a lengthy recently-found inscription to Rawlinson, Hincks, Fox Talbot, and Oppert, requesting them to translate the text quite independently of each other and to send in their versions. The answers were read out and compared at a formal meeting of the society and it was found that they agreed with each other in all essential details. The four translations – of an inscription of Tiglath-pileser I of Ashur – proved that the new science of Assyriology had been built on a reliable scientific basis. Much ground had been covered since the Italian explorer Pietro della Valle brought back the first cuneiform texts to Europe in 1621.

Why did the Mesopotamian scribes use so complicated a script? To explain why, it is necessary to give a short survey of the history of the art of writing as practised in the civilised territory of the Euphrates and Tigris. When men there began to record their thoughts in writing, the secret of spelling had not been discovered. The possibility of analysing a language into twenty-five to thirty letters was not realised. That is why the most ancient writing of the Sumerians was a pictographic script; in other words, when they meant to convey the idea of a fish they actually drew a fish. Where the Sumerians proved their ingenuity was in their ability to denote abstract ideas by the use of symbols, such as a star for heaven or the deity, or by the combination of two signs, such as those for 'mouth' and 'water' to render the verb 'to drink'. Their material, soft clay, did not lend itself to curved lines;

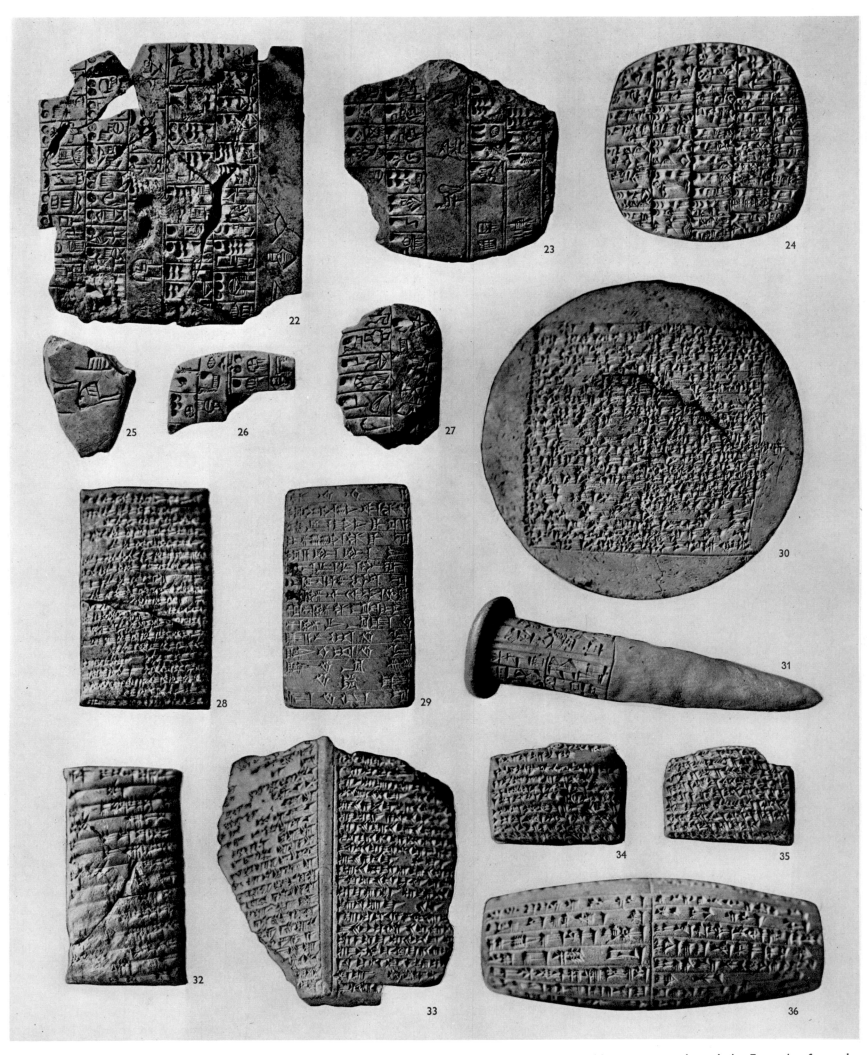

22-3, 25-7. 'Archaic' tablets found at Ur clearly show how cuneiform writing originated in recognisable pictures and symbols. Examples from the De Liagre Böhl Collection at Leiden. **24.** Undamaged tablet found at Lagash, from the period before Sargon. **30.** Head of a clay nail of Rim-Sin of Larsa. **28.** Hymn to Hammurabi or Shulgi. **29.** Tablet of dedication by Kudur-Mabug to the goddess Nana. **31.** Clay nail. **32.** Old Babylonian letter from Shamshu-iluna about redeeming citizens who had fallen into slavery. **33.** Fragment of a clay prism containing annals of Ashurbanipal. **34-5.** Two contracts dating respectively from the reigns of Nebuchadnezzar II and Darius, i.e. the last period of cuneiform. **36.** Cylinder of Nebuchadnezzar II, a handwritten foundation inscription from the temple of the Sun at Sippar. **37.** Stone building inscription found at Abu Habba in 1881. The beautifully engraved inscription states that Nabu-apal-iddin (885-825 B.C.) restored the temple of Shamash which had been destroyed by enemies.

	I	II	III	IV	V	VI	VII	VIII			I	II	III	IV	V	VI	VII	VIII
sag = head									ka+a=nag=to drink									
ka=mouth dug=to speak }									du=to walk gub=to stand }									
ninda= bowl food }									muschen=bird									
ka+ninda=ku=to eat									cha (kua)=fish may }									
a= water									gud=ox									

Drawings to illustrate part of the origin and development of some cuneiform characters from ca. 3000 to ca. 600 B.C.

all lines became straight and gradually the combination of lines became so stylised that the original symbol could hardly be recognised. When this script, evolved to record a non-Semitic tongue, was adopted by the later inhabitants of Mesopotamia, it underwent a new development which, so far from simplifying it, had the opposite result. This historical development explains the polyphonic character which makes mastery of cuneiform such a laborious mental exertion. The sign 𒌓, for instance, can be read as *ud*, *ut*, *tu*, *tam*, *par*, *pir*, *lakh*, or *khish*, and it can also have the meaning of *umu* = day or *shamshu* = sun. Anyone who has ever had to transcribe a cuneiform text with a complete list of signs by his hand must think with pity of the pupils at Babylonian schools for scribes and with even more admiration of the perseverance, brilliant intuition, and learning of the decipherers.

Once one type of Mesopotamian writing system had yielded its secrets, it was not difficult to work out the other systems of earlier periods. There were sufficient texts available in which linguists of antiquity had recorded their knowledge in comparative lists for the benefit of their pupils. Hincks, who was mentioned above, had already shown that two inscriptions, one in the Old and one in the New Babylonian cuneiform script, represented different versions of the same text.

Even when the Phoenicians had discovered ca. the thirteenth century B.C. that language could be recorded in a simple alphabetic cuneiform, as texts from Ugarit have proved, Mesopotamian scribes persisted in their use of the old complicated script, which was regarded as a god-given magic enabling men to send their souls out into the world and to be effective at distant places and in distant ages.

THE TECHNIQUE OF THE WRITING

As we have already seen, the material available to the Mesopotamian scribe was soft clay. Some very old tablets made of baked gypsum and sand were found in Erech, but in general tablets were shaped by hand from clay. For documents which did not need to be preserved for long no attempt was made to remove impurities; pebbles and even date stones can therefore sometimes be found in tablets. For documents of special importance and for literary works the clay was purified, with the result that the clay shows as much variety of quality as modern papers do.

The conditions a simple tablet had to satisfy were few: the material had to remain soft and workable for a short time, and it must not adhere to the stylus. Once the text was inscribed, the tablet was dried in the sun. It was possible to use the tablet again for another text by soaking it in water. It then served the same purpose as the slates formerly used in school, from which writing could be erased with a sponge. There was, however, the disadvantage that this method lent itself to forgery. Par. 48 of the Code of Hammurabi refers to a tenant farmer who is prevented by floods from meeting his obligations. He is released from them or, as the Code literally says, 'he shall wipe his tablet clean'. In the case of a contract drawn up on a tablet, the custom was to break the tablet together with the contract on the day the latter expired.

Not till a later period did it become usual to bake tablets in an oven so that their durability became practically unlimited. Holes were bored in them to prevent them from cracking during this process.

Tablets of many shapes are known (see Pls. 22-36). They may be oblong, square, or round. The round shape was preferred for school work, where the diameter could separate the teacher's example from the pupil's exercise. Tablets could also be oval or wedge-shaped, the latter form being favoured for dedication inscriptions which had to be set into temple walls. The size of the tablets also varied widely. Sometimes they had room for only a seal consisting of a few characters; but the tablets on which the Middle Assyrian laws were recorded have the relatively enormous dimensions of more than $12 \times 8 \times 1$ inches. One of these tablets holds 828 lines arranged in eight columns, four on either side. For tablets of any considerable size it was necessary to take precautions to prevent premature hardening. Scribes took a long time over their delicate work. It was impossible to let a tablet lie about for several days, and the scribe had to do his job as quickly as possible, ensuring all the time, by means of wet cloths, that the clay remained workable. The impression of these cloths can sometimes still be made out on tablets. Accounts covering any considerable period of time had to be prepared for by laying in a stock of small tablets, on which the progress of business was recorded from day to day.

The texts were written with a sharpened reed. As a definitely identifiable example of this instrument has never been found, its shape and the material it was made from have been a subject of extensive discussion. It has still not been definitely established how the scribe manipulated his stylus or how the latter was made. Most indications nevertheless suggest that a hard variety of reed still found in southern Mesopotamia was used, which could be sharpened on a grindstone. It is true that some Assyrian reliefs show scribes at work, but the sculptors did not succeed in illustrating clearly how the scribes set about their task (see page 27).

The art of writing flourished in and about the temple, though this does not mean that the oldest texts were religious in character. On the contrary, it was rather economic necessity which demanded the recording of goods and numbers on tablets, and this fact reflects the administrative function which the temple performed in antiquity. The earliest scribes recorded their signs in a vertical direction. They started in the top right-hand corner, i.e. the point most convenient for the right hand, and wrote from top to bottom and then in columns from right to left. In the course of development the direction of writing rotated through an angle of 90° and became horizontal, but now running from left to right. This change in the direction of writing greatly influenced the form of the characters for words, syllables, and letters. The art of engraving texts in mirrored writing and using them for duplication was mastered at an early date. There is even evidence that loose movable letters were sometimes used, early forerunners of the art of typography.

It is no surprise to learn that writing styles changed in the course of the centuries, so that the script is a valuable evidence in dating texts. Allowance must nevertheless be made for a powerful conservatism which results in ancient types of script, and even vertical writing, being found in more recent times. It seems that the scribes with an archaic style of this sort did not have the slightest difficulty in employing it. The ties with tradition were weakest where the art of writing developed away from its original home. The tendency towards cursive writing, for example, is clearly visible on tablets from Assyrian settlements in Cappadocia. Thus, while it is possible to detect remarkable dissimilarities in contemporaneous scripts, it is also important not to underestimate the influence of various schools for scribes. Apart from the idiosyncrasies of individual scribes, these schools conventionalised the combinations of characters according to certain standards of calligraphy. The scribes continued to regard themselves as the practitioners of a noble art of divine origin, at which the layman gazed with the awe of the uninitiated.

What has been said so far about writing techniques applies to the normal clay tablet. Other materials, such as hard stone, were also used for inscriptions on monuments. Texts were even recorded in lapis lazuli, and on silver, gold, and ivory. In later times abundant use was made of papyrus, leather, and parchment, materials which were doomed to total destruction in a climate such as that of Mesopotamia.

Assyrian reliefs show us various scribes. One of these has attracted particular attention. It dates from the time of Sennacherib (end of eighth century B.C.) and shows a scribe writing notes in a 'tablet book' coated with wax. Beside him stands another scribe, handling a roll (of papyrus or leather?). We now know what such a tablet book looked like. At Nimrud in 1953 sixteen ivory tablets and an equal number of small walnut-wood plates were found at the bottom of a well. On the tablets were found traces of beeswax containing 25 % of arsenic sulphide. This substance, which is found in natural form in the vicinity of Nimrud, makes wax easier to work. The combination of the two was spread in semi-molten condition over the surface of the writing tablets. It was then possible to engrave texts in it.

The ivory tablets were joined together with hinges so that they formed a single volume – a book of thirty pages with a front and rear cover. The front cover also served as title-page, and on it, carved into the ivory, could be read: 'Palace of Sargon, the king of the world, the king of Assyria. He caused the series of texts, *When Anu-Enlil*, to be written on an ivory writing-tablet and brought to his palace at Dur Sharrukin.' The intention of this king, who ruled at the end of the eighth century B.C., was apparently never carried out. The tablets remained in Nimrud and were dropped in a well where they were preserved by water until their discovery in 1953. The metal hinges have disappeared, and as no trace of rust has been found they are thought to have been of gold. In that case they probably fell a prey to gold-hungry looters. The find constitutes a valuable addition to our knowledge of the techniques employed by scribes. A notebook of this kind was useful when prisoners were brought in, the numbers of the slain were counted, or a record of booty had to be kept. In this book, consisting as it did of small plates coated with a wax preparation, the scribe possessed an efficient aid which was easier to work with than a clay tablet.

The art of writing in Mesopotamia was a complicated matter and the scribe's training must have lasted a long time. He had to acquire a mastery of several languages, scripts, and techniques under the patronage of Nabu or Nebo, whose emblems included the cuneiform character and the tablet. Nabu was known as the inventor of writing, the scribe without a peer and the secretary of the gods, he who wielded the reed pen. It is to Nabu's guild and to those who deciphered his cuneiform writing that we owe a knowledge of the ancient Mesopotamian civilisation which has grown beyond our power to survey. Yet this knowledge will continue to grow by the discovery of new texts and the interpretation of texts still unedited.

The top illustration is a reconstruction of the 'tablet book' that was found in Nimrud in 1953. Below it are two examples of Assyrian reliefs showing scribes using tablets of this kind to record the number of enemies slain and the spoils of war.

38. A bronze lion guarding a white stone tablet bearing a foundation inscription of the petty king Tishari of Urkish. Inscriptions of this kind were buried under temples from early times. They contained architectural indications useful to posterity if the building had to be restored, the dimensions being read from the *templum*. This was an area of the sky mapped by the priests and projected onto earth as a piece of microcosm intended to reflect the macrocosm. The ancients believed that it was impossible to ignore such sacred dimensions with impunity. This particular tablet is $4\frac{1}{4}$ in. wide. The script is typical of the 24th to 22nd centuries B.C. The tablet was found at Larsa and is now in the Louvre. **39.** A small stone stele ($14\frac{1}{2}$ in. high), a fine example of a genre that is represented by several other pieces in the British Museum. It shows in relief the figure of Ashurbanipal or his brother Shamash-shum-ukin as a builder. Although the script is characteristic of the Neo-Assyrian period, the theme is based on very old traditions. Ur-Nanshe of Lagash also, who lived nearly 2000 years earlier, is represented with a basket full of bricks on his head. This was the method used by Ashurbanipal to proclaim himself restorer of the temple of Esagila in Babylon. The inscription, too, recalls the king's pious architectural activities: 'He has rebuilt Esagila with wood of cypresses and of cedars; he has fitted new doors and has presented vessels of gold, silver, copper, and iron.' The text ends with the usual curse on those who might dare to alter the monument. **40.** Clay tablet found in Ashurbanipal's library; it is among the most famous inscriptions in the British Museum. It is a fragment of Tablet XI of the Gilgamesh epic in the later Assyrian version and contains the description of the Flood, which Utnapishtim survived. The text was identified by the Assyriologist George Smith among the tablets sent home by Layard in 1872 and was the subject of his lecture in London on 3 December, which caused a great sensation and awakened public interest in cuneiform literature. In 1873 the *Daily Telegraph* financed an expedition to Nineveh under his leadership. He discovered the missing fragments of the Flood episode, and brought back an important collection of objects and inscriptions. The tablet measures $5\frac{3}{4} \times 5\frac{1}{4}$ in. The right-hand column of the obverse side seen here contains lines 165-214, the left-hand column lines 218-267 (damaged) of the story of the Flood; the rest (the preceding lines) is on the front of the tablet.

Excavations in the Twentieth Century

UP TO THE SECOND WORLD WAR (see Map 2)

While the French excavators were successfully at work in Susa, on Persian territory, the German Orient Society, which was under the patronage of the Emperor Wilhelm II, decided to excavate the mound of Babylon, and leadership of the expedition was entrusted to Robert Koldewey. Digging continued without intermission through all seasons of the year from 26 March 1899 to the spring of 1917. The main assistance that Koldewey called in during that time was from architects, and Assyriologists were kept at a distance. This underestimation of the usefulness of epigraphists, who are able to read any texts found and thus help in the dating of the various habitation layers, was also typical of the excavation at Ashur. Koldewey nevertheless succeeded in resurrecting the city of Nebuchadnezzar to life again. The older cities on the site of Babylon, for example that of Hammurabi, could not be reached because the ground-water had risen considerably since those days. No impressive museum pieces came to light during the eighteen years of excavation; but anyone who has visited the Staatliche Museen in Berlin and stood before the Ishtar Gate which Koldewey reconstructed from original fragments, with its glazed blue bricks and its ochre reliefs of bulls and dragons, will not readily forget the impression made by this magnificent monument (see Pl. 241). But probably the main achievement of Koldewey's lifework lies in the fact that we can now form an accurate idea of what Daniel 4 describes as the great city that Nebuchadnezzar built.

A few years after it has been excavated a tell generally presents the cheerless sight of a deserted town buried in sand. Not so Babylon. Koldewey made Nebuchadnezzar's city a permanent monument to German skill in excavation work. Nor should it go unmentioned that between times a number of mounds in the vicinity were visited and described, while test digs which benefited later research were conducted at Birs Nimrud, Tell Fara, and Abu Khatab.

Another expedition under the auspices of the German Orient Society was sent out to Sharqat, where the remains of the ancient Ashur lay buried. The leadership was entrusted to Walter Andrae, a pupil of Koldewey. Work on this site, too, continued without intermission from 1903 until 1914. Generally speaking, Andrae's methods are esteemed even more highly than those of his teacher. The systematic excavation of this enormous mound made it possible to describe the history of the city in detail from about 3000 B.C. until the rule of the Sassanids in the third century A.D. But a lay visitor to the site of Ashur will find less to see than the tourist does in Babylon. From Ashur the mound of Kar-Tukulti-Ninurta (thirteenth century B.C.), a few miles away, was explored. Of very special value was the excavation of Tell Halaf; this was led by Baron Max von Oppenheim, who had originally been a diplomat. As a result of preparatory work on the Baghdad Railway he had been confronted with finds from the mound by Bedouin as early as 1889. Since Tell Halaf will figure prominently in the next chapter, we will merely mention here that von Oppenheim also had successful results when he led an expedition to Jebelet el-Beda, forty-four miles from Tell Halaf. These excavations bring us into the region which was named Subartu by the Assyrians, and which, with Sumer, Akkad, Elam, and Amurru, formed their 'world'.

During this period of glory for German archaeology representatives of the other leading nations were not absent from the excavation sites. On the western bank of the Euphrates, also in the vicinity of the Baghdad Railway, the English set up their archaeological site. This was at Carchemish, where digging went on from 1911 to 1914 under the direction of Campbell Thompson and Sir Leonard Woolley. It was resumed in 1920, but had soon to be abandoned again because of Franco-Turkish disputes about the demarcation line between Turkey and the mandated territory of Syria as it then was. The town mentioned in Jeremiah 46 : 2 and in 2 Chronicles 35 : 20 proved to be what might have been expected, an important strategic point on the road joining Palestine and Mesopotamia, with habitation layers ranging from the Stone Age to the sixth century A.D. About the same time a French expedition under Henri de Genouillac was working at Tell el-Oheimir, which was successfully identified as the ancient Kish, a capital of four dynasties in antiquity. This spot is not far from Babylon and was frequently visited at the beginning of the nineteenth century by travellers who sometimes regarded it as a suburb of Babylon, believing too literally the legend which credited the latter with an exaggerated size. The break that the First World War caused in the peaceful work of the diggers provided a useful opportunity to draw up a balance sheet. Soon afterwards the English in especial took advantage of their privileges in the newly independent Iraq and concentrated all their attention on the exploration of Ur and its environs. How much more favourable were the circumstances in which work could be undertaken! Transport facilities were vastly improved and the personal safety of the scientists was guaranteed by increasing central authority. But above all the excavator possessed a method, the fruit of practical experience, which could lead to the astonishing results obtained by Sir Leonard Woolley when he dug the treasures from the Royal Tombs of Ur during his campaigns of 1927 and 1928. Since then a history of the excavations in Mesopotamia would be inconceivable without the expedition mounted by the British Museum and the Museum of the University of Pennsylvania. The yield of twelve campaigns between 1922 and 1934 is immeasurably great (see Pls. 65 and 96-103). Anyone who wishes confirmation of that statement need only visit the appropriate section of the British Museum. The treasures from Shub-ad's tomb are some of the finest museum pieces ever to have been taken from the soil of Mesopotamia. But even without them the excavation of Ur would have been a success for having uncovered the ziggurat, the temples, and the scribes' house with their long history of neglect, destruction, and restoration. At the same time admiration for the achievements of the archaeologists at Ur should not distract attention from a small but important excavation at Tell el-'Obeid, a tell slightly more than 1,100 feet long and from 20 to 25 feet high, situated about four miles west of Ur. The pottery from this mound gave its name to a characteristic period of Mesopotamian civilisation. About the same time a joint Anglo-American expedition was working at Kish (where de Genouillac had started) and Jemdet Nasr, which will be found fifteen miles to the northeast of Kish. Activity increased very rapidly about this time. Der, where Rassam and Budge had searched, was again explored by Andrae and Jordan. The great problem of the site of ancient Agade was, however, still not solved. The Pennsylvania Museum was responsible for digging at Tell Fara (Shuruppak) in 1931. The Germans resumed operations at Erech, where eleven campaigns under the leadership of Julius Jordan, Arnold Nöldeke, and Ernst Heinrich were carried out between 1928 and 1939. French excavators moved into Larsa (now

41. The French excavator Victor Place in Part III of his work *Ninevé et l'Assyrie* (Paris, 1867) has left an impressive picture of the conditions in which archaeologists worked in the middle of the 19th century. In 1853 he performed the feat of transporting a number of huge statues of bulls, each of the colossal weight of 32,000 kg., in their entirety from Khorsabad to the Tigris. Botta, his predecessor, had similar items cut into six pieces before daring to transport them. The drawing shows that the feat was only possible by the use of hundreds of workers encouraged by drummers and spectators.

42-4. The excavator realised that he was doing exactly what the Assyrian kings had done. The latter had their sculptors produce reliefs showing vividly how a sculpted bull of colossal proportions was transported from the workshop to its destination. The reliefs revealed how it was possible to convey the enormous statues in one piece. Sleighs were used which were pulled by dozens of workers by means of ropes. To facilitate movement wooden beams were placed in succession under the sleighs. Comparison with the Assyrian reliefs shows that technical progress in 3,000 years had not been great.

45-7. More difficult still than transport to the river was that by water to Baghdad and thence to the port of Basra. A shipwreck on the Tigris had already caused an important collection of antiquities from Khorsabad to vanish to the bottom of the river. We possess a description of these objects which have still never been recovered. Even in the matter of river transport Place was inspired by the method by which the former inhabitants had solved the problem. Reliefs showed rafts supported by inflated animal skins. Very heavy loads were floated downstream in this way. The Assyrians' method was put to the test at the end of April 1855, when Place's eight rafts moved off, reaching Baghdad by 4 May. This *kelek* stood up better to the caprices of gales and the river than the steamboat which had already been used in experiments. The paddleboat *Tigris* had been lost with all hands in the spring of 1836 as a result of a sudden squall. The memory of this catastrophe at the confluence of the Euphrates and the Khabur was still very fresh when Place wanted to transport the treasures of Khorsabad by way of the river. The success of his undertaking was yet another proof that the well-tried methods of the ancients were still, in 1855, the best for transport of heavy objects.

45

46

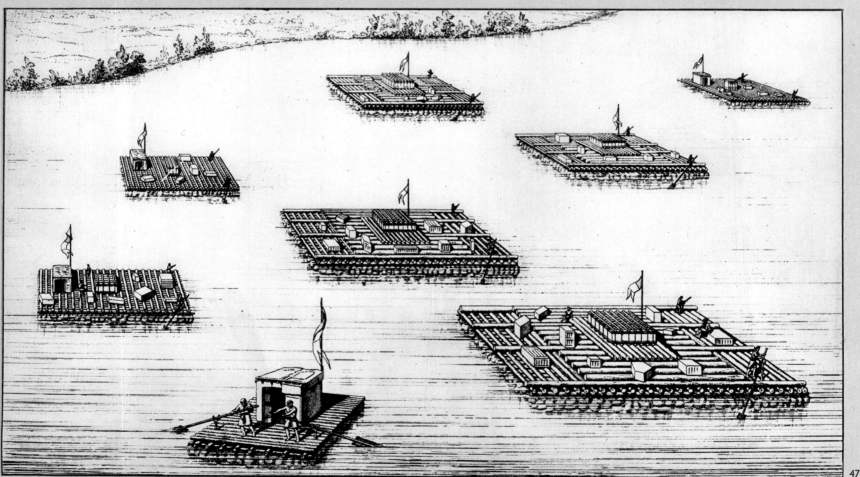

47

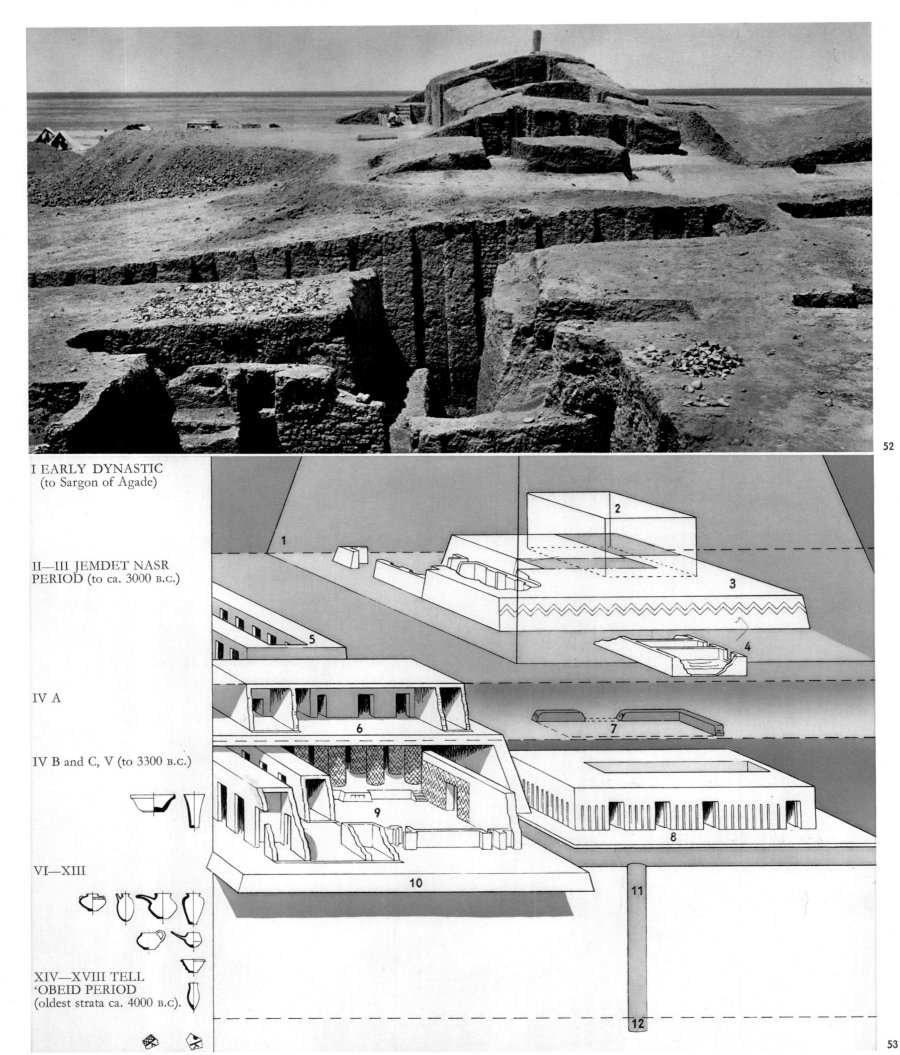

52

I EARLY DYNASTIC
(to Sargon of Agade)

II—III JEMDET NASR
PERIOD (to ca. 3000 B.C.)

IV A

IV B and C, V (to 3300 B.C.)

VI—XIII

XIV—XVIII TELL
'OBEID PERIOD
(oldest strata ca. 4000 B.C.).

53

48. This composite photograph gives an impression of the cultural layers at Eridu, which were excavated between 1946 and 1949. At the top we see the remains of the ziggurat erected about 2000 B.C. by Ur-Nammu. Beneath this temple tower were discovered the remains of sixteen temples built one above the other in various periods, the oldest dating from the Tell'Obeid period, and beneath these again traces of still older habitation. **49.** The tell of Eridu with its two distinctive peaks. **50.** The wind has already buried Eridu under sand again. **51.** The tell of Eridu as seen from the Akitu house outside the walls. **52.** Tell 'Uqair during the 1940-1 excavations. **53.** Civilisation layers at Erech: 1. ziggurat of Ur-Nammu; 2. temple; 3. platforms; 4. sacrificial basins; 5 and 6. temples; 7. red temple; 8. temple on limestone base; 9. inner court with mosaic stone floor; 10. foundation of older building layer; 11-12. test dig town to virgin soil, depth 53 ft.

54
55
56

57

54. In the campaigns of recent years very careful work has been done on the tells of Erech under the leadership of Professor Lenzen. The buildings are of clay bricks which differ little from the grit in which they were buried. The task therefore has been not excavation but preparation. In recent years work has been largely confined to the Eanna group of temples, which has representatives of all archaeological layers. **55.** A wall is carefully brought to light with the aid of brushes and pins under expert supervision. **56.** The difficult work is done by a trained worker who separates the grit from the wall with a pin. **57.** This building, a small object outside the town precincts, attracted attention by its semicircular shapes. The conjecture that it was a mithraeum has slowly become certainty, especially since the discovery in London of a similar building which was undoubtedly a mithraeum. This is an indication of the presence here of Roman legions.

58

59

60
61

62
63

58. The old walls of Erech, with a perimeter of almost 6 miles, lie hidden beneath the surface of the ground; but in the morning, when the atmosphere is damp, their course stands out dark against the light background. The saline content of the clay bricks makes the ground hygroscopic, which explains the mystery of this brief duration of the visibility of the walls. Bright moonlight also sometimes brings out the outlines, and the unexpected discovery of the Akitu house at Erech was due to this. Returning from an outing by car, the staff on an expedition were delayed by tyre trouble and passed by the tell late at night. Then for the first time, in the light of the moon, dark outlines were visible; these proved to be those of the festival building, the site of which was then unknown although it was realised that it must lie outside the walls. The entire building with its numerous rooms and inner courts was subsequently excavated.

59. The semicircular bastions of the outer wall also become clearly visible.

60-1. These photographs show the traces of a violent fire which destroyed a temple on this site after Persian times. The clay walls of the building were vitrified by the heat, and bitumen poured from the roof on to the floor, where the burning furniture fell into it, leaving clear impressions from which the original shapes can be reconstructed.

62. A peculiar wall decoration consisting of mosaic-like arrangements of cones was found in some buildings in Erech. The photograph, taken soon after the discovery, shows a detail.

63. In Erech as elsewhere the courses of clay bricks were separated by straw. The layers of straw gave the necessary elasticity to large buildings such as ziggurats.

64. The excavation site at Ur where Sir Leonard Woolley achieved such sensational results is still dominated by the ziggurat of Ur-Nammu and the near-by 'house of tablets'. **65.** The most impressive single discovery during the excavation at Ur was that of the 'Royal Tombs'. Excavation techniques here reached their zenith, as demonstrated by the meticulous preservation of objects found and the accuracy with which the circumstances surrounding the sealing of the tombs were reconstructed. Particularly astonishing was the discovery of Shub-ad's grave, where no fewer than 74 people, 68 of them women, had met their death. Many problems still surround this drama: in the lands where Mesopotamian culture dominated it was not the custom to bury courtiers alive with their dead king; the dating of the event is uncertain and the names of the buried kings do not occur on any list. A. Forester made the above reconstruction of the moment when Shub-ad's attendants were about to be united with her in death.

66 67

68 69

70

66. The enormous mound at Nineveh regularly provides surprises such as this recent find: a winged guardian of the gate, whose face is still intact. **67.** This discovery led the Iraqi Department of Antiquities to reconstruct the original gate building on its actual site. **68.** During excavations at Nimrud in 1955 the statue of a man holding a square tray in his hands was found. Half of the head is missing, but the regular pattern of the beard and hair makes reconstruction easy. **69.** The ruins of Ashur, long the scene of German excavations, now lie deserted beside the Tigris. Traces of the bastions are still clearly visible. **70.** At Nimrud, where investigations are still regularly pursued under the leadership of Professor Mallowan, these remains of the quay walls of ancient Calah were exposed, proving that the city was on the river then, whereas its distance from the Tigris nowadays is quite considerable.

called Senkereh, southeast of Erech and twelve miles north of the Euphrates), where clandestine digging was beginning to create such havoc that the Department of Antiquities called in the assistance of the Royal Air Force in the spring of 1931 to drive off Arab treasure-seekers. The French archaeologists, who included André Parrot, had already achieved creditable results here and were planning to continue in the winter of 1933-4 when a change in Iraq's attitude to archaeological missions caused France and Britain to choose a different scene of operations. The essentially not unreasonable restriction imposed by the Government of Iraq, to the effect that unique finds must not leave the country and that only half of other finds might be exported, had a remarkable and in some respects a very useful result. The British Museum abandoned the excavations at Ur and Arpachiya, and the Louvre those at Tello. Woolley went and dug at 'Atshanah, in the Plain of Antioch; Mallowan, who had been digging at Nimrud, transferred his search to Chagar Bazar and Tell Brak; by the end of 1933 Parrot was in Tell Hariri, where he discovered Mari, which has since become famous. We will dwell for a moment on the excavation of Mari, because it proved such a typical combination of chance, knowledge, and favourable political circumstances (see Pls. 77-9).

In 1933, while digging a grave, several Arabs had found a large and heavy statue near Tell Hariri to the west of the Euphrates, near its middle course. It was disfigured, but gave the impression of having once been beautiful. The find was brought to the notice of the French Archaeological Service, and René Dussaud, curator at the Louvre, advised further investigation. The very first campaign uncovered the ancient city of Mari. The name was known from various sources, including the prologue to the Code of Hammurabi, but its position had until then been a matter for conjecture. A series of surprises emerged from the campaign of 1934-5 after the area containing the royal palace was reached. Until 1939 Parrot was in charge of these excavations, which added to the fame of French archaeology. After the Second World War the work was resumed in 1950 for several more campaigns. Mari is outside Iraq but belongs entirely to Mesopotamian culture. With its palace and its royal archives dating from the eighteenth century B.C., it is unusually well preserved. In Mari as elsewhere, archaeology has been able to reap the benefit of disasters which struck the ancient world. The fact that Mari was destroyed at the end of the eighteenth century B.C. by Hammurabi and so thoroughly that it never rose in glory again, is the reason why, when the palace was excavated thirty-six centuries later, the sewage system proved able to cope perfectly with a tropical shower. The slow wear and tear of peaceful history sometimes frustrates the archaeologist, whereas a war or a natural catastrophe often supplies him with the material he needs.

To complete the survey, there are two sites that must be mentioned: the Diyala region and the upper course of the Tigris. The Diyala flows into the Tigris not far from Baghdad, and in antiquity its banks were inhabited by a dense population, who owed their prosperity to an excellent irrigation system. Expeditions to this region were undertaken under the auspices of the Oriental Institute of the University of Chicago. They were led by the Dutch scholar, Henri Frankfort, and with the assistance of a large staff and ample financial means they worked in Tell Asmar, Khafaje, Ishchali, and Tell Ajrab from 1930 until 1937. Tell Asmar was identified as the site of the ancient city of Eshnunna, the residence of Bilalama, of whom we shall have more to say in connection with his law code (twentieth century B.C.). Khafaje has become known chiefly for its temple oval, which was perhaps dedicated to Inanna.

When excavations started in the vicinity of Kirkuk, they too were

71. The mound of Nimrud now lies on the edge of a cotton plantation. **72.** From an elevated point there is a wide view of the excavation site and its immediate surroundings. **73.** In the foreground is part of a sewer. **74.** The city was rich in inscriptions recording the deeds of its kings. Shown here are large stone tablets which have just been cleared of rubble and sand; the authentic information carved on them in handsome cuneiform now contributes to our historical knowledge of Assyria.

under American direction. The Yorghan Tepe mound proved to be the ancient Nuzu, now generally famed for its legal-commercial texts, which reveal remarkable parallels with the history of the patriarchs in Genesis. Here, too, was found the world's oldest known map; it was drawn before 2000 B.C., on clay, and shows rivers, canals, and mountains.

Of the many other tells that were uncovered before the start of the Second World War, one at least, Arpachiya, must be mentioned. Mallowan, assisted by his wife, Agatha Christie, worked here in 1933 under the auspices of the British School of Archaeology in Mesopotamia. The greatest sensation here was provided by the discovery of the *tholoi*, round buildings with a rectangular forecourt, which are regarded as the prototypes of the Mycenaean *tholoi*.

DURING AND AFTER THE SECOND WORLD WAR

In the thirties of the present century an interest in pre-Islamic civilisation was aroused among native Iraqi archaeologists. The latter had taken part in expeditions from abroad and had acquired an expertise which was displayed towards the end of the Second World War and afterwards. This interest is in fact steadily spreading to wider sections of the population, as the visitor to the Baghdad or Mosul museums can see for himself. Charge of the Department of Antiquities, which was long in the trusted hand of Dr Naji-al-Asil, has now been passed on to Dr S. Fuad Safar, who achieved such fine results at Hatra and Eridu. The excavation of the awkwardly situated Eridu in particular brought surprises in the form of more ancient civilisation strata than had been expected. Also worthy of mention are the excavations at Tell 'Uqair (1940-1), Hassuna (1943-4), and 'Aqarquf (1943-5), all of which were the result of Iraqi initiative. In addition to these activities, Mallowan resumed his investigation of Nimrud, the Americans returned to Nippur under the leadership of McCown and Haines, while the Germans, now led by Heinz Lenzen, have been working continuously on the Erech mound again since 1954 (see Pls. 54-63).

Denmark has been participating in the archaeological work on the island of Bahrain and in northeast Iraq. In the course of this work Peter Vilhelm Glob of Aarhus found confirmation of the conjecture that the island can be identified with Dilmun, where, according to the Gilgamesh epic, Utnapishtim, the Noah of the Assyro-Babylonian story of the Flood, lived. This was the centre of the worship of Enki, the god of the primeval ocean, who was also venerated at Eridu. But Dilmun's chief importance is as a link in the chain between the Sumerian civilisation and the related culture in the Indus valley, traces of which were found at Mohenjo-Daro. In 1957 a Danish expedition under Harald Ingolt visited the sixteen tells in the valley of the Little Zab, which will soon be flooded permanently when the reservoir at Dokan is completed. First reports mention tablets whose contents provide interesting background material to the stories of the patriarchs.

The latest nation to be represented on the excavation scene in Iraq is Japan, an expedition led by Namio Egami having been sent out by the University of Tokyo in 1956. At Telul ath-Thalathat, a mound thirty-seven miles west of Mosul, they discovered, among other things, the remains of a temple thought to be one of the oldest and best preserved in all Mesopotamia.

The end of the excavations is still not in sight. Thousands of uninvestigated tells have been recorded and are awaiting visits by archaeologists. Many problems dating from the classical era of archaeology, for example the site of Agade, have still not been solved. But attention has, in particular, been transferred from the classical periods of Nineveh and Babylon to Sumerian civilisation, and more especially to times of which the only evidence is artefacts and pottery.

75. A stone relief of a bull slowly comes to light in Nimrud. In the background is a cuneiform inscription. **76.** Detail of a monument at Ur photographed during excavation. The British Museum contains several other examples of this genre dating from the 9th century B.C.; they all show a bracelet with a rosette, a bag in the left hand, and in the right usually a cone-shaped object used in a rite at the sacred tree.

75

76

77. Aerial photograph of the palace at Mari after excavation by French archaeologists under the leadership of André Parrot. The exposure of this, the largest royal residence of the 2nd millennium B.C., also attracted attention by the discovery of its archives, containing tens of thousands of clay tablets. The photograph shows a system of over 250 rooms with inner courtyards, the whole covering an area of more than 6 acres. **78.** This detail of the excavation shows one of the passages, the walls of which are still surprisingly high. At the end of the passage is a room where scribes were taught. The light entered not by windows but through inner courts and gates, so that twilight prevailed which was barely sufficient to read by. Alongside the benches were water-troughs in which to soften the clay tablets again after use. **79.** A piece of sculpture as it was found on the site in 1937; it proved to be a fine example of skill from the 18th century B.C.

The Pre-literary Period

The most drastic change in the history of human civilisation took place when man ceased to live exclusively by hunting and fishing and on the chance offerings of nature and engaged in agriculture and cattle breeding. Not until a recent period of the excavation work in Iraq did it prove possible to localise the scene of this transition. The remains of the oldest farms in Mesopotamia were obviously not to be sought on the alluvial river plains. The men who settled there had already acquired considerable experience of agriculture, otherwise they could not possibly have undertaken the difficult struggle against the water. Before Professor Robert J. Braidwood succeeded in identifying the site of man's transition from food gatherer to food producer, something was known of cave-dwellers who lived about 10000 B.C. and village-dwellers who lived about 4500 B.C.

That does not mean that the former should be regarded as the most ancient inhabitants of Iraq. At Barda Balka in Kurdistan simple stone implements have been found which must have been made by a representative of *homo faber* about 100,000 years ago. In a cave at Khazar Merd, not far from Sulaimaniya, traces were found of human beings who must have lived there 50,000 years ago. In the Shanidar valley Ralph S. Solecki, leader of the expedition mounted by the Smithsonian Institute, found a fourth Neanderthaler in 1956-7, whose age he estimates at 60,000 years! But there was a gap between the cave-dweller of Zarzi, likewise not far from Sulaimaniya, estimated at ca. 1000 B.C., and the civilised village-dwellers of Hassuna. The honour of filling the gap fell to Professor Braidwood, archaeologist of the University of Chicago. He pinpointed man's vital transition in Mesopotamia – a process more drastic than the industrial revolution after James Watt – as having occurred on the plateau of Jarmo, not far from the village of Chemchemal (see Pl. 80).

The site had already been recognised as a valuable one for prehistory by the Department of Antiquities of Iraq. This discovery was due to a fortunate coincidence. In 1946, when an official of the Department had offered a cigarette to a village sheikh, he noticed that the sheikh struck a light with a flint and steel. He recognised the flint as a finely wrought specimen of the late Stone Age. When the sheikh indicated the spot where this artefact had been found, Jarmo was discovered. In the spring of 1948 Braidwood carried out a preparatory investigation here which led to the notable expedition of 1950-1, in the course of which it proved possible to distinguish fifteen different cultural layers over a small area. Only the five top layers showed any traces of pottery. The others contained traces of people who were unable to make earthenware but used tools made from flint and obsidian. Obsidian is a vitreous lava which must have been brought from a distant source, the nearest place where it is found being Lake Van. The presence of this material indicates that trading took place over great distances. When the radio carbon test, an extremely important tool in the absolute determination of age, was applied to snails' shells, it showed that this site had been inhabited between 5077 and 4537 B.C. One of the most remarkable implements found there was a sickle made of flint. It was fastened into a wooden handle with bitumen. The houses consisted of rectangular rooms with ovens and chimneys and hollows in the clay of the floor. Although the walls were constructed in a simple style and of mud, they gave the impression that building had a centuries-old tradition behind it. Unfired clay figures representing animals and pregnant women testify to an

80. The exposed foundations of a house at Jarmo. The mud walls were erected above the stones, which indicate the lay-out.

ancient religion which had given rise to fertility rites. Ornaments of stone, such as beads, rings, and armbands, had also been made.

From their base at Jarmo Braidwood's staff also conducted research at Karim Shahir, not much more than a mile away. Here a more primitive stage of habitation was found, in which there was no evidence of a closed village community, no obsidian, and no sickles. The settlement of Karim Shahir is therefore dated about 6000 B.C. and is also regarded as an important historical link between the cave-dwellers and Jarmo. The Palegawra cave lies in the same area. The material discovered here suggests a period filling the gap between Karim Shahir and Zarzi. Thus the pieces are slowly being fitted together, adding more and more detail to the history of Mesopotamian man between 10000 and 5000 B.C., even though he himself has left no written word or piece of earthenware to make the task easier. At any rate it is certain that the great revolution of the Neolithic age took place in Kurdistan. The excellent climatic conditions at that time were the main reason why this particular part of Mesopotamia witnessed the change of the hunter and fisher into a farmer and cattle breeder, even if the nomad continued his migrations in the countryside surrounding the villages (see Map 6).

THE EVIDENCE OF POTTERY

All the same, there is still a gap of 2,000 years between the rising agricultural civilisation of Jarmo and the first Sumerian to make himself understood with the aid of written characters. This period – equal in length to the time that elapsed between the Emperor Augustus and the discovery of atomic energy – can be examined only briefly here. Nonetheless, it is possible to mark this period out into subdivisions on the basis of its pottery (see Map 7).

It seems fairly certain that the objects uncovered during Iraqi excavations at Hassuna, not far from Ashur on the Tigris, follow chronologically upon those from Jarmo. The date of the excavations was 1943-4. The bottom layer, immediately above the virgin soil, contained the remains of flint tools but also coarse earthenware jugs.

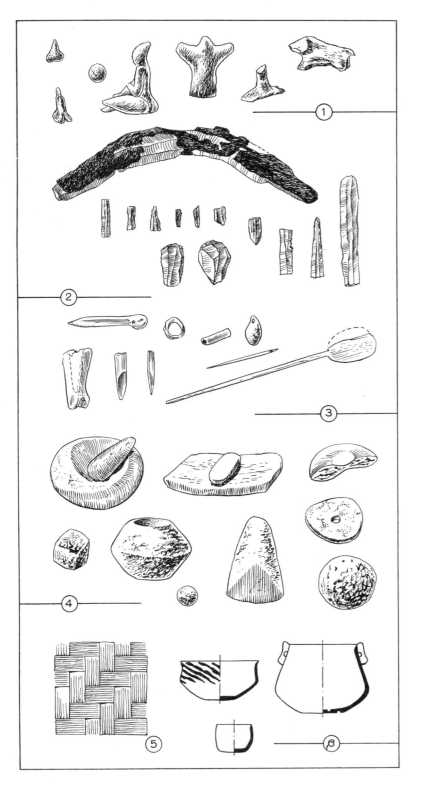

This layer was followed by seven others containing ruins of houses, which showed some evolution and did not differ basically from the mud huts which can be seen to this day in any Iraqi village – an obvious example of the static character of life in the East. The great difference between the culture of Hassuna and that of Jarmo is the appearance of pottery. The latter is of a particular character which enables it to be identified in habitation strata of mounds in Cilicia, Syria, and Palestine. In other words, we are dealing not with a sudden manifestation of skill on the part of an isolated potter in Hassuna, but with a movement among an entire people. This nation can also be recognised from the shape of its skulls, so that it seems probable that in the Neolithic age a nation in mass migration swept over an area stretching from the mountains of Kurdistan to the Mediterranean.

More recent strata at Hassuna revealed pottery of a type that was first found in Samarra by Herzfeld and Sarre during the German excavations of 1912-14. This pottery is decorated with drawings of plants, animals, and human beings, painted in bright-red and purple-brown colours. Samarra earthenware, which is characterised by great artistry, has now also been found at various sites between the Tigris and northern Syria.

The pottery next in antiquity to that found at Hassuna and Samarra is called after the mound Tell Halaf in the vicinity of Ras el-'Ain, near the headwaters of the Khabur. The old name of the town was Gozan. In 1931 von Oppenheim, who dug here from 1911 to 1913 and again in 1929, published a book with the subtitle of 'A new culture in earliest Mesopotamia', which drew the attention of a wide circle of interested admirers to the magnificent earthenware from one of the oldest strata at Tell Halaf. Its variety of form and its decoration appeared to lend it great appeal to the modern imagination. Von Oppenheim was able to produce whole or pieced-together earthenware in the form of beakers, bowls, basins, plates, and jugs. The clay of which the pottery was made was extraordinarily pure, the walls of the dishes unusually thin. The decoration had been applied in two or three colours; it was sometimes a geometrical pattern, but mostly it consisted of figures of human beings or animals, or human beings with birds' heads. A great variety of animals was found: horses with short manes, flying birds, and many kinds of ungulates. The finds at Tell Halaf ceased to be an isolated phenomenon when earthenware apparently representing the same culture turned up elsewhere. It was found at Hajji Muhammad near Khidhr and even in Eridu. The discovery of the Tell Halaf culture in southern Mesopotamia was particularly surprising because it showed that the lowland had been inhabited at a much earlier date than had been assumed hitherto. The Iraqi excavations at Eridu in 1946-9 thus caused a further sensation among those who considered themselves familiar with the history of Mesopotamia in the fifth millennium B.C. For although the absolute date of the Tell Halaf culture has not yet been established by radio-carbon tests, there is a general tendency towards the conviction that it developed shortly after 5000 B.C.

Yet the most impressive addition to the still scanty information came from Arpachiya, about four miles north of Nineveh. In the course of a test dig at Nineveh it had been noticed that although the virgin soil was not reached until a depth of about 90 feet, Tell Halaf pottery could be found at a depth of about 60 feet. In these circumstances it was impossible for the diggers to uncover the stratum they were interested in without irreparable damage to the others. Meanwhile, however, it had been learned that Tell Halaf potsherds lay at the surface of the small mound at Arpachiya. The British School of Archaeology therefore began investigating this site in 1932, with spectacular results. It proved possible to distinguish sixteen habitation

Top left: objects found at Jarmo in 1948 and 1951. 1. Unfired clay figures; 2. flint implements; 3. objects of bone; 4. grindstones; 5. reed mat; 6. pottery (only in the more recent layers); 7. reconstruction of a farm at Hassuna ca. 5000 B.C. Opposite page; top, view of Erbil, situated on a mound containing many habitation layers; lower left, landscape in Kurdistan near Jarmo; lower right: minaret of the Friday Mosque near Samarra, built ca. A.D. 850.

layers, of which the sixth to the tenth, counting from the surface, were characterised by Tell Halaf earthenware. The sixth layer was the most interesting because a craftsman's shop was discovered in it. His shop had been razed to the ground by fire and his wares lay charred in the ash. But sherds of earthenware painted in white, black, and red were found. These included a bowl, which it was possible to reconstruct completely from seventy-six pieces. Among the other finds were a piece of red ochre clay, flat palettes for mixing the paint, and bone tools for shaping the clay. Here, again, the jugs and bowls were decorated with both geometrical patterns and images of flowers, trees, and dancing girls.

Tholoi were found in the older layers of the Tell Halaf period at Arpachiya. A *tholos* is a building of circular ground plan, with a rectangular passage in front of it. It was obvious that subsequent generations had treated with particular reverence the ground on which these *tholoi* had been built. This suggests that these remarkable buildings were shrines.

As in Jarmo, the ancient inhabitants had used flint and obsidian for their implements. We can therefore be sure that in the Tell Halaf period a trade route was maintained as far as Lake Van, i.e. over a distance of some 190 miles. But, as another mound in the vicinity proved, there were also links with the Persian Gulf, necessitating a journey of over 810 miles. It is, of course, not certain that any individual trader covered such great distances without intermediate calls, although it is not beyond the bound of possibility.

The finds at Arpachiya raised the question of relationship with the Greek world. The *tholoi* certainly turn up again in the cult of Mycenaean Greece. The potter's workshop at Arpachiya contained stone figures representing phalanges, parallels with which have been encountered among the prehistoric remains of the Almerian culture in southern Spain. The impression given is that a movement starting in Mesopotamia spread by way of Cyprus and Crete to western Europe and finally reached the Atlantic Ocean. The British School of Archaeology, which on leaving Arpachiya worked at Chagar Bazar from 1934 to 1937, found again here traces of the Tell Halaf culture which confirmed and complemented the theory formed at Arpachiya. The mound is on the bank of the Dara, once more near the head of the Khabur. The sixth to fourteenth habitation layers in succession displayed the magnificent multi-coloured pottery characteristic of the Tell Halaf period, which seems to have lasted longer here than in Arpachiya. The nation responsible for the destruction of the sixth layer at Arpachiya probably moved westward without bothering about the less accessible highlands to the north. A building of the *tholos* type was found in level nine, and the other finds were in accordance with expectations for the period: clay figurines of the mother goddess, amulets in the form of a double axe, and images of domestic animals.

The impression is given that several metals (e.g. gold, lead, and silver) were known in the Tell Halaf period. That few traces of these are to be found is not surprising. Metal was so rare that as soon as an object made of it was no longer serviceable it disappeared into the melting-pot. Nevertheless, a copper bead was found in one of the Tell Halaf levels at Chagar Bazar. The over-all impression left is that the period we have just described was typified by great artistic skill and closely-knit social organisation.

The sixth habitation level at Arpachiya is thought to provide evidence of a movement of population to which the Tell Halaf civilisation fell a prey. The new inhabitants, who radically changed the face of civilisation as reflected in the pottery, are named after Tell el-'Obeid, a small mound to the west of Ur. Traces of the Tell 'Obeid culture can be found from Eridu in southern Mesopotamia to Tepe Gawra in the north and to Ras Shamra in the west. Tell 'Obeid earthenware occurs in Ur, Erech, Lagash, Susa, Persepolis, and many other places. The discovery of Tell 'Obeid pottery in Eridu, where it was not expected, caused a sensation. A chance discovery at Hajji Muhammad in 1937 had led to the realisation that even the south Mesopotamian plain might have been inhabited at that very remote

period. The Eridu excavations between 1946 and 1949 brought incontrovertible proof. In fact, Tell 'Obeid ware of such a peculiar type was found in the fourteenth to the eighteenth levels that some investigators believed there had been a proto-Tell 'Obeid or even a pre-Tell 'Obeid period which was contemporary with the Tell Halaf period.

Anyone making a superficial acquaintance with Tell 'Obeid ware gets the impression that from an aesthetic standard it represents a decline. The pottery of this period actually falls into two different types: a coarse kind, made by hand, and a fine kind, made with the aid of the wheel. Here was visible proof of a technical improvement. In addition the art of keeping the heat in a closed oven uniform had been acquired, and grease was removed from the clay, which was then mixed with sand, straw, and lime. But technical advances are not a guarantee of finer design, while we must also make allowance for the possibility that the peoples of Tell 'Obeid culture had burst into the river plain from the highlands and had, so to speak, to start from the beginning again.

The use of copper must have meant momentous changes. The oldest brass axe known was found in the Tell 'Obeid level of Tepe Gawra, a small mound to the north of Nineveh. This metal was imported from the mountain country – the exact source is not yet known – and at first it was used solely for the manufacture of weapons. For domestic purposes stone implements continued to be used, while even sickles and nails during the Tell 'Obeid period were still made of stone or baked clay. A number of gold beads were also found at Tepe Gawra. Some time was still to elapse before copper was alloyed with tin and men could use the much harder and much more useful bronze.

One of the characteristics of the Tell 'Obeid civilisation was the shape of the stone seal impressed on soft clay as a mark of ownership. In the Tell Halaf period this had been flat, but now we find a dome-like shape. The decorations become more complicated and illustrate unknown myths involving human beings, animals, and dragons. About this time there is a change in burial customs. The dead are no longer buried together under the floors of the houses but taken to cemeteries outside the town. A cemetery containing over a thousand family graves was found near Eridu. Burial presents, such as figures of gods and small clay boats, accompanied the dead. The houses are made of clay bricks baked hard in the sun. Of the buildings the small temples are the most outstanding, as at Tepe Gawra, where three temples were erected round a large inner square, and at Eridu, where a rectangular shrine was surrounded by a number of smaller rooms. The temple was the central building in the city. Upon a platform in the shrine stood a statue of the deity who was regarded as the lord and ruler of the community. This is another reason for believing that the foundations of the later Sumerian civilisation were laid in the Tell 'Obeid period.

To avoid making this survey too complicated let us now turn to the Erech period. It might perhaps be worth while to abandon the traditional classification and to replace it by a system of periods based on the eighteen habitation levels which at Erech separate the early dynastic period, with its written material, from the virgin soil. We should then be able to accord the renaissance of Tell 'Obeid pottery a definite place. In any case, the Erech and Tell 'Obeid cultures existed side by side until the former took the upper hand. Once more, it is virtually certain that newcomers turned the stream of tradition into a new channel. They built temples which greatly resemble the shrines at Eridu, yet at the same time show a striking difference. For the first time in the architectural history of Mesopotamia the column makes its appearance. Terracotta cones of various colours were used to decorate the walls and columns. Red, white, and black, these were driven into the clay while it was still soft, and arranged to form geometrical shapes (see Pl. 62). Anyone who visits the excavation site at Erech can still lift these cones - very like our sticks of chalk - in hundreds from the ground. The result of the decoration is to be seen in the Iraq Museum in Baghdad. It is remarkable that this attractive ornamentation fell into disuse not long after the Erech period. Also known about this time was the art of fresco painting, magnificent examples of which were found at Tell 'Uqair in a temple erected on a D-shaped platform. Another novelty was the use of cylinder seals instead of stamp seals. The figures which they impressed in the soft clay include animals and human beings. But what chiefly makes this period important are the first attempts at writing. At Erech were found the 'archaic' tablets, bearing a multiplicity of characters. These tablets are the forerunners of the literary period. It is for this reason that the era which now follows is spoken of as the proto-literary period. It is, however, even more usual to call it after the pottery which first enabled it to be characterised. This was first found and identified at Jemdet Nasr, a tell south of Baghdad, which was investigated by an Anglo-American team in 1925-6 and 1928. The Jemdet Nasr civilisation, however, appeared in its most mature form at Tell Brak in the north, about half a mile west of the River Jaghjagha, which was called the Hermas in antiquity. The old Mesopotamian name of the city which became the mound of Tell Brak is unknown. During the British School of Archaeology's expedition here in 1937-8 thousands of small figures of gods were found, which have one or two pairs of eyes instead of a head. They lay in the remains of temples which had been built, each on the site of its predecessor, in the south of the city. This ruin is called the 'Eye Temple' and, like Erech, had wall decorations in the shape of cones.

The meaning of the black and white alabaster figurines with the eyes pierced in them is not known; they are not unique, having been found in Susa and Syria, as well as in Tell Brak. The Eye Temples were visited 3,000 years ago by marauders who sank at least eight vertical shafts right through the habitation layers. Beneath the oldest temple they dug a network of tunnels. The fact that these could still be inspected by the light of flash-lamps in the twentieth century without danger to life is a proof of the competence with which men built in those days with their primitive implements.

The general impression left by the proto-literary or Jemdet Nasr period is one of great economic and cultural progress, in both the north and the south. There was regular traffic between Tell Brak and Sumer although the distance downstream along the Euphrates was over 625 miles. The excavator of Tell Brak, Professor Mallowan, thinks that the legends of a prehistoric time in which heroes such as Lugalbanda and Gilgamesh made long journeys have a historical background in the Jemdet Nasr period. It is also typical that the glazed earthenware and steatite beads found in hundreds of thousands at Tell Brak also occur in the Indus valley, although there they belong to a more recent period. Men's horizon in those days was continually widening, and we must not underestimate the distances they dared to cover for the sake of commerce.

A completely new phenomenon during this period is sculpture. The reliefs on the splendid vases seem almost to detach themselves from their background and lead an independent life. On 22 February 1939 the nearly life-size head of a woman was found in the Jemdet Nasr level at Erech. It was made of limestone and almost intact (see Pl. 253). This discovery, one of the most important in the history of Mesopotamian excavations, revolutionised ideas about this last phase of the pre-literary period. The serenity and aloofness of this full-face portrait suggest a goddess or a priestess. As an artistic performance it is one of the peaks of the period we have reviewed. But the alabaster vase (see Pl. 92) found as long ago as the 1933-4 campaign is also beautifully designed. It was reconstructed on the basis of fifteen fragments. The men advancing with baskets before the goddess Inanna are drawn with great lifelikeness. A number of pictographic inscriptions containing lists of sacrificial animals also date from this period. These administrative documents compiled for purposes of religion mark the start of a new era which has left us a written literature.

The illustrations on this page are of votive offerings from the archaic layers of Erech. **81.** Figurine of a goat. **82.** Gazelle lying down. **83.** Small bird. **84.** Lion-headed bird. **85.** White stone pendant with two fishes. **86.** Copper lion. **87-8.** Seal impression showing animals and the symbols of the goddess Inniss. **89.** Libation jug. **90.** Jug reconstructed from fragments found. **91.** Silver jug.

The Civilisation of the Sumerians

INTRODUCTION

We know very little about the origins of Sumerian civilisation. The Sumerians inhabited a region between the Euphrates and the Tigris, extending approximately from modern Baghdad to the Persian Gulf, and their historians write as if they had been there since the creation of the world. They called their country Shumer, and this name is perhaps identical with the Biblical Shinar of Genesis 11 : 2. The area of Sumer was not more than that of two provinces of modern Iraq and was roughly equal to that of Holland. The region to the north of Sumer was called Agade, usually written Akkad. Sumer and Akkad together comprised the whole of Mesopotamia. From the epic *Enmerkar and the Lord of Aratta*, written ca. 2000 B.C., we can deduce the Sumerians' conception of the world. North of Sumer lay 'Uri', that is, Akkad as it was later known; to the east 'Shubur-Khamazi' (Iran); to the west 'Martu', that is, the territory between the Euphrates and the Mediterranean, including the Arabian peninsula. The Sumerians regarded their own country as the southern limit of this world. And although their own territory was so limited in size, there were periods in its history when it almost entirely dominated the 'world' (see Map 8).

It is true to say that the influence of their civilisation extended farther than their political ascendancy. Their history as a power has two main periods. The first, or 'early dynastic', lasted until the appearance of Sargon of Agade. After the latter's interlude of Semitic supremacy, Sumer's might reached a new peak under the third dynasty of Ur. The founder of this dynasty was Ur-Nammu, whose son, Shulgi, was able to call himself the 'king of the four quarters of the world'. When the last king of this dynasty, Ibi-Sin, was overthrown ca. 1950 B.C. by the Amorites from the northwest, the political domination of the Sumerians ceased. In matters of culture and religion, however, they continued to play a leading rôle for many centuries, while as an ethnic group they were slowly absorbed into their Semitic environment. We do not know when this process of absorption was completed.

THE 'EARLY DYNASTIC' PERIOD

The 'early dynastic' period lasted about four centuries. It is difficult to reconstruct its history with any certainty, although the Sumerian scribes left much information about it, including a number of lists of kings' names. One of these kings was called Mesannipadda. This name cropped up again in an inscription found in the temple at Tell el-'Obeid, which ran: 'A-anni-padda, son of Mesannipadda, king of Ur, built this for his goddess Ninhursag.' This provided a reliable point of departure for a history of a period which was to produce famous monarchs such as Eannatum and Urukagina. The community they ruled, however, already showed all the characteristics of an ordered society with a long history of development behind it, a development which we are only able to describe tentatively.

We may possibly find a number of landmarks in the epic poems of the Sumerians. Of the nine such poems which we now possess five are devoted to Gilgamesh, two to Enmerkar, and two to Lugalbanda. These heroes are also mentioned in the Sumerian king list which was probably compiled between 2250 and 2000 B.C. There they appear as kings of the first dynasty of Erech, which followed the first dynasty of Kish. The latter must therefore have been preceded by the Flood, a catastrophic event which was still remembered as the dividing line between two periods in world history. The fame of the kings of the first few dynasties is thus handed down in the form of a myth with a historical background. In other words, there is a Sumerian 'heroic

92. Alabaster vase for religious purposes (height 3 ft. 7¼ in.), Jemdet Nasr period, found at Erech. The three rows of reliefs represent a sacrificial scene: naked men bringing baskets containing offerings; and below it animals, probably sacrificial, plants, and water.

age' comparable with that of the Greeks, the Indians, and the Germans. The great expert on the civilisation of Sumer, Professor Kramer of Philadelphia, thinks that far-reaching conclusions can be drawn from this heroic age. In this he subscribes to the views of Hector Munro Chadwick, an English scholar, who saw 'heroic ages' as the literary consequence of a social phenomenon. According to him, the heroic age coincides with national migrations and with the encounter of tribes of a low standard of culture with civilised states on the point of disintegration. If this law is true, the Sumerians were not the earliest inhabitants of Mesopotamia. There was a pre-Sumerian period characterised by a peasant civilisation which had penetrated from Iran. This civilisation merged with that of the Semitic immigrants and conquerors from the west and must have dominated political and cultural life for a long time. According to Kramer, a Mesopotamian empire had in fact been formed which could be considered the first empire in the history of civilisation.

In the Near East the decay of a central authority always offers the nomads an easy opportunity to invade the cultivated country. Kramer therefore also thinks that the Sumerians came originally from an area near the Caucasus, conquered Lower Mesopotamia after much skirmishing, and became a settled nation there. The historical background to the Sumerian epics should therefore be sought in the period of struggle for the cultivated country. After a certain degree of pacification had been reached, the natural talents of the Sumerians, he argues, must have had such a fructifying effect on the existing cultural achievements that civilisation blossomed in a way which fills the modern observer with admiration. The two main representatives of that civilisation are architecture and literature.

At the dawn of Sumerian history we see a group of city states of varying sizes. One of the largest cities in Sumer was Erech with its wall of plano-convex bricks, five and a half miles in circumference. Round the city lay a limited area which was subject to an *ensi* ruling in the name of a *lugal*. Both the *ensi* and the *lugal* considered themselves as reigning on behalf of their deity. Each city had as its centre the temple consecrated to the divine protector of the population. Ur was the city of Nanna, the moon god, and his wife, Ningal; Erech belonged to Anu and Inanna, Nippur to Enlil and Nin-lil, and Lagash to Ningirsu and Baba. Every war a king waged was a war waged by his deity against the deity of the enemy city. That is why the rule of the Sumerian city kings is called theocratic.

The community was organised down to its smallest division, and in some cases over-organised. It is obvious that effective irrigation of the country could only be guaranteed by close organisation. If this apparatus fell into the hands of ambitious rulers and grasping officials freedom was threatened and the burden of taxation made heavier. The tax-collector was always a much-feared man in ancient Sumer. In a series of proverbs forming part of Sumerian didactic literature, we read: 'You may have a lord, you may have a king, but the man you really have to fear is the tax-collector.' This situation was accepted like the many arbitrary acts by king or deity that the citizen of ancient Mesopotamia had to endure. It seems, however, that in the days preceding the reign of the reformer Urukagina in Lagash in the twenty-fourth century B.C. personal initiative had been stifled and the weight of taxation had become unbearable. The citizens banished the last ruler of the ancient Ur-Nina dynasty and elected Urukagina, scion of a new house, to be their *ishaku* or city governor. He fulfilled the hopes of his people, as we know from a text composed in honour of the king for the inauguration of a new canal.

The scribe, who perhaps fell into the error of oversimplifying matters, but had personal experience of all he relates, tells how the inspector of taxes confiscated everything, including boats and cattle. If a man wished to divorce his wife, he had to pay tax, and if a salve-maker had made up a preparation of oil, he had to pay tax. Why, even at funerals officials stood by, ready to requisition quantities of oats, bread, and beer from the next of kin. But Urukagina put an end to this pillage by the revenue authorities. He restored the *amargi* or freedom of the land. He also cleared the city of usurers, thieves, and murderers,

and protected the poor, widows, and orphans against their oppressors. Even in his own time these deeds of Urukagina were considered so important that they were recorded in a number of inscriptions, four of which were found in Lagash in 1878 by French excavators. Alas, the just Urukagina came to a bad end. He was overthrown by Lugal-zaggisi, king of the still unexcavated Umma (Tell Jokha), which lay fifteen and a half miles to the north-west of Lagash. The reformation, by coming too early or too late, had apparently weakened the structure of the state.

The enmity between Lagash and Umma was, in any case, deeply rooted in history. We are fully informed of it by the archivists of the temple and palace at Lagash, some of whom were not content to chronicle incidental happenings, but attempted to explain their interconnection. One of them wrote at the time of Entemena, the fifth ruler of the Ur-Nina dynasty. Entemena was a nephew of the Eannatum familiar to us from the famous 'Stele of Vultures', on which he is shown moving off at the head of his troops after a victory over the inhabitants of Umma (see Pl. 117). The archivist describes how his city's struggle for power dates back to the time of Mesilim, who was king of Kish about 2600 B.C. Mesilim mediated in a border dispute between Lagash and Umma, and after consulting the oracle erected a stele to mark the frontier for all times. This was of little avail, for shortly afterwards Ush, the *ishaku* of Umma, pulled up the stele and occupied the northern territory of Lagash. This was the start of a complicated story, which the involved style of the Sumerian scholar makes difficult to follow. It ended eventually after a settlement, satisfactory for Lagash, was apparently imposed by a third power; Mesilim's boundary was restored in the time of Entemena.

As we have said, Umma regained power in the reign of Lugal-zaggisi. An unknown Lagash scribe has left us a lament for his destroyed city, ending in a curse upon the king of Umma who desecrated the temple and made himself guilty of sin against Ningirsu. But Lugal-zaggisi also conquered Erech, become master of all Sumer, and later boasted of ruling from the Persian Gulf to the Mediterranean. After reigning for twenty-five years, however, he was compelled to bow the knee to Sargon of Agade, who about 2250 B.C. established a Semitic domination that was to last for a century and a half. Thus the pre-dynastic period came to an end and the ancient civilised land was ruled from Agade by a Semite calling himself *sharru kenu* or the 'rightful king'. Lugal-zaggisi's prayer, the text of which we now possess, therefore remained unfulfilled. It reads: 'May Enlil, the king of the gods, convey my request to Anu, my beloved father, and add life to my life. May he make the lands to live in safety and entrust to me there a people as numerous as the herbs of the field! May he make the celestial sheepfolds prosper and gaze with kindness upon the land! The kind fate that the gods have destined for me – let them not change it! May I always remain the shepherd who leads his flock!'

A separate chapter will be devoted to the dynasty of Agade and its downfall as a result of invasion by the barbarous Gutians (see pp. 73ff.).

THE SUMERIAN RENAISSANCE

After the Gutians had ruled Mesopotamia for a century, their yoke was shaken off by Utu-hegal of Erech, who had successfully organised an army of liberation during the occupation. According to an inscription of much later date, 'The god Enlil, the king of the land, commanded Utu-hegal, the strong hero, the king of Erech, the king of the four quarters of the world, whose word is without its peer', to wipe out even the name of the Gutians. Yet this liberator was not to become the lord of Sumer. The period of the Sumerian renaissance was, politically speaking, to be that of the third dynasty of Ur, beginning with Ur-Nammu.

Those who excavated at Ur, Erech, Eridu, Lagash, and Nippur found traces of Ur-Nammu's activities and fame. This king, who reigned from 2044 to 2027 B.C., deliberately set out to restore the

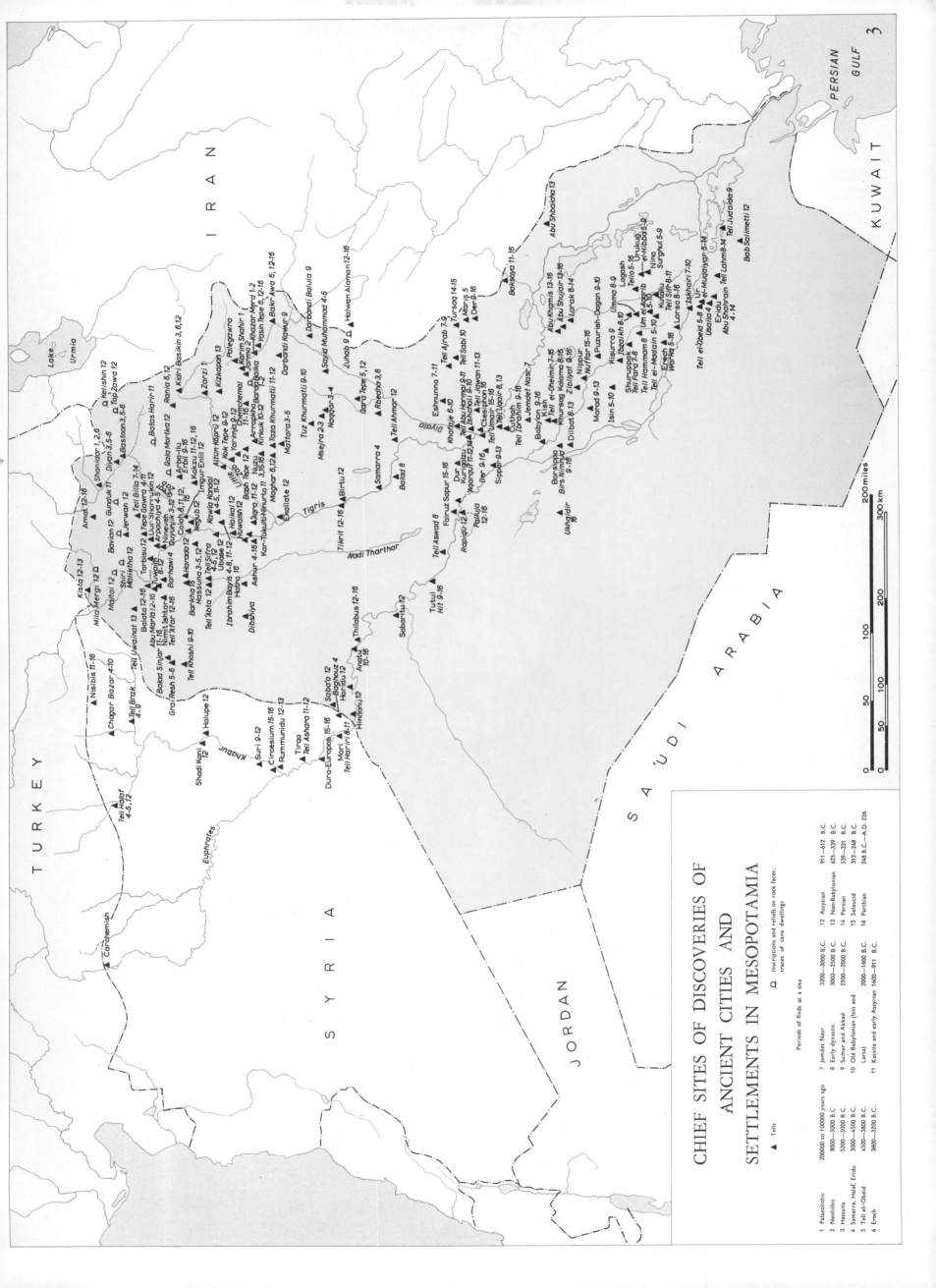

3

PERSIAN
GULF

KUWAIT

IRAN

Lake
Urmia

TURKEY

SYRIA

JORDAN

SAUDI ARABIA

Euphrates

Khabur

Diyala

Tigris

Wadi Tharthar

Carchemish

Tell Halaf 4-5,12

Nisibis 11-16
Chagar Bazar 4-10
Tell Brak 4-9
Graï Resh 5-6
Balad Sinjar
Shadi Kapri 12
Halupe 12
Suri 9-12
Circesium 15-16
Rummunidu 12-13
Tirqa
Tell Ashara 11-12
Mari
Tell Hariri 8-11,

Dura-Europos 15-16
Sabata 12
Baghouz 4
Haridu 12
Hindanu 12

Anatu 10-16
Thilabus 12-16

Sabaritu 12

Tutul
Hit 9-16

Kista 12-13
Miid Mergi 12
Maltai 12
Tell Uwainat 13
Bavian 12
Jerwan 12
Amat 12-16
Shanidar 1,2,6
Shiri
Maliktha 12
Tarbisu 12-16
Abu Maria 12-16
Nimit Ishtar 4
Tell Afar 12-16
Tell Khoshi 9-10
Ibrahim Bayis 4-8,11-12
Dibshiya
Hotha 16
Barhalik 15
Hassuna 3-5,12
Horada 12
Tell Abta 12
Tell Shira 4-5,12
Ubase 12
Ashur 4-16A
Calah 6,11,12
Nineveh
Quyunik 3-12
Imgur Enlil 12
Arpachya 15
Abu Shahrain 15-16
Tepe Gawra 4-11
Gunduk 11
Balata 12-16
Kar-Tukulti-Ninurta 11 3,15-16
Maqra 11-12
Huwaish 12
Haikal 12
Kowla Kandal
Negub 12

Kelishin 12
Top Zawa 12
Diyan 3,5-6
Bastoon 3,5-6
Batas Harir 11
Rania 6,12
Kidri Baskin 3,6,12
Zarzi 1
Kizkapan 13
Polegawra
Karim Shahin 1
Jarmo 2
Khazan Merd 1-2
Bard Balka 1-2
Yasin Tepe 6,12-16
Arba-ilu
Erbil 9-16
Kok Tepe 9-12
Yarimja 9-12
Tell Billa 7-14
Qala Mortka 12
Kakzu 11-12,16
Altun Köprü 12
Arrapkha
Bard Balka
Kirkuk 10-12
Taza Khurmatli 11-12
Maghar 6,12A
Exkallate 12

Bakr Awa 6,12-16
Darbandi Balula 9
Mattara 3-5
Tuz Khurmatli 9-10
Sayid Muhammad 4-5
Halwan Alaman 12-16
Zunab 9

Mejra 2-3
Naqsan 3-4
Qara Tepe 5,12
Rbedha 3,8
Tell Ahmar 12
Samarra 4
Balad 8

Tikrit 12-16
Birtu 12

Tell Aswad 8
Fairuz Sapur 15-16
Rapiqu 12
Der 9-16
Dur Kurigalzu
Aqarquf 11-12,14
Sinchari 9-10
Tell Ojavan 11-13
Ctesiphon 16
Tell Umair 15-16
Sippar 9-16
Tell Ibrahim 9-16
Cuthah
Tell Ibrahim
Babylon 9-16
Kish
Tell el-Oheimir 7-16
Khursag Kalama 8-16
Jemdet Nasr 7
Dilbat 8-13
Ziblyat 9-16
Marad 9-13
Borsippa 9-16
Birs Nimrud

Eshnunna 7-11
Khafaje 6-10
Tell Abu Harmal 9-11
Mari 5
Den 9-16
Tell Ajrab 7-9
Tell Sabi 10
Tursaq 14-15

Boksaya 11-16
Abu Shbaiaha 13

Abu Khamis 13-16
Abu Shujain 8-16
Larrak 8-14
Nippur 15-16
Nuffar 15-16
Puzurish-Dagan 9-10
Kisurra 9
Isin 5-10
Jbzalkh 8-10
Shuruppak
Tell Fara 7-8
Tell Hammam 8
Umma 8-9
Lagash
Tello 5-16
Nina
Surghul 5-9
Uruk
e-Warka 8-16
Ereck
Kutalu
el-Aqrib
Tell el-Madain 5-10
Tell Sifr 8-11
Larsa 8-16
Iskhain 7-10
Tell el-'Obeid 5-8
Ur 5-14
Usaila 4
Eridu
Abu Shahrain 4-14
el-Muqaiyar 5-14
Tell Lahm 8-14
Tell Judaida 9
Bab Salimeti 12

PERSIAN GULF

KUWAIT

0   50   100   200 miles
0   50   100   200   300 km

CHIEF SITES OF DISCOVERIES OF
ANCIENT CITIES AND
SETTLEMENTS IN MESOPOTAMIA

▲ Tells

Ω Inscriptions and reliefs on rock faces;
     traces of cave dwellings

Periods of finds at a site

1 Palaeolithic	200000 to 100000 years ago	7 Jemdet Nasr	3200—3000 B.C.	12 Assyrian	911—612 B.C.
2 Neolithic	8000—5000 B.C.	8 Early dynastic	3000—2500 B.C.	13 Neo-Babylonian	625—539 B.C.
3 Hassuna	5200—5000 B.C.	9 Sumer and Akkad	2500—2000 B.C.	14 Persian	539—331 B.C.
4 Samarra, Halaf, Eridu	5000—4500 B.C.	10 Old Babylonian (Isin and		15 Seleucid	312—248 B.C.
5 Tell el-Obeid	4500—3800 B.C.	Larsa)	2000—1600 B.C.	16 Parthian	248 B.C.—A.D. 226
6 Erech	3800—3200 B.C.	11 Kassite and early Assyrian	1600—911 B.C.		

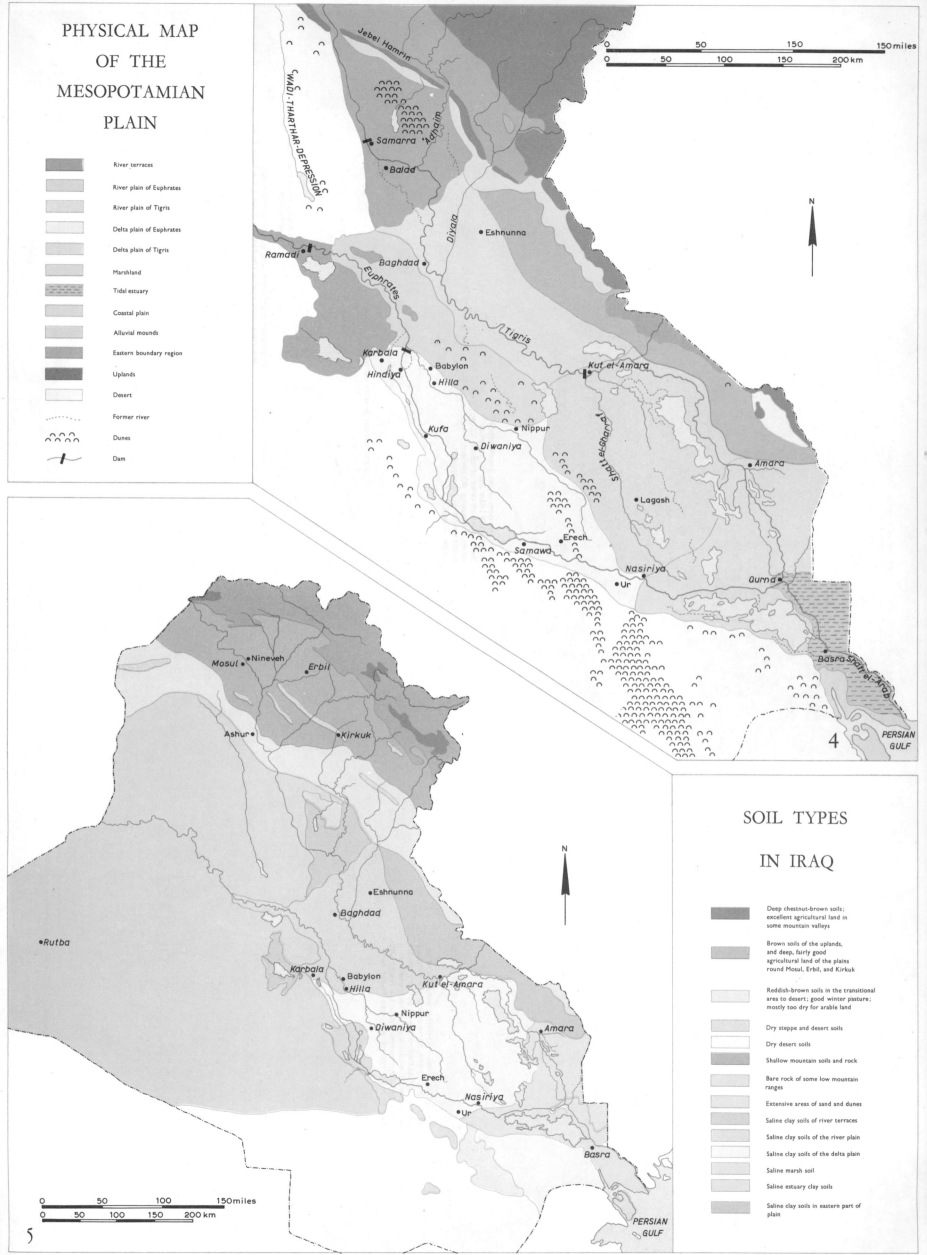

PHYSICAL MAP OF THE MESOPOTAMIAN PLAIN

River terraces
River plain of Euphrates
River plain of Tigris
Delta plain of Euphrates
Delta plain of Tigris
Marshland
Tidal estuary
Coastal plain
Alluvial mounds
Eastern boundary region
Uplands
Desert
Former river
Dunes
Dam

50 150 150 miles
50 100 150 200 km

N

Jebel Hamrin
WADI-THARTHAR-DEPRESSION
Samarra 'Adhaim
Balad
Diyala
Eshnunna
Ramadi
Baghdad
Euphrates
Tigris
Karbala
Babylon
Kut el-Amara
Hindiya
Hilla
Kufa
Nippur
Shatt el-Gharraf
Diwaniya
Amara
Lagash
Erech
Samawa
Nasiriya
Qurna
Ur
Basra Shatt el-Arab
PERSIAN GULF

4

Mosul Nineveh
Erbil
Ashur
Kirkuk
Rutba
Eshnunna
Baghdad
Karbala
Babylon
Hilla
Kut el-Amara
Nippur
Diwaniya
Amara
Erech
Nasiriya
Ur
Basra
PERSIAN GULF

N

0 50 100 150 miles
0 50 100 150 200 km

5

SOIL TYPES IN IRAQ

Deep chestnut-brown soils; excellent agricultural land in some mountain valleys

Brown soils of the uplands, and deep, fairly good agricultural land of the plains round Mosul, Erbil, and Kirkuk

Reddish-brown soils in the transitional area to desert; good winter pasture; mostly too dry for arable land

Dry steppe and desert soils

Dry desert soils

Shallow mountain soils and rock

Bare rock of some low mountain ranges

Extensive areas of sand and dunes

Saline clay soils of river terraces

Saline clay soils of the river plain

Saline clay soils of the delta plain

Saline marsh soil

Saline estuary clay soils

Saline clay soils in eastern part of plain

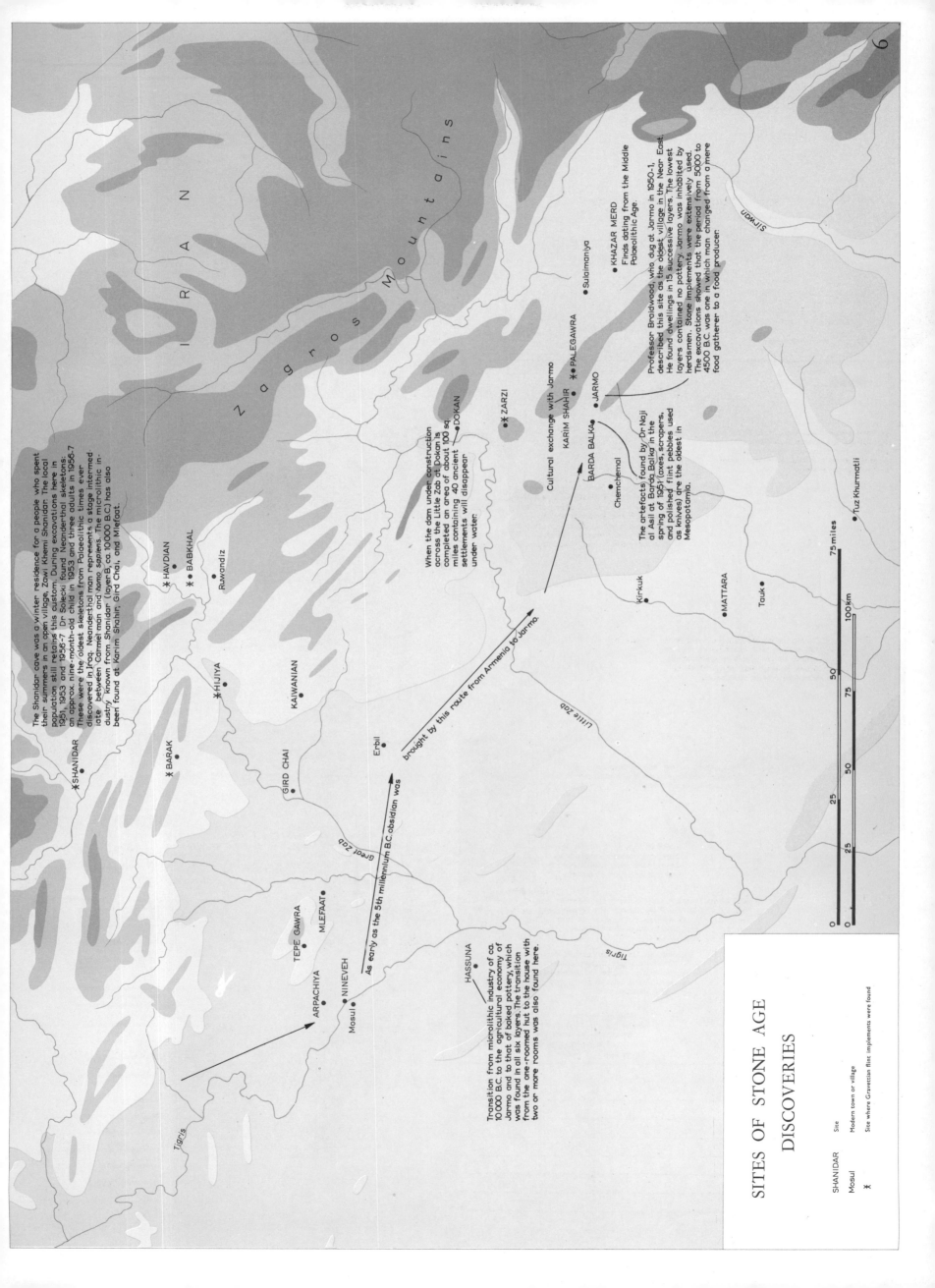

The Shanidar cave was a winter residence for a people who spent their summers in an open village, Zawi Khemi Shanidar. The local population still retains this custom. During excavations here in 1951, 1953 and 1956-7 Dr Solecki found Neanderthal skeletons: an approx. nine-month-old child in 1953 and three adults in 1956-7. These were the oldest skeletons from Palaeolithic times ever discovered in Iraq. Neanderthal man represents a stage intermediate between Carmel man and *homo sapiens*. The microlithic industry known from Shanidar (layer B, ca.10000 B.C.) has also been found at Karim Shahir, Gird Chai, and Mlefaat.

When the dam under construction across the Little Zab at Dokan is completed an area of about 100 sq. miles containing 40 ancient settlements will disappear under water.

Cultural exchange with Jarmo

KHAZAR MERD
Finds dating from the Middle Palaeolithic Age.

Professor Braidwood, who dug at Jarmo in 1950-1, described this site as the oldest village in the Near East. He found dwellings in 15 successive layers. The lowest layers contained no pottery. Jarmo was inhabited by herdsmen. Stone implements were extensively used. The excavations showed that the period from 5000 to 4500 B.C. was one in which man changed from a mere food gatherer to a food producer.

The artefacts found by Dr Naji al Asil at Barda Balka in the spring of 1951 (axes, scrapers, and polished flint pebbles used as knives) are the oldest in Mesopotamia.

As early as the 5th millennium B.C. obsidian was brought by this route from Armenia to Jarmo.

Transition from microlithic industry of ca. 10,000 B.C. to the agricultural economy of Jarmo and to that of baked pottery, which was found in all six layers. The transition from the one-roomed hut to the house with two or more rooms was also found here.

SITES OF STONE AGE DISCOVERIES

SHANIDAR   Site

Mosul   Modern town or village

✳   Site where Gravettian flint implements were found

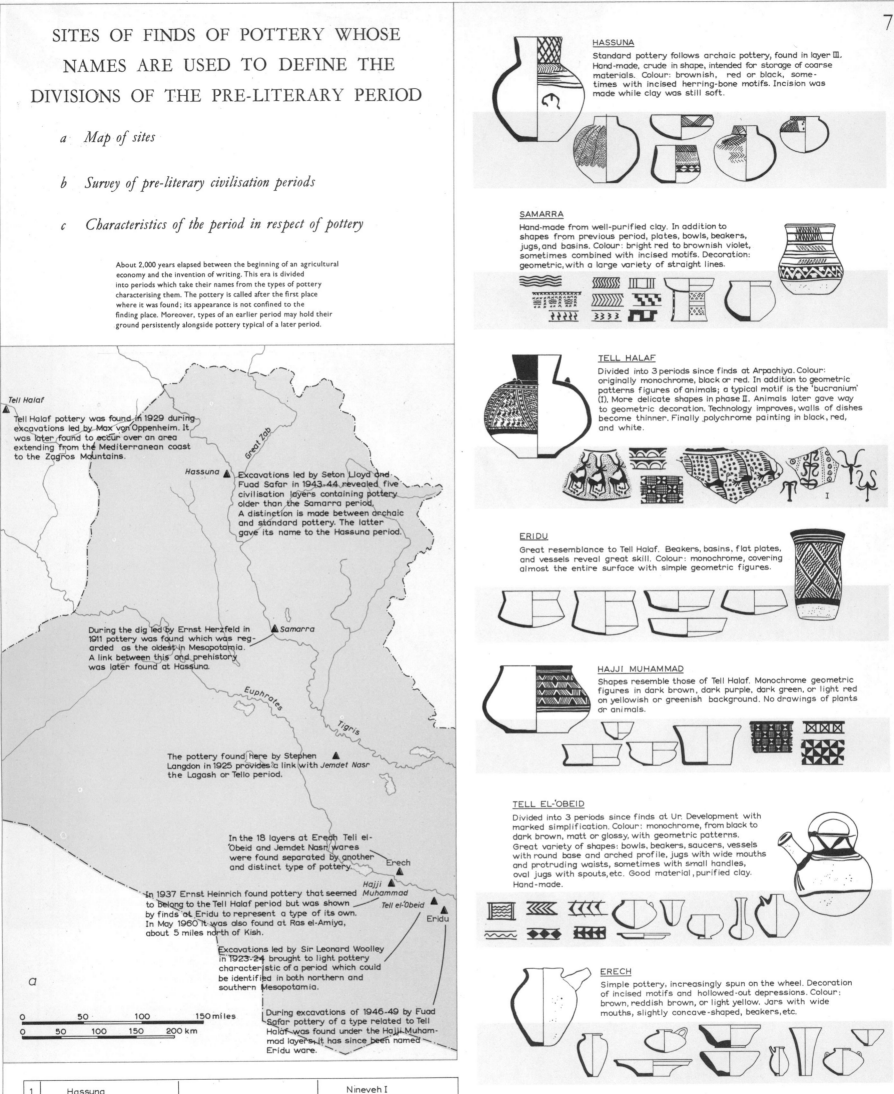

SITES OF FINDS OF POTTERY WHOSE NAMES ARE USED TO DEFINE THE DIVISIONS OF THE PRE-LITERARY PERIOD

a   Map of sites

b   Survey of pre-literary civilisation periods

c   Characteristics of the period in respect of pottery

About 2,000 years elapsed between the beginning of an agricultural economy and the invention of writing. This era is divided into periods which take their names from the types of pottery characterising them. The pottery is called after the first place where it was found; its appearance is not confined to the finding place. Moreover, types of an earlier period may hold their ground persistently alongside pottery typical of a later period.

Tell Halaf

Tell Halaf pottery was found in 1929 during excavations led by Max von Oppenheim. It was later found to occur over an area extending from the Mediterranean coast to the Zagros Mountains.

Great Zab

Hassuna

Excavations led by Seton Lloyd and Fuad Safar in 1943-44 revealed five civilisation layers containing pottery older than the Samarra period. A distinction is made between archaic and standard pottery. The latter gave its name to the Hassuna period.

During the dig led by Ernst Herzfeld in 1911 pottery was found which was regarded as the oldest in Mesopotamia. A link between this and prehistory was later found at Hassuna.

Samarra

Euphrates

Tigris

The pottery found here by Stephen Langdon in 1925 provides a link with the Lagash or Tello period.

Jemdet Nasr

In the 18 layers at Erech Tell el-'Obeid and Jemdet Nasr wares were found separated by another and distinct type of pottery.

Erech

Hajji Muhammad

In 1937 Ernst Heinrich found pottery that seemed to belong to the Tell Halaf period but was shown by finds at Eridu to represent a type of its own. In May 1960 it was also found at Ras el-Amiya, about 5 miles north of Kish.

Tell el-'Obeid

Eridu

Excavations led by Sir Leonard Woolley in 1923-24 brought to light pottery characteristic of a period which could be identified in both northern and southern Mesopotamia.

During excavations of 1946-49 by Fuad Safar pottery of a type related to Tell Halaf was found under the Hajji Muhammad layers; it has since been named Eridu ware.

| 0 | 50 | 100 | 150 miles |
| 0 | 50 | 100 | 150 | 200 km |

a

1	Hassuna		Nineveh I
2	Samarra	Hassuna III–VI	Nineveh II a-b
3	Tell Halaf	Hassuna VI–XII	Nineveh II c
4	Eridu	Eridu XV–XVII	
5	Hajji Muhammad	Eridu IX–XIV	
6	Tell el-'Obeid	Eridu VI–VIII	Erech XIV–XVIII
7	Erech		Erech V–XII
8	Jemdet Nasr		Erech III–V

b

HASSUNA

Standard pottery follows archaic pottery, found in layer III. Hand-made, crude in shape, intended for storage of coarse materials. Colour: brownish, red or black, sometimes with incised herring-bone motifs. Incision was made while clay was still soft.

SAMARRA

Hand-made from well-purified clay. In addition to shapes from previous period, plates, bowls, beakers, jugs, and basins. Colour: bright red to brownish violet, sometimes combined with incised motifs. Decoration: geometric, with a large variety of straight lines.

TELL HALAF

Divided into 3 periods since finds at Arpachiya. Colour: originally monochrome, black or red. In addition to geometric patterns figures of animals; a typical motif is the 'bucranium' (I). More delicate shapes in phase II. Animals later gave way to geometric decoration. Technology improves, walls of dishes become thinner. Finally polychrome painting in black, red, and white.

ERIDU

Great resemblance to Tell Halaf. Beakers, basins, flat plates, and vessels reveal great skill. Colour: monochrome, covering almost the entire surface with simple geometric figures.

HAJJI MUHAMMAD

Shapes resemble those of Tell Halaf. Monochrome geometric figures in dark brown, dark purple, dark green, or light red on yellowish or greenish background. No drawings of plants or animals.

TELL EL-'OBEID

Divided into 3 periods since finds at Ur. Development with marked simplification. Colour: monochrome, from black to dark brown, matt or glossy, with geometric patterns. Great variety of shapes: bowls, beakers, saucers, vessels with round base and arched profile, jugs with wide mouths and protruding waists, sometimes with small handles, oval jugs with spouts, etc. Good material, purified clay. Hand-made.

ERECH

Simple pottery, increasingly spun on the wheel. Decoration of incised motifs and hollowed-out depressions. Colour: brown, reddish brown, or light yellow. Jars with wide mouths, slightly concave-shaped, beakers, etc.

JEMDET NASR

Well-fired pottery, hard, often glazed. Reliefs formed by excision of soft clay. Vases with spouts, dishes with flat bottoms, etc. Characteristics: thick-set jars with sharply-defined shoulders and overhanging rim.

c

cities of southern Mesopotamia which had fallen into ruin under the Gutians. He had temples and ziggurats built, the most famous of these being the ziggurat of Ur, which he erected in honour of the moon god Nanna, in Babylonian Sin. On the third terrace of the lofty ziggurat, the best-preserved in Mesopotamia, stood a small temple built of glazed blue bricks, the bridal chamber of Nanna and Ningal. The outer covering of the lowest terrace was formed of bricks in each of which the name of Ur-Nammu was impressed (see Pl. 274).

Fragments of a legal code of the same Ur-Nammu, the earliest documents of the kind so far discovered, are known. In the Sumerian text, inscribed on light-brown sun-baked bricks measuring 8 by 5 inches, only five paragraphs are legible, of which three are important because they refer to the application of the *jus talionis*. These lay down the amount of the fine that anyone must pay who has inflicted corporal injury on another. Thus, at least three centuries before Hammurabi, the rule of 'an eye for an eye' which we find in Exodus 21 : 23 as well as in the Code of Hammurabi, had been rendered humane by conversion into a system of fines. Under Ur-Nammu's law, a man who had, for example, cut off another's nose was not forcibly deprived of his own nose but could make amends by putting down two-thirds of a mina of silver. There is an important prologue which is better preserved than the actual code. In it the king's deeds are summed up in the following words: 'He slew Namkhani, the priest-king of Lagash. He brought the temple boat of the moon god back to the eastern canal, on the order of Nanna, the king of the city, and made Ur resplendent again. Then Ur-Nammu, the strong hero, the king of Ur, the king of Sumer and Akkad, upon the order of Nanna, the king of the city, established law and justice in the land and put an end to rebellion and tyranny. Throughout Sumer and Akkad he abolished the tolls levied by the master mariners. He caused the dimensions of the bronze shekel and the silver mina to be fixed, and assigned a standard weight to the silver shekel, being one-sixtieth of a mina. He made the banks of the Euphrates and Tigris safe once more. He put down injustice: the orphan might no longer be the prey of the rich, or the widow the prey of the powerful, or the man who had one shekel the prey of him who possessed a mina.' So, approximately, allowing for lacunae in the damaged text, runs the declaration of principles of a king who tried to restore the order of earlier times.

Many letters and documents of the third Ur dynasty have survived. And as every business deal in those days was recorded on a small clay tablet, the number of contracts extant is large. Altogether they give a picture of a time in which trade has revived, thanks to law and order in the state and safety on the roads. It was probably this fact and not the levying of high taxes that enabled Ur-Nammu to find the means to build so many monuments. His foundation inscriptions and his inscribed clay 'nails' have been found everywhere. Also familiar from his period are bronze figurines about ten inches high representing the king with a basket of building material on his head. Similar figurines in the shape of nails and bearing inscriptions were also placed in foundation stones for documentary purposes.

We speak of a Sumerian renaissance; but it is obvious that the Semitic influence in Sumer and Akkad could no longer be annulled. A statesmanlike policy was probably also at work to bring the Semitic and Sumerian elements as close together as possible. One gets the impression that Ur-Nammu and his successors were truly guided by the principle of mutual benefit by co-operation. In addition, they accorded the city rulers in their territory a great degree of independence, as we know from information referring to one of the most likable princes of the period, Gudea of Lagash.

Gudea was nominally a vassal of Ur-Nammu or the latter's successor, but being animated by the same ideals as to the Sumerian renaissance as Ur-Nammu, he could safely be entrusted with considerable freedom of action. The French excavators at Lagash (Tello) recovered various likenesses of this ruler which seem to reflect his personality faithfully (see Pls. 135 and 136). They are all in character and conjure up the picture of a deeply devout man. Such texts as we have by him or about him confirm this impression. The most impor-

tant is the poem in which the building of the temple E-ninnu ('house of the fifty') in honour of the god Ningirsu is described. It is written on two large clay cylinders divided up into 1,365 sections.

In this fine work Gudea placed on record how the god had informed him in a dream of his desire for a temple. Then he had turned to the goddess Nanshe, interpretress of dreams, for her advice as to the details of the shrine. There follows a description of the actual construction and an appeal to the citizens to complete the temple not only by the work of their own hands but more especially by devotion and virtue. The very long poem is a unique source of information about the pantheon and, consequently, about the religious ideas of Sumer in Gudea's time. In addition, it contains a detailed description of the rites observed during the building of a temple. Practically nothing remains of the temple, and the images of the gods, adorned with gold and precious stones, were a welcome haul for the looters; a text containing such a wealth of information is all the more valuable for that fact.

Gudea was not a king; he called himself the *ensi* of Lagash. But the 'world' of those days was open to him in the fullest sense. When he himself in one of his inscriptions states that Ningirsu, his beloved king, opened all the trade routes from the Upper Sea to the Lower for him, it is no idle boast. The diorite of which his statues were made came from Oman, the precious cedar wood from the Amanus Mountains in Syria, the gold dust from Khakhu, and the asphalt from Magda. His city, though not the residence of a *lugal*, was a flourishing commercial centre where land and water trade routes met. He paid tribute to Ur, like his successor, but was able to embark independently on campaigns, for instance against the Elamites. He planted forests; by his own account he expelled the wicked magicians from Lagash; and he ruled like a faithful shepherd over his 216,000 subjects. Whom he included among the latter is not quite clear from the text.

THE CODE OF LIPIT-ISHTAR

A good example of how the Sumerian and Akkadian civilisations were synthesised in the legal field is offered by the code of Lipit-Ishtar, who belonged to the dynasty of Isin and ruled from 1864 to 1854. We have now, it is true, reached a period later than the decline of the third dynasty of Ur, but the code is recorded in Sumerian and is generally thought to have its roots in a more remote past. The kings of Isin, like the rulers of the contemporaneous dynasty of Larsa, have Semitic names, betraying their Amorite origin, but their legislation is strongly influenced by the customary law of Sumer. Indeed, they felt themselves to be the universal heirs to the kings of the third dynasty of Ur. So it is not surprising to find a hymn of Lipit-Ishtar, written in Sumerian, in which he not only deifies himself but also assumes the sacred titles of 'shepherd' and 'husbandman' used by the earlier kings. It proved possible to reconstruct the text of Lipit-Ishtar's code from fragments found in Nippur and now housed in the museum of the University of Philadelphia. These were linked up with a text from the Louvre in Paris, which was originally thought to be a hymn to Lipit-Ishtar but was now found to be the prologue to his code. A paragraph from his code, written in Akkadian, had been previously found on a tablet used for writing practice in school.

To what degree Lipit-Ishtar felt himself to be the continuer of the most ancient traditions is obvious from the prologue, in which he calls himself 'the humble shepherd of Nippur, the true husbandman of Ur who ceaselessly looks after Eridu, the lord who gives good rule to Erech, the king of Isin, the king of Sumer and Akkad, the man after the heart of Inanna, who at the command of Enlil established justice in Sumer and Akkad'. Like Urukagina, he brought his subjects *amargi* (freedom, especially from foreign oppressors). Then he says: 'By means of excellent administration I made the father maintain his children while I made the children maintain their father; I caused the father to be helped by his children and the children to be helped by their father.'

The tablets on which the law is recorded are badly damaged, so

93
94

95

93. Copper relief of a lion-headed eagle and two stags, from the temple of Nin-hursag at Tell el-'Obeid, Dimensions 6 ft. 6¾ in. × 2 ft. 6½ in. 94. Frieze of cows from the same temple. 95. Part of the same frieze. On the right the cows are being incompetently milked from behind; on the left butter is being made and stored. The two groups are divided by a door made of reeds and two young cows. The limestone figures are set against a black bitumen background and framed in copper. Dimensions 6½ in. × 3 ft. 9 in. 96. Reconstructed lyre taken from Shub-ad's tomb at Ur. It was originally made of shell, lapis lazuli, red limestone, gold, and wood. Height 3 ft. 11 in. 97. 15-carat gold helmet, found in the grave of Mes-kalam-dug at Ur. Small holes are still visible through which laces were threaded to secure an inner lining. 98 and 99. Gold sheath for the dagger below. Dagger with lapis lazuli hilt decorated with gold, from a tomb at Ur. An owner's mark is visible on the blade.

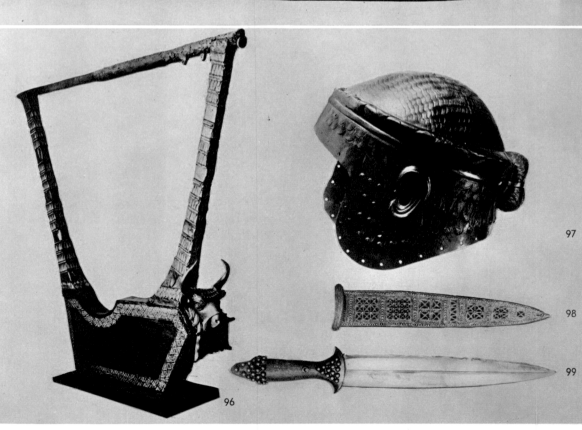

96

97

98

99

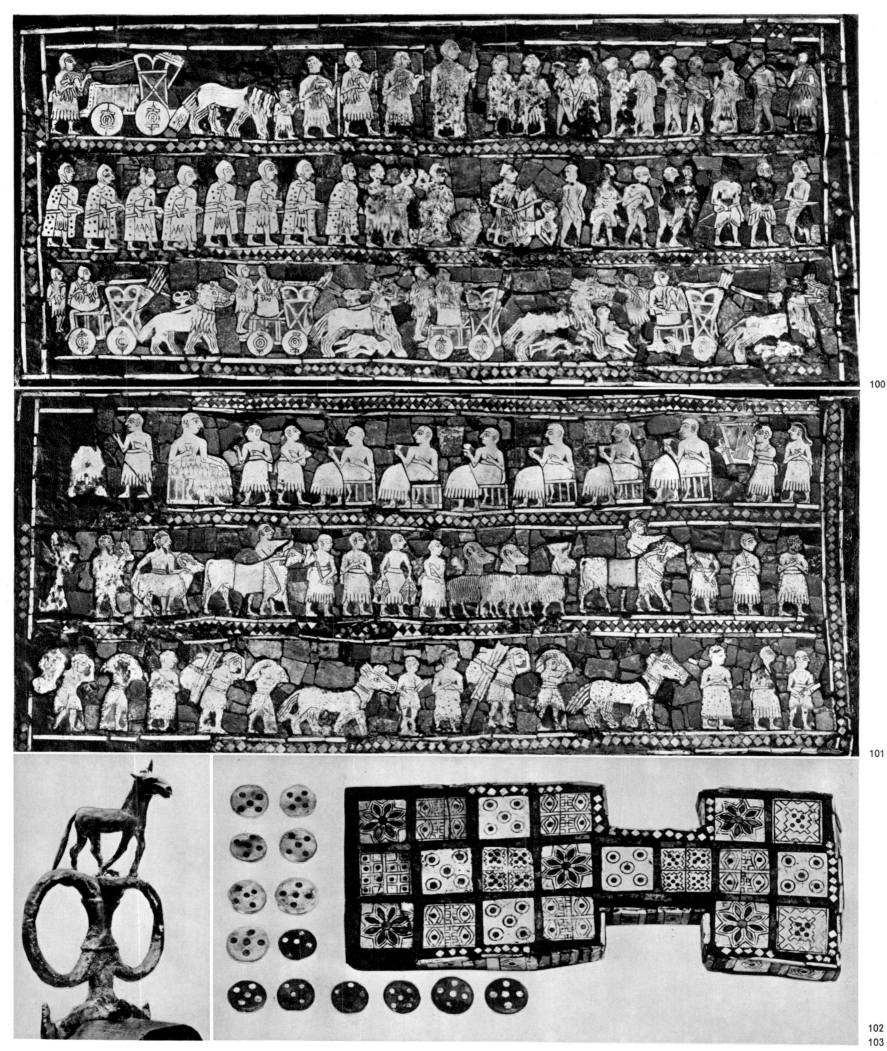

100

101

102
103

100. Fragment of a mosaic panel from Ur (8 in. × 18½ in.) showing a king's victory over his enemies. The chariot wheels have no spokes but are made from semicircular pieces of wood. The chariots are drawn by four asses or mules. At the bottom we see chariots pulled by galloping asses over a corpse-strewn battlefield. **101.** This panel is associated with the preceding one and depicts a peaceful scene. The two parts together are generally known as the 'Standard of Ur'. The figure at the top left probably represents the king; at the top right we see a musician and a woman singer. The panels are of shell, lapis lazuli, and red limestone set in bitumen. **102.** Rein-ring figure of a wild ass, intended for fitting to the pole of a chariot, from the 'Royal Tombs' at Ur. **103.** Gaming-board and pieces from the same tombs, made of bitumen inlaid with shell, bone, red limestone, and strips of lapis lazuli. Length 9½ in., diameter of pieces ¾ in. Rules of game unknown.

53

that the beginning is missing. There is a lacuna of about 120 lines, and then we find rules for the chartering of ships. The paragraphs after that concern date-palm plantations, and here we read: 'If a man has given fallow land to another to make an orchard of it, and the latter man does not complete the task of making the fallow land into an orchard, then the man who made the orchard shall receive for his share the fallow land that he neglected.' And also: 'If anyone cut down wood in another's orchard, he shall pay half a mina of silver.' Then follow provisions for the protection of adjoining properties, for the punishment for illegal retention of runaway slaves, and relating to the *miktum*, that is, a citizen with certain rights. Attention is paid to false accusations and to the law of property, inheritance, and marriage. It states, for instance, that 'if someone has taken a wife and she has borne him children and these children remain alive, but if the slave woman has also borne her master children and the master has freed the slave with her children, the children of the slave woman shall not share in the possessions of the master'. There is a remarkable paragraph which says that 'if a son-in-law has gone into the house of his prospective father-in-law and has handed over the purchase price of the bride and is then chased from the house and his wife given to his friend, then the purchase price which he took with him shall be paid back to him. But his friend may not marry the woman'. The situation provided for here is somewhat similar to that of Samson towards the end of Judges 14; yet it is not quite clear why this marriage impediment should apply particularly to 'his friend'.

After dealing with compensation for damage to hired oxen, the code ends with an epilogue in which the blessing of Enlil is besought in the usual way for those who adhere to the law and a curse called down on such as might infringe the law or cause it to be infringed.

The code of Lipit-Ishtar is as unsystematically arranged as the other ancient Mesopotamian codes that we know. It should perhaps be regarded rather as a collection of traditional verdicts pronounced by judges under the primeval customary law. That would account for the haphazard arrangement of the paragraphs. Nevertheless, we possess very little in the way of judicial opinions, and we may be all the more grateful for the written record of a judgment in the following particularly difficult case.

It had happened in the area under the jurisdiction of Ur-Ninurta, Lipit-Ishtar's successor in Isin. Ur-Ninurta transferred the case to the popular assembly at Nippur. It concerned the guilt or innocence of a woman whose husband had been murdered. The murder had been committed by a barber, a gardener, and a third man whose occupation is not stated. The murderers had informed the wife of the victim, Nin-dada, and she had delayed in reporting the crime. At the popular assembly nine citizens considered her to have been an accessory, but two men spoke in her defence. She had had reasons for not mourning her husband's death very much, as he had refused to maintain her. The defenders had their way: the murderers were condemned to death but the wife went free. The names and usually the occupations of all those concerned were given. The proceedings were recorded so that the case might serve as a precedent on a future occasion, if necessary. We may join Kramer in calling it a standard judgment.

THE REIGN OF SHULGI

We now return to the centre of Sumer. Ur-Nammu was succeeded by his son Shulgi, who not only calls himself 'king of the four quarters of the world' but also, like Naram-Sin, precedes his name with the determinative for 'deity'. He was the founder of the famous royal tombs at Ur, where he buried the mortal remains of his father and mother and where a total of four kings of the dynasty found their final resting place. Sir Leonard Woolley discovered the graves in a rectangular vaulted building of brick, measuring 100 feet by 83 feet, and 33 feet under the ground. The rites performed round this subterranean tomb seem connected with the cult of the spring god Tammuz (Dumuzi in Sumerian) and the celebration of his resurrection. By his solemn marriage with the goddess Inanna the king was iden-

tified with Tammuz. A chance discovery in Puzurish-Dagan (Drehem, six miles southeast of Nippur) showed Shulgi in a different light. He appears to have founded there a farm where animals of the most diverse kinds were bred, mainly, no doubt, for the royal table. We have far less information about him as a person than about Gudea of Lagash, although he must have been the most important king of the third dynasty of Ur. His rule extended from Susa to Alalakh in Syria and Kanish in Cappadocia; he gained victories in the Zagros Mountains and restored and founded temples like his father. Power and prosperity continued under his son Bur-Sin (or Amarsin), but while the latter's descendant and successor Shu-Sin was reigning signs of decline began to be visible.

THE DECLINE

Shu-Sin built a defence wall called 'Murik Tidnim' ('to keep Tidnim away') along the middle course of the Euphrates for the purpose of warding off the Semitic Bedouin sweeping in from the western desert. The fall came in the reign of Ibi-Sin. He was the last of the celebrated third dynasty of Ur, and though not incompetent he was no match for Ishbi-Irra of Mari. His city was destroyed in 1936 B.C. and he either fled or was taken captive to Elam; what became of him we do not know. A long poem of lamentation running to 435 lines has survived, in which the fall of Ur is related. Its main theme is the complaint of the goddess Ningal. Twice she tried to dissuade the gods Anu and Enlil from their decision, taken in council, to destroy the city. The gods who decide fate are not persuaded, however, but send Kingaluda, the lord of the evil storm-winds, to carry out their decree. Then comes another lament by Ningal, after which a singer implores first Ningal and then Nanna to have the gods return to a new Ur with its temples restored. But the king of Sumer has fled to the mountains like a bird whose nest has been destroyed, and all her children have raised a lamentation.

For a time it may have seemed that Ishbi-Irra of Mari had established domination over entire Mesopotamia. But a dangerous competitor called Naplanum came along, who also belonged to the invading West Semites. Naplanum occupied Larsa and gained control of a large proportion of the existing trade, because his new capital was traditionally the most important market town in the marshland. Another period of central administration was thus over for the empire. A large number of independent city-states now sprang up, which were ruled by kings from the west or the east. The ruling class was Amorite or Elamite, as the names of the rulers show. The latter, however, largely adopted the civilisation of the Sumerians, so that despite political disintegration continuity in cultural matters was maintained.

THE SUMERIAN CULTURE

Having thus summarised the main happenings in the two Sumerian periods, which were separated by the Akkadian dynasty and the rule of the Gutians, we will now take a closer look at the main intellectual movements so far as these can be deduced from literary remains. In the first place we are struck by the increased competence of scribes to express themselves in an attractive way despite the complexity of the cuneiform script. Writing is no longer, as it was in the beginning, confined to the service of economic interests, but increasingly becomes the vehicle of *belles-lettres*. That is why the scribes' school flourished, and we have a text which introduces us in almost a modern humorous manner to the trials of a pupil amidst his teachers. The conditions described are those of about 2000 B.C., and we should probably have known nothing about them if the inhabitants of Mesopotamia themselves had not enjoyed story-telling. Twenty-one copies of the tale are now known to exist, their scattered fragments being housed in the museums of Philadephia, Istanbul, and Paris.

That the 'children of the house of tablets' had not an enviable life will be clear from the following extract. 'Pupil, where have you been

104. Perforated slab of slate (height 7½ in.) from Nippur. The hole enabled this votive tablet to be fastened to the wall. According to the inscription the donor was Ur-Enlil, a superior merchant. At the top, in duplicate, is a naked priest offering a libation to a bearded god seated on his throne with his arms folded and his hair tied up, and wearing a crown of vegetation. The lower half shows two goats driven by a man carrying a milk-pail and another with a stick in his hand. 105. Soapstone dog found at Lagash. The inscription says it was offered to the goddess Nin-Sin by a high Lagash official for the preservation of the life of Sumu-El, king of Larsa. A small stone beaker for libations was fastened to the dog's back at a later period. 106. Soapstone lamp bearing two intertwined serpents, also found at Lagash. This theme is a fairly frequent one, as for example on sacred beakers (cf. Pl. 139).

107. Perforated votive tablet of white sandstone (height 15¾ in.) from Lagash, with the 'family relief' of King Ur-Nina. In the upper panel he carries a basket containing the foundation stone of a temple which he is about to build. Opposite the king stand his wife and their four sons; the foremost of these is his successor Akurgal. Underneath we see Ur-Nina, probably at the consecration of the temple. He is faced by a high official and three other sons, all of them named. In both cases the small figure of a cupbearer is seen behind the king. **108.** Copper statuette of a chariot and four (height 3 in.), found in a temple at Tell Ajrab. **109.** Copper statuette of a bison, a Sumerian work of art but found near Van in eastern Turkey. **110.** Volcanic stone statue (height 15¼ in.) representing a scribe of the period of Ur-Nina. On the back an inscription is engraved from which it appears that this Sumerian scribe of the 25th century B.C. was called Dudu.

111
112
113
114

115
116

111. One of a group of 10 male and 2 female worshippers from the temple of Abu at Tell Asmar. Alabaster figures, height from 8 to 27½ in. The eyes are of shell and bitumen, and the hair and beard were blackened with bitumen. The figures, which are geometrically formalised, were buried under the floor of the temple. **112.** Figurine of woman, from Khafaje. **113.** Candlestick from Kish, with base in the form of a frog (height 18 in.). **114.** Copper statuette (height 16 in.) of a worshipper, on a four-footed standard. **115.** Perforated limestone votive tablet (height 12½ in.) depicting a festive scene, from Khafaje. **116.** Votive tablet (height 6¾ in.) from Lagash, on which a priest makes a libation to a goddess. He pours the liquid from a jug with a spout into a vase from which a plant and bunches of dates protrude. The goddess wears her hair in three plaits, with a crown of feathers. Beneath the feet of the completely naked priest and the goddess there is a stylised mountain.

117. Fragment of the 'Stele of Vultures' of Eannatum of Lagash, so called from a part not shown here on which vultures are seen carrying off limbs of the slain. The height of this limestone relief is 6 ft. 2 in. At the top right we see the king leading his heavily armed troops over a road formed by conquered enemies. Below, Eannatum in his war chariot. The text speaks of a great victory over neighbouring Umma. The front of the relief, not shown here, represents a deity who has collected the enemy in a net.

118. Fragment of a votive tablet of black stone showing a likeness of Enannatum of Lagash (height $7\frac{1}{2}$ in.), ruler of almost entire Sumer. This descendant of Ur-Nina presents the typical appearance of a Sumerian: clean-shaven face and head, protruding nose extending in a straight line from a low, sloping forehead, bare torso, and kilt. He is a representative of the first period of Sumerian domination in southern Mesopotamia.

119. Stone bowl bearing reliefs of bulls and stalks of corn (height 2 in.). **120.** Limestone tablet showing wrestlers on left and boxers on right, found at Khafaje (5¼ in. × 9¾ in.). **121.** Crystalline limestone monster (height 3¼ in.), in the Guennol Collection, Brooklyn Museum. **122.** Copper statuette of two men wrestling, with heavy jugs on their heads, from the temple of the goddess Nintu at Khafaje (height 4 in.). **123.** Alabaster bas-relief (height 9 in.) of man carrying fishes, from a period certainly earlier than Sargon of Agade; found at Lagash. **124.** Silver vase (height 13¾ in.) of Entemena of Lagash, with animals engraved on it and mounted on a brass pedestal. One of the most beautiful products of the Sumerian silversmith's art. Found at Lagash. The lion-headed eagle holding two lions in its claws is perhaps intended to symbolise the victory of Lagash over its neighbours. The vase has been preserved intact.

all this time? At the house of the tablets. What did you do there? I read the clay tablet and ate. I covered my tablet right to the edge with writing. When school was over, I went straight home and recited to my father what I had learned. I read out to him what I had written and he was satisfied. Next morning I had to get up early. I went to my mother and said to her: "Give me something to eat, for I have to go to school." She then took two rolls from the oven and she sat by me as I drank. I ran off with my lunch bread. But the school janitor said: "You are far too late." Then I was afraid and my heart began to thump. I went to the teacher and he said: "Go to your place!" He looked at my tablet and was angry and he beat me.' The sorely-tried pupil then suggests to his father that he should invite the teacher home, and this is done. In addition, the father gives the teacher a dress, a gold ring for his finger, and a sum of money. The teacher then encourages his pupil with the words: 'Boy, because you have paid heed to my words and did not ignore them, you may attain the peak of the scribe's art and master it entirely. You will become the leader of your brothers and the captain of your friends, you will be the best among the pupils. You have done your school tasks well. You are now a man of knowledge.' Thus the difficult time the pupils spent in the 'house of tablets' was rewarded. The scribe was a respected figure in Sumerian society. The entire administrative order of the country depended on his ability. Frequently he specialised, perhaps because he was an expert at engraving monumental inscriptions or because as a mathematician he was at home in the maze of the sexagesimal system.

On the other hand the scribe was conscious of the dignity of his position and often appended his personal name and surname. In texts of an economic and administrative nature from ca. 2000 B.C. about 500 scribes state their name and the name and profession of their father. From this it appears that they belonged to the well-to-do middle class. They could therefore afford the school fees that had to be paid to the *umonia* or headmaster. There is no evidence to suggest that women were admitted to the scribes' school.

That the doctor was next in dignity to the scribe in Sumer follows almost as a matter of course. The seal of his personal physician was found in the tomb of Ur-Ningirsu of Lagash. This shows the god of healing wearing a beard, a tall turban, and a long garment, and with medicine in his right hand. The accompanying text reads: 'O god Edin-mugi, vizier of the god Gir, who attends mother animals when they drop their young! Ur-lugal-edinna the doctor is your servant.' The doctor is called *azu* or *ia-zu*, a word meaning 'water expert' or 'oil expert' which passed by way of Akkadian into Greek as *hiaomai*. A tablet measuring 2 inches by 4 and containing a number of prescriptions in its six columns was found at Nippur. It is no longer possible to test their efficacy, mainly because the names of the diseases concerned are missing, yet this fragment from a medical manual is important because it shows that the physician was already distinct from the medicine man and did not rely on exorcism or spells.

Agricultural science is represented mainly by a tablet measuring 3 inches by 4½ also found at Nippur. The text supplemented by fragments contains 108 lines and opens with the following words: 'In days of yore a farmer gave his son the following advice.' This advice refers first to the irrigation water which must not be allowed to rise too high. After the water has drained away, the fields must be weeded. Then the soil has to be turned over, twice with a pick-axe and once with a hoe. Lumps of hard earth should be broken up. Then ploughing and sowing take place simultaneously, for the plough is fitted with a box from which the seed drops to the ground through a funnel. The seed must be planted everywhere at the same depth. After sowing, the furrow must be cleared of heavy clods. Little effective remedy was known against field-mice and other vermin, so advice in this direction is limited to the recitation of a prayer to the goddess Ninkilim. The birds have to be scared off. Exact details as to the timing of the next irrigation are given. Grain for the king has to be watered a third time (cf. Am. 7 : 1). This is followed by advice on harvesting and threshing. Man was taught all these things by the god Ninurta, the son and faithful husbandman of the god Enlil. Deeply rooted in the Sumerians was

the consciousness that all arts and sciences had been revealed to man by the gods and were not the fruit of practical experience. Enlil, chief among the gods in the Sumerian pantheon, who had taken the place of the sky god Anu, was also the creator of the pick-axe and the plough. That is why a hymn to Enlil of Nippur goes: 'But for Enlil, the high mountain, cities would not be built, fortresses would not be erected, stables would not be built, sheepfolds would not be set up, a king would not be raised to the throne, a high priest would not be born, ... the workers would have no supervisor, no inspector over them, ... the rivers – their waters would bring no floods, the fishes of the sea could not spawn in the creek, the birds of the air would build no nests on the wide earth, in the sky the passing clouds would withhold their rain from us ....'

But, according to the Sumerian way of thinking, it was not only the tools and the skills in handling them that had been presented by the gods to man. Far more important still were the divine laws which from the day of creation had controlled the cosmos and kept it in motion. The Sumerian word for this kind of law is *me*. Even human civilisation was preserved by a number of laws. A scribe has left us a list of these laws which we might regard as the characteristic elements in Sumerian culture. They are not all clear and translatable, but what is comprehensible helps us to build up a picture of the ancient civilisation. Omitting a number of somewhat obscure elements but observing the sequence deliberately followed by the author of a hymn to Inanna, we obtain the following list: sovereignty, divinity, the sublime and enduring crown, the royal throne, the sublime sceptre, the royal insignia, the sublime sanctuary, the function of shepherd, the kingship, lasting feminine majesty, the priestesses, the priestly dignities, truth, the descent into the Underworld, the return from the Underworld, the eunuch, the war standard, the deluge, sexual intercourse, prostitution, art, the shrine, music, heroism, power, enmity, righteousness, the destruction of cities, lamentation, the joy of the heart, lying, the rebellious land, goodness, justice, the wood-worker's art, the metal-worker's art, the profession of scribe, the trade of blacksmith, the trade of leather-worker, the trade of mason, the trade of basket-maker, wisdom, attentiveness, sacred purification, fear, consideration, the troubled heart, judgment, and musical instruments.

We shall probably never succeed in finding the rule on which this particular order was based, but in any case it is remarkable to note that in addition to positive elements such as truth and peace there is no lack of negative ones like lying, destruction, and dissension. It seems almost to suggest that civilisation will always consist in the interplay of the most conflicting forces. It is impossible to derive moral guidance from the list of laws. That, however, does not mean that moral ideals were lacking. From Urukagina onwards all the kings continually boast in their inscriptions that they have served the cause of justice.

Nevertheless, the basis of their outlook on life is that man was formed of clay in order to serve the gods. His fate is decided for him by the gods, who are capricious and unpredictable in their actions. In fact, therefore, no thought is devoted to free will or responsibility, for they do not exist. Yet the sages of Sumer taught that man's suffering is the consequence of his failings. If a man is struck by misfortune, it is always because he has in some way or another deserved it, for a sinless man has never been born. If a man felt that he had been compelled to suffer undeservedly, his only course was to raise his voice in lamentation. One such lamentation grew into a piece of literature, nowadays appropriately named the 'Sumerian Job'. The fragments of this book, found in Nippur, are now housed partly in the museum of the University of Philadelphia and partly in the Istanbul Museum.

The name of the man visited by misfortune is not given, but he is said, like Job, to have been rich, righteous, and surrounded by friends and relatives. When he was stricken by disease and suffering, he turned to his guardian deity in supplication and complaint. The greater part of the poem consists of a description of the wretched treatment he receives from everyone. His relatives and professional singers are invited to join in his lament which ends in a confession

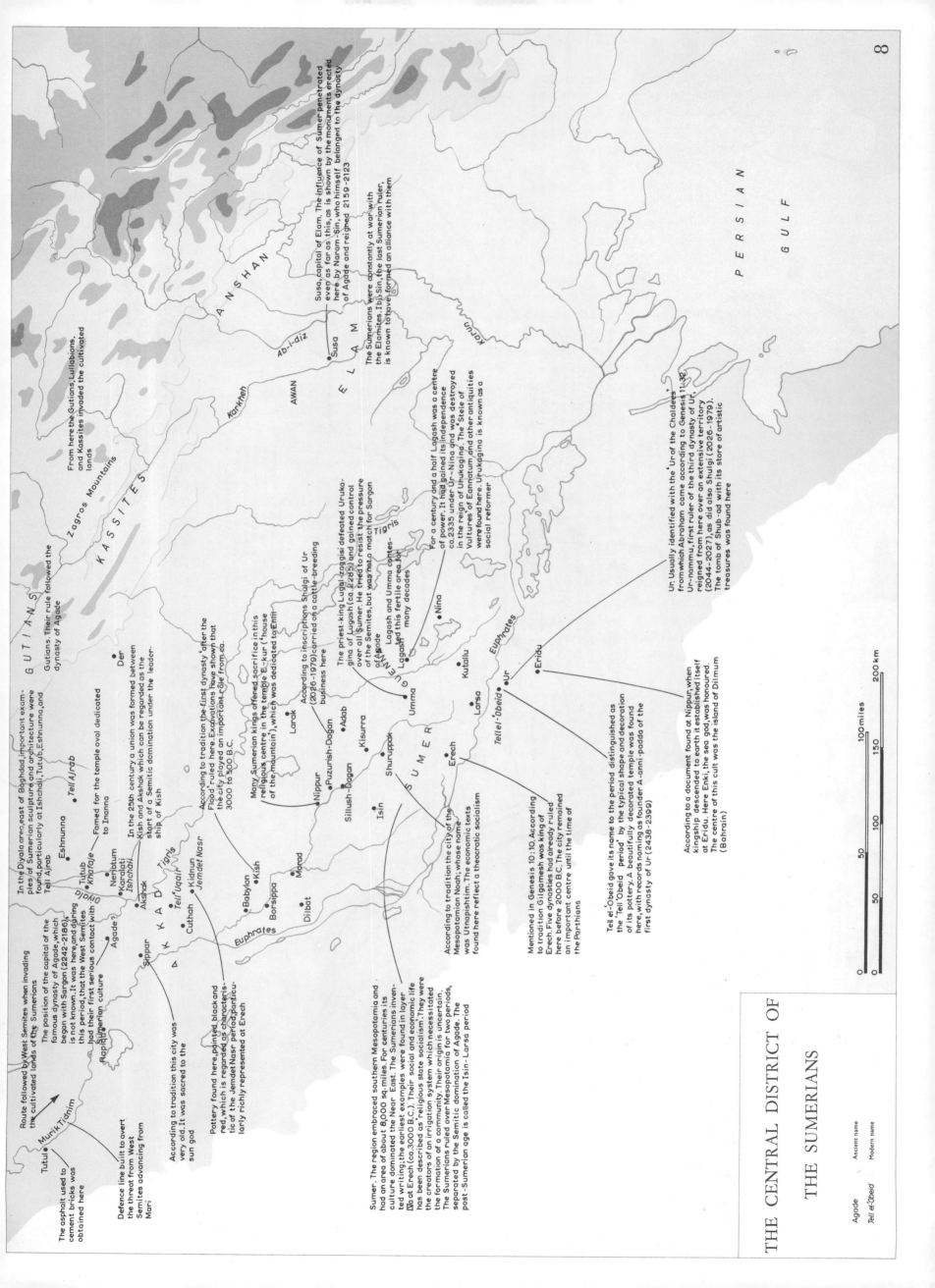

THE CENTRAL DISTRICT OF

THE SUMERIANS

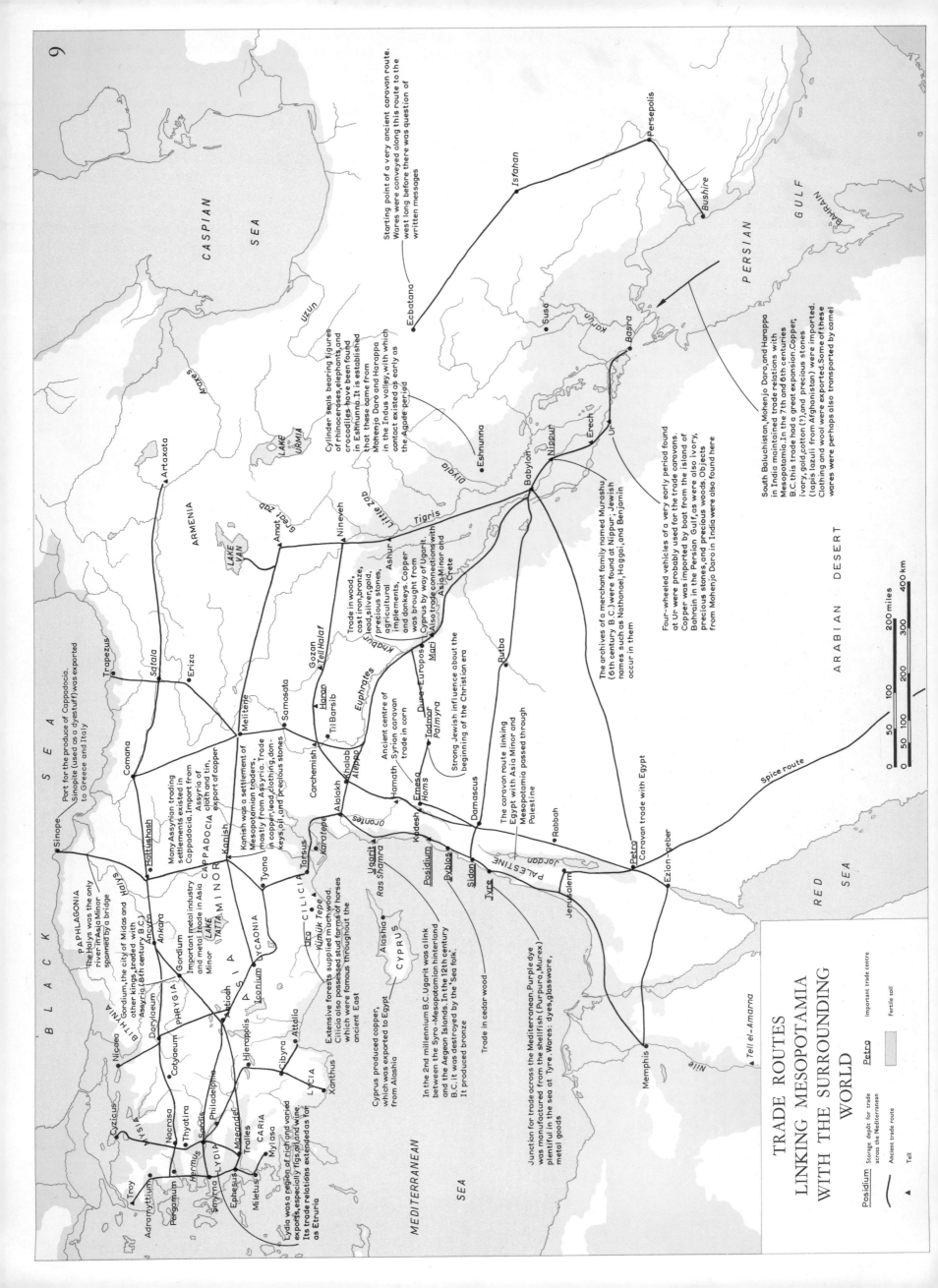

TRADE ROUTES
LINKING MESOPOTAMIA
WITH THE SURROUNDING
WORLD

Posidium Storage depôt for trade across the Mediterranean

Petra Important trade centre

——— Ancient trade route

▲ Tell

Fertile soil

Starting point of a very ancient caravan route. Wares were conveyed along this route to the west long before there was question of written messages

Cylinder seals bearing figures of rhinoceroses, elephants, and crocodiles-have been found in Eshnunna. It is established that these came from Mohenjo Daro and Harappa in the Indus valley, with which contact existed as early as the Agade period

Trade in wood, cast iron, bronze, lead, silver, gold, precious stones, agricultural implements, and donkeys. Copper was brought from Cyprus by way of Ugarit. Also trade connections with Asia Minor and Crete

Ancient centre of Syrian caravan trade in corn

Strong Jewish influence about the beginning of the Christian era

The archives of a merchant family named Murashu (6th century B.C.) were found at Nippur. Jewish names such as Nathanael, Haggai, and Benjamin occur in them

Four-wheeled vehicles of a very early period found at Ur were probably used for the trade caravans. Copper was imported by boat from the island of Bahrain in the Persian Gulf, as were also ivory, precious stones, and precious woods. Objects from Mohenjo Daro in India were also found here

South Baluchistan, Mohenjo Daro, and Harappa in India maintained trade relations with Mesopotamia. In the 7th and 6th centuries B.C. this trade had a great expansion. Copper, ivory, gold, cotton (?), and precious stones (lapis lazuli from Afghanistan) were imported. Clothing and wool were exported. Some of these wares were perhaps also transported by camel

Port for the produce of Cappadocia. Sinopite (used as a dyestuff) was exported to Greece and Italy

The Halys was the only river in Asia Minor spanned by a bridge

Gordium, the city of Midas and other kings, traded with Assyria (8th century B.C.)

Important metal industry and metal trade in Asia Minor

Many Assyrian trading settlements existed in Cappadocia. Import from Assyria of CAPPADOCIA cloth and tin, export of copper

Kanish was a settlement of Mesopotamian traders, mostly from Assyria. Trade in copper, lead, clothing, donkeys, oil, and precious stones

Extensive forests supplied much wood. Cilicia also possessed stud farms of horses which were famous throughout the ancient East

Cyprus produced copper, which was exported to Egypt from Alashia

In the 2nd millennium B.C. Ugarit was a link between the Syro-Mesopotamian hinterland and the Aegean Islands. In the 12th century B.C. it was destroyed by the 'Sea folk'. It produced bronze

Trade in cedar wood

Junction for trade across the Mediterranean. Purple dye was manufactured from the shellfish (Purpuro, Murex) plentiful in the sea at Tyre. Wares: dyes, glassware, metal goods

The caravan route linking Egypt with Asia Minor and Mesopotamia passed through Palestine

Lydia was a region of rich and varied exports, especially figs, oil, and wine. Its trade relations extended as far as Etruria

Caravan trade with Egypt

Spice route

Labels on the map

BLACK SEA

CASPIAN SEA

MEDITERRANEAN SEA

PERSIAN GULF

RED SEA

ARABIAN DESERT

ARMENIA

PAPHLAGONIA

BITHYNIA

PHRYGIA

ASIA MINOR

CAPPADOCIA

LYCAONIA

CILICIA

LYCIA

CARIA

LYDIA

CYPRUS

PALESTINE

LAKE URMIA

LAKE VAN

LAKE TATTA

Halys *Hermus* *Maeander* *Uzun* *Araxes* *Great Zab* *Little Zab* *Tigris* *Euphrates* *Khabur* *Diyala* *Orontes* *Jordan* *Karun* *Kerun* *Nile*

Troy Adramyttium Pergamum Cyzicus Nacrasa Thyatira Sardis Smyrna Philadelphia Ephesus Tralles Miletus Mylasa Xanthus Cibyra Attalia Hierapolis Iconium Antioch Cotyaeum Dorylaeum Nicaea Gordium Ancyra Comana Sinope Trapezus Satala Eriza Artaxata Amat Zob Nineveh Melitene Samosata Hattushash Kanish Tyana Tarsus Karatepe Yümük Tepe Ura Alashia Ugarit Ras Shamra Posidium Byblos Sidon Tyre Kadesh Hamath Homs Emesa Alalakh Khalab Aleppo Carchemish Til Barsib Haran Gozan Tell Halaf Ashur Dura-Europos Tadmor Palmyra Damascus Jerusalem Rabbah Rutba Petra Ezion-geber Memphis Eshnunna Babylon Nippur Erech Ur Basra Bushire Persepolis Isfahan Ecbatana Susa Memphis

Tell el-Amarna

0 50 100 200 miles
0 50 100 200 300 400 km

of guilt. His prayer is heard and the poem concludes with a hymn to the deity who has helped him in his wretchedness. The main theme of the poem obviously runs parallel to that of the Book of Job.

As in the Old Testament, no hope of life in a world to come could be held out. When a man died his clay returned to the earth it came from and his spirit descended into the nether regions, a country from which no return was possible and the descriptions of which are reminiscent of the Sheol in the Old Testament. The Sumerian name for the Underworld was Kur. This word originally meant 'mountain' and then 'foreign country', because the tribal home of the Sumerians bordered on the hostile highlands in the west. Then the name was also applied to the world of the dead, a change in meaning which is also found in Egypt. The practice of conjuring up the dead, as in the incident of the Witch of Endor (1 Sam. 28), is familiar from the Sumerian poem, *Gilgamesh, Enkidu, and the Underworld*, which tells how the shade of Enkidu can return from Kur. There is a detailed description of Kur in the myth of *Inanna's descent into the Underworld*.

It is extremely difficult to co-ordinate the religion of the Sumerians into an acceptable system, for they themselves never felt the need for systematic treatment of cosmogony or theology. They had hundreds of different gods, whose names are known from the long lists they compiled for the use of schools for scribes. The personal names of the Sumerians were often combinations of names of gods. Names of deities also occurred on votive tablets, in the royal inscriptions, and in numerous hymns, prayers, songs, and myths. It is hard to say what associations the faithful attached to particular names. The existence of a world of gods was for him an indisputable fact. He might complain to the gods of his lot; it never occurred to him to doubt their existence. The chief gods created the world and all that exists and moves in it. A reflection of this power could be seen in the behaviour of the king whose word was obeyed as soon as uttered.

Some deities are always very prominent; they occupy places of honour at the banquets of the gods, they are found at the top of lists of the gods, and they do the greatest deeds. Among these was the sky god Anu, honoured in Erech, whose place was later taken over by Enlil. Enlil is called 'father of the gods', 'the king of heaven and earth', and 'the king of all lands'. It was to Enlil, worshipped in Nippur, that kings owed their authority.

He was followed by Enki, who ruled over Apsu, the primeval ocean. Enki was as wise as he was resourceful, and therefore capable of carrying out Enlil's decrees in every detail. One myth describes how he filled the Euphrates and Tigris with water and the rivers with fishes. He establishes laws for the sea and wind to obey and as often as is necessary appoints gods to be responsible for their maintenance. But he also takes care of the plough, the houses, the stables, and the sheepfolds, while yet other gods are appointed to assume permanent care of these things. Behind these various beliefs we see the deep religious conviction that a creative orderliness is continuously revealed in the vital phenomena of nature and the community.

The life of the Sumerian, like that of the entire ancient world, was permeated by religion. This is obvious in the first place from the very many temples, which though small in the earliest times – the floor of the shrine in Eridu was only thirteen feet square – slowly grew in extent and magnificence. The Sumerian temples in the fourth level of Erech were very roomy and were surrounded by dwellings for the priests, storehouses, and offices. A temple in its completed form was not unlike a complicated business undertaking. The faithful came here with their sacrifices; here the priests performed the rites which they had learned to perfection. Although the temples were destroyed and pillaged, their remains still give some impression of the rich ornamentation they once possessed. But more impressive still than the statues of gods, the votive offerings, or the decoration of the temple is the piety of the Sumerians as we can observe it in hymns and prayers, lamentations and myths.

In general the hymns are monotonous, repeating the name of the divinity besought and listing his titles and works. The prayers sometimes take on a fervent tone, as in the prayer of Gudea of Lagash to

Tentative reconstruction of the temple of Ninhursag at Tell el-'Obeid. For the decoration of the wall above the platform, cf. Pls. 94 and 95.

the goddess Gatumdug, in which he says: 'My queen, daughter of the clear sky, who gives good advice, who occupies the first place in heaven, who gives life to the land! You are the queen, the mother who founded Lagash! In the people on which you deign to look power is super-abundant; the devout man on whom you deign to look is given length of days. I have no mother; you are my mother. I have no father; you are my father. In the shrine you have caused me to be born. My goddess Gatumdug, you know all that is good, you have admitted the breath of life into me. Under the protection of my mother, in your shadow I wish to stand in reverence.' Such expressions of individual piety are rare; but then the writer is still struggling to give literary expression to what is almost ineffable.

What is more, very few overcame the crippling effect of the belief that evil spirits roamed the space between heaven and earth. There was, for instance, the dangerous demon Udug, who had to be restrained by exorcist formulae. Then there were the Gallu demons, who being as thin as a stylus were able to perform their wicked deeds secretly. They could not be dissuaded by food or drink, but 'pulled the wife from the husband's embrace and the child from the nurse's breast'. There was therefore scope for magicians, and if they became too powerful, they had, as Gudea of Lagash informs us, to be driven from the land. But the exorcist knew the formulae for protection against the devils, he knew how the amulet had to be made up and how it had to be worn for effective protection. On the testimony of written texts the spiritual life of the Sumerians had an unparalleled variety. But the great and guiding beliefs were passed on from generation to generation and, as we shall see, gave religious life forms which have persisted up to the present day.

129

130

131

132

133

125. Fragment of a black stone vase showing a tightly bound prisoner of war being led away naked. 126. Shell on which is engraved a naked priest holding a jug for the libation ceremony. Found at Ur. 127. Sumerian woman, of the ruling class to judge by her dress and jewellery. 128. Votive tablet offered, the inscription states, by Dudu, priest of the god Ningursu. The priest, wearing a skirt, stands facing right. To the left is the familiar representation of the lion-headed eagle grasping in its talons the backs of two lions, which lift up their heads to bite the eagle's wings. To the left is a calf and below is a braid decoration. The eagle with outspread wings is the emblem of Lagash. The tablet dates from the first half of the 3rd millennium. Made of bitumen; height 9¾ in. From Tello. 129-133. These illustrations are impressions of cylinder seals. The cylinders, made of all kinds of stone, had mirror images of figures and texts engraved in them. The methods of the *purkullu* (stone-cutter) have been known since the finding at Eshnunna of a pot filled with half-finished seals and tools. The cylinder was originally fitted with a handle, then later a hole was made in it so that the owner could hang it round his neck. When he rolled it over soft clay, it made an impression which could serve as an owner's mark, an ex-libris, or a signature. The thousands of cylinder seals which have been found depict mythological and religious scenes, and are therefore indispensable as sources of information about the religious world of the inhabitants of ancient Mesopotamia, particularly the Sumerians. 129. Cylinder seal from Erech, ca. 3000 B.C. (as is also Pl. 132). This seal was of marble with a bronze shaft and a bronze ram for a handle. The scene shows the feeding of animals intended for temple rites. Observe the naturalistic attitude of the animals. 130. On this cylinder impression we see in the centre a hero engaged in battle with mythological animals. 131. Seal bearing figures of animals and religious symbols. 132. A boat laden with objects for the sacrificial service. The men propelling the boats are naked; the man in clothes in the centre is probably a priest. The cylinder which made this impression was about 1¾ in. high and of lapis lazuli, and had a bronze shaft ending in a silver handle in the shape of a calf. It comes from Erech and must have been made ca. 3000 B.C. 133. This cylinder is of jasper and shows a goddess leading a worshipper to a god's throne. Between the goddess and the god stands the jug used for libations, and above it can be seen the attributes of the deity — a disk inside the crescent moon, and a staff. The text above the kneeling bull reads: 'Ur-Nusku, son of Kaka, a merchant.' Date about 2000 B.C.

134

134. Top part of a stele, probably from Lagash, showing Gudea being led before a god by two other gods. The panel is 2 ft. 3½ in. high and of grey limestone. Gudea holds a palm branch in his hand. The god leading him by the hand – probably Nin-gish-zi-da – wears a robe revealing one shoulder; round this god's shoulders we see two serpents, each wearing a horned crown. The central figure has disappeared; all that can be seen is a stream of water, probably poured from a vase held by the god. Beside the throne is a lion and behind it another god in an attitude of respect.
135. Blue diorite statue of Gudea of Lagash seated and holding the plan of a temple in his lap. The beautiful cuneiform inscription which runs round his skirt and stool states that the statue is dedicated to Gatumdug.
136. The only undamaged statue of Gudea, also made of diorite. He is wearing the turban that is character-istic of all the images we possess of this *ensi* of Lagash. The eyebrows follow a typical fishbone pattern. This statuette is just over 19 in. high.
137. Human-headed bull from Lagash (4 in.), an example of late-Sumerian art.
138. This relief (width 24¾ in.)

135
136

also dates from the period of Gudea. The top panel represents worshippers, but more interesting is the lower panel where a musician is seen playing an eleven-stringed harp. The figure on the other side of the finely carved harp is probably a female singer.

139. Dark-green soapstone ceremonial beaker with a decoration consisting of upright dragons and curled serpents (height 9 in.). It dates from the period of Gudea of Lagash. The inscription between the two figures states that Gudea dedicated the beaker to Nin-gish-zi-da, the god of healing. The intertwined serpents are enigmatic. Perhaps they were typical symbols of Nin-gish-zi-da. The monster on the left has a snake's head but the claws and wings of an eagle and a spotted body. The head is covered by a crown from which two horns protrude and a mane hangs down. The monster's tail is like a scorpion's. The monster holds a staff in his claws, and this is thought to be the earliest representation of the symbol of the god of healing. In this extraordinary and elaborate decoration the artist has combined fantasy with a certain realistic quality, the serpent's scales, for instance, being suggested by inlaid pieces of marble.

137

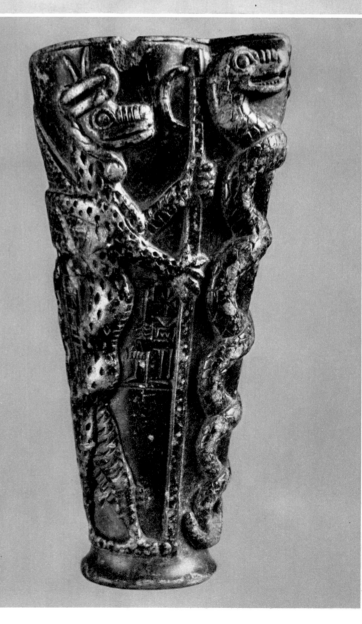

138
139

69

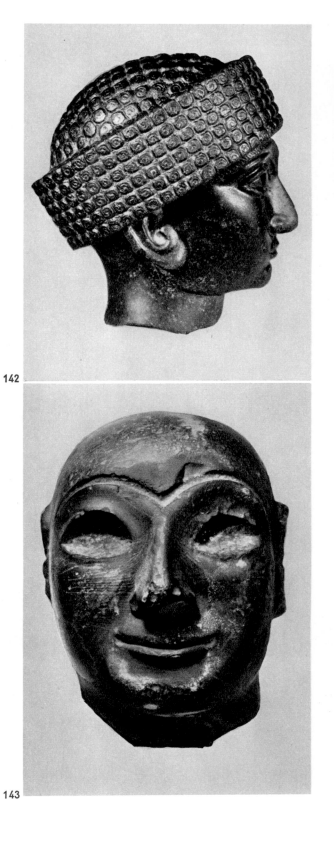

142

143

140

141

140. Back view of a statue of Ur-Ningursu, son of Gudea and his successor as *ensi* of Lagash. It is 18 in. high and made of gypsum-like alabaster. Found during clandestine digging which caused the treasures from the tell of Lagash to be scattered far and wide. The text states the subject's name and contains a dedication to Nin-gish-zi-da. **141.** The base on which the statue stands shows the figures of eight bearers offering their tribute in baskets. The leaders of the group are bearded and wear headbands with plumes projecting from them. **142.** This diorite head represents Gudea or his son Ur-Ningursu. **143.** This head of a bald king is older than the preceding one. Whom it represents is not known. Both heads are in the Museum of Antiquities at Leiden. **144.** A white alabaster statuette (20¾ in. high) of the master of ceremonies Ebih-il, found at Mari. The well-preserved eyes are of black stone, lapis lazuli and mother-of-pearl. It is thought to have been made about the middle of the third millennium B.C.

145. Woman's head with a covering in the form of a *polos*. Length nearly 6 in. Found in the temple of Ishtar at Mari (ca. 2500 B.C.).

146. Gypsum head of a woman wearing a tiara ($1\frac{1}{3}$ in.), found in the temple of Shamash at Mari; probably represents the goddess Ninhursag.

147. Mother-of-pearl figurine of a man with a sacrificial goat in his arms, found in the temple of Ninhursag at Mari. Length $3\frac{1}{4}$ in.

148. Gypsum head reconstructed from fragments from the temple of Ishtar at Mari; height nearly $5\frac{1}{2}$ in. It cannot be identified for lack of an inscription, but probably represents a high official or king.

149. Shell and ivory figurine of a man at a feast, holding a beaker in his hand. His hair is long and falls down in waves.

150. This figurine is the counterpart of the preceding, but with a striking difference: this man has a clean-shaven head and a beard. The images are respectively 3 and $2\frac{1}{2}$ in. high and were found at Mari, to the south of the temple of Shamash.

145

146

147

148

149

150

Sargon of Agade

A SEMITIC INTERLUDE

Seen in retrospect, the Semitic period was the briefest of interludes in the Sumerian drama. Semitic supremacy came suddenly, lasted only a century and a half – not long in the history of ancient Mesopotamia – and ended in catastrophe when the barbaric hordes descended from the mountains in the east. Yet historians of later generations look back upon that period as one of the most important because it was the first to give shape to a great empire with a single central authority (see Pl. 155). From then on the re-unification of all the territories conquered by Sargon of Agade into a Greater Mesopotamia remained a living aspiration and many subsequent conquerors sought to emulate his example.

Who was this Sargon of Agade? One answer is found in the legend of his birth as handed down in the form of *naru* literature. This term denotes monumental literature, deriving its material from historical tradition and appending to it a blessing or a curse, according as the result of the events narrated is good or bad. The text referring to Sargon dates from the seventh century, which proves how long after his death he continued to exercise the minds of scribes. It is written in the first person and tells of his birth in the following terms: 'My mother was an *enitum*, my father I know not, and my father's family dwells in the mountains. My city is Azupiranu on the bank of the Euphrates. My mother the *enitum* conceived me, in secret she bore me. She laid me in a basket of rushes and closed my door with bitumen. She placed me on the river, which rose not over me. The river bore me up and carried me to Akki the irrigator. Akki the irrigator lifted me out when he had cast in his pail. Akki the irrigator accepted me as his son and reared me. Akki the irrigator made me his garden-lad.'

This legend, of which various versions are known, attracted the attention of Old Testament scholars because of its resemblance to the story of the birth of Moses in Exodus 2 : 1ff., where a child, destined to play an important part, is laid in an ark of bulrushes and entrusted to the river. The difference is that Sargon was born out of wedlock; his mother the *enitum* was probably a priestess under obligation to remain celibate. She therefore abandoned him, and he was reared by an irrigator towards whom the court at Kish was well disposed. The king of Kish, named Ur-Zababa, made Sargon his cupbearer-in-chief, from which position the foundling succeeded in seizing the throne of Kish, how we do not exactly know. This was the start of domination by the Semites, who differed from the Sumerians in appearance and also, and still more, in language. The Sumerians had long been accustomed to Semites in their midst, and there had even been some city kings with Semitic names, although Sargon was the first to become supreme ruler. Cuneiform texts now appeared for the first time in Akkadian, a language cognate with Hebrew, Aramaic, and Arabic. The religion and culture of Semites dwelling in Mesopotamia were not very different from those of the Sumerians. They worshipped the same gods under different names, while as to culture the Semites were still appreciative pupils dependent on their masters. Nevertheless, the Semitic Ishtar, goddess of fertility and identical with the Sumerian Inanna, was now accorded an important place. She became the spouse of Anu, the sky god, and was eventually the principal goddess of the pantheon during the dynasty of Agade.

Sargon seems very soon to have abandoned Kish as his residence and to have moved to Agade, which he himself had founded. The site of this town has never been established with certainty. It has sometimes been identified with Der, twelve miles west of Baghdad, but no clear evidence in support of this hypothesis has ever been found during excavations there. For Mesopotamian archaeology this is a completely baffling riddle, although it may still be solved one day. For our knowledge of the architecture of the Akkadian period we are still mainly dependent on the results obtained during the excavations at Tell Brak in the north and in Tell Asmar, which was found to conceal the remains of ancient Eshnunna.

The reconstruction of Sargon's campaigns and deeds is made more difficult by the nature of the literature in which they have been handed down. Our chief sources of knowledge are the historical omens, which presupposed a parallelism between events and signs and were therefore used to forecast the future. The occurrence of natural phenomena in the sky, for example, foreshadowed the events which were held to be parallel with these signs. The only copies of Sargon's omens are from the Assyrian and Neo-Babylonian periods, and were therefore written at a much later date than the events they purport to describe. Nevertheless, it is legitimate to form the following general picture of Sargon's conquests.

He led his first campaign upstream along the Euphrates, where he captured Tutul, the site of modern Hit, famous for its asphalt springs. The god Dagan was honoured here, who is perhaps identical with the Dagon worshipped by the Philistines according to 1 Samuel 5. Sargon invoked his help and took it as a sign that his prayer had been heard when he succeeded in capturing Mari and subduing a region bordering on the Amanus and Taurus mountains. He appears to have brought the entire west under his control by the eleventh year of his reign. A text from the historical omens, which is, however, not confirmed by the chronicles, actually makes it appear as if he crossed the Mediterranean to Cyprus and Crete. This is improbable; but he and his armies did at any rate reach the Mediterranean coast. It was these conquests which brought him into conflict with Lugal-zaggisi of Erech. The latter regarded the territory in the west as part of his sphere of influence, and laid tribute on the countries in and about Palestine. Sargon's attack on Erech was so unexpected that he managed to take Lugal-zaggisi alive. Lugal-zaggisi was humbled and led off to Nippur like a dog on a lead. Then Sargon conquered and dismantled the second city of Sumer, Ur. He captured E-ninmar and Lagash, washed his weapons in the Persian Gulf in token of annexation, occupied Umma, destroying its walls, and then crossed over to Dilmun, which was probably the island of Bahrain.

The information available suggests that Sargon did not destroy the cities he captured, but allowed their princes to remain in power if they were prepared to pay him tribute as their overlord. It also gives the impression that trade flourished as a result of the lengthening of the caravan routes, which had become much safer in an extensive kingdom with a fixed central authority. That Sargon honoured local customs is apparent from a relief on an alabaster disc representing his daughter in her function as a priestess of the moon god in Ur. Yet this does not mean that all the countries willingly submitted to Sargon's rule; the chronicles mention a dangerous rising which, according to the Babylonian version, was caused by Marduk's wrath. Sargon, it says, had built a second city, Babylon, over against Agade and thus incurred the city god's displeasure. But although, according to the chronicles, the entire land rose up against him, the dynasty was not overthrown. Sargon died after a reign of forty-four years and the throne was ascended by his son Rimush, who ruled for ten years and was then murdered in a palace revolution. Even then the dynasty did not fall: Rimush's brother Manishtusu assumed control and

151
152

153

151. Red sandstone stele, ca. 6 ft. 6 in. high, found at Susa. It represents Naram-Sin conquering the Lullubians. He stands before a stylised mountain, with a tree to indicate a wooded area. The king is leading the soldiers who stand below him. He wears a helmet with two horns, a symbol of his divinity, protruding from it. His feet rest on two fallen enemies, a third falls into the abyss, a fourth has been transfixed by a spear, a fifth pleads for his life, and a sixth stands helpless with a broken spear. Naram-Sin is armed with axe, spear, and bow. **152.** Fragment of a stele on which only the image of Naram-Sin is preserved. He is holding two weapons, of which only the shafts remain, and wearing a heavy bracelet on each wrist. The sculptor has succeeded in giving the king an impressive dignity of bearing. **153.** Terracotta lions from Tell Harmal. They guarded the entrance to the temple of Nisaba, goddess of fertility.

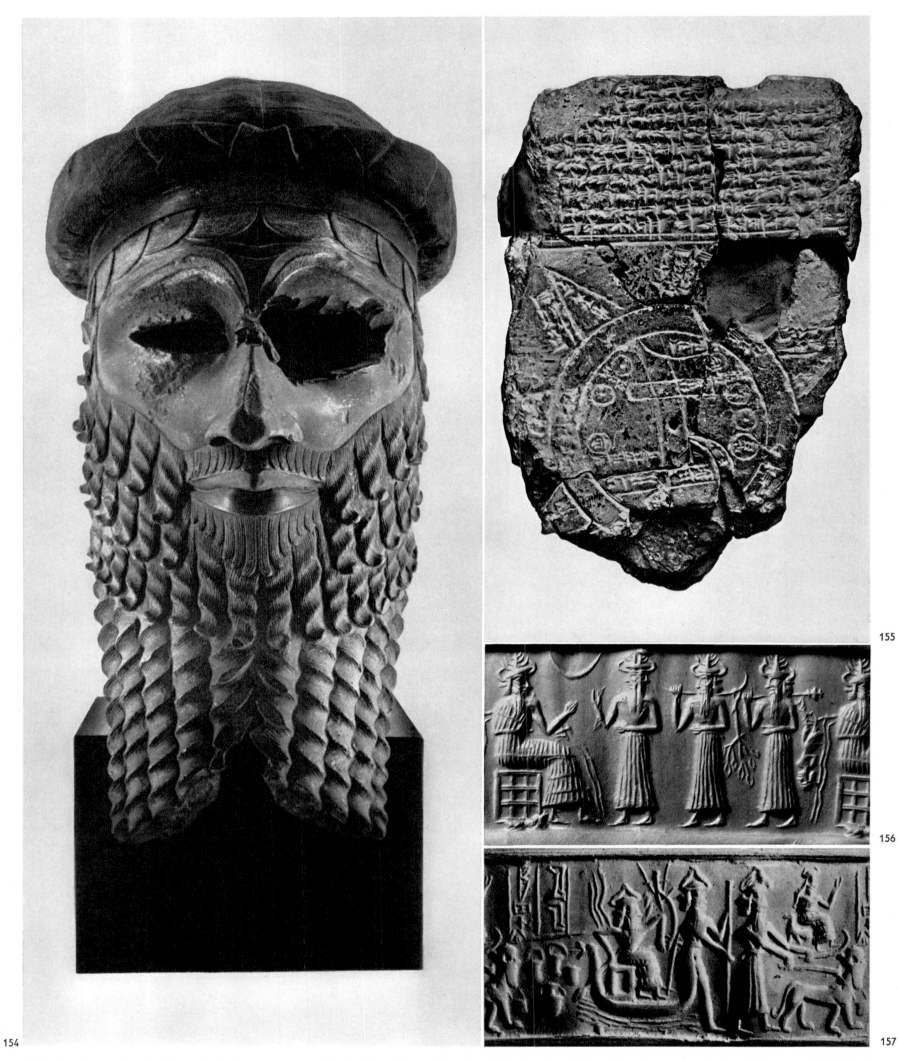

154. This bronze head, 14¼ in. high, from the second half of the third millennium B.C., found at Nineveh, and now in the Iraqi Museum, Baghdad, is probably of Sargon of Agade. Although the eyes are missing, the sculpture has an air of distinction which is further strengthened by the beautifully curled beard and moustache, the lips, and the powerful nose. **155.** This Babylonian world-map, drawn on a clay tablet about 600 B.C., demonstrates how Sargon's fame lived on among later generations. For not only does it illustrate the Babylonian concept of the world but the inscription mentions the conquests of this king who lived many centuries earlier. **156.** Impression of a seal from the time of Sargon; it shows a two-faced deity and lesser gods. **157.** This impression of a cylinder seal is also from the period of Sargon. In the centre is the sun god seated upon a throne in his boat and holding a plough with his hand.

reigned for fifteen years. He, too, was an energetic ruler and a successful general. But their fame was far exceeded by that of Naram-Sin ('the favourite of Sin'), who, after Sargon, is the greatest representative of the Agade dynasty. He reigned for thirty-six years.

THE PERIOD OF NARAM-SIN AND HIS SUCCESSORS

In the texts of Naram-Sin the character for 'deity' appears for the first time preceding the king's name, a proof that he was the first to lay claim to divine honour. He calls himself not only king of Sumer and Akkad but also 'king of the four quarters of the world' and even *shar-kishshatim,* 'king of the entire world'. His campaigns took him to the north and the east, where he waged war against the Lullubians in the Zagros Mountains and the Gutians invading from the north. He had reliefs carved in the mountain rocks as a permanent symbol of his presence. One of these was found at Diyarbekir on the Tigris in the extreme north, and another on the walls of a pass south of Sherizor near Darbandi Kawur, to the south of Sulaimaniya in the territory of the Lullubians. He is shown here as a larger than life-size warrior, holding a club in his right hand and a bow in his left. Beneath his feet lies a defeated enemy. With the powerful muscles of his shoulders and upper arms the king gives the impression of overwhelming might. We may regard this relief as the prototype of the 'Victory Stele' which was found at Susa (see Pl. 151).

Nevertheless, it was during Naram-Sin's campaigns that the future conquerors made themselves known. The Lullubians were defeated, but Naram-Sin suffered a crushing defeat at the hands of the barbarian Gutians. This had no serious consequences for him personally, and when he died he was succeeded by his son, who bore the proud name of Shargalisharri, 'king of all kings', but in his inscriptions always confined himself to the modest title of 'king of Agade'. This was also a sign of a changing situation, for it became clear early in his reign that the power of the dynasty of Agade was on the wane. In the west Elam was lost. Naram-Sin had appointed a certain Puzur-Ishushinak as governor there. The latter began to conquer territories on his own account, and when Naram-Sin died immediately proclaimed his independence, without Shargalisharri being able to do much about it. But the Gutians in particular had been greatly heartened by their victory, and we now see them starting to stream into Mesopotamia from the north. The king of Agade died in the course of the struggle against the infiltrating mountain nation, and the dissolution of his empire was soon in full swing. A chronicler sums up the situation in the phrase: 'Who was king, who was not king?' In three years four kings are named who reigned shortly after each other or possibly tried to reign simultaneously. There was a temporary recovery in the reigns of Dudu and his son Shudural, who respectively ruled for twenty and fourteen years. Then the proud dynasty of Agade was extinguished for ever. Agade was captured and destroyed by the Gutians, after which it disappears from history. Little is known of the Gutian régime in Mesopotamia. Information in the king lists suggest that they were never in firm control of the country. The upstart masters are spoken of disparagingly in the inscription of Utu-hegal, king of Erech, who says: 'Gutium, the mountain dragon, who attacked Agade with hostile deeds, who took the wife from her husband and the children from their parents.' This text appears to be inspired by more than the disdain of a civilised people for barbarians. Economic texts from the time of the Gutians indicate that trade was crippled and agriculture neglected. But the cities of southern Babylonia, which had maintained their own regional character under the domination of Agade, declared their independence and were destined soon to lead a Sumerian renaissance which appropriated the achievements of the Agade period.

In the eyes of the Sumerians the Semites, to whom Sargon belonged, were not barbarians. They had absorbed the culture of the Sumerians too long for that. But some excavations also revealed that the Agade period had been characterised by activities other than military. The most impressive example of Agade architecture came to light when temple and palace buildings and the residential areas adjoining them were excavated at Eshnunna. In one part of the palace a water closet with a pedestal-type lavatory pan in the western fashion was found; it was made of brick and connected by waste pipes to a sewage system. The water closet also contained, built into the floor, an earthenware jar which could be used for rinsing and washing; an earthenware baler still lay beside it. The drain, which had a diameter of over a yard and a length of over fifty yards, was angled steeply to facilitate flushing. If necessary, a small slave could have wormed his way through the drain to clean it thoroughly. The palace at Eshnunna also had five bathrooms. Thus, during the Agade period, hygienic practices were observed which were unknown in the West, even in the palace of Versailles, up to relatively modern times.

Another example of a large palace of this period was found at Tell Brak, northeast of Nineveh, near one of the tributaries of the Khabur. The bricks of the wall are stamped with the name of Naram-Sin. This was a huge building, erected on the ruins of a temple belonging to the Jemdet Nasr era. It had walls 33 feet thick, erected round five interior courts. Covering an area nearly 400 feet by over 300 feet, the palace was both a citadel and a store for tribute from the west. Its discovery brought confirmation of the traditions current among the Hittites of an Akkadian domination of Anatolia. As a supplier of the metals needed for arms the latter territory was becoming increasingly important. No temples of the Agade period have yet been found, although a hand-stamp was recovered at Nippur which bore in mirror writing the inscription: 'Naram-Sin, who built the temple of the god Enlil.' It was about this time that the custom of recording the name of the royal builder on hand-stamps began, a practice to which archaeology is much indebted. Thus, although there was a great measure of continuity in history, it is possible at this distant date to distinguish some of the characteristics of the Agade period. They can even be found in the reliefs: in the dress of men and women, in the way people wore their hair and men their beards. The plastic arts occasionally have a naturalistic liveliness which seems inspired by the products of the Jemdet Nasr period. The cylinder seals are remarkable for their powers of composition and the boldness of their subjects: a rite or a myth, daily life, and religious representations. Even beast fables are illustrated, as we can see on a seal from Eshnunna. This shows a lion and a horse seated opposite each other, sucking beer through a straw. The design of the popular cylinder seal provides a standard by which to judge the artistry and craftmanship of the sculptors of a particular period (see Pl. 156-7).

But even in other respects the age of Agade as it emerges from the chronicles and the mounds of ruined cities presents an attractive appearance. It was an era of wide horizons, which offered trade and commerce prospects previously unknown. Comparison of the finds at Mohenjo-Daro and Harappa in the Indus Valley with those made at Eshnunna and Ur in Mesopotamia proves that trade relations must have existed between these two regions, distant as they were from one another (see Map 9). For example, imprints of a seal showing a procession of animals, with a rhinoceros and an elephant beside each other and a crocodile above them, were found at both Mohenjo-Daro and Eshnunna, while a piece of clay bearing the head, horns, and neck of an Indian zebu was also discovered at Eshnunna.

The Agade period was a productive interlude in the Sumerian age: the practicability of a strong central authority accompanied by great regional freedom, and freedom, too, for the citizen, as well as better guarantees of his safety, had been demonstrated. A return to these ideal conditions long remained a national ambition. The Sumerian chronicler was conscious of this longing, which is apparent in a lament for the downfall of Agade. An explanation is sought for the disaster. The lament says: 'It is a punishment for the sacrilegious deed of Naram-Sin, who plundered Nippur and did not spare even E-kur, the shrine of Enlil.' To pacify Enlil's rage eight gods had pronounced a curse on Agade, and therefore it was depopulated for all time: 'He who said, "I would live in that city", could find there no good place to live in; he who said, "I would rest in Agade", could find there no good place to rest in.'

The Age of Hammurabi

THE FIRST DYNASTY OF BABYLON

Hammurabi was the sixth king of the first dynasty of Babylon. This dynasty had first come to power in the person of Sumu-abu in a period of decentralisation. A strong authority capable of uniting the cities of southern Mesopotamia for common action was entirely lacking. The area subject to the control of any one of the various city kings was limited. One of these cities was Bab-ilu, which even then boasted a long history going back until it disappeared in the mists of time. What the name originally meant cannot be said with certainty. The Bible story links it with a Hebrew verb *balal* meaning 'to confuse', and with the origin of the multiplicity of tongues (Gen. 11 : 9). Excavations on the site of Babylon did little to lift the veil of ignorance concerning the remotest past of the city. The subsoil water has risen here, rendering the Babylon of Hammurabi almost inaccessible, and only the much more recent habitation layers were successfully uncovered.

It is legitimate to deduce, however, that the city flourished in the eighteenth and nineteenth centuries B.C. thanks to efficient irrigation of a fertile soil still unaffected by salinisation. Moreover, the city lay on the Euphrates, which was sufficiently navigable to be a great boon to trade and traffic. When Hammurabi ascended the throne in 1724 B.C., Babylon was probably a prosperous, unpretentious provincial town. There was nothing to indicate that it would shortly develop into the metropolis of an extensive empire (see Map 10).

Among the small city states by which Babylon was surrounded, Larsa, Isin, and Eshnunna were most prominent. Our knowledge of this period is mainly due to the discovery of the archives of Mari, with their hundreds of clay tablets containing authentic information about the events which preceded the capture of Mari by Hammurabi. They show that in the first year of his reign Hammurabi was contemporaneous with the powerful Shamshi-Adad I of Ashur, who also controlled Mari. After Shamshi-Adad had died and been succeeded by his son, Ishme-Dagan, there was a considerable shift of the balance of power in the Mesopotamian world. The city of Mari succeeded in regaining its independence, and a native ruler Zimri-Lim was able to occupy the throne there. With that event Assyria's ascendancy in Mesopotamia was temporarily at an end. Hammurabi had now only two real rivals: Rim-Sin, king of Larsa, and Zimri-Lim of Mari. With the information culled from the Mari archives it is possible to follow the expansion of Hammurabi's empire in broad outline. Generally speaking, Hammurabi initially strengthened his position by political rather than by military means. He joined coalitions, but would break an alliance whenever he saw profit in doing so. Together with other southern Mesopotamian cities he fought against the Elamites in the east, but eventually turned against Larsa which had been one of his allies. In 1693, after a reign of sixty years, Rim-Sin saw his city pass into the hands of the Babylonians. Zimri-Lim of Mari had for a time been an ally of Hammurabi in campaigns against the Bedouin tribes who took advantage of every weakening of the central authority to invade the cultivated territory. In 1690 B.C. Hammurabi captured the town, which had developed a brilliant culture on the western bank of the Euphrates. It was probably on the occasion of a second conquest that the city was so completely destroyed by Hammurabi that there could be no question of rebuilding it. To this catastrophe the French expedition led by André Parrot later owed the successful excavation which displayed to us in a manner unparalleled elsewhere the civilisation of a city on the fringe of Mesopotamia in the eighteenth century B.C.

In the last few years of his reign Hammurabi also conquered the kingdom of Eshnunna and a weakened Assyria, which in the reign of of Ishme-Dagan I (1723-1693) had quickly shown unmistakable signs of decline. Thus, towards the end of his life, Hammurabi ruled over the whole of Mesopotamia. His officials had the caravan routes and their junctions under their control from the Taurus Mountains in the north to the Persian Gulf. It looked as if the old empire of Sargon of Agade's day had returned, thanks to rigid organisation under the powerful leadership of a single man. There are even vague indications that Hammurabi's troops pushed on through Palestine to the Mediterranean coast. A theory which attempted to identify the great king of Babylon with 'Amraphel king of Shinar' in Genesis 14 : 9 is now generally rejected, so that a possible link that would have helped to date Abraham has been lost.

Who was this Hammurabi? The name, pronounced Khammu-rabi ('the god Khammu is great'), was not an uncommon one about this time. The archives of Mari have acquainted us with a namesake in Aleppo and another in Kurda, and it is sometimes difficult to know which of the three is being referred to. Hammurabi belonged to the Amorites, who had originally lived as nomads but had invaded the cultivated region several generations earlier and settled there. These western Semites had gradually established themselves in a position from which they could dominate the original Sumero-Akkadian population. It is difficult to describe Hammurabi's character, for such representations of him as we possess are stylised and conceal personal traits behind the mask of a king (see Pls. 158 and 160). The information from written sources is somewhat more useful. Zimri-Lim of Mari had at the court of the Babylonian king various representatives whom we know by name because they regularly sent reports to their lord. The most important of these appears to have been Ibal-pi-el, but others are also named. They kept Zimri-Lim informed of the movements of Hammurabi's troops and of the king's doings. They were frequently in the king's presence and so gained an impression of his personality. It is sometimes possible to read something of this impression between the lines of their businesslike yet sometimes far from clear reports. La'um, for instance, writes to Zimri-Lim of trouble caused by members of the embassy at a court reception. They felt they had been slighted in a matter of precedence by the master of ceremonies and complained to Hammurabi personally about it. The king, however, is reported to have given them a haughty and very dictatorial reply. Even at the beginning of his rise to power he showed himself to be a man who knew what he wanted.

We learn even more about him from the letters he sent to his officials. These were composed by the chancellory scribes, but they have the tone of personally dictated messages. They are addressed to Sin-idinnam and Shamash-hasir and refer to the most varied range of subjects such as religion, judicial procedure, taxation, government and the army, public works, trade and agriculture. In them he reveals himself as a man who kept in close and detailed touch with events. Little escaped his notice. In particular he paid attention to those who came to him with their complaints, seeking justice at the highest level. Here are details of one such case which he dealt with in one of his letters: 'Tell Sin-idinnam, thus speaks Hammurabi. The official, Lalum, has informed me as follows: the judge Ali-elatti has laid claim to ground which I have long possessed; he has even con-

158
159

160
161

158. Limestone relief with a likeness of Hammurabi. This stele was offered by one of the king's high officials for the preservation of Hammurabi's life. The work reveals some personal characteristics, e.g. the long, crooked nose. The unshaved upper lip is typical of the Amorites. **159.** This head from a diorite statue, found in Susa, possibly represents Hammurabi. The headgear is like that worn in 160. **160.** The top part of the stele bearing the Code of Hammurabi. The sun god Shamash is seated on his throne, with a ring and staff in his hand; the king faces him with his right hand raised as a mark of respect. **161.** Diorite statue of Puzur-Ishtar, governor of Mari. It was found at Mari where it had been taken as a war trophy. The head is now in Berlin, the body in Istanbul. **162.** Bronze statuette of a worshipper, a votive offering for the preservation of Hammurabi's life made in a temple at Larsa; height $7\frac{3}{4}$ in.

fiscated the grain harvest from my ground. Thus he has informed me. The charter has been examined in the palace and indeed thirty acres are registered there in Lalum's name. Why then has the judge Ali-elatti laid claim to Lalum's ground? Investigate this matter. If Ali-elatti has done Lalum wrong, repair the damage he has suffered. Then punish Ali-elatti for the harm he has done him.' Such a letter reveals not only a sense of justice but also the strict organisation of an empire in which land ownership is registered on an almost cadastral basis. But many other types of cases were submitted to the king, such as that of a grain merchant who is owed money by a provincial governor, a cattle-owner who has been wrongly held responsible for a debt, or a baker who has become involved in a lawsuit over a field.

THE CODE OF HAMMURABI

The background to Hammurabi's actions is found most clearly stated in his code of law, a copy of which was found in the vicinity of Susa by French excavators. This discovery during the winter campaign of 1901-02 was the most sensational of the early years of this century. The stele of polished black diorite, which is now in the Louvre, is 7 feet 6 inches high. At the top is a bas-relief showing Shamash, the sun god and patron of justice. He is seated on his throne and bears his insignia in his hand. Opposite him, in an attitude of respect, is the king, receiving the law. A prologue in poetical language is followed by 282 paragraphs containing a case-by-case formulation of customary law and occasionally giving a new turn to that law. The text concludes with a poetical epilogue in which Shamash's blessing is invoked upon those who preserve the law and ruin is prophesied for the king who fails to uphold the system of justice recorded in it. The entire text represents the zenith of the Mesopotamian scribe's art (see Pl. 160).

The cuneiform script engraved in the stone is particularly beautiful and clear, the language is pure and expresses succinctly what has to be said. Probably several copies of the stele existed, to be erected in public places so that the citizen of Hammurabi's empire might know his rights, either through his own ability to read or by getting someone

---

PARAGRAPHS FROM THE CODE OF HAMMURABI

1. If a man has accused another and arraigned him of murder, and is then unable to prove it, he shall be put to death.

2. If a man has accused another of sorcery, and is then unable to prove it, the accused shall go to the holy river. He shall jump into the holy river, and if the holy river overwhelms him, the accuser shall take his house and keep it. If the holy river proves that the accused is to be acquitted and he returns safely, then he who accused him of sorcery shall be put to death, and the accused shall take and keep his house.

55. If a man has opened his irrigation channel and has been negligent, allowing the ground on the field of his neighbour to be removed by the water, he shall pay corn to the value of the damage suffered by his neighbour.

108. If an ale-wife refuses to accept grain in payment for strong drink, but takes silver by the heavy weight, or if she reduces the value of beer that is served upon payment in grain, she shall be denounced and cast into the water.

109. If ruffians are assembled in the house of an ale-wife, and she does not cause these ruffians to be seized and taken to the palace, she shall be put to death.

138. If a man wishes to divorce his first wife who has borne him no sons, he shall pay her money to the value of her bridal present and he shall compensate her for the dowry which she took from home; then he may divorce her.

---

to read to him the paragraphs relevant to his own case. The stele which was found so far from Babylon had originally been erected in the temple of Shamash at Sippar. Invaders from Elam had carried it off as a trophy of war, an example followed by Nebuchadnezzar if he in fact removed the stone tables of Moses from the temple at Jerusalem to Babylon. King Shutruk-Nahhunte, who ruled Elam about 1160 B.C., appears to have intended adding an inscription of his own to the stele, for several legal paragraphs have been chipped off. If this theory is correct, the intention was never put into effect, so that the Code of Hammurabi has survived almost undamaged until the present day.

The first editors of the inscription possibly thought that they were dealing with the oldest recorded law code in the world, not only because the dates assigned to Hammurabi at that time were several centuries earlier than we now know to be the case, but also because no text of a similar nature was known. The interest of Old Testament commentators in this code was particularly great because until the beginning of the twentieth century the law of Moses existed in complete isolation owing to the lack of comparative contemporary material. But here was an authentic text, older than the oldest traditions to which the law of Moses could be traced back, and forming part of the wide field of ancient Eastern jurisprudence. Comparative study gave rise to a new subject on which many scholars have since worked with so much success that it has been accorded a place of its own in the lecture syllabus of universities.

Thus, although we can no longer say that the Code of Hammurabi is the oldest or the most original known to us in the history of Eastern jurisprudence, it is still one of the most detailed and the most interesting. It introduces us to a world where the Sumerian principle of order is combined with many technical achievements. Paragraphs 215-23, for instance, relate to the surgeon, and are followed by provisions for the veterinary surgeon and the barber. The surgeon, we find, is able to perform eye operations with copper knives – several centuries before the Iron Age! His fee is defined as 10 shekels for a citizen of the ruling class, 5 for a second-class citizen, and 2 for a slave, to be paid by the latter's master. A successful leg operation brings him a fee of 5, 3, and 2 silver shekels respectively. If the eye operation fails and the leading citizen loses his eye, the surgeon's hand has to be cut off. The death of a slave entails repayment of his value, while the loss of his eye is punished by the obligation to pay half that value. A veterinary surgeon is allowed to charge up to one-sixth of the value of the animals he has cured.

Paragraphs 228-33 are concerned with the master builder. For building a house he may charge a sum proportional to the cubic content of the house. If the house collapsed and the owner was killed, his death was avenged by the death of the builder. If the owner's child was killed, the builder answered for it with the life of his own child. What we now know of the application of the *jus talionis* in the laws of Ur-Nammu and Eshnunna makes acceptable the hypothesis that even in Hammurabi's time it was possible to compound for death and injury by a fine.

THE JUS TALIONIS

The text of the law code of Bilalama, who reigned ca. 1950 B.C., was found during excavations initiated by the Iraqi Department of Antiquities at Tell Harmal, where remains of ancient Shaduppum, the administrative centre of Bilalama's kingdom, were uncovered. The little mound, in which some of the ancient buildings have been reconstructed, is now surrounded by a suburb of expanding Baghdad. In 1948 Albrecht Goetze published the text of a law which must be about two centuries older than that of Hammurabi. It is written in Akkadian on two tablets, one measuring 4 × 8 inches and the other 4¾ × 4½ inches and both containing the same text. Even under this law the literal interpretation of 'an eye for an eye and a tooth for a tooth' had been replaced by a milder system of fines. Thus we read in Paragraphs 42-8 (in all 61 have survived): 'If one man bites or cuts

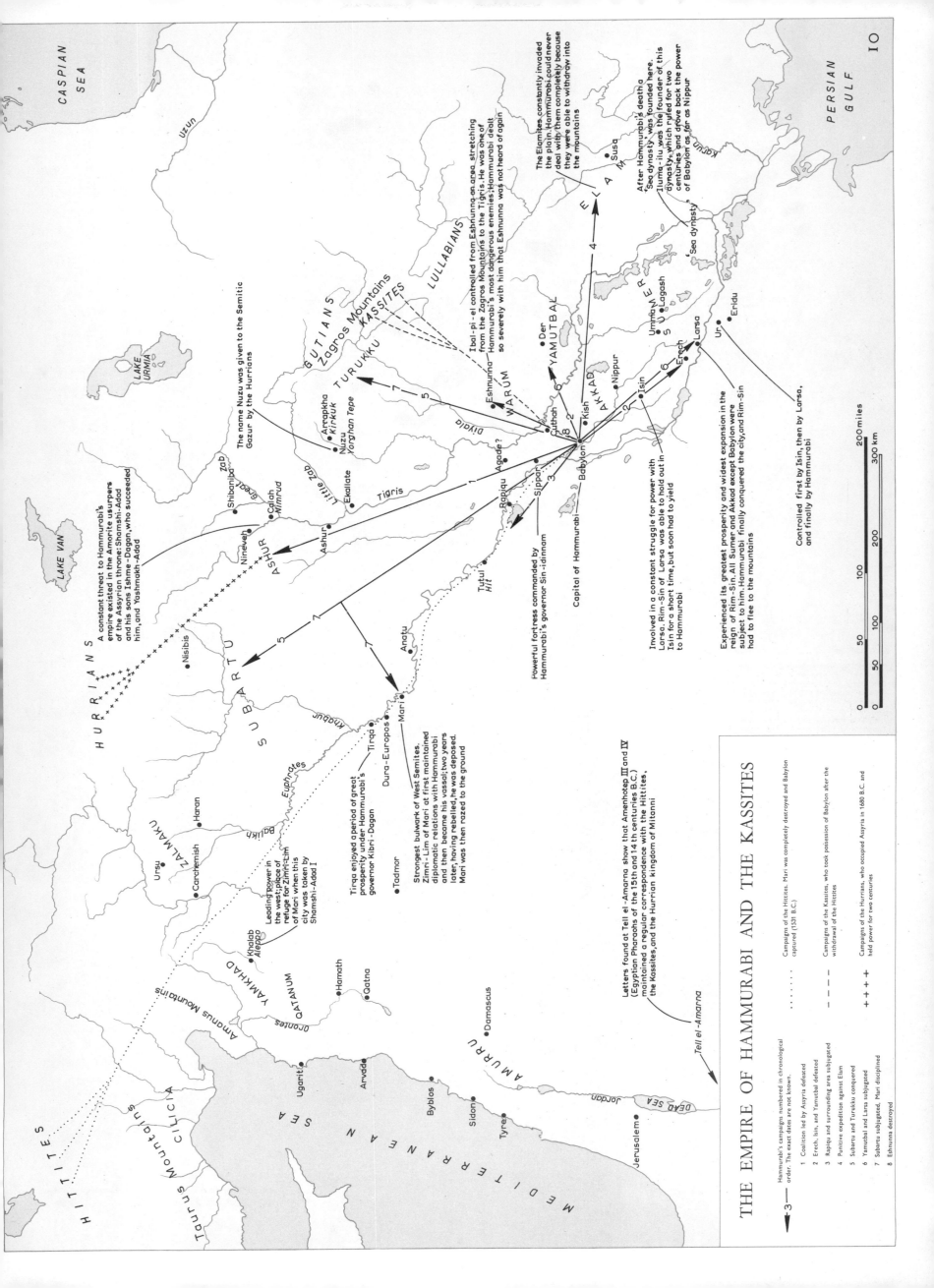

THE EMPIRE OF HAMMURABI AND THE KASSITES

CASPIAN SEA

LAKE VAN

LAKE URMIA

HURRIANS

Uzun

A constant threat to Hammurabi's empire existed in the Amorite usurpers of the Assyrian throne: Shamshi-Adad and his sons Ishme-Dagan, who succeeded him, and Yashmakh-Adad

The name Nuzu was given to the Semitic Gazur by the Hurrians

GUTIANS
Zagros Mountains
KASSITES
TURUKKU
LULLABIANS

Ibal-pi-el controlled from Eshnunna an area stretching from the Zagros Mountains to the Tigris. He was one of Hammurabi's most dangerous enemies; Hammurabi dealt so severely with him that Eshnunna was not heard of again

The Elamites constantly invaded the plain. Hammurabi could never deal with them completely because they were able to withdraw into the mountains

After Hammurabi's death a "Sea dynasty" was founded here. Ilumа-ilu was the founder of this dynasty, which ruled for two centuries and drove back the power of Babylon as far as Nippur

E L A M
Susa

Nisibis

Shibaniba
Balawat

Calah
Nimrud

Nineveh

Ashur
ASHUR

Ekallate

Arrapkha
Kirkuk

Nuzu
Yorghan Tepe

Zab

Little Zab

Tigris

Agade?

Rapiqu

Sippar

Diyala

Der

Eshnunna

Cuthah
Kish
Babylon
AKKAD

Nippur

Isin
Umma
Lagash
Erech
Larsa
Ur
Eridu

YAMUTBAL
WARUM

S U M E R

"Sea dynasty"

Karun

Powerful fortress commanded by Hammurabi's governor Sin-idinnam

Capital of Hammurabi

Involved in a constant struggle for power with Larsa. Rim-Sin of Larsa was able to hold out in Isin for a short time, but soon had to yield to Hammurabi

Experienced its greatest prosperity and widest expansion in the reign of Rim-Sin. All Sumer and Akkad except Babylon were subject to him. Hammurabi finally conquered the city, and Rim-Sin had to flee to the mountains

Controlled first by Isin, then by Larsa, and finally by Hammurabi

SUBARTU

Tutul
Hit

Euphrates

Khabur

Anatu
Mari
Tirqa
Dura-Europos

Strongest bulwark of West Semites. Zimri-Lim of Mari at first maintained and then became his vassal; two years later, having rebelled, he was deposed. Mari was then razed to the ground

Tirqa enjoyed a period of great prosperity under Hammurabi's governor Kibri-Dagan

Leading power in the west: place of refuge for Zimri-Lim of Mari when this city was taken by Shamshi-Adad I

ZALMAKU

Ursu
Carchemish
Haran

Balikh

Tadmor

Khalab
Aleppo

YAMKHAD

Hamath
Qatna
QATANUM

Orontes

Damascus

AMMURU

HITTITES

Taurus Mountains
CILICIA

Amanus Mountains

Ugarit
Arvad
Byblos
Sidon
Tyre
Jerusalem

M E D I T E R R A N E A N   S E A

DEAD SEA
Jordan

Letters found at Tell el-Amarna show that Amenhotep III and IV (Egyptian Pharaohs of the 15th and 14th centuries B.C.) maintained a regular correspondence with the Hittites, the Kassites, and the Hurrian kingdom of Mitanni

Tell el-Amarna

PERSIAN GULF

IO

─3➤ Hammurabi's campaigns numbered in chronological order. The exact dates are not known.

.... Campaigns of the Hittites. Mari was completely destroyed and Babylon captured (1531 B.C.)

─ ─ ─ Campaigns of the Kassites, who took possession of Babylon after the withdrawal of the Hittites

+ + + + Campaigns of the Hurrians, who occupied Assyria in 1680 B.C. and held power for two centuries

1 Coalition led by Assyria defeated
2 Erech, Isin, and Yamutbal defeated
3 Rapiqu and surrounding area subjugated
4 Punitive expedition against Elam
5 Subaru and Turukku conquered
6 Yamutbal and Larsa subjugated
7 Subaru subjugated, Mari disciplined
8 Eshnunna destroyed

0   50   100   200 miles
0 50 100 200 300 km

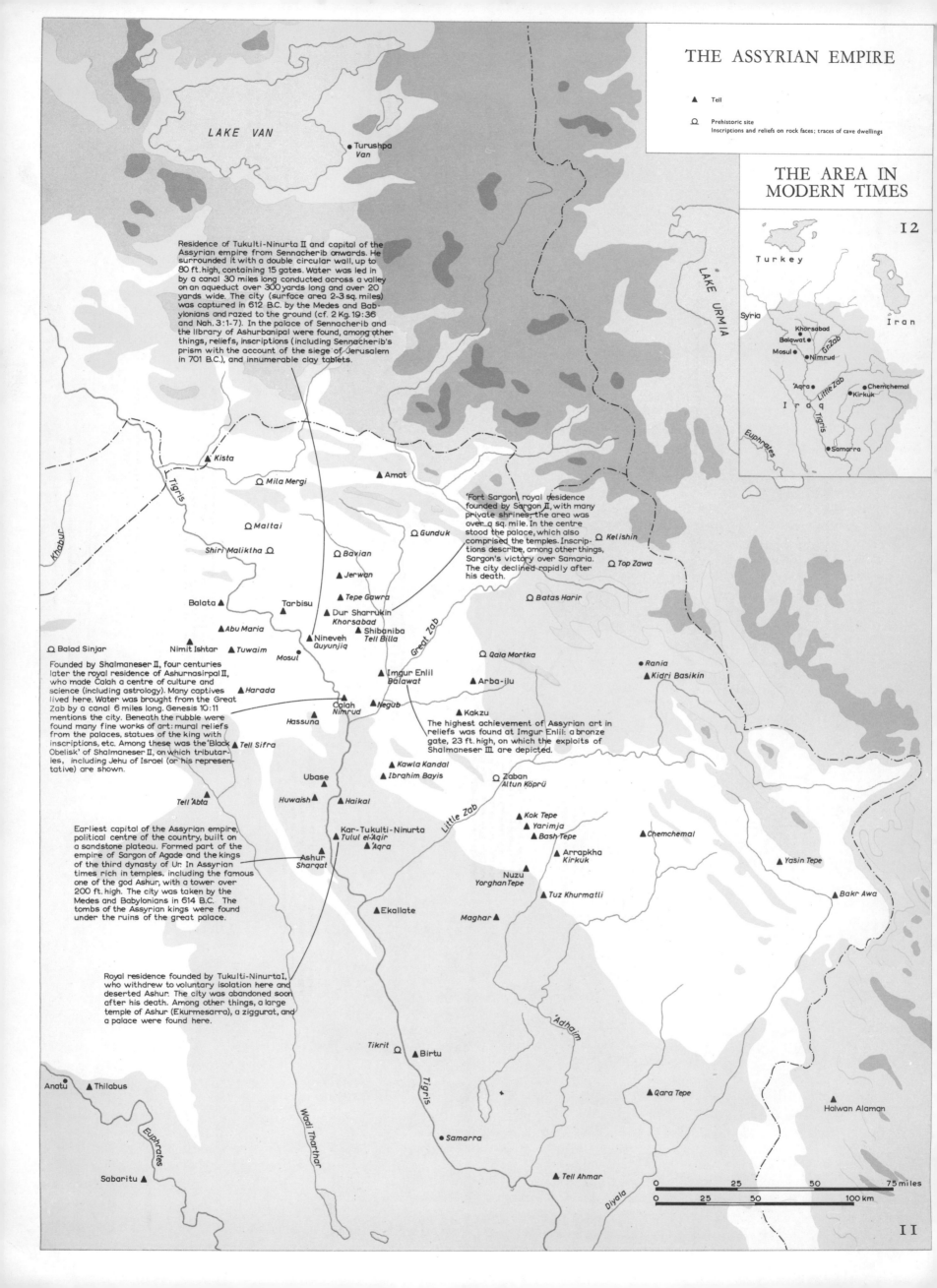

THE ASSYRIAN EMPIRE

▲ Tell

Ω Prehistoric site
Inscriptions and reliefs on rock faces; traces of cave dwellings

THE AREA IN
MODERN TIMES

12

LAKE VAN

• Turushpa
Van

LAKE URMIA

Turkey

Iran

Syria

Khorsabad
Balawat ●
Mosul ●   ● Nimrud

'Aqra ●

Chemchemal ●
Kirkuk ●

Iraq

Euphrates

Tigris

● Samarra

Residence of Tukulti-Ninurta II and capital of the
Assyrian empire from Sennacherib onwards. He
surrounded it with a double circular wall, up to
80 ft. high, containing 15 gates. Water was led in
by a canal 30 miles long conducted across a valley
on an aqueduct over 300 yards long and over 20
yards wide. The city (surface area 2-3 sq. miles)
was captured in 612 B.C. by the Medes and Babylonians and razed to the ground (cf. 2 Kg. 19:36
and Nah. 3:1-7). In the palace of Sennacherib and
the library of Ashurbanipal were found, among other
things, reliefs, inscriptions (including Sennacherib's
prism with the account of the siege of Jerusalem
in 701 B.C.), and innumerable clay tablets.

▲ Kista

Ω Mila Mergi

▲ Amat

'Fort Sargon' royal residence
founded by Sargon II, with many
private shrines; the area was
over a sq. mile. In the centre
stood the palace, which also
comprised the temples. Inscriptions describe, among other things,
Sargon's victory over Samaria.
The city declined rapidly after
his death.

Ω Maltai

Ω Gunduk

Ω Kelishin

Shiri Maliktha Ω

Ω Bavian

Ω Top Zawa

● Jerwan

▲ Tepe Gawra

Ω Batas Harir

Balata ▲

Tarbisu ▲

● Dur Sharrukin
Khorsabad

▲ Abu Maria

● Shibaniba
Tell Billa

Ω Balad Sinjar

Nineveh
Quyunjiq

Nimit Ishtar ▲ Tuwaim

● Rania

Ω Qala Mortka

Ω Kidri Basikin

Mosul

▲ Arba-ilu

Founded by Shalmaneser II, four centuries
later the royal residence of Ashurnasirpal II,
who made Calah a centre of culture and
science (including astrology). Many captives
lived here. Water was brought from the Great
Zab by a canal 6 miles long. Genesis 10:11
mentions the city. Beneath the rubble were
found many fine works of art: mural reliefs
from the palaces, statues of the king with
inscriptions, etc. Among these was the 'Black
Obelisk' of Shalmaneser II, on which tributaries, including Jehu of Israel (or his representative) are shown.

▲ Harada

▲ Imgur Enlil
Balawat

● Negub

Calah
Nimrud

▲ Kakzu

The highest achievement of Assyrian art in
reliefs was found at Imgur Enlil: a bronze
gate, 23 ft. high, on which the exploits of
Shalmaneser III are depicted.

Hassuna ▲

▲ Tell Sifra

▲ Kawla Kandal

▲ Ibrahim Bayis

Ω Zaban
Altun Köprü

Ubase ▲

Little Zab

▲ Kok Tepe

Huwaish ▲

▲ Haikal

▲ Yarimja

Tell 'Abta ▲

▲ Bash Tepe

▲ Chemchemal

Kar-Tukulti-Ninurta
● Tulul el-'Aqir

▲ Arrapkha
Kirkuk

Earliest capital of the Assyrian empire,
political centre of the country, built on
a sandstone plateau. Formed part of the
empire of Sargon of Agade and the kings
of the third dynasty of Ur. In Assyrian
times rich in temples, including the famous
one of the god Ashur, with a tower over
200 ft. high. The city was taken by the
Medes and Babylonians in 614 B.C. The
tombs of the Assyrian kings were found
under the ruins of the great palace.

▲ 'Aqra

Ashur
Sharqat

▲ Nuzu
Yorghan Tepe

▲ Yasin Tepe

▲ Tuz Khurmatli

▲ Ekallate

▲ Bakr Awa

Maghar ▲

Royal residence founded by Tukulti-Ninurta I,
who withdrew to voluntary isolation here and
deserted Ashur. The city was abandoned soon
after his death. Among other things, a large
temple of Ashur (Ekurmesarra), a ziggurat, and
a palace were found here.

'Adhaim

Tikrit Ω ▲ Birtu

Anatu Ω ▲ Thilabus

▲ Qara Tepe

Halwan Alaman

Euphrates

Wadi Tharthar

Tigris

● Samarra

Sabaritu ▲

▲ Tell Ahmar

Diyala

0   25   50   75 miles

0   25   50   100 km

II

CHRONOLOGICAL TABLE OF THE PERIOD OF HAMMURABI
(see page 87)

First dynasty of Babylon		Contemporaries of Hammurabi	
		Larsa:	
Sumu-abu	1826-1813	Rim-Sin	1753-1693
Sumu-la-ilum	1812-1777		
Zabum	1776-1763	*Assyria:*	
Apil-Sin	1762-1745	Shamshi-Adad	1744-1724
Sin-muballit	1744-1725	Ishme-Dagan	1723-1693
Hammurabi	1724-1682		
Samsu-iluna	1681-1644	*Mari:*	
Abi-eshu	1643-1616	Yashmakh-Adad	-1722
Ammi-ditana	1615-1579	Zimri-Lim	1722-1690
Ammi-zaduga	1578-1558		
Samsu-ditana	1557-1526		

off the nose of another, he shall pay one mina of silver, for an eye one mina, for a tooth half a mina, for an ear half a mina; for a slap in the face he shall pay ten shekels of silver. If a man cuts off the finger of another, he shall pay two-thirds of a mina of silver. If a man knocks down another in the darkness of night (?) and the latter breaks his wrist, he shall pay half a mina of silver. If he breaks his foot, he shall pay half a mina of silver. If a man breaks another's . . . (?), he shall pay one-third of a mina of silver. If a man spits upon (?) another, he shall pay ten shekels of silver. Moreover, in cases where the sum involved is between one-third and one mina of silver, the accused shall be summoned before the court. A capital offence comes before the king.' The language of this code is excellent, but the arrangement is so disorderly that the 'code' is thought nowadays to consist of examples of legal language for use in the schools for scribes. In that case the clay tablets would represent only fragments of the Code of Eshnunna. Despite that fact, however, great interest was aroused by the finding, right at the beginning of the code, of price lists for primary necessities of life and tables of fixed rents and wages.

BIBLICAL AND BABYLONIAN LAW

From the law as it applied to the surgeon it is obvious that we are dealing with a typical class society, distinctions being drawn between the *awilum*, the *mushkenum* (both freemen), and the *wardum* (a slave). This distinction is unknown in Biblical law, for the Mosaic code presupposes a peasant community in which everyone is born with the same rights. A closed community of this kind has difficulty in absorbing foreigners, however, and so we find them divided into two groups: the *ger* with rights and the *nokri* without rights. Under the law of Moses anyone who had had to sell himself into slavery was freed in the sabbatical year, that is, every seventh year; under the Code of Hammurabi he had to be freed after three years. Despite the resemblances, therefore, there is also considerable difference between Old Babylonian and Biblical law, and this is partly due to the difference in social background between the city on one hand and the agricultural country on the other.

While Biblical law contains no article relating to trade, Paragraph 7 of the Code of Hammurabi reads: 'If an *awilum* has bought or taken custody of silver or gold, a slave, an ox, or ass, or anything else from an *awilum* or the slave of an *awilum* without witnesses or a contract, then that *awilum* is like unto a thief and shall be put to death as such.' This paragraph explains the overwhelming quantities of contracts that the soil of Mesopotamia has preserved and which are so instructive not only on account of the personal names that occur in them but also for the writing of economic history. This will be clear from the following example.

Although Hammurabi followed old traditions in regulating the community he ruled over, there was a lack of uniformity in the cities of southern Mesopotamia with regard to the right to private property. The situation was in fact one of coexistence – not necessarily peaceful –

between different economic systems and social institutions. Thus great adaptability was demanded of the citizens of Larsa, accustomed as they were to the rule of Rim-Sin, when Hammurabi took over authority. The consequences of the new order for a well-to-do family in this city can be read in authentic documents, the archives of Sanum and his successors. These show that Sanum was able originally to make a profit on many transactions and then to purchase possessions of stable value such as land. Private citizens could become large landowners in this way. In Hammurabi's empire this was not possible, for ground there belonged either to the temple, as a sort of monastic property, or to the palace, in which case it was at the free disposal of the king, who could reward his army captains and soldiers with *ilku* (land held in fee). After Hammurabi had incorporated the kingdom of Larsa, Sanum's grandson was no longer able to invest his profits in land. He retained his great estate and was allowed to bequeath it to his five sons, but the contracts show that no more land was bought. Sanum's great-grandson, however, devised a new means of attaining prosperity, namely as a purchasing agent for the state. Documents left by him show that he was a wholesale dealer in fish, dates, onions, and wool. Trade in fish, a perishable commodity, was particularly risky, and only those with considerable capital behind them could bolster themselves against the setbacks of this sensitive trade. Sanum's archives are an example of how genuine source material throws light on the joys and sorrows of citizens swept along by the tide of politics and not deemed worthy of interesting mention in official annals.

Thus Hammurabi has gone down into history as the 'king of justice', who was familiar with traditional law, applied it, and, when he saw fit, dared to reform it. The sun god Shamash was the patron of justice and hence of all the necessitous. Hammurabi had received the law from Shamash, yet strangely enough this did not result in the sun god occupying a predominant place in the pantheon. The city god of Babylon was Marduk, and Marduk was proclaimed the highest of the gods.

In the fine language of the epilogue it says that Hammurabi has inscribed his precious words on this monument 'that the strong might not injure the weak and that the widow and the orphan might receive justice'. The text continues: 'Let the oppressed citizen who is involved in a lawsuit come before my image as king of justice, let him have my inscription read out to him, and let him hear my precious words. Let this monument throw light upon his case, and may he discover his rights and his heart be made glad.' This is the court poet speaking, and it is impossible to form a reliable picture of Hammurabi from a text of this nature. An abundance of other sources enables us, however, to see this king against the background of his time. They show that he must be counted one of the greatest figures in Mesopotamian history.

THE DECLINE

Hammurabi had no successor who was in any way comparable to him. His son, Samsu-iluna, began granting freedom from taxation in the second year of his reign. Ur and Erech nevertheless defected and were only forced back into the empire by severe countermeasures. A son of Rim-Sin, who had fled to Elam, became the leader of a stubborn revolt. Eventually Babylon split into a northern and a southern kingdom. Hammurabi's dynasty contrived to remain on the throne of Babylon until the Hittites, extending their expeditions in search of booty far from their native Asia Minor, put an end to it. Under the last king of the first Babylonian dynasty, Samsu-ditana (1557-1526), Babylon had declined into a provincial town whose only significance was as a religious centre to which pilgrims flocked for the New Year festival. The memory of its glory under Hammurabi survived, however, and with it a latent aspiration to recover its former power once more. It was to be over 1,000 years before Nebuchadnezzar II achieved this in unequalled fashion. Meanwhile we see foreign invaders establishing themselves in Babylon.

The Period of the Kassites

The Kassites or Cossaeans ruled Mesopotamia for over four centuries. The number of inscriptions they have left is extremely small in relation to this lengthy period. The result has been a tendency to form a low opinion of their civilisation and to regard the Kassite period generally as one of decline. Several excavations, however, particularly that at Dur Kurigalzu and a block of temple buildings in Erech, showed that the Kassites have in fact made a positive contribution to the cultural history of Mesopotamia.

This ruling race came in all probability from the mountain country which is now called Luristan. The success with which they descended from the northeast and pushed into the river plains of the Euphrates and the Tigris they owed to the political situation. In the course of a bold campaign the army of the ancient Hittite empire under Murshilish I had penetrated as far as Babylon and might have put an end to the first dynasty there. But their lines of communication extending back over 600 miles to the heart of Asia Minor were too long to maintain. In Mesopotamia, therefore, they left behind them a trail of destruction and a vacuum which was filled by the Kassites. That the latter were able to hold their ground for so long can also be explained by the international situation in Asia Minor, which they exploited with great political skill. It was more by adopting a neutral attitude than by waging war that they maintained the status quo in the territory they held, although there are records of campaigns against Elam and the 'Sea land' (see Map 10).

Virtually nothing is known of the Kassites' language. Such texts as they left are in Akkadian and only a few words in these can be identified as Kassite. They likewise appear to have had little difficulty in adapting their religion to that of Babylon. At any rate they call their gods, of whom Kharbe, Buriash, and Shuriash are the most prominent, by Sumero-Akkadian names. That their internal policy was directed towards reconciling the population with their régime is seen from their expedition to Khalab (Aleppo) to fetch back the statues of Marduk and his wife Sarpanitum, which had been taken there by the Hittites. We get the impression that the Kassites felt themselves culturally inferior to the Babylonians and therefore appropriated their

civilisation as far as they were capable of doing so. Nevertheless, a period of humiliation started for the original population when proud Babylon was ruled under the new name of Kar-Duniash by the barbarians. Their first residence was not Babylon but Hana ('Ana) on the middle course of the Euphrates. Kurigalzu II (1337-1313) appears finally to have moved his capital to Dur Kurigalzu, which he himself built on the site now occupied by 'Aqarquf, about fifteen miles west of Baghdad. Here, like a beacon in the wide expanse of flat land, the weathered temple tower, which had long attracted attention but was not the subject of close examination until after the end of the Second World War, rises to a height of 165 feet (see Colour Plate facing p. 142).

When it was finally excavated by the Department of Antiquities of Iraq, not only was the stairway of this ziggurat laid bare, but three temples and a part of a palace were also discovered. The temples were consecrated to the old familiar gods Enlil, Nin-lil, and Ninurta. The most striking artistic objects found there were terracotta statuettes (see Pls. 165-8), while fragments of a larger than life-size statue of the founder Kurigalzu were also found. The walls of the palace were decorated with frescoes, and one architectural novelty not previously encountered elsewhere was a gallery with square pillars. Thus Dur Kurigalzu helped to make up for the lack of inscriptions during the Kassite period. Yet the Kassites also took particular pains to touch up and restore the shrines they found in their territory. Traces of these activities can be found in Nippur, Larsa, Ur, and Erech. In the last of these cities Karaindash restored the Eanna group of temples in the middle of the fifteenth century B.C. A small temple was found here which is typical of Kassite architecture: reliefs consisting of modelled bricks stand out against the walls of the small temple to the goddess Inanna. These bricks were fitted together to form the figures to be portrayed, in this case gods and goddesses (see Pl. 164). This technique was to flourish again at a much later period, in the time of Nebuchadnezzar in the sixth century B.C. The façade with 'water gods' in Erech is thus another example of the original work that the Kassite period was capable of producing.

A certain light was shed on the Kassites from a totally unexpected

164

165

166

163. Clay model of a liver, inscribed with magic formulae, now incomprehensible, for the use of soothsayers, a practice to which Ezekiel 21:21 alludes. Probably dates from 19th-18th century B.C. **164.** Façade incorporating water gods made of bricks modelled and cemented together; found in the temple of Inanna at Erech and typical of the Kassite period. **165.** Terracotta man's head, found at Dur Kurigalzu; it dates from the period of the Kassites. **166.** Full-face view of the same head, with its beard and clean-shaven upper lip. **167.** Terracotta lioness of the same period, also found at Dur Kurigalzu. **168.** Detail of the head of the preceding statuette.

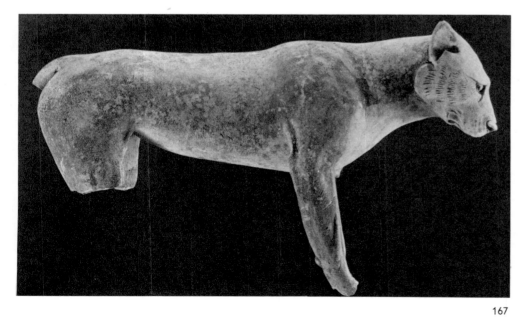

167

168

quarter. The archives of letters of the Pharaohs Amenhotep III and Amenhotep IV (Akhenaton) were found at Tell el-Amarna (the ancient Akhetaton) in 1887. This find of clay tablets revealed first that Akkadian was used in the fourteenth century B.C. as an international language of diplomacy. The letters showed that princes and governors resident in Palestine, which was still nominally ruled by the Egyptian Pharaohs, corresponded with Egypt in the Assyro-Babylonian cuneiform writing. It is true that their language is interlarded with Canaanite words and idioms, but in the main it is Akkadian. That this language was accepted as a *lingua franca* by Egypt, which generally guarded itself against foreign influences, is proof of the dominating position that Mesopotamian culture had maintained, even under the Kassites.

Among the letters recovered are a number sent by Kadashman-Kharbe (Kadashman-Enlil) I and Burnaburiash II, and copies of the replies of the Egyptian court. The impression the reader gets is of begging letters from parvenus unable to overcome their feeling of inferiority before the ancient traditions of the Egyptian dynasties. In them the Kassites asked Egypt to send gold for the decoration of their temples and palaces, wives for their harems, and strange animals to display in their menageries. In exchange for these they were able to offer lapis lazuli which they themselves could get from areas which are now part of Afghanistan. The women sent should, if possible, be princesses, but ladies of the court would at a pinch also be acceptable, as the difference would scarcely be noticed in Babylon. They asked animals for their zoos but would not be shocked if the animals sent had by some artifice been made more fantastic than they were in nature. They valued the Pharaoh's personal interest in their welfare and complained when their illness evoked no token of sympathy from Egypt. The following are some examples of fragments from this correspondence. Kadashman-Kharbe writes to Amenhotep III: 'To Nibmuwaria, King of Egypt, my brother. Thus spoke Kadashman-Kharbe, King of Karduniash, your brother: it goes well with me, may it go very well with you, your house, your wives, your entire land, your coaches, your horses, your nobles. As for the girl, my daughter, whom you wrote you wanted to marry, the woman is now grown up, she is marriageable, send for her. My father once sent you a messenger and you did not detain him long; you dispatched him quickly back hither, and sent my father a fine present. But when I sent you a messenger you kept him for six years and for those six years you paid me thirty minas of gold with the value of silver. This gold was tested before the eyes of Kasis, your messenger, and he was a witness. When you prepared a great feast you sent me no messenger to bid me come, eat and drink, and you sent me no festive present. Behold what I did! In my house I prepared a great feast, your servants watched and in the portal of the house I put up a notice saying: "Come! Eat with me and drink!" I did not do what you did.' Another letter by the same writer reads: 'Behold, when you, my brother, not wishing to give me one of your daughters in marriage, write: "Since ancient times no daughter of a king in Egypt has been given to any man," I reply, "Why do you speak thus? Are you not king and may you not act as you please? If you give, who shall speak against it?" When they told me your answer, I wrote the following to my brother: "There are grown daughters and beautiful women enough. Send me then any beautiful woman you think fit. Who shall say, That is no king's daughter?" '

Burnaburiash was not ashamed to admit his ignorance of geography. In a letter which strikes the modern reader as rather comical he informed the Pharaoh that he had been slightly ill. The Egyptian ambassador had paid him a visit but his illness had prevented him from dining convivially and drinking a glass of wine. Since then he had been looking in vain for some sign of interest from the Pharaoh. He had complained of this indifference to a member of the Egyptian diplomatic mission. This appears to have been a tactful man who explained that the distance to his country was rather great and that this was no doubt the reason for the delay in receiving sympathy. In fact he exclaimed: 'Can you imagine that your brother would hear of your illness and show no interest in it?' The still mistrustful Burnaburiash then instructed his own ambassadors to report on the length of the caravan route to Egypt. Their information, he wrote, had reassured him.

Also found in the archives were lists of presents which had been sent by the Pharaoh to Mesopotamia and those which streamed in the reverse direction from Mesopotamia to Egypt, and the impression one gets is that Kadashman-Kharbe and Burnaburiash did not do too badly. The lists that were kept of these imports and exports contribute greatly to our knowledge of barter traffic along the busy caravan routes running through Palestine from Mesopotamia to the land of the Nile. The extent of this traffic depended mainly on how peaceful conditions were in the intervening territory and on the supervision the two states were able to exercise on the trade routes. Burnaburiash was therefore greatly troubled by a powerful rival who crossed his path, and bitterly reproached the Pharaoh when he found he was maintaining diplomatic relations with Ashur.

For a long time Ashur had been a province of the kingdom of Mitanni, which was ruled over by the Hurrians. The centre of this kingdom lay between the Khabur and the Euphrates and it dispatched armies into Palestine, where Egypt fought against them until relations became more friendly in the reign of Tushratta (contemporary with Amenhotep III and IV). But when King Suppiluliumas of the Hittites had brought the western part of Mitanni under his sway, Ashur became independent, and its king, Ashur-uballit I, was also able to initiate a correspondence with the Pharaoh which soon centred on the familiar theme – gold. In one of the letters recovered from Tell el-Amarna, he writes: 'Gold in your country is like dust; one only needs to pick it up. Why then can you not part with it? I am building a new palace. So send me gold for mural decorations and other needs.' Burnaburiash, who watched the changing political scene and continued the Kassite tradition of neutrality, could see no better solution than to marry the king of Ashur's daughter. But when Burnaburiash lost his life in a palace revolution, it became clear how much greater the power of Ashur was than that of Babylon: Ashur-uballit intervened and placed a puppet king on the throne of Babylon. The Kassite dynasty, however, had still a long time to run, and it was after this shift of power that Dur Kurigalzu was built. Yet it marked the start of a process which, after centuries of which we know little, was to establish the undisputed power of Ashur. Nevertheless, it was not Ashur which put an end to the Kassite period. Here the Elamites played a rôle comparable with that of the Hittites in the sixteenth century B.C. They invaded southern Mesopotamia and wreaked great destruction but were compelled to withdraw by the dangers threatening them from the east. One of their kings, Shutruk-Nahhunte, carried the column bearing the Code of Hammurabi off to Susa. These events took place in the middle of the twelfth century B.C., and in Babylon a dynasty from Isin ascended the throne.

As we have seen, the details available to us about the Kassite period are scarce and they will have to be supplemented before it is possible to form a reasonably complete picture of the Kassite contribution to Mesopotamian civilisation. A few remarks may, however, be added to what has already been said. It was in the time of the Kassites that the horse was introduced into Mesopotamia, not for riding, but for pulling war chariots. This ushered in a new era so far as warfare was concerned, whilst a speeding-up of commercial traffic also resulted. The use of *kudurru* stones also dates from their time (see Pls. 256–60). These were boundary stones which were stacked in the temples as proof of ownership. They show reliefs, frequently of interest for the history of religion, and also a text containing a declaration that a piece of ground has been gifted to the citizen named, the dimensions of the ground and the easements to which it was subject being clearly stated. Witnesses are also recorded and curses on anyone who might dare to remove, alter, or destroy the *kudurru*. Examples of this remarkable form of document are known from various centuries, but its origin dates back to the period of the Kassites, which is worthy of thorough investigation for other reasons besides.

Problems of Chronology

THE BASIS OF CHRONOLOGY

From an early period the Mesopotamians divided time into minutes, hours, days, months, and years. The smaller units of time were measured by means of a sundial or a water-clock. The latter was a vessel from which water was allowed to flow at a constant rate from the moment a star rose one evening until the same star rose the following evening. This quantity of water was weighed and divided by twelve. Thus fixed divisions of the day were established and generally accepted.

The length of the month was determined by the period of revolution of the moon, and as this is roughly 29 days the month lasted 29 or 30 days, starting from the time the crescent moon became visible. It was soon observed that a year consisting of twelve such months fell short of the solar year, and to make up for this the Babylonians intercalated a 'leap' month every second or third year, while the Assyrian calendar fell a month behind over the same period. The Babylonian system was introduced by Tiglath-pileser I (1114–1076 B.C.), so that thenceforth the Assyrian year also began with the spring month of Nisan. Israel adopted this calendar, and the Jews have continued to use the Babylonian reckoning, the only change being the displacement of the New Year from the first of Nisan to the first of Tishri, the seventh month. The fact that the Mesopotamian year from about the middle of March to about the middle of April in the following year is on the average the same length as the Julian year gives us a starting point for a reasonably reliable chronology.

A considerable time after they had mastered the art of writing the Sumerians drew up lists of successive years, naming each of them after an important event in the year that preceded it. Thus, if a canal was dug, a wall built, or a temple erected in a certain year, the following year might be named correspondingly. Such lists were drawn up for individual royal reigns or individual dynasties, so that the length of the latter is easily found. A relative chronology is thus obtained which needs only a reliable starting point for conversion into an absolute list of dates.

The Assyrians had the custom of compiling *limmu* lists, a *limmu* being a magistrate chosen each year by drawing lots. The ballot was known by the name of *puru*, a word which has survived in the Jewish feast of Purim (Est. 9 : 26). The year was named after the *limmu* chosen. Lists are known which contain only the names of the office-holders; but more helpful in arriving at an absolute chronology are those that refer to important events which took place in the year of a particular *limmu*. The following statement is of great importance: 'During the office as *limmu* of Pur-Shagale, governor of Gozan, there was rioting in the city of Ashur. In the month of Sivan there was a solar eclipse.' This eclipse in the third month of the year has been dated by astronomical calculation as having occurred on 15 June, 763 B.C. This provides us with the fixed point from which to work backwards. Pur-Shagale was the eighth *limmu* in the reign of Ashur-dan III. By Assyrian custom Ashur-dan himself must have been *limmu* in the first or second complete year after his accession to the throne. In addition to the *limmu* lists the Assyrians had others which stated how long each king had reigned. The most detailed of these is the one found at Khorsabad in the 1932-3 campaign. According to the colophon it was compiled by Kandalanu, a scribe of the temple of Arba-ilu, during the second tenure of the office of *limmu* by Adad-bela-ukin, governor of Ashur. The reliability of the information has been confirmed by comparing it with the *limmu* lists. Of the 69 kings from Shamshi-Adad I to Ashur-nirari V there are 14 for whom we also have *limmu* lists. A list of Assyrian kings which appeared suddenly several years ago and is now in the possession of the Seventh Day Adventist Seminary appears to be related to, and agrees with, the Khorsabad list. Working back from Ashur-dan III it is possible to date Shamshi-Adad I's reign accurately within ten years as 1744 (or 1734) to 1724.

DATING HAMMURABI

As the Mari archives show that Shamshi-Adad I must have been contemporaneous with Hammurabi, it has been necessary to put the latter's dates forward several centuries. Previously the main source of chronological information about Hammurabi had been the Venus tablets of his grandson, Ammi-zaduga. There we read: 'When the planet of Venus disappears in the west on the fifteenth day of Shabatu, remains invisible for three days and re-appears in the east on the eighteenth day of Addaru, it has the same meaning as in the first year of Ammi-zaduga: kings will be dismayed, Adad will bring rain and Ea floods, and one king will send greetings to the other.' The original purpose of such texts is clear; the aspect of the sky determines the course of events on earth, and conclusions as to the future can be drawn from past records of both. Thus astrological notes may sometimes serve as a basis for scientific calculations. As the planet Venus repeats the appearance described at regular intervals, a wide range of different periods could have been assigned to the reign of Ammi-zaduga and likewise to that of his grandfather Hammurabi. Since the information found in the Mari archives has been known, the general trend has been to place Hammurabi in a period much more recent than that previously accepted, and the Venus tablets, like other reports associated with them, have played only a minor rôle in the determination of chronology.

Despite what has been said above, the problems of chronology are still not solved. This is obvious from the variety of dates assigned to Hammurabi by scholars who have devoted much research to chronology and who have drawn widely differing conclusions from the same set of data. The fact that dynasties which may have ruled simultaneously are listed consecutively, ignorance as to whether the start of the Kassite period coincided with the end of the last Babylonian dynasty, and other uncertainties make Mesopotamian chronology a complicated subject. The following list of dates for Hammurabi will demonstrate this point: Albright 1728-1686 (and so de Vaux), Sidney Smith 1729-1750, de Liagre Böhl 1704-1662 (and so Weidner), van der Meer 1724-1682.

Anyone who compares the various published works of these specialists will also see that they have frequently revised their estimates. To facilitate the use of the present atlas, it has been decided to use the chronology of Professor van der Meer of the University of Amsterdam, an explanation of which will be found in his *Chronology of Ancient Western Asia and Egypt* (2nd rev. ed., Leiden, 1955). The great advantage of this chronology is that it is the one which fits in best with the known sequence of events in the countries round Mesopotamia, for example in Iran, Palestine, Egypt, and the Hittite empire.

169

170

169. Statuary such as this lion, which forcibly reminds us of the art of the Hittites, was found at Malatya, north of Carchemish, on the edge of the sphere of Mesopotamian culture, The spiral mane and the form of the eyes are very reminiscent of the sculpture found at Boghaz Köi. Local variation makes dating difficult, and this statue can only be assigned to the rather wide period from the 12th to the 9th century B.C. **170.** Relief of a wild boar, found at Miletus. **171.** At Sakje Geuzi, west of Carchemish, the well-known figure of the 'guardian' attracts attention by its individual form. **172.** Relief from Alaya Huyuk, 19 miles northeast of Boghaz Köi, where the art of the Hittites, though often dependent for its themes on Mesopotamia, developed a character of its own. This interesting *huyuk* (tell) was first excavated by British, and from 1935 onwards by Turkish, archaeologists. The Hittite palace uncovered here is considered to be one of the last Hittite monuments in Asia Minor in the 13th century B.C. This relief is part of the decoration of a gateway formed by upright stones. It shows a sword-swallower, and two acrobats climbing an unsupported ladder. The sculpture is lively and narrative in character. The subject the sculptor chose is rare in the art of the ancient world and consequently possesses great intrinsic charm as well as being of interest in showing something of a scene from ordinary life in contrast to the almost invariably hieratic and ceremonial art of the palaces.

171

172

The Rise of the Assyrians

THE EMPIRE OF SHAMSHI-ADAD

The shift of political power to the north now compels us to turn our attention to the development of Ashur (Hellenised as Assyria). The kings of Akkad and those of the third dynasty of Ur spoke of the homeland of the later Assyrian world power as 'Subartu'. The influence of the Semites had been very strong here from ancient times, while the written language was Akkadian, although it acquired characteristic features divergent to some extent from Babylonian. The city of Ashur lay about sixty miles south of the present Mosul and its kings ruled over a neighbouring area of limited extent. Not until the decline of the third dynasty of Ur did they extend their power and take over trade with Cappadocia and other areas. This brought prosperity to Ashur, but when the trade settlements such as Kanish (Kültepe) were lost, a period of impoverishment again set in for the narrow strip of territory along the Tigris (see Map 11).

That Ashur's power expanded and the city flourished was due to Shamshi-Adad, who has been a much more familiar figure to us since documents from the Mari archives were published. He was the son of Ilakabkabu, prince of the town of Tirqa on the Euphrates. He succeeded in subjugating Mari, which can probably be regarded as one of the most important centres of the time, and placing his son Yashmakh-Adad on the throne. This enabled him to exercise control over the caravan routes to the Mediterranean coast and Asia Minor. The Mari letters give an impression of the powerful character of this king, who believed himself the chosen servant of Enlil, the god worshipped at Nippur. By implication he also considered himself called to continue the traditions of the kings of Sumer and Akkad. In him we have the fountain-head of an urge for power inspired by religious motives, which was to have a great effect on the history of the Near East.

On the foundations of an old shrine in Ashur Shamshi-Adad built a large new temple in honour of Enlil, which was given the name of 'house of the wild bull of all lands'. He also bestowed the name of Shubat Enlil ('dwelling of Enlil') on a town. But he had no successors capable of maintaining the empire he had established, so that it was a long time before the aspirations that Shamshi-Adad had aroused were once more realised. This takes us to the period of Ashur-uballit I, whose name, as already mentioned, occurs in the letters from the Tell el-Amarna archives.

This king is the first to use the word Ashur, preceded by the determinative for 'country', as the name of his kingdom; it occurs on a cylinder seal. The older name of Subartu was now confined to a part of Mitanni in the north of Mesopotamia. It was under Ashuruballit I that the Assyrians started the campaigns which spread panic in Asia Minor from the fourteenth to the seventh century B.C. and left behind a trail of destruction, while we know from their own inscriptions and, so far as the later period is concerned, from the Old Testament that they scattered terror among the surrounding tribes and nations by their massacres, tortures, and carrying off of prisoners.

The Assyrians treated the conquered territories in a more brutal and indiscriminate way than the Babylonians had done. They made hardly any attempt to build up a well-organised empire. They imposed tribute and despatched punitive expeditions if it did not come in on time. A lack of organised supervision allowed revolts to break out frequently, and the history of Assyria is without its equal as a military chronicle. Unlike the annals of the Babylonians, those of the Assyrian kings recorded these war operations in detail and without scruple, while the palace reliefs provided the illustrations to accompany them. Although court historians were in principle not allowed to mention defeats, a critical examination of the facts they relate shows that Assyria experienced its ups and downs and that there were periods of peace for the surrounding lands, for example the one during which David was able to establish a great kingdom in Palestine.

The Assyrians were faced with a problem which has kept recurring in waves in world history, namely invasion by tribes from the steppes. These sometimes gained a footing in the cultivated areas and tried to extend their power by means of raids. When they failed in their attempts and also lost their strategic bases, they withdrew to the vastness of the steppe between the Euphrates and the Tigris, beyond the reach of the Assyrian punitive expeditions. The Assyrians knew no other means than extermination by which to defend their border regions where the only natural barrier – an ineffective one – was the steppe. The tribes, which were thus constantly on the move for several centuries and yet founded powerful states, are grouped together under the name of Aramaeans. Abraham, Isaac, and Jacob belonged to one of these tribes.

Avoiding so far as possible a monotonous list of campaigns and battles won or lost, we will now mention the kings who by their monuments and inscriptions attained some prominence.

TUKULTI-NINURTA I

The first worthy of such mention is Tukulti-Ninurta I (1242-1206), who was called Ninos by the Greeks. He is known to have deported 28,800 men from Syria and to have conquered entire southern Mesopotamia as far as and including Bahrain. He dragged the king of Babylon to Ashur in chains, and on another punitive expedition destroyed Babylon entirely and removed the statue of Marduk to Ashur, an act which was regarded even by his own people as sacrilege. The typical attitude of Ashur towards Babylon was in general one of respect for both the culture and religion of the south and the relative independence and age-old tradition of the city. Tukulti-Ninurta's act was an exception to the rule.

The king apparently could also not get on well with his fellow-townspeople. At least he moved his residence to Kar-Tukulti-Ninurta, which he himself built, slightly to the north of Ashur and on the other bank of the Tigris. Shifts of capitals occurred rather frequently in the ancient East and were usually a sign of strained relations. In the case of Tukulti-Ninurta subsequent events seemed to confirm this interpretation: he was assassinated in his palace in a revolt led by his own son, and the capital which he had founded was abandoned.

TIGLATH-PILESER I

This event was followed by a century of decline for Assyria. The power of its kings was overshadowed by that of the south, where Nebuchadnezzar I in particular gained prominence towards the end of the twelfth century B.C. The first to make the name of Assyria dreaded again was Tiglath-pileser I (1114-1076). It was he who built the large temple with two ziggurats in Ashur. One was dedicated to Anu, the other to Adad. Clay prisms of this king were also found in the temple. So far as we know, the custom of Assyrian kings of recording their chronicles on six-, eight- or ten-sided prisms began with him (see Pl. 33). Tiglath-pileser is also known to have been a great hunter of lions, wild bulls, and elephants. The god of hunting was Ninurta, and it is perhaps this same name which is rendered as Nimrod in Genesis 10 : 8. We are already familiar with the royal custom, con-

173

174

173. The favourable situation of Ashur (Sharqat) is still visible to anyone who visits the deserted tell nowadays. Its position on the western bank of the Tigris gave it security against attacks from the east. In the west the endless steppe extended to the city, and still does. Between the two the city enjoyed all the advantages of the fertile valley to its north and south. Moreover, Ashur lay on one of the caravan routes of antiquity. The abandoned house of the expedition and the tell can be clearly seen in the photograph. The excavated tell, now largely filled in again by the agency of wind and rain, is about 60 miles south of Mosul, from which it can be easily reached. There is little left of the excavated temples and palaces which is recognisable on a superficial visit, but above the shabby ruins projects a ziggurat from which a wide view of the landscape can be obtained. The bastions of the stout walls round the city are still discernible (see Pl. 69).

175. Sandstone figure (height 3 ft. 4¼ in.) of Ashurnasirpal II, from Nimrud. The king carries in his hand an object normally found in the hand of a god. The inscription is engraved on his breast. **176.** Amber statuette of Ashurnasirpal II. **177.** Guardian at the entrance to Ashurnasirpal II's palace at Nimrud. This tutelary genius combines the body of a lion, the wings and breast of an eagle, and a human head crowned with a mitre and four horns. The beast is represented with five legs, probably to give the impression of having four when viewed from front and side. The vision recounted in Daniel 7 was probably inspired by the sight of similar figures. **178.** Relief from Ashurnasirpal II's palace at Nimrud, representing a winged genius with an eagle's head. As this imaginary creature is called not only *lamassu* and *shedu* but also *kuribu*, it is thought to be related to the Biblical cherubim above the Ark of the Covenant (Exod. 25 : 20).

179. The Black Obelisk of Shalmaneser III, found at Nimrud; height 6 ft. 7½ in., width at foot about 2 ft. This magnificent piece from the British Museum is best known for its connection with the Old Testament, the second strip showing the king receiving tribute from 'Jehu, the son of Omri' (cf. 2 Kg. 9-10). The monument ends in a stepped pyramid. There are 20 panels in all, each framed between inscriptions containing some of the annals of Shalmaneser III. All the details are remarkable, particularly for the animals they show, such as camels, lions, an elephant, and monkeys. **180.** Detail showing Jehu or his representative prostrate before the supreme king. **181-3.** Bronze reliefs which adorned the gates of Shalmaneser III's palace, found at Balawat (Imgur-Enlil). The strips were only $\frac{1}{16}$ in. thick, about 8 ft. 10 in. long, and 11 in. wide. They mainly illustrate military scenes such as the arrival of an expeditionary force at the sources of the Tigris, the offering of sacrifice (top), and the construction of a statue of the king (below). **182.** A city being stormed. **183.** Manacled men and women being led into captivity.

180

181

182

183

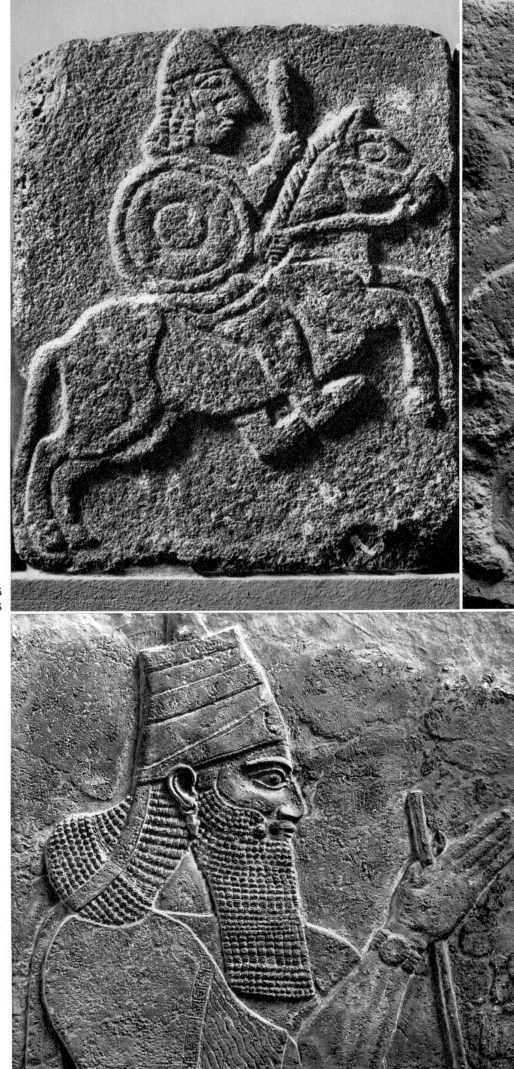

184
185

186

184. Basalt relief of a horseman with shield and club, 2 ft. 3½ in. high, found at Tell Halaf (9th century B.C.). The man is clean-shaven and has long hair. Tell Halaf art was markedly different from contemporaneous Assyrian art.

185. Limestone relief of a man riding a camel, also from Tell Halaf (9th century B.C.); the colours are red and ochre, the height is 2 ft. ½ in.

186. Fragment of a gypsum tablet from the palace of Nimrud, 3 ft. 7¼ in. high, bearing a portrait of Tiglath-pileser III. The king wears a pointed crown; his hair and beard, long and undulating, are held in position by ribbons. He wears bracelets round his wrists and carries a staff in his right hand.

187. Alabaster relief from Nimrud, 2 ft. 10 in. high, showing Ashurnasirpal II on a lion hunt. The king and the charioteer are in a chariot drawn by two horses, although the head of a third horse is also visible. Beneath the horses' hoofs lie two lions transfixed by arrows. To judge by reliefs lion-hunting was a favourite distraction of Assyrian kings. The six-spoked chariot wheel is worthy of note.

188. The artists who carved the reliefs in the palace at Nimrud had a particular preference for representation of the winged genius (see Pl. 178), who is here seen carrying out the fertilisation rite at the sacred tree.

189. White limestone sculpture from Nimrud, 6 ft. 11 in. high, showing Shamshi-Adad V of Assyria. Especially interesting are the symbols of divinity above him and the cross on his breast. His right hand is raised in command and he carries the sceptre in his left.

96

187

188
189

firmed by the Mari letters, of keeping a menagerie for this purpose. The Assyrian rulers maintained one, not so much in order to exhibit exotic animals as to have a reserve for the hunting season. We also see that the release of lions from their cages and the actual hunt are regularly recurring themes for sculptors from now on. Assyrian armies first reached the Mediterranean again under Tiglath-pileser I. We even possess an account of how the king took to sea with ships for a seal hunt. The time to consolidate the empire had not yet come, however, and when Adad-Nirari II acceded to the throne in 910 B.C. Assyria had again shrunk to a narrow strip of land bordering the Tigris, barely ninety-five miles long, threatened from the west by Aramaeans and from the east by the Gutians and the Lullubians. But now began an expansion which was to continue unbroken until decline set in during the second half of the seventh century B.C.

ASHURNASIRPAL II

The kings who felt themselves chosen to restore the ancient glory also bore the glorious ancient names: Adad-Nirari II (910-889) and Tukulti-Ninurta II (889-884). The latter's son and successor, Ashurnasirpal II, was to be the greatest conqueror of all. He inherited a territory stretching from the Khabur to the Zagros Mountains and from Nisibis to Samarra, in which order prevailed and whose frontiers were consolidated. And now began a series of aggressions which were to be accompanied by a ruthlessness harsh even by Assyrian standards. The inscriptions make no attempt to disguise their lack of humanity. When the town of Kinabu on the Hulai fell, the chronicler wrote: 'Of the soldiers I slew 600 with the sword, 3,000 prisoners I burned in the fire, I kept no one alive as a hostage. The city king fell into my hands alive. I piled their corpses as high as towers. The king I flayed and hung his skin on the wall of Damdamusa.' And as the chronicler relates it, so the reliefs depict it.

Meanwhile, a chance discovery has shown us this cruel king from another side, so that we now also know him as the most lavish host antiquity has yet produced. He was particularly interested in the city of Calah (Nimrud), founded by Shalmaneser I in the middle of the thirteenth century B.C. Calah lay where the Great Zab joins the Tigris. The city had fallen into decay but was rebuilt by Ashurnasirpal. His father had preferred Nineveh, and though he did not neglect this city or, for that matter, Ashur, his main favours were bestowed on Calah. He had the whole of the old town demolished and the canal Pati-khegalli ('which gives access to abundance') dug for defence and irrigation. Then he built the palace that was partly uncovered by Layard from 1849 to 1851, at the time when excavation was still in its treasure-hunting stage. It was then filled in again owing to lack of funds, but the excavations of the British School of Archaeology led by Professor Mallowan have now systematically laid bare the foundations. The palace was found to have occupied an area of about 4,000 sq. feet. No trouble or cost had been spared in fitting out and decorating this palace; it was even air-conditioned. It was here, in 1951, that the 'Banquet Stele' was found which is now preserved in the Museum of Antiquities at Mosul. This is a large rectangular stone on which the king is shown surrounded by the symbols of the sky gods. A detailed inscription states that the completion of the palace and the surrounding parks was celebrated with a great feast to which 69,574 guests from all parts of the empire were invited. For ten days they were wined and dined at the royal table. For this special occasion alone 2,200 oxen and 16,000 sheep were slaughtered, while 10,000 skins of wine and 10,000 barrels of beer were drunk. The enumeration of the various delicacies consumed uses many words which are hard to understand. The text ends thus: 'For ten days I regaled the happy peoples of all lands together with the populace of Calah, treated them to wine, provided them with baths and ointments, and showered honours upon them, and then I sent them home in peace and joy.' The military annals form a macabre background to this statement.

The decoration of the palace appears to reveal the influence of artists from Asia Minor. For instance, all the walls of the rooms and courtyards had large alabaster panels bearing reliefs, some with and some without inscriptions, a few of the inscriptions being in a magnificent Assyrian cuneiform. Ornamentation of this kind, though unknown in the south, occurs in Hittite buildings of the fourteenth and thirteenth centuries B.C. and, after the collapse of the Hittite empire, at a later period in Syria. The erection of colossal figures in the form of winged lions or bulls to guard the palace was also a custom copied from the Hittites. Ashurnasirpal therefore seems to have acquired the services of sculptors from the west and to have obtained from them an original treatment of his own country's art. Most of these artists and craftsmen had probably been taken captive from their native land. If so, the devotion with which they ornamented the palace at Calah is all the more astonishing.

There is a complete absence of epistolary literature in Ashurnasirpal's time, and so we know little about his officials. We know by name his minister Gabbi-ilani-eresh, who represented him in the capital when the king was away at the wars. His burden must have been an onerous one, for Ashurnasirpal took the field every spring with his army, as we are told David did 'at the time when kings go forth to battle' (2 Sam. 11 : 1). The army had been made more efficient by the independence of action granted to the cavalry, who were now also allowed to operate without war chariots, and by an improvement in the battering rams. On the training and organisation of his officials we have little information. This, in fact, was probably at all times the weak point of the Assyrian empire, which was kept together more by the dread of its legions than by competent administration.

SHALMANESER III

Ashurnasirpal was succeeded by his son, Shalmaneser III, who was to reign until 824 B.C. He was a conqueror of the same school as his father. We are abundantly informed of his methods of waging war by the 'bronze gates of Balawat' (see Pls. 181-3). These were found in the mound of ancient Imgur-Enlil, only a few miles from Nimrud. The gates of the palace there were ornamented with bronze strips in which reliefs were hammered out in repoussé. They give a lively picture of the manoeuvres of the Assyrian army and are incidentally of great artistic value. But this king's name was made even better known in Europe by the famous black obelisk found by Layard at Nimrud. Both the reliefs and the text of the obelisk provided links with Bible history. Jehu of Israel, or his representative, is pictured as a bringer of tribute, kneeling before the Assyrian king. At this point in time the Bible story emerges from the vacuum in which it has been taking place, and non-Biblical texts start illuminating and accompanying its incidents.

The armies of the Assyrian kings had several times penetrated 'unto the land of Khatti and unto the Great Sea where the sun sets', as it says in an inscription of Tiglath-pileser I, without the peoples of Israel and Syria appearing to take much notice of the fact. Even Ashurnasirpal II, who levied tribute on Tyre, Sidon, and Arvad, left the territory south of a line from Nineveh to Tyre unmolested. At any rate neither the Bible nor Assyrian sources mention any attempt to conquer Damascus. It was Phoenician kings who were compelled to bring the valuable products of their land in tribute to the Assyrian king and to embrace his feet as a sign of their subjection. Meanwhile the kings of Israel, Aram, and other territories or cities had realised that danger threatened them from the east and they joined in a confederation. Thus, when Shalmaneser III (858-824) turned southwards after laying Phoenicia under contribution, he found a coalition of eleven kings facing him. It is now, for the first time, that a non-Biblical source mentions a king of Israel, Ahab being listed among the confederate kings. The 'Monolith Inscription' from Kurkh records that Adad-idri of Damascus threw 1,200 chariots, 1,200 cavalry, and 20,000 foot-soldiers into the battle, Irhuleni of Hamath 700 chariots, 700 cavalry, and 10,000 foot-soldiers, and Ahab of Israel 2,000 chariots and 10,000 soldiers. This battle, fought in northern Syria at Qarqar, opens a new chapter in the history of the Near East.

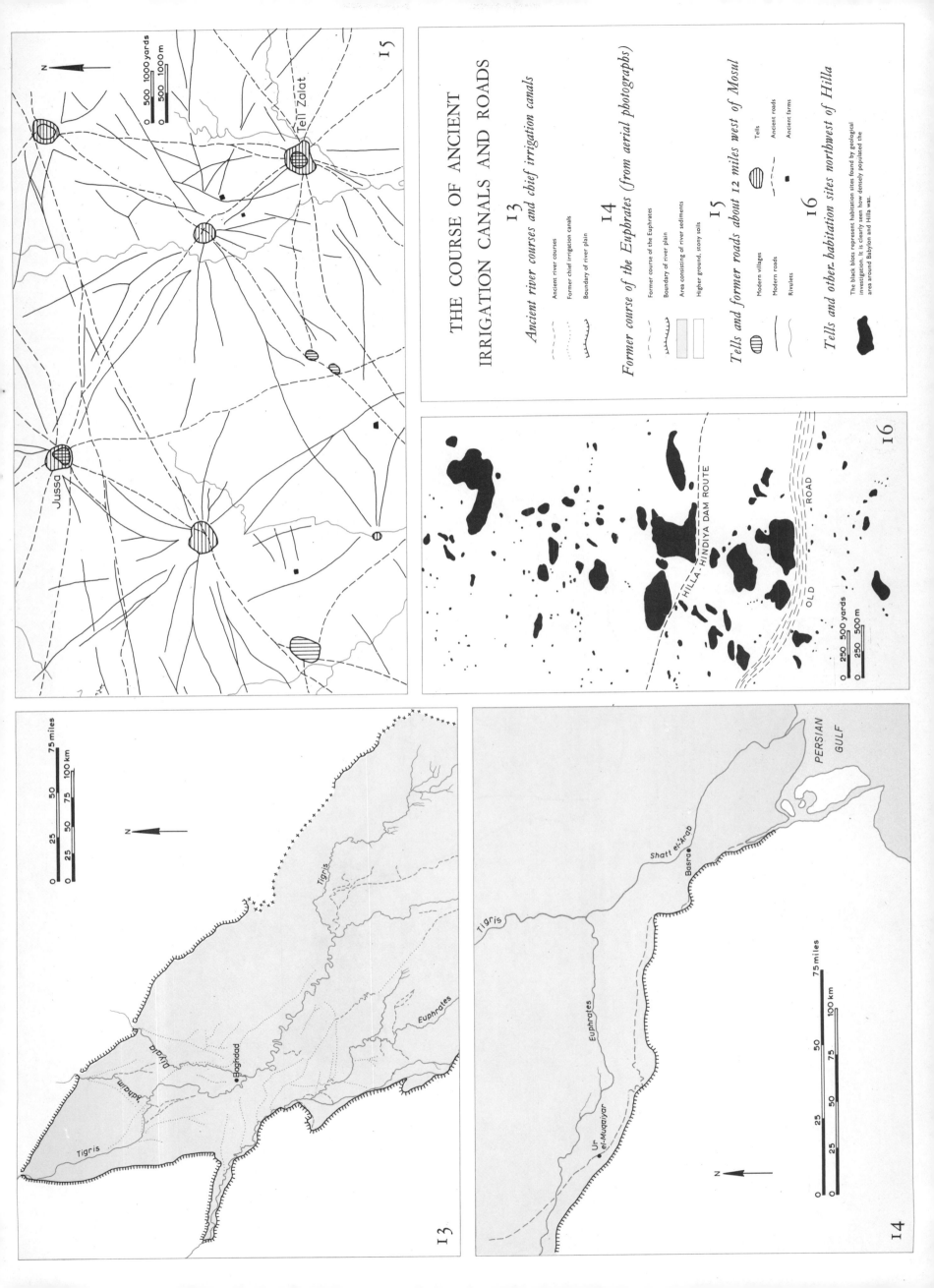

THE COURSE OF ANCIENT IRRIGATION CANALS AND ROADS

13

Ancient river courses and chief irrigation canals

— — — Ancient river courses
· · · · · Former chief irrigation canals
—‖‖‖— Boundary of river plain

14

Former course of the Euphrates (from aerial photographs)

— — — Former course of the Euphrates
—‖‖‖— Boundary of river plain
▨ Area consisting of river sediments
▧ Higher ground, stony soils

15

Tells and former roads about 12 miles west of Mosul

⊞ Modern villages
— — — Modern roads
——— Rivulets
⊞ Tells
- - - - Ancient roads
■ Ancient farms

16

Tells and other-habitation sites northwest of Hilla

◼ The black blots represent habitation sites found by geological investigation. It is clearly seen how densely populated the area around Babylon and Hilla was.

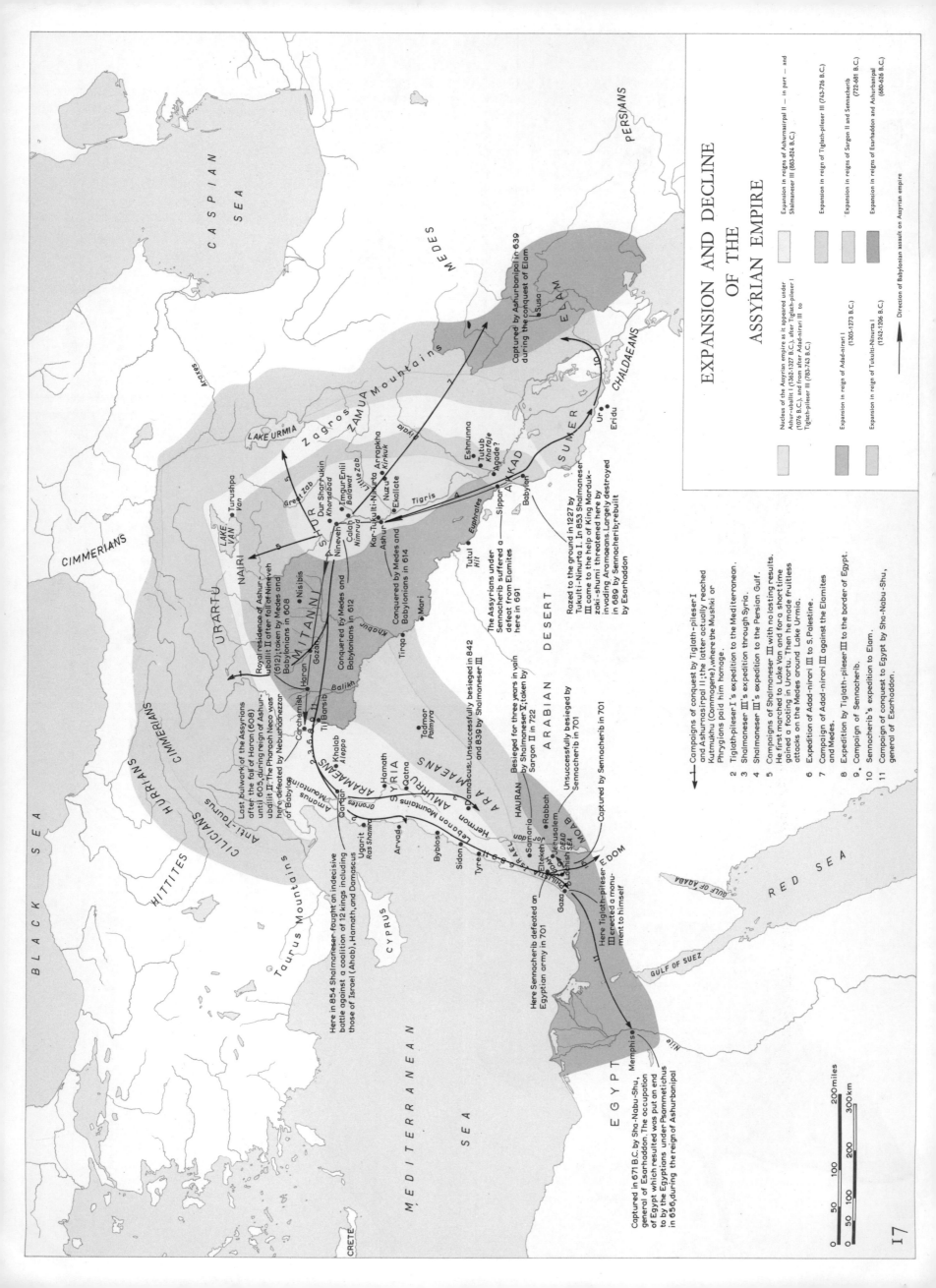

EXPANSION AND DECLINE
OF THE
ASSYRIAN EMPIRE

Nucleus of the Assyrian empire as it appeared under Ashur-uballit I (1362-1327 B.C.), after Tiglath-pileser I (1076 B.C.), and from after Adad-nirari III to Tiglath-pileser III (783-743 B.C.)

Expansion in reign of Adad-nirari I (1305-1273 B.C.)

Expansion in reign of Tukulti-Ninurta I (1242-1206 B.C.)

Expansion in reigns of Ashurnasirpal II — in part — and Shalmaneser III (883-824 B.C.)

Expansion in reign of Tiglath-pileser III (743-726 B.C.)

Expansion in reigns of Sargon II and Sennacherib (722-681 B.C.)

Expansion in reigns of Esarhaddon and Ashurbanipal (680-626 B.C.)

Direction of Babylonian assault on Assyrian empire

1 → Campaigns of conquest by Tiglath-pileser I and Ashurnasirpal II; the latter actually reached Kutmukhu (Commagene), where the Mushki or Phrygians paid him homage.

2 Tiglath-pileser I's expedition to the Mediterranean.

3 Shalmaneser III's expedition through Syria.

4 Shalmaneser III's expedition to the Persian Gulf.

5 Campaigns of Shalmaneser III with no lasting results. He first marched to Lake Van and for a short time gained a footing in Urartu. Then he made fruitless attacks on the Medes around Lake Urmia.

6 Expedition of Adad-nirari III to S. Palestine.

7 Campaign of Adad-nirari III against the Elamites and Medes.

8 Expedition by Tiglath-pileser III to the border of Egypt.

9 Campaign of Sennacherib.

10 Sennacherib's expedition to Elam.

11 Campaign of conquest to Egypt by Sha-Nabu-Shu, general of Esarhaddon.

The Encounter of Israel and the Assyrians

THE FALL OF THE KINGDOM OF THE TEN TRIBES

According to the annals of Shalmaneser III the battle of Qarqar was a great victory for the Assyrians. He says explicitly: 'With the august power that my Lord Ashur lent me, with the powerful arms accorded me by Nergal, who walks before me, I fought against them. From the city of Qarqar to Gilzau I routed them. By force of arms I scattered 14,000 soldiers of their army; like the god Adad I rained a deluge upon them; I piled up their corpses; I scattered their numerous troops like seeds over the plain. By force of arms I made their blood to flow in the furrows. The plain was too small to let their corpses fall; the outspread ground was not large enough to bury them; with their bodies I filled the Orontes as with a dam. In this battle I took their chariots, their cavalry, their horses, and their armour.'

The battle of Qarqar was not such a great success for the Assyrians as the court historian makes it seem. At least there is no evidence that it had serious consequences for the allegedly defeated kings, and this makes us suspicious of an account by a chronicler whose task it was to ignore his king's reverses and record only his victories. More remarkable is the fact that the Old Testament makes no mention of a battle of such great significance. At any rate, the Assyrian danger was temporarily averted at Qarqar. The writer of the Bible devotes his entire attention to the struggle between Ahab and Aram. Ahab had apparently withdrawn from the anti-Assyrian coalition, and kings in Palestine as a whole could again permit themselves the luxury of war against each other.

The need for a common front was no longer felt. The Biblical writer's interest is particularly reserved for the struggle between Elijah and Elisha on one hand and the house of Omri on the other. And that is why the annals of the latter are rarely quoted by the Book of Kings. Otherwise they would have told us about the expansion of Israel under Omri, the general and king. The depth of the impression made by this king on neighbouring countries may still be gauged from the characteristic way in which the chronicles of the Assyrians use his name. They speak of Israel as the house of Omri and of the Israelites as the sons of Omri long after his dynasty has been eradicated by the usurper Jehu. The latter is mentioned on a fragment from the annals of Shalmaneser III, which runs: 'Then I took tribute of the Tyrians, of the Sidonians, and of Ja-u-a (i.e. Jehu), of the house of Hu-um-ri-i (i.e. Omri).' This humiliation of Jehu is also illustrated on the famous black obelisk of Shalmaneser (see Pls. 179 and 180). The accompanying text reads: 'Tribute of Jehu, of the house of Omri. I received from him silver, gold, a golden bowl, a vase(?) of gold, golden beakers, pitchers of gold, tin, a sceptre, and *purukhtu* wood.'

Adad-nirari III (809-782) also mentions that he received tribute from various states in Palestine, among which Israel is listed: 'From the Euphrates to the Great Sea where the sun sets I subjugated the land of Khatti and that of Amurru in its entirety, and the lands of Tyre, Sidon, Omri, Edom, and Philistia. I laid heavy tribute upon them.' Yet to judge by the Bible, kings in Palestine were still free to wage war on one another until Tiglath-pileser III's campaign in 745 B.C.

During Jeroboam II's reign in Israel (781-753) the prophet Amos appeared at the shrine of Bethel with a gloomy prophecy in which he foretold that the king would be led into exile. Nothing seemed to justify his pessimistic view of coming events. In fact, Jeroboam succeeded in the course of his long rule (which the Old Testament actually sets at forty-one years, including the years of his regency;

see 2 Kg. 14 : 23) in taking advantage of the weakness of the northern states to extend Israel's territory 'from the entrance of Hamath as far as the Sea of the Arabah' (2 Kg. 14 : 25). Azariah, king of the more southerly Judah, was able to bring Solomon's old road to the Gulf of 'Aqaba under his control again (2 Kg. 14 : 22). Indications are to be found in the Assyrian annals that Azariah was for a time the most important king in Palestine. He is described as head of the confederation set up to oppose the Assyrian penetrations. Amos's prophecies did not start to be fulfilled until Menahem ruled over Israel (752-742).

The Bible states (2 Kg. 15 : 19-20) that the supreme king Pul had appeared on the Palestinian scene during the reign of Menahem. The king of Israel purchased a relative degree of independence for the price of a thousand talents of silver, which he collected by levying fifty shekels of silver from every landowner in his realm who owed him allegiance. Pul is Tiglath-pileser III, who had ascended the throne of Babylon as Pulu. Menahem is listed as Me-ni-khi-im-me of Sa-me-ri-na-a (Samaria) in the annals of Tiglath-pileser III, together with Rezin of Damascus, Hiram of Tyre, and a great number of other kings. Tiglath-pileser also says that Menahem paid a great price to save his royal residence from destruction.

The wretched condition to which Israel was reduced by the military campaigns of the Assyrians is reflected in the frequency with which the throne was usurped. After ruling for two years Menahem's son was slain by his army commander Pekah. The latter was killed by Hoshea, the last king to sit on the throne of northern Israel. Meanwhile the kings of Israel and Aram had clearly realised that only a strong alliance of Palestinian princes could dam the Assyrian flood. They also tried to attract Judah into this defensive alliance. When Ahaz, residing in Jerusalem, refused to contribute his share, Pekah of Israel and Rezin of Aram marched on Judah in order to force it into the coalition. These events, which took place between 735 and 732, are usually grouped together under the heading of the Syro-Ephraimitic War. We have two views of this war, a northern and a southern. Hosea alludes to the advance of the allied armies in 5 : 8 to 6 : 6 and Isaiah 7 describes the reaction in Jerusalem.

From the point of view of international politics, Ahaz was justified by the course of events. When he called in Tiglath-pileser's help against his kinsmen in the north he was siding with the stronger party. Their superiority in man-power, military organisation, and equipment made the Assyrians invincible. Damascus fell in 732, thus putting an end to the existence of Aram for all time. Large parts of Israel were incorporated in an Assyrian province whose governor had his residence at Arvad. The whole of Galilee was lost to Israel, inhabitants of the occupied territories were deported, and colonists were established by compulsory emigration in the areas thus evacuated. These were the circumstances in which Ahaz sent messengers laden with costly presents to Tiglath-pileser to ask for help against the northern kingdoms of Palestine. Later Ahaz went personally to Damascus to do homage to the Assyrian king (2 Kg. 16 : 7-11). Tiglath-pileser himself makes only passing reference to Ahaz. A text found at Nimrud contains interesting details of his campaign against the Philistines. According to it, the king of Gaza in his flight left not only all kinds of valuables behind but also his wife. Another text, also from Nimrud, lists 'Ia-u-ha-zi (i.e. Ahaz) of Ia-u-da-a-a' (i.e. Judah) between the kings of Ashkelon and Moab as payers of tribute. Israel continued its existence as a truncated state surrounding Samaria for several years more. Events had destroyed any trust in Pekah that still existed. He was slain by Hoshea, who as a vassal of

190

191

190. Relief from Tiglath-pileser III's palace at Nimrud. According to the inscription the city of Astartu has been captured. It stands on a hill and is surrounded by a double wall containing towers. In the outer wall there is a rectangular gateway, in the inner, which projects above the first, an arched gateway. The captured inhabitants and their flocks of fat-tailed sheep are being led off by soldiers. The men are carrying their provisions and humble possessions in bags on their backs. **191.** Relief from the same palace depicting the siege of a fortified city. The iron-clad wooden battering-ram has two beams fitted with iron tips to break bricks from the wall. Behind it, on the wall, can be seen a man in suppliant attitude; beside him are naked captives impaled on stakes, while fallen soldiers lie in a wooded background. The army commander, wearing a sword, is firing an arrow; beside him stands a soldier with a large rectangular shield.

102

192. Relief found in Ashurbanipal's palace at Nineveh. Soldiers are leading prisoners past the king, while women are conveyed in a cart. The relief is part of a large alabaster slab which shows the king in his state chariot reviewing a parade of his troops returning laden with booty from a campaign. The cart, which is being pulled by men, has ten-spoked wheels. **193.** Another relief from Ashurbanipal's palace. The cart seen here is drawn by oxen. Four women are sitting on it but only one is visible in this detail. The woman ahead of the cart is carrying the water supply in a skin. Art in Ashurbanipal's time excelled particularly in the portrayal of animals, in this case the oxen pulling the cart. The total height of the relief is 3 ft. 2¼ in. The relief as a whole presents a lively picture of how a defeated nation was led into captivity. In Ashurbanipal's time the art of Assyria, like its literature and its empire, reached its magnificent peak, and after him all three collapsed with dramatic suddenness.

194

195
196

197

194. This Assyrian relief of the 8th century B.C., made of alabaster, shows sacrificers approaching their deity.
195. A winged genius, another Assyrian work of the 8th century B.C.
196. This relief, sculpted in alabaster, was found at Khorsabad. It served to adorn the walls of Sargon II's palace and is now in the Louvre, Paris. It is 9 ft. 6½ in. high. It shows six boats being propelled across a river. The oarsmen on two of the vessels are clearly seen. The sculptor has conveyed the idea of a river by means of stylised eddies and more especially of fishes and other creatures living in the water. To the left of the panel there is a remarkable creature: a fish with a human head. The main task of the boats is to drag very heavy loads of wooden beams. They have very high prows and sterns, the former being in the form of horses' heads. The sterns end in fish-tails. The sculptor is representing what he saw on the river.
197. This relief from Sargon II's palace at Khorsabad shows archers hunting in a wood. The clean-shaven man on the left is shooting at birds, but the bearded men facing the right have taken a hare and a gazelle. This relief is now in the British Museum.
198. This limestone sculpture, with a height of 2 ft. 11 in., is also from Khorsabad and is now in the Museo di Antichità, Turin. It represents Sargon II and gives the impression of being a portrait study. The nose, eyebrows, and eyes are distinctive. Sargon's hair is dressed in the royal fashion. His beard is curled all over, his moustache at the sides; his ear-ring is in the form of a cross.

198

199

200
201

199. Stone bas-relief from Khorsabad, now in the Louvre, Paris. It is a fragment of a larger relief showing men bringing tribute; their clothes and hair reveal that they are foreigners. Two of them are leading horses, and two others carry small boxes decorated with towers and probably containing valuables. Observe that the left arms of the latter two men end in right hands. By its composition and liveliness of presentation this relief is the finest found at Khorsabad. **200.** This winged bull with a human head guarded the gate of a Khorsabad palace. The head with its long curled beard has a serene expression. Its headgear is adorned with two pairs of horns as a symbol of divinity. Such mythical monsters, Esarhaddon tells us, were propitious beings placed on either side of doorways 'to repulse the wicked'. **201.** Detail of 194. The sacrificer, probably a priest, is carrying a bunch of plants in his right hand, while in his left arm he holds the gazelle which will shortly be offered to the god.

202

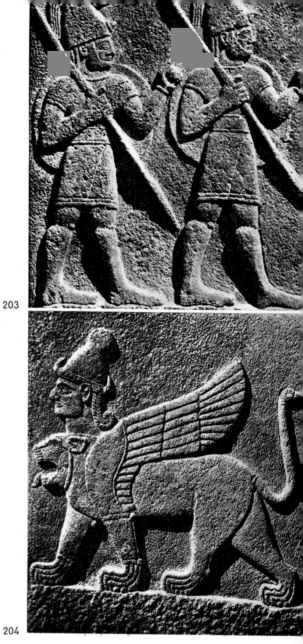

203

204

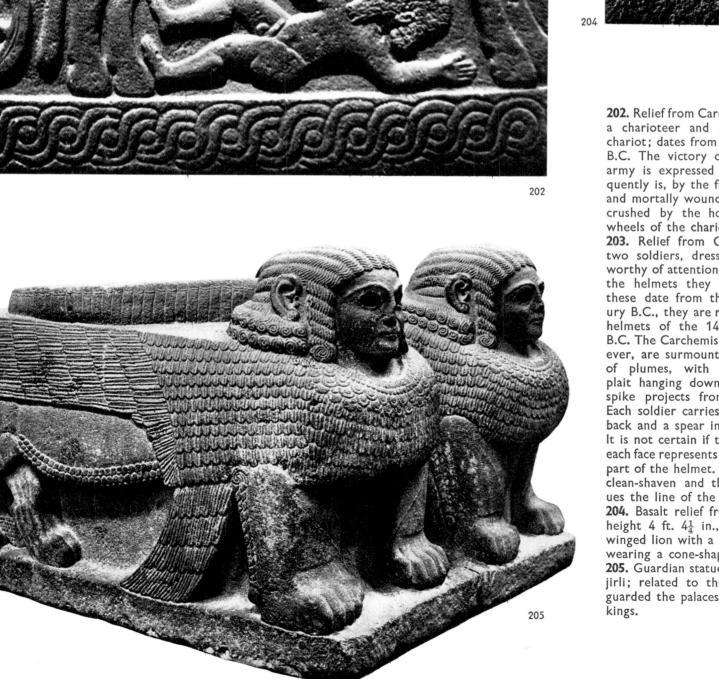

205

202. Relief from Carchemish showing a charioteer and an archer in a chariot; dates from the 8th century B.C. The victory of the invincible army is expressed here, as it frequently is, by the figure of a naked and mortally wounded enemy being crushed by the horses' hoofs and wheels of the chariots.

203. Relief from Carchemish. The two soldiers, dressed in kilts, are worthy of attention, particularly for the helmets they wear. Although these date from the 9th-8th century B.C., they are related to Hittite helmets of the 14th-13th century B.C. The Carchemish helmets, however, are surmounted by two rows of plumes, with a four-stranded plait hanging down from them. A spike projects from each helmet. Each soldier carries a shield on his back and a spear in his right hand. It is not certain if the object round each face represents a beard or forms part of the helmet. The upper lip is clean-shaven and the nose continues the line of the forehead.

204. Basalt relief from Carchemish, height 4 ft. 4¼ in., consisting of a winged lion with a human head and wearing a cone-shaped horned cap.

205. Guardian statues found at Zenjirli; related to the figures which guarded the palaces of the Assyrian kings.

the Assyrians was allowed to accede to the throne (2 Kg. 15 : 30). According to the Assyrian account in Tiglath-pileser's annals: 'The land of Omri ... all its inhabitants and their possessions I carried off to Assyria. They deposed their king Pa-ka-ha (Pekah) and I appointed A-u-si (Hoshea) over them. I received from them ten talents of gold and a thousand talents of silver in tribute, and I took them to Assyria.'

Hoshea ruled in name for nine years, and during this time he paid tribute to Shalmaneser V (727-722), the successor of Tiglath-pileser III. But when the supreme king at Nineveh learned that Hoshea had been in touch with Egypt and failed to send tribute, he immediately had him taken prisoner. We have no Assyrian account of this event, but it is reported in 2 Kings 17 : 3-6 and 18 : 9-11. It was apparently not difficult to capture the king of Israel; he had perhaps been invited to answer for his actions at a place appointed by Shalmaneser and had gone there unsuspectingly. Be that as it may, the Assyrians had more difficulty in conquering Samaria. This strategically situated fortress town was besieged for three years and finally captured by Sargon II (see Pl. 186). The theory, held by some, that it was Shalmaneser who captured the city is unacceptable.

THE SARGONID DYNASTY

Sargon II (720-704) took six years to build a new royal residence at Dur Sharrukin, on the site of the modern Khorsabad (see Pls. 199 and 200). At the entrance to this city, which was abandoned by his successor, he erected 'display inscriptions' giving an account of his capture of Samaria. There we read: 'I besieged and conquered Samaria. I carried off into captivity 27,290 of those who dwelt therein. I took possession of 50 chariots that were there ... The rest I allowed to take back their share. I placed my commander-in-chief over them and imposed on them the same tribute as on the former king.' The fall of Samaria was thus followed once more by mass deportations to Mesopotamia and Media. The exiles' final destination was near the Khabur and at Nimrud on the Tigris. In the course of time they disappeared from history and it is idle to speculate whether these ten lost tribes of Israel could possibly have crossed Europe and ended up in England. There is a complete absence of scientific support for this hypothesis, which is based on fantasy. The depopulated land of Israel was settled by colonists from other areas, who included townspeople from Babylon, Hamath, and Cuthah (2 Kg. 17 : 6 and 24), although the king of Assyria did accede to the request to send at least one priest of the God of Israel back to his own country to instruct the new population in the ritual with which the god of the country wished to be worshipped. Thus was founded the community known as Samaritans who were later to oppose Jerusalem with a national and religious self-consciousness of their own.

By its policy of subjection Judah had escaped destruction, but there was no question of its being able to lead an independent existence. Not only had tribute to be raised on an undiminished scale for the foreseeable future, but even spiritually the Assyrians exerted a great influence. The erection of an altar of an Assyrian type in front of the Temple building may be regarded as an example of this. Ahaz had seen such an altar in Damascus and sent a drawing of it to Jerusalem with instructions to the high priest Uriah to replace the brazen altar by an altar of the new type. This was not, as some think, the altar of the god Hadad, who was venerated in Damascus, since the text clearly states that the changes were wrought 'for the king of Assyria' (2 Kg. 16 : 10-18). Thus the Assyrian period, which was to last about a century, had dawned in Jerusalem.

Ahaz was succeeded by Hezekiah, who is praised by the author of 2 Kings 18 : 1-8 because he tried to restore to the Temple of Jerusalem its special character as the shrine of the God of Israel. During his rule there must have a strong movement in favour of an active policy of anti-Assyrian coalitions. Support was expected from Egypt in particular. At that period Isaiah was the prophet who expressly warned against trusting in Egyptian military power. For three

years he submitted himself to the indignity of going about naked and barefoot, as a silent sermon that 'the king of Assyria shall lead away the Egyptians captives and the Ethiopians exiles, both the young and the old, naked and barefoot, with buttocks uncovered, to the shame of Egypt' (Isa. 20 : 3-4). Thus he prophesied against alliance with Egypt and the smaller states in the south of Palestine. He was equally hostile to a coalition with Babylon, which assumed independence for a short time under Merodach-baladan, who even sent envoys to Hezekiah to examine the possibility of common action (Isa. 39 or 2 Kg. 20 : 12-19). This Babylonian king (whose name was actually Marduk-apul-iddin II) successfully warred against Sargon II for over ten years, according to a statement on a cylinder which he had erected in Erech and was found in Nimrud. When the *turtanu* or commander-in-chief of the Assyrian army had besieged and captured Ashdod (Isa. 20 : 1), the city kings of Palestine had again to pay homage and tribute to the Assyrian supreme king. Besides Philistia, Moab, and Edom, Judah is also mentioned in this connection. A critical situation arose when Sargon II was killed on a military expedition to the land of Tabal, north of the Taurus. Perhaps Isaiah 14 : 4-19 is an allusion to this event, which awakened hopes of a coming liberation. What we read here is a hymn beginning with the words, 'How the oppressor has ceased! the insolent fury ceased!'. It sings of the emotion that was aroused by the arrival of the tyrant in the kingdom of the dead. It may be that the form of this majestic song was influenced by older examples, such as a Sumerian song narrating the descent of Ur-Nammu into the Underworld. The song of Isaiah mentions a king of Babylon, and that is why it has been taken to refer to another king of a later date. It should, however, be remembered that after defeating Merodach-baladan in 709 Sargon was also king of Babylon. However that may be, hopes were shattered. True, Sargon's body was not taken to his capital, and rebellions took place in all parts of the empire; but Sargon's son Sennacherib managed to stay on the throne. The revolts were put down, and the Assyrians continued to dominate from the mountains in the east to Cyprus and the border of Egypt.

SENNACHERIB AND JERUSALEM

Hezekiah, it appears, had meanwhile allowed himself to be involved in the independence movement of the kings of Palestine. He had also taken measures which suggest that he was expecting a siege. According to 2 Kings 20 : 20, he made a conduit, or tunnel, which was redis-

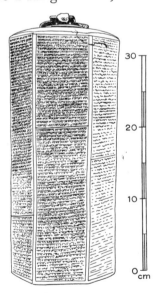

As was the custom of the Assyrian kings, Sennacherib had his annals recorded on a clay prism. The drawing gives an idea of the famous six-sided prism on which the siege of Jerusalem during the reign of Hezekiah is mentioned along with other campaigns. It was found in the tell of Nineveh in 1830 by Colonel Taylor and is now in the British Museum.

covered in 1862 thanks to an inscription in ancient Hebrew characters, the historical veracity of the Bible being thus confirmed. This tunnel was completed by 701 B.C. when Sennacherib laid siege to Jerusalem. The circumstances leading to this siege are described in dramatic detail in 2 Kings 18-19, where a number of remarkable details concerning cultural history are also given. We read there that Sennacherib had conquered Lachish, a city which for size of population and strength was more important than Jerusalem. Sennacherib then had his artists depict the conquest of Lachish on the walls of his palace

206. The 'Mona Lisa' of Nimrud, made of ivory, probably adorned a throne or a table. The head was found in a deep well in the northwestern palace during the 1952-3 campaign.

at Nineveh in reliefs which are related in style to those of Tiglath-pileser III (see Pls. 190 and 191). From Lachish the conqueror sent his envoys with an army to Jerusalem to compel the surrender of the town and denunciation of the alliance with Egypt. On this mission the Assyrian envoys deliberately did not use Aramaic – which apparently already had the status of a diplomatic language – but Hebrew, the language spoken by the people of Jerusalem, so that they might understand the terrifying words. The envoys tried to shake their confidence in the god of the country; for were not the gods of Hamath, Arvad, and Samaria powerless against the might of Sennacherib? This was indeed plain speaking, and it did not fail in its effect on Hezekiah. Isaiah, however, advised him not to accept the Assyrian proposals as they would be forced to withdraw. Subsequent events proved Isaiah right and the authority of the prophet was thus established for all time.

Nevertheless, it is far from easy to reconstruct the actual course of events from the description. Nor has it become any easier now we possess Sennacherib's annals, recorded in cuneiform on a six-sided prism of clay. A copy of it was in fact found recently which deviates from it only in details and accords completely with it on the siege of Jerusalem. Sennacherib's court historiographer writes as follows: 'As for Hezekiah of Judah, who did not submit to my yoke, forty-six of his fortified towns and fortresses, and countless small places in their neighbourhood I besieged and captured by escalade and by bringing up siege engines, by storming with shock troops, by breaches, mines, and battering-rams; 200,150 people, young and old, men and women, horses, mules, asses, camels, cattle, and sheep without number I took away from their midst and counted as spoil. Himself I shut up like a caged bird in his capital Jerusalem. I enclosed him with earthworks to turn back(?) all who came out through the city gate. His cities which I had despoiled I cut off from his land and gave them to Mitinti, king of Ashdod, Padi, king of Ekron, and Silli-bel, king of

Gaza, and thus I diminished his land. To his former annual tribute I added further tribute and presents due to my majesty, and imposed these upon him. Hezekiah himself was overcome by the splendour of my majesty, and the Arabs and his best troops, which he had brought in to reinforce his capital Jerusalem and had received as support, deserted him. He sent after me to Nineveh, my royal city, together with 30 talents of gold, 800 talents of silver, jewels, antimony, large pieces of red stone, couches of ivory, state chairs of ivory, elephants' hides, elephants' tusks, maple-wood (?), yew-wood (?), all kinds of valuable treasures, his daughters, his harem, and male and female singers. To pay tribute and acknowledge his subjection he sent his envoy.'

That, then, is Sennacherib's account, which though authentic and contemporary need not necessarily be more credible, for we know that in his annals an Assyrian king is never the loser. Nevertheless, it is worth while to consider what siege Sennacherib is talking about here. 2 Kings 18 : 14-16 does in fact state that Hezekiah sent 30 talents of gold and 300 of silver, as well as presents, to Lachish and that he did homage. 2 Kings 19 : 8-13 adds that Sennacherib was diverted from the Palestine fortresses by a campaign against Tirhakah, the king of Ethiopia. These Bible statements can also be read between the lines of Sennacherib's annals. Quite divorced from them, however, are the contents of 2 Kings 19 : 35, which tells with surprising brevity how Jehovah's angel slew 185,000 men of the Assyrian army in a single night. It is legitimate to wonder whether this last statement is a boast copied from a Sennacherib myth and incorporated in the liturgy with which the liberation of Jerusalem was celebrated annually.

The miracle can be found related in a somewhat modified form in Herodotus (*History*, ii, 141), who recounts that according to Egyptian tradition the Pharaoh Sethos during his despairing struggle against Sennacherib had a vision in which he saw his god Hephaestus, who promised him assistance. One night the Assyrian camp was invaded by a multitude of field-mice, which destroyed their weapons. Then the enemy fled and many fell. We find the mouse as a symbol of the plague in 1 Samuel 5 : 6ff. and 6 : 1ff. There is no reason to suspect that the legend recounted by Herodotus has been influenced by the Bible story, although the historical event – a sudden withdrawal of Sennacherib's army – is the basis of them both. We may also wonder whether Jerusalem was besieged a second time. If it was, Sennacherib's annals are silent about it. Perhaps the siege was lifted because of the outbreak of an epidemic among the Assyrians or because of events at home. It is possibly significant that Sennacherib was murdered shortly afterwards and succeeded by his son Esarhaddon.

It was under Esarhaddon that the Sargonid empire, which was ruled, except for a short break, from Nineveh, attained its greatest extent. Even Egypt became an Assyrian province – in 671 B.C. – and it is probable that thenceforth foreign rule in the land of the Nile was maintained by military settlements which drew some of their reinforcements from Judah. It is, in fact, not impossible that the prohibition in Deuteronomy 17 : 16 which states that the king 'shall not multiply horses to himself, nor cause the people to return to Egypt, to the end that he should multiply horses', refers to the historical situation in the reigns of Hezekiah's successors, Manasseh and Amon. The military colony at Elephantine (Yeb) which left papyri dating from the fifth century B.C. must already have had a long history when it fell a victim to nationalistic movements under the leadership of priests of Khnub towards the end of that century, since it was already in existence before the campaign of Cambyses, more than a century earlier.

The Assyrian period certainly did not cease with Sennacherib's astonishing raising of the siege at Jerusalem in 701 B.C. Babylon's attempts to make itself independent were bloodily suppressed in 689 B.C. by Sennacherib, who captured and destroyed the holy city and left it at the disposal of the nomads from the steppes. The next ten years, during which Babylon lay desolate, are forgotten when the prophecies of Isaiah 13-14 are declared to be 'false'! At any rate Isaiah had been proved right in his warning against Merodach-baladan.

Seen from this great distance in time, it is surprising that Esarhaddon was able to remain in power. According to 2 Kings 19 : 37 and Isaiah 37 : 38 his father had been murdered by his sons Adrammelech and Sharezer, obviously with the intention that their brother Esarhaddon should not become king. The Bible story is confirmed by a text of Sennacherib's grandson Ashurbanipal, who states that the murder took place in a temple in Babylon. It has also been suggested that Esarhaddon himself had a hand in the murder, because in the prism in which he alludes to the events no curse is pronounced on the perpetrators of the deed. Be that as it may, Esarhaddon (see Plate 210) acceded to the throne in the spring of 680 B.C. and held it until his death in 669 B.C., during an expedition to Egypt. The Old Testament makes no further mention of Esarhaddon. Jerusalem was ruled for many years by Manasseh, who according to 2 Chronicles 33 : 11 was a prisoner for some time in Babylon. In fact, Esarhaddon invited kings, occasionally as many as twenty-two at a time, to Nineveh to answer for their actions. Manasseh is not mentioned in this connection, although 'Me-na-si-i' of 'Ia-u-di' occurs in a list of subject kings. Esarhaddon ruled with extraordinary cruelty. Of his vassal in Sidon he relates: ' 'Abdi-Milkutti, who fled before my weapons on to the sea, I pulled out of the sea like a fish and I cut off his head.' Another passage reads: 'To give the people an example of the power of Ashur, my lord, I hung the heads of Sanduarri and 'Abdi-Milkutti round the necks of their most prominent citizens, whom, thus adorned, I made walk in procession along the streets of Nineveh, to the strains of singers accompanying themselves on harps.' Atrocities of this kind made attempts at revolt anything but attractive.

In outward appearance Assyria was the most powerful land that the ancient world had ever known. Particularly the fact that Esarhaddon had successfully penetrated far into Egypt and occupied Memphis in 671 must have made a deep impression. The wife, sons, and daughters of the Pharaoh were taken as prisoners to Assyria. Under the mound of Nebi Yunus at Nineveh three Egyptian statues were found which probably formed part of the booty brought home by the Assyrian army on that occasion. But the Assyrian lines of communication were becoming much too long, and the subject nations were merely waiting for an opportunity to shake off the yoke.

Intellectual life shows clear signs of decay in the reign of Esarhaddon. This was the time when 'hemerologies' flourished; these were lists of days with their good and bad omens. Some of the latter have survived to this day, when superstitious fear prevents some people from taking important decisions or actions on a Friday or the thirteenth of a month. The following passage from a hemerology devoted to the month of Tishri may be quoted as an example: 'On the first day he shall not expose himself to the gale on the field. He must not eat garlic, otherwise a scorpion will sting him. He must not eat white garlic, otherwise he will suffer a heart attack. On the second day he must not climb upon a roof, for Ardat Lili (an evil demon) would find him. He must not eat roast meat, otherwise he will be covered with sores. On the third day he shall have no sexual intercourse with a woman, for the woman would rob him of his virility. He shall not eat fish; it is disrespectful and a crocodile would attack him. He shall not eat dates, for they would give him a stomach illness. He shall not irrigate a sesame field, for the sesame caterpillar would overcome him. A woman shall not visit him, for his plan would not succeed. On the fourth day he must not cross a river; the fullness of his strength would depart from him. He shall not go to outlying places, otherwise an enemy would fight with him. He shall not eat beef, goat's meat, or pork, for he would suffer headaches. He shall not set foot where an ass has walked, otherwise he will develop sciatica.' These texts give a lively picture of daily life among the Assyrians. They are sometimes anything but clear, because they mention names of demons and diseases which cannot be identified. Behind them stands the figure of the priest-magician, whose task it was to neutralise evil influences by exorcisms and magical acts.

The dangers to which people and particularly the king were exposed assumed gigantic proportions when the sun or moon was wholly or partly eclipsed. The change in the celestial regime of the macrocosm about the New Year's feast was also a time fraught with danger. To preserve the king there was a custom of appointing a substitute king, which has survived in the guise of a carnival king. Usually some simple man was chosen to occupy the throne and thus divert attention away from the real king. Certain indications seem to suggest that the substitute king was put to death after his short rule. A text from an earlier period tells us that a gardener Ellil-bani, who was destined for a similar fate, retained the throne because the real king choked to death with a bowl of porridge during the ritual festive banquet. The morbid and superstitious Esarhaddon meted out the hard lot of the substitute king to the simple Damki, together with a lady of the court. The texts which refer to it, though not clear in every detail, are interesting because they speak of Damki's death in words reminiscent of the Song of the Servant of the Lord in Isaiah 53.

THE DECLINE AND FALL OF ASSYRIA

The only Old Testament mention of Esarhaddon's successor Ashurbanipal is cursory and occurs in Ezra 4 : 10, where a letter from Rehum to Artaxerxes refers to 'the great and noble Osnappar'. The latter name is a corruption of Ashurbanipal. Conversely, the annals of the Assyrian king make scarcely any mention of Judah. When he has to march against an Egypt in revolt, where Tirhakah has recaptured the city of Memphis, he demands tribute of twenty-two kings on the coast of Phoenicia on the way, and 'Mi-in-si-e' (Manasseh) is named among those who brought gifts, supplied troops, and embraced Ashurbanipal's feet. It is clear that not the slightest political importance was attached to Judah at that time.

We shall return to Ashurbanipal and his forty-two-year reign (668-626) when we discuss the emergence of literature, for it was he who founded and maintained the great library at Nineveh. It is in this fact rather than in his campaigns and lion hunts (see Pl. 207) that his lasting importance lies. His death was followed by years in which the power of Assyria rapidly declined. His weak son Ashur-etil-ilani was deposed by an army leader, and another son, Sin-shar-ishkun – called Sarakos by the Greek historians – contrived to occupy the throne. His successes had no lasting result.

In Babylon, meanwhile, a certain Nabopolassar had dethroned Assyria's vassal, Kandalanu, and founded an independent dynasty. In Jerusalem Josiah was suddenly able to effect a religious reform which amounted to a liberation from all foreign influence on spiritual life. The details of this are found in 2 Kings 23, and the event must be placed in the year 626 or shortly after it. About the same time Zephaniah (2 : 13-15) announced the coming fall of Nineveh: Assyria, he prophesied, would be destroyed and Nineveh would become a wilderness.

With the aid of a Babylonian chronicle which is in the British Museum and was deciphered in 1923, we can fairly accurately reconstruct the course of events which led to the downfall of Nineveh. The Babylonians, Medes, and Scythians had united to destroy Assyria. After various campaigns, the first of which took place in 616, they succeeded in the summer of 612 in capturing Nineveh. The destruction of the vast city by fire and water was so thorough that Xenophon with his Ten Thousand soldiers was able to pass by the spot two hundred years later without even suspecting the glory that lay hidden under the rubble and sand. The prophecies of Nahum give expression to the joy that greeted the downfall of the metropolis which had inflicted so much misery on Palestine: 'Woe to the bloody city, all full of lies and booty – no end to the plunder! The crack of whip, and rumble of wheel, galloping horse, and bounding chariot! Horsemen charging, flashing sword and glittering spear, hosts of slain, heaps of corpses, dead bodies without number...' (Nah. 3 : 1-3). Thus when the end of the Assyrian period came it came quickly; but even so another oppressor had already arisen.

The Period of Literary Greatness

The name of Ashurbanipal, the king who built up a vast library in his residence at Nineveh, is inseparably linked with the development of Mesopotamian literature. It is mainly for this that he merits our attention. A description of his life, rich as it was in military campaigns interrupted by lion hunts, would not be complete without mention of his rôle as a patron of the arts and in particular of literature. We will try to conjure up a picture of the man on the basis of the information available to us on clay tablets.

That the dynasty of the Sargonids did not totter in the critical situation created by Esarhaddon's death in Palestine on his way to war against Egypt was due to the energetic action of the queen-mother. We know something of this forceful woman from a letter to her provincial governors in which she asks to be informed immediately of any attempt at rebellion. It was she who made it possible for her grandson Ashurbanipal to take the reins of government firmly in his hands.

He had been properly prepared for his task. In one of his inscriptions he relates the skills taught to him while he was still crown prince. He had learned to ride thoroughbred horses, to shoot with bow and arrow, to hurl the lance, to drive battle chariots, and even to make shields with the skill of a smith. All that was part of the normal education of an Assyrian prince. What is surprising about the inscription is that it mentions other things which belong rather to the education of a scholar. For he had mastered the scribe's art, and become skilled in writing on clay tablets or 'speckling' (the expression he uses for this also applies to the spots on a panther's skin), an accomplishment he owed to Nabu, the patron of scribes, and Nabu's wife, Tashmetum, who had given him 'great ears', that is, a large measure of intelligence. He relates that he was also introduced to the secret science of those who know how to explain signs in the sky or on earth and can predict the future from the lines in the liver of a sacrificial animal. He also learned to count and to solve difficult problems of division and multiplication. He had studied not only Assyrian but also Old Sumerian, so that he was able independently to read and translate very old tablets 'from before the Flood'.

Although we need not accept at its face value what a sycophantic court historian chooses to state, there is nevertheless a remarkable stress on cultural and religious training which is absent from similar inscriptions of other kings. Not only that, but his actions proved that his interest in art and literature was serious. He seems, in fact, to have been a man who could hold his own in conversation with the scholars of his time and could sustain a high level of discussion on astrology and other sciences or pseudo-sciences.

The reliefs show him at his other accomplishments, which is not surprising in view of the conservative character of an art which permitted little deviation from tradition. The hunting scenes left by his sculptors belong to the peak of Assyrian art (see Pls. 223-5). We see the lance thrown, the arrow flying through the air, and the stricken lion collapsing on the ground. Yet even if the artists were confined to the traditional subjects, it is unlikely that they indulged in fantasy. Indeed, Ashurbanipal was probably a king gifted not only with great intelligence but with a strong physique hardened in his youth.

He was also a tragic figure, for despite all his accomplishments he could not swim against the tide of his age. World history is often dominated by powerful movements which even the strongest personalities are unable to arrest, while much weaker figures appear greater than they actually were because they had the tide with them.

In the long run the independence movement in distant Egypt proved irrepressible. When Ashurbanipal died, this part of the empire had been completely lost. He was able to maintain power in his immediate surroundings at the cost of much bloodshed in a campaign marked by dramatic events. Particularly tragic was the revolt of Babylon. Ashurbanipal had had to resign himself to the assumption of the Babylonian throne by his brother Shamash-shum-ukin. The south had always been the home of separatist movements of people who could not resign themselves to domination by the north. Shamash-shum-ukin probably tried to take advantage of this situation in order to eclipse his brother. When the rebellion assumed a more serious character, Ashurbanipal laid siege to the ancient holy capital. Conditions of famine gradually prevailed inside the city, and the distress was further increased when a relieving force of Bedouin were also driven within its walls. The Assyrian armies finally forced their way into the city, and Shamash-shum-ukin threw himself into the flames of his burning palace and died. Babylon was treated with a harshness which made a deep impression on the world of those days. The Assyrians had laid violent hands on the centre of the civilisation they admired so much, the southern city where Ashurbanipal had agents buy up the clay tablets with which he increased his collection.

Ashurbanipal was not the first Assyrian king to accumulate literary texts. In this respect he was the continuer of a work which had begun as long previously as the twelfth century. But no king before him had tried with such fervour to form a complete collection of known literature. All of it had to be assembled in the library built near his royal palace at Nineveh.

The founding and extending of a library were nothing new. The formation of archives by merchants and authorities had long been a familiar practice. Every temple had a room in which clay tablets bearing religious texts were stored. Ashurbanipal, however, aimed at something more than a national archive or a specialised library. In his library he wished to assemble the whole of literature as it was known at that time.

The king makes it appear that he personally copied the texts. Although we assume that he could read and write, we must regard this statement as unworthy of credit, for the skill of a competent scribe took years of training to acquire. He must have had scribes at his disposal who copied the works he wanted. At any rate he had in his service officials whom he spurred on by letters of which authentic copies have been found. One of them was called Shadunu. Shadunu made journeys to centres of the art of writing, such as Babylon and Sippar, and was authorised to commission poets and prose writers to compose original works. One letter sent by Ashurbanipal to Shadunu reads as follows: 'On the day you receive this letter, you shall take with you Shuma, his brother Bel-etis, Apla, and other skilled persons of Borsippa, as many of them as you know. Collect the tablets they have lying at home, and also those deposited in the temple of Eridu.' After naming a number of the texts he wanted, the letter continues: 'You must gather together and bring to me valuable tablets of which there are no copies in Assyria. I have already written to the temple guardian and to the mayor of Borsippa that you, Shadunu, are authorised to keep the tablets in your stores. No one may withhold tablets from you. If you should hear of any other tablet or ritual text which seems suitable for the palace library seek it out, take it with

207

208

207. Detail of a large relief in the British Museum, depicting Ashurbanipal hunting wild asses. The foremost rider is the king, who has released the reins so as to manipulate his bow and arrow. He is followed by two servants, the first carrying a quiver and holding arrows ready for his master; the second bears a lance. The sculptor has succeeded in capturing and fixing the action of the galloping horses in a harmonious composition. The king is clearly drawn on a larger scale than the servants, though not excessively so. The actual dimensions of the detail are 3 ft. 8 in. × 1 ft. 8¾ in. **208.** Relief, now in the British Museum, illustrating the struggle of the Assyrians against the Arabs. **209.** Horse's head, detail from a relief showing a part of the Assyrian army on the march to the accompaniment of music. The special preference which sculptors of the 7th century B.C. display for horses at the gallop is striking.

you, and send it hither.' Ashurbanipal was thus a bibliophile without his like in antiquity, one for whom no trouble was too great when it was a question of acquiring sole existing copies.

Librarianship thus flourished in Ashurbanipal's reign. The strict orderliness that prevailed in his library was deeply rooted in a tradition which went back to the time of the Sumerians. There was a centuries-old familiarity with archives, and there were expert civil servants. As the library itself was completely destroyed by war operations, it is far from easy to reconstruct its outward form with any certainty. Planks and wooden bookshelves were not used, for wood was expensive and had to be brought from afar. Instead, there were probably walls containing niches in which baskets or clay chests were arranged. The baskets contained tablets, the contents of which were briefly indicated on a clay label. Items associated with one another were kept together. When the text of one tablet was continued on another tablet, a catch-line was used, that is, the last few words of the first tablet were repeated at the start of the second. Silent reading as we know it did not exist in the ancient world, so it was necessary to insert catch-lines to prevent interruptions in the spoken delivery.

Tablets which formed a series were numbered like the pages of a book, and each series was given a name which was repeated at the beginning and end of each tablet. This name was usually taken from the opening words of the first tablet. For instance, a series of incantations we know is called 'Shurpu', or 'destruction by fire'. It is in this series that occurs the text to which allusion has already been made: 'Palace of Ashurbanipal, the king of the world, the king of Assyria, who trusts in Ashur and Nin-lil, to whom Nabu and Tash-metum grant great ears, who was endowed with a clear eye and mastered the most distinguished art of writing, as no one among the kings, my forefathers, has ever learned to do. With the wisdom of Nabu and the art of scribes such as are trained to do so, I wrote on tablets, I completed them, I revised them, and placed them in my palace where I might see and read them. Your power is beyond compare, oh king of the gods, oh Ashur! He who takes away this tablet or writes his name beside mine, may Ashur and Nin-lil ruin him with their rage and wrath and destroy his name and seed in the land.'

Texts of this kind show how anxious Ashurbanipal was that his name should go down to posterity as an expert in the field of literature. He had collected the tablets into series and placed related series near to each other, and had even had them catalogued. It is generally thought nowadays that his methods of librarianship became known to the Greeks by way of the islands of the eastern Mediterranean. The custom of keeping manuscripts in jars, familiar to us from the recent discoveries near the Dead Sea (first century A.D.) and from the Gnostic manuscripts of the second century A.D. found in Upper Egypt, is a continuation of similar usages in ancient Mesopotamia. It is believed that the Alexandrian Ptolemies in particular carried on the same tradition of accurate classification. If this is so, our modern libraries are linked to Ashurbanipal's by an unbroken historical chain.

The literature he collected was anonymous. But if the author's name is not given, the copyist's is. If the latter was an important personality, the name of his father and that of his grandfather were also added. Sometimes there is a note about the original from which the copy was made, for example where it was found and how it looked. This is followed by an assurance that the copy and original have been compared. Yet little value was attached to exact transcription. Even religious texts were not copied accurately in every detail. The copy might also be dated, in imitation of commercial and legal texts in which dates were compulsory. The owner of a collection sometimes marked the tablets with his cylinder seal, a custom we may regard as the first stage in the development of *ex-libris*. Thus it is not difficult to recognise in Ashurbanipal's library all the factors that contribute to the formation of a library nowadays.

The greatest service that the bibliophile king did to posterity was to store such a complete collection of literature in a single place. When the great discoveries began in the middle of the nineteenth century

and an astonished Western Europe learned for the first time of the finds at Mosul on the Tigris, the famous library made it possible to lay hands immediately on the classical products of Assyro-Babylonian literature.

THE GILGAMESH EPIC

The most celebrated poetic work to emerge from Ashurbanipal's collection was the epic of Gilgamesh, now a treasured possession of the British Museum. This national epic of Babylonia consists of twelve cantos, the eleventh of which suddenly became a focus of interest in 1873, when George Smith identified the Babylonian account of the Flood on fragments of clay tablets. It was only later on that it was found to be loosely connected with the great epic of Gilgamesh. The latter had survived in anything but a perfect state, but the course of the narrative could be made out in broad outline. Editors of the epic are no longer solely dependent on the fragments from Nineveh. A Sumerian fragment from the period of King Shulgi (about 2000 B.C.) has been found. A somewhat more recent fragment in Old Babylonian has survived, and an eighteenth-century tablet is also known, while two sixth-century Assyrian fragments were found in Erech. In the museum at Istanbul Dr Frankena found several clay tablets which he was able to identify as fragments of the seventh canto. A piece of the sixth canto was found in the vicinity of Megiddo. At Hattushash, the Hittite centre, fifteenth-century fragments in three different languages were recovered. Thus the epic had been known and handed down in writing for over fifteen centuries within the sphere of influence of Mesopotamian culture, which extended from Asia Minor to the Persian Gulf. Knowledge of the epic is still being added to by new discoveries in widely separated sites and the lacunae are slowly being filled.

Gilgamesh, the hero of the epic, was one of the princes who ruled shortly after the Flood. He was king of Erech and a tyrant who did not 'leave the maiden with her mother, the daughter with the hero, or the wife with her husband'. He was two parts god and one part human, and his walk was as dignified as that of an aurochs. But the lamentations of the oppressed were heard by the goddess Ishtar, who then created an adversary for Gilgamesh. This was Enkidu, a faun living in a state of absolute innocence amidst the beasts of the field. When Gilgamesh heard of Enkidu from a hunter, he suggested that Enkidu should be brought into contact with a woman. Her love estranged Enkidu from the beasts of the field.

Remarkable dreams warn Gilgamesh of the coming of the warlike hero. He tells his mother that in his dream he was rushing excitedly up and down among men when the stars in the sky and the entire firmament fell upon him. He could not rid himself of this weight, and meanwhile the whole of Erech came and stood round about in order to pay homage to it. In a second confused dream he saw an axe lying in the road at Erech. He fell in love with the strangely shaped axe and nestled close to it.

Meanwhile Enkidu has become a civilised man, who eats bread, drinks strong drink, and goes about clothed. Arriving in Erech, he meets Gilgamesh and tries to restrain him from an act of violence. After an indecisive but epic battle there follows the story of a friendship which links the two friends and is for Gilgamesh the beginning of his reformation. This is accompanied by a breach with Ishtar and a *rapprochement* with Shamash, the sun god.

The two friends go to the Cedar Forest, where they fight the giant Humbaba, defeat him, and cut off his head. On the return journey Ishtar tries to ensnare the hero in her mesh, but he repels her advances and in fact sneers at the goddess. This was arrogance on his part, for the anger of the gods is always stronger than human power. Ishtar persuades her father Anu to make the Heavenly Bull descend to earth, which he does, dragging seven lean years in his wake. Enkidu slays the Heavenly Bull, but despite Shamash's pleading the council of the gods decides that Enkidu must die. His illness and death are followed by the moving lamentation of Gilgamesh, which is reminiscent of David's lamentation after Saul and Jonathan had fallen at Gilboa (2 Sam. 1 : 17-27).

It is at this point that the main theme of the epic first appears: fear of death and consequently the search for and the finding and losing again of the herb of life. This herb has a vivifying quality: the old man who eats of it is made young again. The tree of life in the story of Eden has the same power, and when Adam and Eve are sent out of the garden of life they are made subject to mortality (Gen. 3 : 22). The quest for the herb of life leads the hero to the island of the blessed which is the abode of Utnapishtim. The ferryman Urshanabi takes him to the man whose name means 'he that has found life'. Now follows a number of philosophic sayings giving a very pessimistic account of man's ability to overcome death. This philosophy is in keeping with the whole conception of the Babylonian Noah. He is also the great sage who left his views to posterity in the form of sayings. Then comes the story of the Flood, which includes an account of how Utnapishtim escaped sentence of death. A special grace of Enlil was granted to him. His victory over mortality is an exception, like that of Enoch (Gen. 5 : 24) and Elijah (2 Kg. 2 : 11) in the Old Testament. When the story of the Flood is terminated, Utnapishtim returns to his philosophy that sleep is a mirror of death. Man, who cannot even do without sleep for six days and seven nights, must not try to conquer everlasting sleep.

During Gilgamesh's sleep Utnapishtim's wife performs a peculiar ritual: each day she bakes a loaf and places it on his head. Some commentators think that the loaves are reminders of the time that Gilgamesh had spent sleeping, others that they are meant to symbolise the ages of man, from infant in arms to greybeard. Then the hero is allowed to bathe in the water of life before setting out again, as he must, in search of the herb of life.

Weighed down with stones, he descends to the depth of the primeval ocean and there he plucks the miraculous herb. When the waves cast him upon the shore again, he still has it in his hand and it seems that his struggle and pains have been rewarded. But on the way back to Erech Gilgamesh and Urshanabi come upon a small lake of cool water, and Gilgamesh goes down to refresh himself in it. While the herb is lying by the water's edge, the serpent wriggles though the grass and eats it up, after which it sloughs its skin and continues on its way renewed. No lamentations ensue. Gilgamesh sits down and weeps and utters a few words of self-reproach; he should, he says, have paid more attention to signs.

So no victory over death is possible and all men must go to the land from which there is no return. The only comfort is that Erech is solid and immortal. Thus Gilgamesh says to his companion: 'Go up, Urshanabi, and walk on the wall of Erech, seek out the substructure, look at the brickwork, whether it is not made of baked brick, and whether its foundations were not laid by the seven sages.' These words had already been said at the beginning, and now they were being repeated. The actual epic ends at this point but there is an appendix which describes how the shade of Enkidu is conjured up from the Underworld. Enkidu tells how the fate of the dead depends on how they have been buried.

Thus the epic of Gilgamesh is concerned with the besetting problem of death, leaving entirely aside the possibility of overcoming mortality by service in the temple and dedication rites.

THE ADAPA MYTH

The myth of Adapa is also concerned with the problem of mortality. A large part of it was found at Tell el-Amarna, but three smaller fragments were recovered from the ruins of Ashurbanipal's library. Adapa is comparable to Adam, he is a man and represents humanity. He possesses wisdom, but not immortality. His calling is that of fisherman, and he supplies fish daily to the temple. On one occasion when the south wind capsizes his boat and he nearly becomes food for the fishes, Adapa utters a curse which proves effective, for the wings of the south wind are indeed broken and Anu observes seven

Selections from the epic of Gilgamesh, the national heroic poem of Babylonia

Tablet I—THE TYRANNY OF GILGAMESH AND THE CREATION OF ENKIDU

*1. He who saw everything [to the ends] of the earth,
Knew [all things, observed] all things,
. . . all together
Who [possessed] wisdom and [executed] all things,*
*5. Who beheld mysteries and [laid open] hidden things –
He brought news from the time before the Flood,
Undertook a far journey, full of toil and [trouble],
After which he engraved all his labours on a stone tablet.
He built the wall of ramparted Erech,
Of consecrated Eanna, the holy treasure house.*
*10. Behold its wall, whose cornice is of copper;
Examine the bastion, which none can rival;
Touch the threshold which is from hoary antiquity.
Approach Eanna, the dwelling of Ishtar,*
*15. Which no future king, no one, shall equal;
Mount and walk on the wall of Erech,
Examine the substructure, view the brickwork.
Is the brickwork not of brick?
Did the Seven Sages not lay the foundation?*

Tablet VIII – THE LAMENT FOR ENKIDU

*1. 'Hear me, ye elders, [listen] to me!
I weep for Enkidu, my [friend],
I lament bitterly like a mourning woman.
The battle-axe at my side, the [bow] in my hand,*
*5. The sword in my belt, the [shield] in front of me,
My festive robe, my joy . . . .
An evil [demon] appeared and [robbed] me of [you].
My younger brother, who hunted wild asses and panthers
in mountains and steppes!
Enkidu, my friend, who hunted wild asses and panthers
in mountains and steppes!*
*10. After we had [achieved] everything, climbed [the mountains],
Seized and killed the Heavenly Bull,
Struck down Humbaba, who [lived in the Cedar Forest],
What is this sleep which has overtaken [you]?
Your eyes are dark, you hear not [my voice]!'*
*15. But he does not raise [his eyes].
He feels his heart; it does not beat.
Then he veiled his friend like a bride.
He raises his voice like a lion,
Like a lioness bereft of her whelps.*
*29. Again and again he turns back [to his friend],
Tears his hair . . . ,
Pulls off and casts away his finery.*

Tablet XI – THE DECISION OF THE GODS

*8. Utnapishtim said to him, to Gilgamesh:
'I will reveal a secret to you, Gilgamesh,*
*10. I will tell you a secret of the gods.
You know the city of Shuruppak, on the banks of the Euphrates.
In this city, already ancient, the gods were met together;
Then by the great gods the decision was taken,
To bring forth a deluge.*
*15. [Thus decided] Anu, their father,
Heroic Enlil, their adviser,
Ninurta, their herald,
Ennuge, their irrigator.'*

210. This stone stele, height 10 ft. 6¾ in., was found at Zenjirli and is now at Berlin. It represents Esarhaddon (680-669), holding two prisoners of war with ropes. According to the inscription one is the king of Egypt and Ethiopia; the other may be the king of Tyre. At the top right can be seen four gods standing on animals, and alongside them their symbols: a crescent moon, a winged solar disk, and objects shaped like stars and spears. **211.** This limestone relief, 19½ in. high, which was found at Ashur, dates from about the same time as 210. A deity who cannot be identified stands on the back of a winged, bull-headed lion. **212.** Assyrian archers of the time of Ashurbanipal. **213.** This representation of a fisherman was found in the south-western palace at Nineveh. It is 19¾ in. high and made of gypsum, and dates from the time of Sennacherib. **214.** The unpractical shape of the boats used has survived till the present in the *gufah*, here seen on an irrigation canal between Babylon and Kish. The author of Exodus 2 : 3 and that of the legend of the birth of Sargon of Agade, which is related to the story of Moses, had the *gufah* in mind when they told of an ark made of bulrushes and pitch which floated down the river and was finally rescued together with its load. **215.** A circular boat propelled by four oarsmen transporting a heavy load across the river. To the right of the boat we see a fisherman floating on an inflated animal skin.

210
211

212

213

214
215

The impressions of cylinder seals provide a fantastic accompaniment to the contents of the ancient myths, although accurate interpretation remains difficult.

days later that there is no more wind from the south. Adapa is called to task for his action. But before he goes up before the throne of the celestial court he is given good advice by Ea.

Ea tells him to don a mourning garment and, when he is asked why he is dressed like that, to answer that it is because the gods Tammuz and Gizzida have disappeared from the land. In this way he will win the favour of the gods and of Anu. He must refuse bread and drink if these are offered to him, but if he is brought a garment and oil to anoint himself with he must accept them. Adapa follows Ea's instructions and at first everything goes as predicted. The mourning garment makes a good impression and he succeeds in making out a good case for himself on the subject of the south wind. Anu now decides to offer him the bread and drink of life so that he may have immortality, but Adapa refuses them. When he is offered the garment of mortality and the oil of transitoriness, he accepts both, to the astonishment of Anu.

The poet does not say in so many words that Ea has consciously deceived his creature. Ea may have made a mistake, for by Mesopotamian ideas even gods have their foibles and to err may be divine as well as human. It is also possible, however, that Ea is a representative of the 'divine deceiver' type, to which Hermes also belongs. When preparations were being made for the Flood Ea betrayed the plan of the gods; in this case it is man he betrays, who, through no fault of his own, is deprived of immortality.

THE DIALOGUE BETWEEN THE MASTER AND HIS SERVANT

Closely related in spirit to the Book of Ecclesiastes, which is so ironical on the need not to be over-wise and not to be over-foolish as a condition for a happy life (Ec. 7 : 15-22), is a dialogue between a master and his servant. It is a pessimistic conversation about the pros and cons of all human activity. The master is a capricious man and the slave approves all his plans. If the master wants his coach prepared to drive to the palace, his decision is applauded because the king will undoubtedly give him a hospitable reception; his decision not to do so is equally applauded. It is also quite possible, the servant comments, that the king will throw him into prison. After washing his hands the master may dine happily, for Shamash gladly watches him do so, but he may equally well not eat and refuse to become his stomach's slave. He can go hunting, build a house, be silent to his enemy, but he may just as well stay at home, not build a house, and start a big lawsuit, for each of these courses has something to be said for it and against it. Thus the relative nature of everything that man does is placed in a mildly humorous light. It is regrettable that this text is badly damaged and has come down to us in a fragmentary state.

WISDOM LITERATURE

More moving and less superficial in content is a great song usually referred to by its first words, *Ludul bel nemeki*, which mean: 'I will praise the lord of wisdom'. This is a text depicting the pitiable state of a Mesopotamian Job. For him the day means lamentation and the night weeping, every month is a silent sitting down, and the whole year is filled with sadness. The god he invokes does not see him, and the goddess he prays to does not even lift her head. There is no comfort for him, neither from the man who examines the sacrificial animal nor from the interpreter of dreams; not even the soothsayer or the magician can help him. Yet he has not been remiss in any respect, either to the king or to the gods. He has faithfully observed the days of worship, taken part in processions, and instructed his fellow-citizens in keeping the commandments of the god and the goddess and in respect for the king's authority. Thus he is unable to understand why he must suffer, and he says: 'What seems good to man is wrong for the deity, the evil in his heart seems good to the deity. Who can ever learn the will of the gods in heaven? Who understands the counsel of the deity?' The second part relates how the just man regains his health, his possessions, and his self-respect, and we are left to debate whether this happy ending is part of the original plan or was added later.

It seems more probable that the conclusion belongs to the original song. The man's suffering is brought to an end by the intervention of Marduk. Completely cured, he can now enter the holy ground of

The same figures keep recurring in all periods, though in varying forms. The animal-man in particular was a favourite subject of the seal-cutter.

Esagila in Babylon. The holy man recites the various names of the gateways of the temple and tells how their meaning was fulfilled. In the 'Gate of Silenced Complaints' his complaint was silenced, and in the 'Gate of Miracles' the miraculous signs were shown to him in all their brilliance. It is almost as if an initiation rite in which the proselyte had to pass through the doors of the temple, was the basis of this song, in which the problem of suffering is presented in much the same way as in Psalm 73.

Comparable with Job is a 'dialogue between two friends' about injustice in the world. In the first stanza 'Job' bemoans his distress and says he has lost his father and mother. His friend replies that everyone must cross the river between this life and the Underworld. It is decreed thus from the beginning, one must accept it, and count on piety being rewarded in this life. To this the afflicted man answers that he suffers hunger and thirst, so that his devout and wise friend urges him to win the favour of Shamash by supplication. The poor man has, however, already done all that can humanly be expected and said prayers or offered sacrifices. The friend says that the rich will also be punished for their bloodthirsty crimes. The sufferer finds no comfort in this answer, which he calls a 'breath of air, as cold as the north wind'. He calls the dogma of retribution in question by exclaiming: 'Those who do not seek the deity follow a happy path, but those who piously pray to the goddess are visited by poverty and care.' The wise friend, who has followed the same line of argument as Job's friends, now arrives at the conclusion that there must be hidden sins for which the sufferer is being punished. The latter refuses to be convinced, and says one might just as well imitate the roving thief or wandering robber preying on the virtuous who take the trouble to build a house and cultivate a field.

The friend agrees with the proposition that the actions of the gods are incomprehensible and their decisions as unfathomable as the depths of the sky. He concedes to the complainer that in heaven the word of the meek who never did wrong does not count. Narru, king of the remotest past and creator of mortals, the famous Zulummur, who cut their clay to length, and Queen Mama, who shaped them, made mankind a joint and everlasting present of lies and deceit. The gods are therefore responsible for all distress and all injustice.

A remarkable thing now happens. The complainer becomes silent and humbles himself like a cringing slave, asking the gods and the king for mercy. Thus, in the religious sense, there is after all a wide difference between the Biblical Job and the Babylonian, although the problem treated is identically the same. Where the two versions agree is that in neither case is there excessive haste to offer a solution. The reason for this is that in Babylon as in Israel the idea of retribution in a life after death did not exist. Righteousness in this earthly existence had to be made public, and from the suffering of the devout there thus arose a deeply reflective literature which owed its existence to philosophic rather than to priestly circles.

THE EPIC OF THE PLAGUE GOD IRRA

Another of the masterpieces of literature represented in Ashurbanipal's library is the epic of the plague god Irra. A remarkable thing is that its author is known. He calls himself Kabti-ilani-Marduk ('Marduk is the most honoured of the gods'), the son of Dabibi. As the name Shamash-Dabibi, of which this is a contraction, occurs frequently but not until later times, it is reasonable to assume that the author, about whom we know nothing more, did not live earlier than the eighth century B.C. At any rate he was a competent theologian and an excellent man of letters. Perhaps he belonged to the priestly class at Babylon, which boasted an ancient literary tradition. It is most unusual for the author of a poem to be known by name. The writer of the Babylonian theodicy concealed his name in an acrostic, from which he has been identified as Saggil-kenam-abbib. The author of the epic of the plague god Irra himself tells us that he was moved to write by divine inspiration. Speaking in the third person, he says that 'in the course of the night he (Irra) showed it to him, and when he rose in the morning he neither omitted nor added a single line'.

It is only in very recent times that, thanks to the Felix Gössmann's great edition of 1956, there has been general interest in this epic. The first fragments had already been published at the end of the nineteenth century, but had been lacking in appeal. This is quite understandable, for the pieces dug up from Ashurbanipal's library contained little that could give a general idea of its contents. The material was con-

THE FLOOD

96. *When something of morning had dawned,*
   There arose a black cloud from the horizon.
   While Adad [the storm god] was thundering within it,
   There went on ahead [the gods] Shullat and Hanish,
100. *Went forth [his] lieutenants across mountain and plain.*
   [Where irrigation dams they found,] Nergal tore out the dam-stays,
   Came Ninurta behind, made the weirs overflow.

   Already the Anunakki had taken up their torches,
   That perchance with their brightness they might illumine the land.
105. *But as the Horror-[cloud] of Adad passed over the heavens,*
   It turned aught that had light into uttermost darkness.
   [What was on] the land fell [sundered in pieces].
   For one day the hurricane raged, [the wind blew],
   The storm roared, so that the water rose above the mountains.
110. *As in a battle [death] overtook [mankind].*

   No man could make out his brother,
   Nor could people be seen from the heavens.
   Even the gods were afeared at the deluge,
   Took to flight and went up to the heaven of Anu;
115. *Cowered they like dogs and crouched down at the outer defences.*
   Ishtar cried out as in pains of travail,
   The mistress of the gods mourned with melodious voice:

   'The world of yesterday is turned to clay!
   In the council of the gods I gave my vote for destruction!
   How can I have enjoined destruction in the council,
   And declared war for the extinction of my race of mankind?
   O my race of mankind, did I myself bring them into the world
   In order to fill the sea with them as with food for fishes?'
125. *The Anunakki wept with her.*
   The gods sat with bowed heads and lamented,
   Their lips veiled [in mourning].

127. *For six days and [seven] nights the wind blew,*
   And the flood and the storm swept the land.
   But the seventh day arriving did the rainstorm subside,
130. *And the flood which had heaved like a woman in travail;*
   There quieted the sea, and the storm wind stood still,
   The flood stayed her flowing.

   I opened a vent and the fresh air moved over my cheek-bones.
   And I looked at the sea; there was silence,
135. *The tide-way lay flat as a roof-top –*
   But the whole of mankind had returned to clay.
   I bowed low; I sat and wept;
   Over my cheek-bones my tears kept on running.
   When I looked out again in the directions,
   Across the expanse of the sea,
   Mountain ranges had emerged in twelve places,

140. *And on Mount Nisir the vessel had grounded.*
   Mount Nisir held the vessel fast nor allowed of any movement.
   For a first day and a second,
   Fast Mount Nisir held the vessel nor allowed of any movement.
143. *For a third day and a fourth day,*
   Fast Mount Nisir held the vessel nor allowed of any movement.
   For a fifth day and a sixth day,
   Held Mount Nisir fast the vessel nor allowed of any movement.

145. *On the seventh day's arriving,*
   I freed a dove and did release him.
   Forth went the dove but came back to me;
   There was not yet a resting place, and he came returning.
   Then I set free a swallow and did release him.
150. *Forth went the swallow but came back to me;*
   There was not yet a resting place, and he came returning.

216. Although it is not known with certainty what is represented by this alabaster sculpture from Khorsabad, 15 ft. 5½ in. high, it is generally referred to as 'Gilgamesh and the Lion'. The man wears Assyrian dress, his hair and beard are long and curled, and he carries a weapon in his right hand. **217.** Typical head of an Assyrian of the 8th century B.C. **218.** This alabaster relief is probably from Nineveh. It was bought from a London art dealer by the Hamburg Museum für Kunst und Gewerbe in 1928. It depicts a prisoner of war and is best dated to the 9th-8th century B.C. **219.** This relief from Sennacherib's palace at Nineveh shows three prisoners of war playing lyres while escorted by a soldier. The lozenged background is meant to suggest wooded surroundings. The scene recalls the complaint of an exile in Psalm 137 : 3: 'They that carried us away captive required of us a song.'

219

siderably supplemented by fragments which had been found in Ashur and were published in 1925 by Erich Ebeling. To these have now also been added fragments from Sultan Tepe and others which Dr Frankena of Leiden succeeded in identifying during his period at Istanbul Museum. We owe it to collaboration by scholars from various parts of the world that out of the five tablets which the whole epic comprised three-quarters of the first, two-fifths of the second, a quarter of the third, and the whole of the fourth and fifth are known. It is now also clear that copies of the work were widely distributed and that several 'critical editions' of it, with variants, existed. The shape of some of the tablets indicated a strange use to which the text had been put. They were fitted with a projection containing an eyelet so that they could be hung round the neck and worn. In other words, they were used as amulets against the disasters that might be unleashed by the dreaded god Irra.

What then is the story of the epic? When it starts, we find Irra enraged because he feels that mankind pays him insufficient respect. In this we see a feature of the Assyro-Babylonian conception of the existence of the gods. Men are dependent on them, but on the other hand the gods cannot do without men's adoration. They need mankind, a fact also illustrated by a passage in Utnapishtim's story of the Flood, in which the gods are terrified by the thought that mankind might be wiped out.

The first canto relates how Irra conveys to Ishum his decision to punish men who ignore him. Ishum is of a kindly nature and well-disposed towards mankind, whose spokesman he often is. He tries in vain to dissuade Irra from his evil plans. Irra's only difficulty is that he has not a free hand as long as Marduk occupies the throne. By every kind of cunning and by taking advantage of the vanity of the monarch of the gods, Irra succeeds in gaining temporary possession of the reins of world government.

Once Marduk has descended to the Underworld, Irra tells Ishum details of his frightful intentions: he plans to let the sun itself fall from the sky and to hide the light of the moon. The small part of the second canto that has been preserved tells us no more. Only a small part of the third canto, too, is still legible, and so far as one can make out the conversation between Ishum and Irra is continued until the former is finally convinced that Irra is quite right. His wrath at man's indifference appears to be fully justified.

In the fourth canto, however, Ishum speaks with horror of the evil that Irra is doing to mankind. Irra has begun to incite the inhabitants of Babylon against the governor and the governor against his subjects. The consequences are so grievous that the progress of the epic is interrupted by a lamentation from Marduk: 'Woe to Babylon which I have planted like an over-abundant garden whose fruit I did not eat; woe to Babylon which I hung like a cylinder seal round the neck of Anu; woe to Babylon which I took as a tablet of destiny into my hands and entrusted to no one!' But now that evil has been unleashed Marduk appears powerless to stop it. Even Sippar, the city of Shamash, Erech, the city of Anu and Ishtar, and Der are affected. The god of Der, Sataran, also intones a lamentation. But more impressive is a speech by Ishum, who tries to make Irra realise what he has done. He has acted cruelly and arbitrarily: 'You have slain the just, you have slain the unjust, you have slain him who sinned against you, you have slain the priest who made the sacrifice to the gods, you have slain the courtier who served the king, you have slain the aged in their rooms, you have slain the young maidens in their beds, and have refused to put an end to these doings, for you said within yourself, "They disregard me."'

In the fifth canto Irra's anger appears to subside suddenly. He praises Ishum for having given him good advice, and Ishum for his part expresses his respect for the violence of Irra's wrath. But in addition he intercedes for the people of Akkad and utters a prayer that they will be allowed not only to return to their former state of prosperity but also, and above all, that they may be liberated from the Luteans. This name refers to the nomads who on occasion invade the settled land, robbing and pillaging. It is tempting to wonder whether this mention of a specific evil is a reference to historical events which may have formed the background to the epic. This is a difficult question to answer. More important is the conclusion where we read: '[The god] who will praise this song, in his temple shall abundance be heaped up, and he who destroys it shall smell no incense; the king who magnifies my name shall rule the four quarters of the world; the prince who utters praise of my heroism shall not see his equal; the singer who sings this song shall not die of the plague, his speech is agreeable to prince and king; the writer who takes it to hand shall remain alive in the hostile land and be honoured in his own; in artists' workshops where my name is uttered unceasingly I will open their ears; in the house where this tablet is erected Irra shall not rage and the Libitti shall not murder; the dagger of the plague shall not come near and invulnerability is conferred with it; may this song be set down for ever and survive for ever, may the lands all hear it and praise my heroism, may the inhabitants of the cities see it and magnify my name.' This makes it clear why some of the Irra tablets had a projection and an eyelet on them. They served as amulets, to carry which was equivalent to worshipping Irra, the god who did terrifying things but whom men did not need to fear as long they honoured him in the proper way.

SCIENCE AND PSEUDO-SCIENCE

The literature assembled in Ashurbanipal's library also included a 'science' section which we would classify nowadays as medicine, astronomy, and philology. These sciences were built on the foundations previously laid by the Sumerians. The latter felt a great and innate need for system, and this need expressed itself in what might not inappropriately be called 'listology'. Titles which in the view of the ancients belonged together were entered on long lists, most of which have survived in a badly mutilated form. It is sometimes possible to follow the reasoning applied in these lists. A work entitled 'If the skull of a man is seized by the demon of fever', for instance, specifies the diseases of the head. Liver, gall bladder, and heart troubles are classified under the heading, 'When excretion is painful' – again the first line of the work. Diseases of the windpipe and lungs are found in a work called 'When one's mouth (i.e. respiration) is difficult'. Diseases of the muscles and joints are also described in a work with the title, 'Large muscles'. Numerous difficulties are encountered in the study of these works because so many of the expressions used cannot be identified. Not that much can be expected in the medical field, for anatomy was scarcely practised if at all. For religious reasons human corpses were not dissected, and any knowledge of human internal organs that existed was derived by analogy from those of sacrificial animals or from wounds received by soldiers in battle. The livers of sacrificial animals were known in particular detail because they were examined for the purpose of divination (see Pl. 163).

A large number of medical texts were collated by René Labat in a book published in 1951 and called *Traité akkadien de diagnostics et prognostics médicaux*. The contents show very clearly that medicine was still struggling to free itself from the chains of magic. There is a characteristic text dealing with discoloration of parts of the body which reads: 'If his right nipple is red he will recover; if his left nipple is red he will die; if both nipples are red there is no *pa-nu-tug* (?). If his right nipple is green his illness will change, if his left nipple is green, his illness is grave; if both nipples are green it is *na-khi-it* (?). If his right nipple is black it is unfavourable; if his left nipple is black it may take long but he will die; if both nipples are black, he will soon die.' Thus only symptoms are given, followed by a prognosis; there is hardly anything resembling a diagnosis, while treatment is entirely disregarded.

Many sorts of healers were known but the most important of them was the *ashipu*, whose treatment was based on the principle that an appropriate word pronounced at the right time could have a direct physical effect. His methods were therefore quite unscientific, yet accurate observation of the symptoms was a matter of life or death for him. It was the *ashipu* class that produced a great work called *Maklu*, a series of exorcisms with notes on the means used by magicians and witches to make their victims fall ill. What they have done anonymously and secretly can be interpreted from the symptoms; it is then a matter of taking appropriate countermeasures. How proficient an *ashipu* could be in describing an illness will be seen from the following text, which clearly refers to a paranoiac, suffering from a persecution mania: 'If a man has an enemy, if wicked calumny pursues him, or people denounce him, distort his words and malign him, if no one tells the truth to him, if he is invisibly surrounded by all manner of sorcery; if god, king, prince, master, police, and the palace guard are incited against him so that they are malevolent....'

The texts which we may consider part of the Assyro-Babylonian pharmacopeia offer the same difficulties as the descriptions of diseases. It is usually impossible to identify their technical terms. Yet there are long lists of names of trees, plants, and flowers from which medicaments were prepared. The effects of these were probably known from practical experience, and in this field medical science might possibly have detached itself from magical practices. Actual evidence shows, however, that cures were in fact expected from combinations of animal and vegetable matter which were entirely based on magic.

We may say that alongside theology there existed a science of astronomy, provided we do not use the term 'astronomy' in its modern sense. The basis of observation of the sky was a belief in a parallelism between the macrocosm and the microcosm. The movements of the sun, moon, and planets were studied to enable deductions to be drawn from them regarding human life. For life depended on the sequence of days, months, and years and hence on the sun and moon; the fate of the community and the individual, therefore, or so people thought, depended on the gods, whose sublime dwelling is in the firmament. That is why, in texts dealing with the celestial bodies, astronomy and astrology are intertwined. Even those who do not share the fundamental belief of the Mesopotamians can nevertheless derive advantage from their accurate observations. From high towers the clear night sky, hardly ever obscured by clouds, was observed with the naked eye. The planets Venus, Jupiter, Mars, Mercury, and Saturn had been known from ancient times; by the seventh century B.C. astronomers could accurately predict a lunar eclipse. The signs of the Zodiac were considered extremely important and each of them was associated with a city. The parts of the world had their counterparts in the sky. Akkad, Elam, and Amurru were each represented by a group of constellations. The heyday of the science of the heavens was the eighth century B.C. A large number of observational reports dating back to that time formed the basis of a primer known from its opening words as 'Plough-handle'. It says that Enlil has command of the thirty-three stars of the northern sky, Anu of the twenty-three stars at either end of the equator, and Ea of the fifteen stars in the southern sky. These stars are listed by name. There is also a list of 'counter-stars', of the periods of revolution of the planets and of the length of the day and night for the first and fifteenth of every month. What was said of medical 'listology' applies equally to all these texts: even if the motives behind them were not scientific, those motives led to extremely accurate observation.

The existence of two languages, the ancient Sumerian and the Semitic tongue of the new ruling stratum of the population, made it necessary to prepare dictionaries. These were arranged not alphabetically but systematically. For the needs of jurists, for example, there was the formulary *Ana ittishu* ('for information of'), in which could be found the Semitic translation of traditional Sumerian expressions and phrases found in contracts. In general writers had a great need of synonyms, for literary standards insisted on the greatest possible variety. A series such as *malku = sharru* (two of the eight synonyms for 'king') was a great help. The same purpose was probably served by a list of etymologies which begins with the words *sigalam = nabnitu* ('creature'). Such etymology has no scientific value, geing guided entirely by arbitrary sound associations, but the information was valuable for anyone practising *belles-lettres*.

SELECTIONS FROM THE BABYLONIAN EPIC OF THE CREATION (ENUMA ELISH)

1. *When the heaven [gods] above were as yet uncreated,*
The earth [gods] below not yet brought into being,
Alone there existed primordial Apsu who engendered them,
Only Mummu, and Tiamat who brought all of them forth.
5. *Their waters could mix together in a single stream,*
Unrestricted by reed-beds, unimpeded by marsh;
For, since none of the gods had at this time appeared,
These had not yet been formed, or been with destinies decreed.
In the depths of their waters the gods were created.
10. *There appeared Lahmu and Lahamu, they [first] were given name.*

. . . .

81. *In the depths of the Apsu the god Marduk was born,*
In the depths of the pure Apsu Marduk was born.
He that begot him was Ea, his father;
Damkina, his mother, was she that did bear him.
85. *He was suckled at the breast of goddesses;*
The nurse who fed him made him such as to inspire awe –
Of attractive figure, with sparkling eyes,
In growth a man while still a child in age.
He looked on him, Ea, his father who begot him,
90. *He rejoiced and was glad, his heart filled with joy.*
Double he made him, twofold divinity imparted to him.
Exceeding tall he was, rising much above them.
But too intricate are his two parts for man to understand;
They are not suited for thinking on, too difficult to contemplate.
95. *He had two pairs of eyes and two pairs of ears;*
When he opened his lips, they breathed out fire.
Large were his two pairs of ears, that he might hear well,
And he contemplated everything with the same number of eyes.
A giant in stature, surpassing all the gods,
100. *A giant in growth, with mighty limbs!*

. . . .

130. *They declare war, rage and bluster,*
They flock together to prepare for the fight.
Then Mother Hubur, who cast every mould of life,
Unleashed the irresistible weapon, bore monster serpents;
Sharp was their tooth and pitiless their fang,
135. *With poison instead of blood she filled their bodies.*
Next, snarling sea-dragons she clothed with terror,
Charged them with aura rays, made them like gods:
'All who shall look thereon they shall dismay!
With bodies reared, ne'er turned shall be their breast!'
140. *She formed the sea-serpent, the dragon and the monster,*
The lion, the mad dog, and the scorpion-giant,
The driving storm, merman, and dragon-fish,
Bearers of weapons unsparing, fearless in battle.
145. *So powerful were her decrees they were unopposable,*
As thus eleven species did she bring forth;
And now from the gods, her sons, who formed [her army],
[As a twelfth] she exalted Kingu, made him chief among them.
To march in the van of the host and to captain the army,
To raise the weapon signalling 'Assault' and launch the attack,
150. *The high command during battle,*
She entrusted to his command, seating him in council:
'I have cast you a spell, made you all-great in the gods' assembly,
The sceptres of all the gods given into your hand.
Yea, supremely great shall you be, you my only husband!
155. *And greater your titles than those of all the Anunakki.'*
She gave him the Tablets of Fate, fastened them on his breast:
'Your command shall be unchangeable, your word shall be fulfilled!'

220. This alabaster relief, 15¼ in. high, comes from Nineveh, and is now in the Berlin Museum. It gives a lively picture of activities in an Assyrian army camp. On the left we see a section through a senior officer's tent, for whom a servant is making up a bed. On the right is a tent in which a meal is being prepared; a servant is busy skinning a sheep. The wall along the top suggests a town in a state of siege. The camels seem to indicate that the whole relief represents a scene from Ashurbanipal's campaigns against the Elamites. Observe the tapered jugs, which are in use in Iraq to this day. The sediment from impure water collects in the cone-shaped bottom. 221. A cavalryman and a foot-soldier of the time of Ashurbanipal. 222. Detail of Pl. 228, second panel, right. Two horses are led by their bridle by a groom. Another example of realistic animal portrayal by the Assyrian artists. This and the preceding relief are in the Louvre.

223. Relief from Ashurbanipal's palace at Nineveh. It is 2 ft. 7 in. high and made of alabaster, and is now in the British Museum. It represents a hunt for wild asses and illustrates Job 39 : 5 ff. Two servants are holding a wild ass captive with a rope, while two asses gallop below. **224.** Ashurbanipal on a lion hunt. After scenes of war, these hunting scenes were the sculptors' favourite themes. Other reliefs, and also a letter found in the royal archives at Mari, show that the lions were captured in advance and kept in cages until it pleased the king to go hunting. The sculptors tried unceasingly to express the ferocity of the lions, the terror of the horses, and the intrepidity of the king. **225.** The degree of artistry sometimes attained in this process is shown by this detail of a relief representing a lion pierced by three arrows. This splendid study also forms part of the mural decoration at Ashurbanipal's palace.

From Nebuchadnezzar
to the Fall of Babylon

231

After the recapture of rebellious Babylon, however, Ashurbanipal restored a semblance of independence to the ancient metropolis. A certain Kandalanu is mentioned after Shamash-shum-ukin in the Babylonian king list, and contracts have been found which are dated by his name and reign. He managed to hold his own until his death in 626 B.C.; but then the Chaldaeans surged up from the south and assumed power in Mesopotamia in conditions of great confusion. Immediately after Kandalanu's death Nabopolassar occupied the city of Babylon. Little is known about this new ruler. He called himself 'son of a nobody', but it is not certain that he meant he was of low birth; more probably it was his way of declaring himself the servant of his god. His name, which was actually Nabu-apal-usur, is pure Babylonian, and it is striking that Nabu or Nebo, who was worshipped in Borsippa, should be so prominent here as apparently to take the place of Marduk. Nabopolassar was not so much an active general as a political opportunist who took advantage of the situation created by the fall of the Assyrian empire. A letter shows that during the destruction of Nineveh he and his troops were no farther away than Bagdadu, which was probably the site of modern Baghdad. From that time onwards the centre of power in Mesopotamia was transferred to the south. So far as the outside world was concerned the only essential change was that the Babylonians took over the traditions and claims of the Assyrians.

In Egypt the new dangers that threatened from Mesopotamia were recognised. The Pharaoh Neco II marched against the truncated Assyrian state ruled over by Ashur-uballit, attacking Judah on his way there. According to the testimony of 2 Kings 23 : 29 and 2 Kings 35 : 20-27, Josiah tried by means of an encircling movement to check the Egyptian army near the pass of Megiddo and was mortally wounded in the engagement. His son Jehoahaz attempted to pursue the anti-Egyptian policy of his father, but he was deposed by the Pharaoh and led off as a prisoner to Egypt. His brother Jehoiakim then reigned in Jerusalem until his death in 597 B.C.

After some initial successes the Egyptian army was overwhelmingly defeated by Nabopolassar's son Nebuchadnezzar (actually Nabu-kudurri-usur) at Carchemish on the Euphrates in 605 B.C. During the pursuit of the fleeing Egyptians news of his father's death reached Nebuchadnezzar at Pelusium. Within a fortnight he had completed the journey from the Egyptian border to Babylon where he assumed power without appreciable opposition. After the demarcation of his frontier with Cyaxares of Media, Nebuchadnezzar began his series of campaigns, some of which were to take him to Palestine. Babylonian sources are very reserved on this subject. Nebuchadnezzar, like his father, certainly mentions the erection of buildings, and the form that these took suggests great piety. It is only from the accounts in 2 Kings 24-5 and Jeremiah that we know how he captured Jerusalem in 597 B.C. and again in 586 B.C., and how he destroyed the Temple and led off the mighty of the land, including Jehoiachin the king and Ezekiel the prophet, into exile.

232

231. On the road from Baghdad, several miles before Hilla, stands the signpost to the excavated area of Babylon. In the background runs the Baghdad-Basra railway line, part of it along a dike constructed by Nebuchadnezzar II. **232.** One of the many lions that adorned the processional street in Nebuchadnezzar's city. It is estimated that there were originally 120 such lions along the walls. The background was blue; the mane, shoulders, and tail were yellow, as was the tongue; the back and paws were white. Height about 3 ft. 3¼ in.

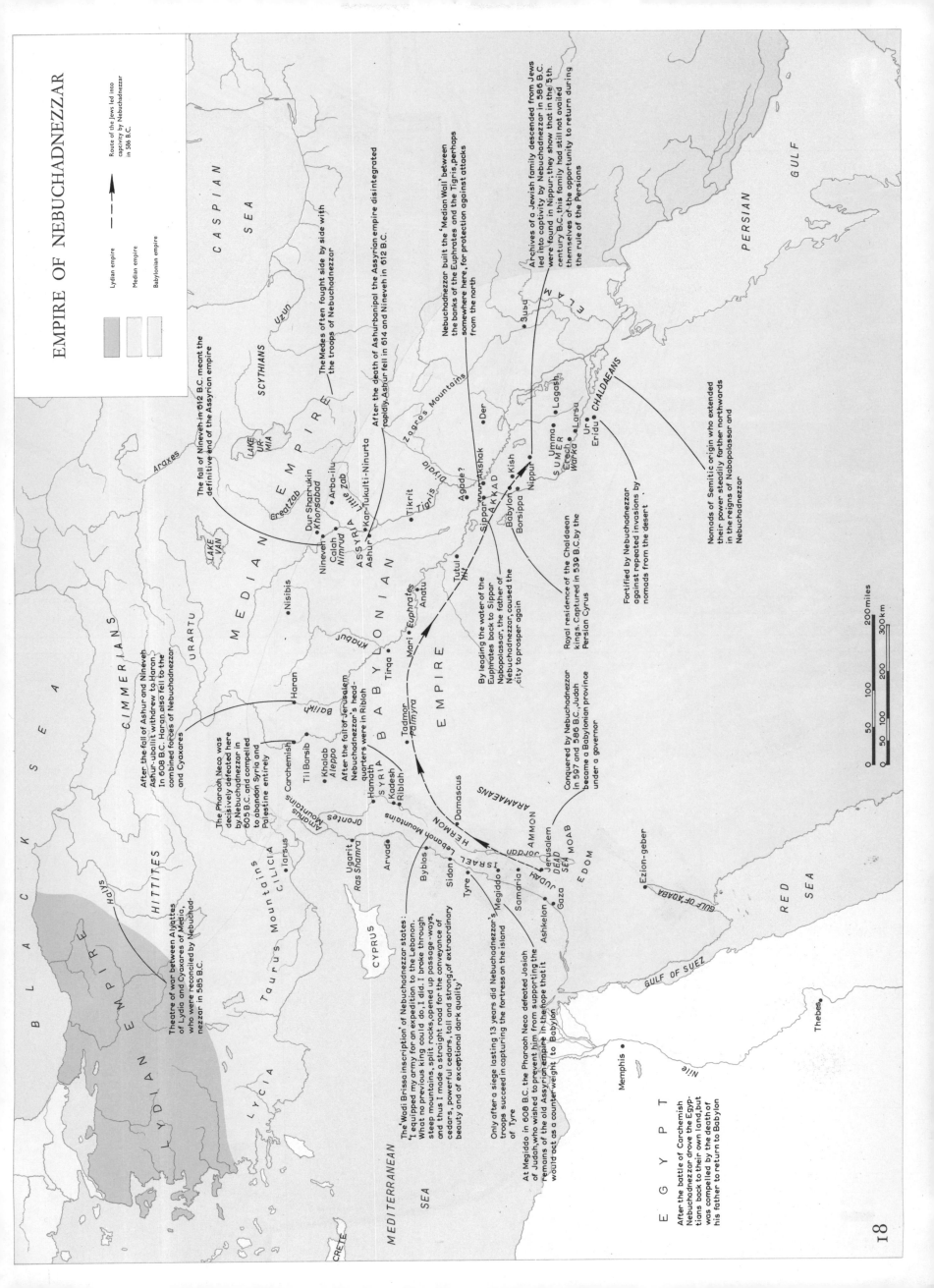

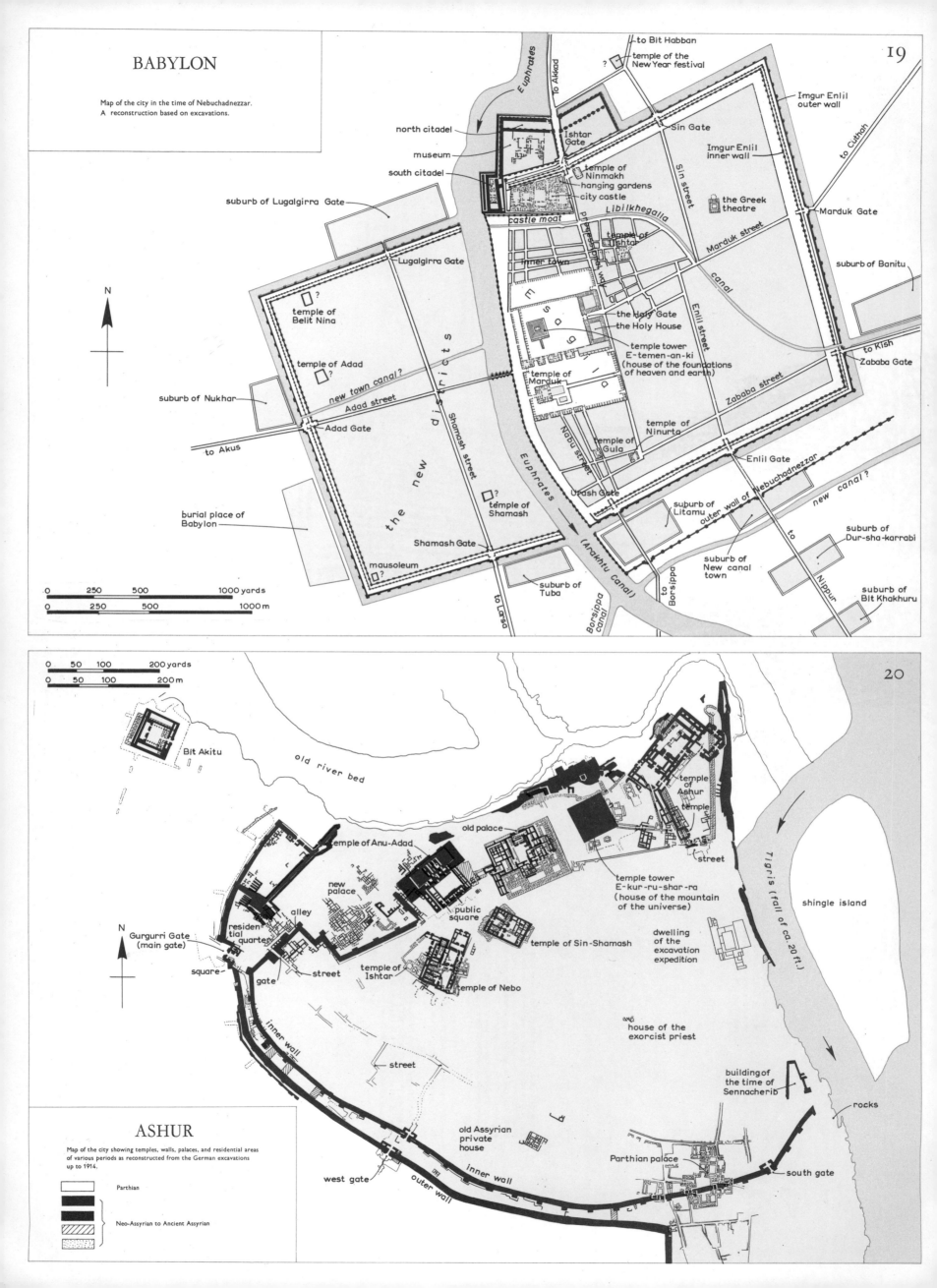

19

BABYLON

Map of the city in the time of Nebuchadnezzar.
A reconstruction based on excavations.

to Bit Habban

temple of the
New Year festival

Imgur Enlil
outer wall

to Cuthah

north citadel

Ishtar
Gate

Sin Gate

Imgur Enlil
inner wall

museum

south citadel

temple of
Ninmakh

hanging gardens

city castle

the Greek
theatre

Marduk Gate

suburb of Lugalgirra Gate

castle moat

Libilkhegalla

temple of
Ishtar

Marduk street

suburb of Banitu

Lugalgirra Gate

inner town

Esagila

Sin street

temple of
Belit Nina

the Holy Gate

the Holy House

Enlil street

temple tower
E-temen-an-ki
(house of the foundations
of heaven and earth)

to Kish

Zababa Gate

temple of Adad

temple of
Marduk

suburb of Nukhar

the new districts

new town canal?

Shamash street

Adad street

Adad Gate

temple of
Gula

temple of
Ninurta

Zababa street

to Akus

Nabu street

Euphrates

Upash Gate

Enlil Gate

outer wall of Nebuchadnezzar

new canal?

to Borsippa

suburb of
Litamu

to Nippur

suburb of
Dur-sha-karrabi

burial place of
Babylon

temple of
Shamash

suburb of
New canal
town

suburb of Bit Khakhuru

Shamash Gate

mausoleum

(Arakhtu canal)

Borsippa canal

suburb of
Tuba

to Larsa

to Akkad

Euphrates

N

| 0 | 250 | 500 | 1000 yards |
| 0 | 250 | 500 | 1000 m |

| 0 | 50 | 100 | 200 yards |
| 0 | 50 | 100 | 200 m |

Bit Akitu

old river bed

temple
of
Ashur

temple of Anu-Adad

old palace

temple

new palace

temple tower
E-kur-ru-shar-ra
(house of the mountain
of the universe)

Tigris (fall of ca. 20 ft.)

shingle island

alley

public
square

Gurgurri Gate
(main gate)

residential quarter

temple of Sin-Shamash

dwelling
of the
excavation
expedition

square

gate

street

temple of
Ishtar

temple of Nebo

house of the
exorcist priest

inner wall

street

building of
the time of
Sennacherib

rocks

ASHUR

Map of the city showing temples, walls, palaces, and residential areas
of various periods as reconstructed from the German excavations
up to 1914.

old Assyrian
private
house

Parthian palace

south gate

west gate

outer wall

inner wall

Parthian

Neo-Assyrian to Ancient Assyrian

N

233
234
235
236

237

233. View of the centre of Babylon as excavated under the leadership of Koldewey and afterwards preserved. **234, 236.** The processional street as it stretched from the Ishtar Gate to the centre of the town. The walls built in the reign of Nebuchadnezzar II still rise to a considerable height. Beneath the level of the street lies a much older Babylon which rising ground-water has rendered inaccessible. **235.** The red figures of dragons and wild bulls stood out sharply against the glazed blue walls. The photograph shows the method followed: special bricks were baked in moulds and cemented together with bitumen. **237.** Of the great Tower of Babel, which was called Etemenanki, little remains except a small island surrounded by a moat. The tower was demolished on the order of Alexander the Great, and the bricks were again used by Seleucus I for the construction of an amphitheatre, a fact proved during a test dig in the 1956-7 season.

131

238

239

238. Clay cylinder foundation inscription of Nebuchadnezzar II. **239.** Inscribed hard green stone, used as a weight. It amounted to a mina (60 shekels), the equivalent of about a kilogram in the time of Nebuchadnezzar II. Height $3\frac{3}{4}$ in. According to the inscription the weight was an accurate copy of a weight belonging to the king and based on Shulgi's standard. It was the property of Marduk-shar-ilani. Origin unknown, now in the British Museum. **240.** Reconstruction of part of Babylon at the time of Nebuchadnezzar. **241.** The outside of the Ishtar Gate at Babylon, reconstructed in the Staatliche Museen, Berlin. The walls were glazed blue, and the reliefs of dragons and bulls red, which later turned ochre owing to oxidation. 13 rows of these animals must originally have comprised 575 figures. **242.** The ground in the vicinity of Babylon is now saline, being in fact sometimes covered with a glittering layer of salt. **243.** The mound of ruins which conceals Nebuchadnezzar II's summer palace.

NEBUCHADNEZZAR AND HIS SUCCESSORS

Return from this exile proved possible, however. And whereas the Assyrians had not even allowed the Israelites to hand on to their children the remembrance of their misery, Nebuchadnezzar's prisoners were able not only to observe their customs in the land by the Chebar, but also to pass on their sorrow and nostalgia to our time in a song such as Psalm 137. The organised abduction of the families by a caravan route nine hundred and fifty miles long must have been an orderly affair, and the consequent tragedy for Nebuchadnezzar was that his comparatively humane behaviour allowed the creation of a literature which represents him as the archetype of the tyrant.

His campaigns of conquest also led him to the Lebanon, where he caused reliefs and an inscription to be set up at Wadi Brissa not far from the Nahr el-Kelb. One relief shows him fighting a lion, the other felling a tree. The inscription makes mention of his care for the people and avows that he was able to complete his task only with the aid of Nabu and Marduk. In reading these texts we may wonder to what extent the scribes were bound by the norms of idealised biography and how much is revealed of the true personality of the king. It was the successful excavations of German archaeologists about the beginning of this century that first identified Nebuchadnezzar as the builder of the great and magnificent Babylon to which Daniel alludes. The discovery of the city brought into relief Nebuchadnezzar's exclamation: 'Is not this great Babylon, that I have built?' (Dan. 4 : 30). The visitor to the partially excavated mound at Hilla will, if he combines imagination with knowledge, see a colourful city emerge, with rose-coloured palaces, white temples, yellow city walls, and a processional street, the blue glazed bricks of which are adorned with red dragons, lions, and wild bulls (see Pls. 232-6 and 241).

Not far from the temple precincts Nebuchadnezzar built an artificial terraced hill, out of love, it is said, for his wife who came from the mountain country and found it hard to get used to the plains of Mesopotamia. Irrigated pleasure gardens and groves were laid out along the terraces. The irrigation waters as they evaporated absorbed heat from the caves hollowed out under the terraces, so that the caves could be used as cold stores. The raw materials for the royal meals

were kept here and issued upon presentation of receipts. The latter are preserved in Berlin and some of them have been identified. It is astonishing to find the name Ia-u-kin or Ia-ku-u-ki-nu cropping up in them. This almost certainly refers to Jehoiachin, who was taken into captivity at the age of eighteen with his family, lived under a kind of house arrest for thirty-seven years, and was then freed by Nebuchadnezzar's successor, Evil-merodach (2 Kg. 25 : 27).

After Nebuchadnezzar's death the Neo-Babylonian empire hastened to its eclipse. Two years later, at the instigation of the priesthood, Evil-merodach (in Babylonian Awil-Marduk) was driven from the throne. His successor, Neriglissar (in Babylonian Nergal-shar-usur), who played an influential part in the capture of Jerusalem (Jer. 39 : 3 and 13), places much stress in his inscriptions on the fact that he was elected by Marduk and Nabu. His son, Labashi-Marduk, was recognised as king only for the months of May and June 556, and then not even by the entire empire. The last king was Nabonidus, whose son Belshazzar acted as his deputy on the throne of Babylon for a time (Dan. 5). A satirical poem which has survived accuses Nabonidus of having used objectionable means to replace the worship of Marduk and Nabu by that of the moon god Sin. It was probably on account of the resultant conflict with the priests in Babylon that he moved his residence to Tema in the Arabian steppe.

This was the situation when Cyrus, the king of the Persians, entered the scene of world history. He had little difficulty, thanks mainly to treachery by Gubaru (written Gobryas in Greek sources), in conquering Babylon in 539 B.C. The city fell without a blow being struck and on this occasion was not destroyed. The destruction and pillage of the city did not take place until 485 B.C., under Xerxes. But 539 B.C. is the year of the fall of Babylon and of the decline of Mesopotamian civilisation. Although the city remained standing for some time to come and the priesthood continued to worship Marduk and Nabu on the same scale as before, an entirely new era had dawned, in which there was soon to be no room left for the priests of Babylon. Their descendants roamed the countries round the Mediterranean where they had a considerable reputations as astrologers but proved poor ambassadors of a civilisation which could boast an interrupted tradition over two thousand years.

The Religion of the Babylonians

THE WORLD OF THE GODS

The religion of the Mesopotamians has been frequently referred to – and stressed – in these pages and illustrated by Plates. This is only as it should be, for the ancient world was, generally speaking, steeped in religion. Culture and science, games, festivities, in fact all human activity on earth, derived their themes from the worship of a superhuman but real being. This supermundane and divine world, on which man knew he depended, has been represented in an infinite variety of ways. That is not surprising; for a long distance in time separates the oldest primitive figurines of the goddess of fertility and the period which saw the composition of hymns and epics so beautiful in form and deep in content that they are still capable of moving us today. Yet even the oldest and almost shapeless figurines give expression to pure religious feelings which animate created man when he knows he is in the sacred presence. Later on there is occasionally a danger that religion will be submerged beneath a mass of aesthetic forms and systematic theology. Then it is aesthetic and intellectual standards which prevail, and art and theology are liberated at the cost of religion.

The excavations at Tell Brak, as we have already related, uncovered figurines with large eyes, a design which is practically unknown anywhere else. The figure of what appears a man is surmounted not by a head but by a pair of large eyes staring at us.

There is not a single text to provide a commentary on the worship that led to the erection of the 'Eye Temple'. The terracotta statuettes were found in hundreds, and they are all thought to date from the early Jemdet Nasr period, about 3000 B.C. They must have stressed one particular aspect of the gods – their all-seeingness as opposed to the circumscribed view of man. For a comparable reason Marduk was sometimes shown at a later period with abnormally large ears – to hear the prayers and hymns of his worshippers. It is only by chance that we know the Tell Brak figurines; yet even if they present a spectacular find, they are only one of innumerable ways in which men sought to express their religious beliefs.

The diversity of form that expression of belief assumed can be partly explained by the extensive area that Mesopotamia covered, the differences in climate and landscape between the rough mountain country in the north and the river plain in the south. Nor should we forget that we are able to survey a period of over four thousand years. During that time powerful movements of populations have taken place. The result of these was not that newcomers cast aside the culture and religion they found among the conquered nations. There was adaptation: widely different elements were merged together but if possible nothing was discarded. Thus the encounter of the city culture of the Sumerians and the nomadic conception of the world of the invading Semites led to a magnificent synthesis. This will be more than a little surprising if we realise that 'encounter' is too euphemistic a term for a succession of military campaigns, sieges, and destructions of cities. That the civilisation of the conquered was higher than that of the new overlords and that it was recognised as such – that is the explanation of this astounding phenomenon.

When the religion of Marduk gained supremacy in Babylon about

1700 B.C., it meant the provisional end of a period during which the Akkadians and the Amorites, though they had supplanted the Sumerians, had also consciously been taking over their culture and their religious conceptions. The Sumerians were their spiritual ancestors and were acknowledged as such. During the aftermath of the empire of Sumer and Akkad a symbiosis had existed and led to a syncretism whose stages of development, despite a wealth of information, can no longer be retraced.

The Sumerian believed that the creation had come about from the union of sky gods and goddesses of fertility. The world and everything in it was thought to be composed of the elements air, earth, and water. The purpose of this creation was mankind, who assumed such various forms as shepherd, farmer, or craftsman, each with his particular tools which he had received from the gods. Sumerian literature has left us disputations between the various callings. One of these in particular is well known because it seems to prefigure the antithesis between Cain the farmer and Abel the shepherd. This dispute is between Dumuzi, the shepherd god, and Enkimdu, the farmer god. There are certainly great differences between the Bible story as related in Genesis 4 and the Sumerian disputation, in which the shepherd is rejected by the goddess Inanna, while the farmer appears to be a peace-loving man. Nor does the dispute end in murder: the shepherd merely feels compelled to assert his good qualities. In disputations of this kind, which have their parallels in conversations between animals and tools, the Sumerians' fancy was given a certain scope, as it was in the liturgical texts of lamentation for Tammuz-Dumuzi and in a temple-building hymn such as that of Gudea, with their carefully managed allusions to mythological conceptions. Tammuz had been betrayed by the sky goddess Inanna and taken off by demons to the Underworld where he reigned like a king and held judgment on the dead. He was addressed from earth in moving lamentations. But he was identified with Dumuzi, 'the true son', who represented the young of the flock and the new harvest and with whom the hope of a regularly rejuvenated nature was associated. This double idea of Tammuz, in which both despair and hope are represented, should put us on our guard against considering the views of the Sumerians as too static.

Yet it was not a dynamism inherent in the Sumerian religion that made the erection of an elaborate polytheistic system necessary. The main driving force was the fact that the incoming Semites were of a particular and different religious stamp. Although they had developed a city culture of some importance in the mountainous north and on the banks of the Khabur and Balikh, they were much more influenced in the matter of religion by the semi-nomads and sons of the desert, for whom the deity and the world of the gods are rather the projection of the sheikh, with his personal power, and his immediate family. The meeting of the religion of the steppes with that of the Sumerian city led to a multiplication of the number of gods and their altars, to complicated genealogies, which sometimes reflect the struggle for power between cities and peoples. Conservatism and tolerance were the formative forces in these ancient theologies.

To illustrate this point let us return to Marduk's elevation to head of the Babylonian pantheon in the age of Hammurabi. To enable this

244. This relief carved in reddish stone was found in Til Barsib and represents the goddess Ishtar standing on a lion with reins in her hand, and her attribute, a star, above her crown. Period 8th century B.C. Height 4 ft. The subject has been identified from an inscription.

245-9. Impressions of seals of the Sumerian period. **245.** 23rd century B.C. **246.** With an image of the sun-god. **247.** 28th century B.C., with a mythological scene. **248.** 25th century B.C., showing a deity seated in a boat. **249.** 28th century B.C., showing a mythological scene. **250.** Seal of the Akkadian period, representing the god Shamash climbing a mountain. **251.** Seal of the period of the Middle Assyrian Empire. **252.** Seal of the 9th-8th century B.C. On the left a hero in combat with an ostrich which is trying to peck him. On the right a sacred tree flanked by two fish-men. **253.** Mask, probably of a priestess, found at Erech, one of the most impressive relics of the Jemdet Nasr period. **254.** Figurine of a priest found at Khafaje. **255.** Gypsum figurine, 8 in. high, found at Mari. The bearded man with his sacrificial animal appears to be a primitive form of the representation of the Good Shepherd.

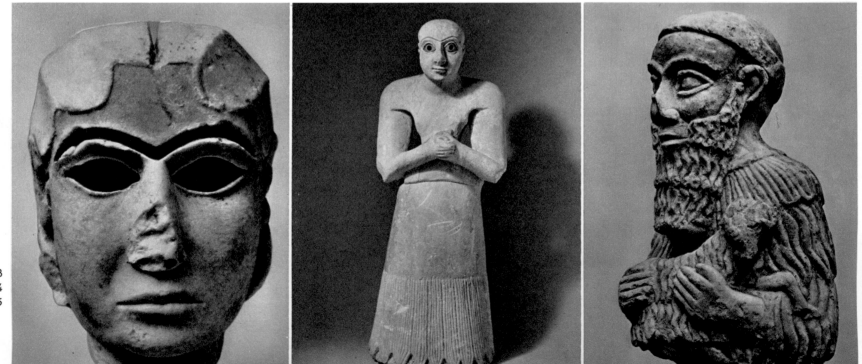

2**!6.** Example of a *kudurru*, originally a boundary stone but later a deed of ownership of immovable property. They are important for the history of religion in Mesopotamia because of the gods and symbols they may show. This one was found at Susa, is 19¾ in. high, and dates from the time of Nazi-Maruttash (1312-1287). **257.** This *kudurru* also was found at Susa. Height 26¾ in. The inscription at the back speaks of a present to Marduk-apal-iddin (12th century B.C.). The stone shows 24 symbols in five rows; the most striking of these is the serpent near the base. **258.** *Kudurru* from the time of Nebuchadnezzar I (12th century), 25 in. high, with 20 symbols arranged in 6 rows. **259.** *Kudurru* of Meli-Shipak. Beneath the symbols of Ishtar, Sin, and Shamash the goddess Nanna is shown receiving the king and his daughter; height 35½ in. **260.** Detail of Pl. **257.** In the third row from the top we note: sceptres in the form of winged dragons, an eagle, a bird, and a lion.

to be done Marduk had first to be identified with the most important deity known to the Sumerians, Enlil. He was the son of the sky god Anu and was worshipped in Nippur. The Marduk cult had therefore to be shifted from Nippur to Babylon. But he was also proclaimed son of Ea, the god of the ocean and wisdom (the Sumerian Enki), who was venerated in Eridu. Such interventions, which appeared extremely revolutionary to contemporaries, had to be accounted for by the adaptation of existing myths. In this the origins of the gods, their mutual strife and finally their common accord with recognition of each other's rights were important considerations. This material was assimilated and enacted in the rites of the religious drama. The striking thing about the innovation is that it was not accompanied by iconoclasm or the destruction of temples. Such acts were generally felt to be sacrilege, to be followed by divine revenge, such as that which struck Sennacherib for his attempts by force to replace the Babylonian worship of Marduk by an Ashur cult.

Marduk's elevation to be head of the pantheon should not be seen as a symptom of a monotheistic trend. Less important deities could be represented as aspects of the main god or even as parts of his body, but the conception of the divine world remained polytheistic. In fact, monotheism and polytheism are imperfect words with which to describe the situation that existed; but it is perfectly obvious that Israel's profession of faith in one God as found in Deuteronomy 6 : 4 would have evoked no response in the religion of Babylon.

The collection of names of gods and the establishment of their genealogical connections therefore constituted one of the main activities of theologians in Mesopotamia. The archives of the Ishtar temple at Erech were found to contain a catalogue of gods listing some 250 names in Sumerian with their equivalents in Akkadian. Unfortunately, only fragments of this text have survived. A list from Shuruppak dating back to the early dynastic period originally contained about 500 names of gods arranged in 20 columns; another from the nineteenth century B.C. lists 473 names and was probably composed by the priests of the Ea temple at Eridu. On this list, which goes back to before the reformation of Hammurabi, Marduk still occupies an inferior position as No. 104. But in his epilogue and prologue Hammurabi names the twelve chief gods of his empire and elevates Marduk to the first position over their heads. Later classifications divide the 600 gods into two categories, those of the sky (the Igigi) and those of the ocean (the Anunnaki). The reformation of Hammurabi, though drastic, did not strip the old lists of their 'canonical' appearance, even when, like the Erech list, they accorded a subordinate place to Marduk or failed to mention a god like Ashur, who later became extremely important.

The three great cosmic gods were originally Anu, Enlil, and Ea, who respectively ruled the sky, the earth, and the ocean. They gradually lost their supremacy, and this process is reflected in the myth. In the Creation epic Anu transfers his leadership to the sun-child Marduk. In Erech he is ousted by Ishtar, who was originally represented as his handmaiden. Not until the time of the Seleucids is he rehabilitated to some extent by his identification with Zeus and the identification of his wife Antum with Hera. As we have already seen, Enlil had to make way for Marduk. He and his wife Nin-lil were retained in the rôle of deities of the storm-winds; in other words, their function now became a purely negative one. Ea was later given a double part to play, for while remaining the god of wisdom, of the art of exorcism and of medicine, he also became the deceiver who delivered mankind, in the person of Adapa, to mortality.

Great significance still attached to the astral gods: Sin (Sumerian Nanna), who represented the moon; Shamash (Sumerian Utu or Babbar, 'the resplendent'), the sun god; and Ishtar (who corresponds to the Ashtoreth of the Bible or the Phoenician Astarte), the goddess of the morning and evening star. The moon god Sin was worshipped in famous temples in Ur and Haran. He was particularly the god of the nomads, who lighted their path through the steppe on their cold nocturnal wanderings. There was a surprising revival of his cult in Babylon's last years under Nabonidus. He was sometimes represented

as old and bearded, and in Ur he appeared also as a bull with a blue beard.

The sun god Shamash daily follows his golden path across the sky, uncovering injustice even in the darkest and remotest corners. He is the protector of the oppressed, and that is why a hymn composed in his honour reminds us in its choice of words and line of thought of Psalms from the Old Testament which sing of the God of Israel as the protector of the poor, the widow, and the orphan. The following is a fragment from such a hymn.

1. [Who] descends into the depths except you?
   You bring to judgment the good and the wicked.
   [Over all the innocent who lie sleepless]
   You pour [refreshment and give them sleep].
5. You hold in check the evildoer, who does not [rest even] at night.
   You sweep away [the violent] who takes the law into his own hands,
   By the righteous judgment, O Shamash, which you pronounce.
   Clear is your utterance, [subject to] no doubt or change.
   . . . .
   He who on unrighteous plea [is taken into custody],
   The prisoner who [languishes] in the house [of his creditor],
   Whose god was [angered against him without cause],
20. [Him you free], as soon as you see this.
    You stand by the [innocent];
    You investigate the offence with which he is charged [and acquit him].
    You bring him [back to his family];
    Out of the land from which there is no return [you rescue him].
25. [You appease] the angry goddesses [and gods].
    You are exalted, [and do not leave him in the lurch].
    . . . .
35. Your sword reaches him, and none escapes it.
    At his trial his father will not stand by him;
    To the verdict of the judge even his brothers will make no answer.
    As by a brass trap he is caught unawares.
    You strike off the horn of him who plans iniquity;
40. The ground crumbles beneath him who practises deceit.
    You cast the unjust judge into chains;
    You inflict punishment on him who allows himself to be bribed to pervert justice.
    He who does not allow himself to be bribed [but] takes the part the weak,
    Is pleasing to Shamash and shall live long.

The external similarity of such hymns to Psalms from the Bible may suggest a literary dependence. At a time when literature was closely bound to traditional forms, the themes circulated in all the regions of the Near East and kept recurring like familiar formulae in ever-changing contexts. Each text must nevertheless be interpreted according to the centre from which it emanated, and in that respect there was a vast difference between Israel and Babylonia. Yet just as the God of Israel, the protector of the rights of the poor and preserver of social equilibrium, is above all a lawgiver, so the worship of Shamash in Larsa and Sippar has juridical as well as moral aspects.

The cult of Ishtar is of quite a different nature. She is the Sumerian Inanna, the daughter of the moon god, who was elevated by Anu to be queen of the sky and was venerated in Erech in the temple Eanna ('house of the heavens'). The fact that she became more particularly the goddess of fertility and, as mother-goddess, also the patroness of sexual love meant that her cult sometimes degenerated into offensive sensuality associated with the temple prostitution which brought such evil repute to Babylon by way of the one-sided and probably also incorrect account of Herodotus (History, i, 199). That there was a conflict between the worship of Shamash and that of Ishtar can be seen from certain trends in the Gilgamesh epic, where the course of the hero's purification leads him away from Ishtar to Shamash. Ishtar was venerated by the Assyrians in Ashur, Nineveh, and Arba-ilu. The famous Ishtar Gate formed the entrance to the processional street in Babylon (see Pl. 241).

Of the other gods who manifested themselves in natural phenomena the following may be regarded as the most important. Ninurta was a Sumerian god of life in nature, who as the son of Enlil was particularly worshipped at Nippur. For the Assyrians he was the god of war and the hunt, and it is possibly the latter aspect that is hinted at in the reference to Nimrod in Genesis 10 : 8. His wife was Gula, the great healer. Adad, who replaced the Sumerian Ishkur, is the same as the Palestinian Hadad and was also called Ramman. He was the god who sent thunder, beneficent rain, and storms. Gibil was the god who unleashed the mysterious steppe fires and struck light. Nusku, Sin's son, who was venerated in Haran, was also a god of light.

Although this list is anything but complete, only three more gods will be discussed: Nabu, Ashur, and Marduk. Nabu is called Nebo in the Old Testament (Isa. 46 : 1); he was the herald and scribe of the gods and was worshipped in the Ezida temple in Borsippa. He was the patron of scribes and astrologers, and also of trade and commerce. At one time attempts were made to place him at the head of the hierarchy of the gods. A similar attempt was made by the Assyrians on behalf of their national god Ashur, whose name is really the same as that of their chief city and their country. In Ashur he was venerated in the temple E-kur-ru-ki-shar-ra ('house of the mountain of the universe'). His identification with Anu's father Anshar raised him to a position above all other gods in the hierarchy, including Marduk. It was probably Sennacherib who promoted this nationalistic religious development, but he was unsuccessful. Yet a fragment of a hymn by Ashurbanipal to Anshar is known in which the national god of Assyria is addressed by this name. Nevertheless, the majesty of Marduk (Sumerian 'Amar-utu', 'sun-calf'), the Babylonian god of the spring sun, to whom the E-temen-an-ki ziggurat (see Pl. 237) in the Esagila temple area was dedicated, remained intact. Originally only the city god of Babylon, with a limited sphere of authority, he became from the time of Hammurabi onwards the undisputed head of the pantheon and his city the pre-eminent place of pilgrimage. His name is given as Merodach in Jeremiah 50 : 2, a form which also occurs in the Old Testament as Merodach-baladan (Isa. 39 : 1). Usually, however, he is referred to as Bel (*belu*, 'lord') (Isa. 46 : 1, Jer. 50 : 2, 51 : 44), and an addition to the Book of Daniel, the oldest detective story in the world, tells how the priests of Bel-Marduk were unmasked by the wise Daniel. To the decipherment of cuneiform, however, we owe another light on the devotion that characterised the cult of Marduk, for the pious author of the hymn, 'I will praise the lord of wisdom', already referred to, makes this prayer.

Who commanded that he should behold his divinity?
To whose heart did it occur to let him go free?
Who except Marduk called him from death to life?
What goddess except Sarpanitum bestowed life upon him?
Marduk can recall from the grave to life,
Sarpanitum takes thought to rescue from destruction.
So far as the earth lies and the sky extends,
The sun shines and fire burns,
Water flows and wind blows,
Where created beings exist, whom Aruru has moulded from clay
In a twinkling, the producer of life –
All things which draw breath glorify Marduk!

This is a fragment of a hymn composed by a devout man who in time of suffering retained his undoubting trust in Marduk and upon deliverance called upon his fellow-creatures to praise Marduk, the lord of wisdom, and his wife Sarpanitum for their mercy. And once again the style reminds us of the Psalms of the Old Testament.

The gods were venerated in temples, of which there were dozens in any considerable city. Ashur possessed thirty-four such shrines, while Babylon boasted fifty-three important temples in addition to chapels and street altars. They varied greatly in design and size, but they were usually rectangular and sometimes, as at Khafaje, oval. In their arrangement into main buildings and secondary buildings with preliminary courtyards and rooms for the priests and stores, they displayed a cosmic symbolism not always easy to comprehend. The temple performed the important function of economic centre or bank, where documents, contracts, and valuables were in safe keeping; it was a powerful institution possessing estates, and therefore had great vested interests in the national economy. The temple was also the centre of learning, and as such was in the hands of the priests.

Although there was originally a powerful bond between the temple and the state – if only because the *ensi* acted as priest-king in the same way as the high priest in Jerusalem after the captivity – a separation of temple and palace slowly took place, which was completed by the time of Hammurabi. There were thirty classes of priests. A most important man in Babylon was the *urigallu*, or what we might call high priest. The priestesses, of whom twenty classes are known, were headed by the *entu* or bride of the gods. The priest who was concerned with

Left: Marduk with a crown of feathers, sword, staff, and ring, and with a dragon at his feet; below, the waters of Apsu, the primeval ocean. Top centre: sacrificial rite copied from an obelisk from Nineveh. Lower centre: procession in which Assyrians bear images of gods; after a relief from Nimrud. Right: the storm god Adad with three forkedlightning in his right hand and in his left reins attached to fabulous animals.

261. Musicians performing in a procession. Ivory, $25\frac{1}{4}$ in. high. Found at Nimrud. **262.** Terracotta tablet with image of the 'divine mother'. It is Old Babylonian in design but difficult to date to a particular period. **263.** Socle of an altar, on which Tukulti-Ninurta I (13th century B.C.) is shown both standing and kneeling. **264, 266.** Fragments of a clay tablet containing part of the text of the Adapa myth. **265.** Tablet containing part of the Babylonian account of the Flood, dating from the middle of the 7th century B.C. **267.** This basalt stele was found at Susa. It is similar in subject to the scene on the Code of Hammurabi and is assigned to about the same period. The worshipper stands with his arms folded facing his god. **268.** An Assyrian in prayer before the image of a god, perhaps Shamash. The locust above the worshipper is especially remarkable.

261
262

263
264

265
266

267

268

269. In many places in Mesopotamia the eroded remains of ziggurats still project above the plain. A number of examples are shown on this page. This illustration is of the ziggurat of Ashur. 270. This ziggurat is a good example of a fascinatingly solitary tower rising from a wide expanse of landscape. 271. The vast excavation area at Erech is also dominated by the ziggurat. This tower on the sacred area of Eanna was originally topped by a white temple. 272. The malwiyah of Samarra is a 9th century A.D. minaret which played an important part in discussions about how the Tower of Babel looked. Illustrations on old cylinder seals suggest that this Muslim building may have been inspired by Assyrian and Babylonian versions of the ziggurat. 273. The oblong ziggurat of Ur is still in a relatively undamaged condition. 274. Stamped bricks sometimes facilitate identification of the royal builder and consequently dating.

religious rites (*sangu*) was distinguished from the exorcists and sooth-sayers. The activities in a temple must have been of an extremely varied nature, comprising not only sacrificial rites and the liturgy but also the expulsion of demons from sick people and the possessed and prophesying the future from the liver of the sacrificial animal or from oil dripped into a beaker.

THE NEW YEAR FESTIVAL

There were festivities at intervals throughout the year, and of these the most important was the Akitu festival. This was a New Year festival which was celebrated in Babylon in the spring month of Nisan and lasted twelve days. The first week was one of religious significance, a week of purification, in which the sins that had sullied the temple, the priests, and the people during the past year had to be washed away. In character the ceremonies were not unlike those described in Leviticus 16 in connection with the Day of Atonement. Although the Babylonian texts referring to the rites contain gaps and obscure passages, it is still possible to reconstruct the course of events in broad outline.

In the night preceding the Akitu festival the chief priest of Esagila had to rise and, clad in a linen garment, recite texts before the image of Marduk. The contents of the prayers were secret and might not be told to anyone. We do know, however, that he had to repeat the entire text of the Creation epic on the evening of the fourth of Nisan. This is the central religious theme of the festival. The idea that the events of Creation, when the world arose from nothingness, are relived in religion runs through the entire festival from the first to the eleventh of Nisan. At the beginning of the festival the powers of chaos are in command; in this chaos Marduk is born and given the task of combating Tiamat.

The king had an important part to play. His sceptre was taken from his hands and his crown from his head. In the hymns recited meanwhile the king is innocent or he confesses his guilt, which is also that of the people. He is a mediator between the gods and the people and atones for the sins of the community.

Between the sixth and eighth of Nisan took place the procession of the gods to the Akitu temple, in the course of which there were seven stops. The fourth stop was in the 'room of destinies' where Marduk under the name of 'king of the gods of heaven and earth' determined the fate of the coming year. It must have been an impressive sight when, Nabu being deemed to have rescued his father Marduk from the Underworld, the gigantic procession of gods and their followers moved out into the processional street, led by the king holding the hands of Marduk's statue and accompanying it to a point beyond the walls. Then they boarded ships which took them to the Bit Akitu, the festival building that every city in Mesopotamia had somewhere outside its walls. It could, as at Erech, be extremely capacious, with numerous rooms and courtyards, but it was erected to be used only once a year. In and around the Bit Akitu, in tents or huts, in the midst of wooded parks that gave refreshing shade, the festivities were continued until, on the eleventh of Nisan, the people returned by the same way they had come. This led up to the triumphal procession in honour of Marduk between the glazed blue walls and figures of animals in red that lined both sides of the processional street. Beautiful hymns were sung to mark the joyful arrival, at which the king once more grasped the hands of the divine statue. Marduk now hastened to his marriage with Sarpanitum, which was celebrated on the twelfth of Nisan. The festival was then in effect over. The gods were carried back to their temples and Marduk re-occupied his lofty throne, from which he reigned over a purified city and a renewed world. Only by delving deeply into the rites of the New Year festival and their cosmic significance is it possible to appreciate to the full the offence and alarm caused by the refusal of Nabonidus, the last king of Babylon, to take part in the procession to the Bit Akitu.

THE ZIGGURAT

We have not yet spoken of the function of the most remarkable monument for which the Mesopotamian city was famed, the tower whose top, according to Genesis 11 : 4, was to reach unto heaven. Part of the background to the story of the Tower of Babel is also provided by the temple which topped the ziggurat. From the earliest times small temples unsuitable for everyday worship were erected on elevated terraces. Ancient examples were found at Erech and Eridu. Ur-Nammu of Ur, however, turned the terrace there into a tower with a number of storeys and a steep stairway leading straight to the top. The remains of ziggurats of later date can be found from north to south over the whole length of Iraq and even in Persia (see Map 21).

The name ziggurat which was given to these towers is connected with a verb meaning 'to rise up high'. It is debatable whether the older, simple terraces can be considered as ziggurats, because they lacked the multiple storeys and the stairways which were later so characteristic. If these are regarded as essential features of the ziggurat, we must agree with Professor Lenzen that the history of the ziggurat begins with the monuments of Ur-Nammu and Shulgi, kings of the third dynasty of Ur. It is certain, nevertheless, that their awe-inspiring

Reconstructions of ziggurats based on data obtained by excavation. From left to right: Ur (ca. 2000 B.C.), Babylon (6th century B.C.) after Busink, and Babylon after Dombart. As yet little can be said with certainty about the method of access to the temple at the top.

The ziggurat of Dur Kurigalzu, built in the 14th century B.C., rises to a height of over 165 ft. from the plain, like a beacon for the traveller.

towers, the construction of which was made possible by the large number of workmen available in the growing towns, draw heavily on ancient traditions. Thus, if we wish to grasp the aim of the ziggurats, we must ask ourselves the motives that led the earliest inhabitants of Mesopotamia to build shrines on artifically elevated terraces. Were they also intended to serve as places of refuge when the rivers rose and the river plain was flooded? Or were they symbols of the world mountain that came into view when the waters fell and were separated from the land at the time of the Creation? In the course of the years many theories have been put forward to account for the temple towers, but there is an increasing tendency to stress their religious significance. The first travellers from the West in the eighteenth and nineteenth centuries, greatly impressed by the ruins rising from the face of Mesopotamia, thought of them as night quarters for priests desirous of the refreshment their altitude afforded, or as observatories for astrologers, or saw in them analogies with the Egyptian pyramids. These rationalistic explanations are contradicted by the facts; but even now that a rich store of literary information is available there is still scope for widely varying interpretations of the ziggurat's symbolism.

The names given to the various ziggurats underline their importance as contact surfaces between the earth below and the heaven inhabited by deities above. The ziggurat at Borsippa was called E-ur-me-imin-an-ki or 'the house of the seven leaders of heaven and earth' – a reference to the sun, the moon, and the five planets which determine the lot of macrocosm and microcosm alike. In Nippur, Larsa, and Sippar people spoke of E-dur-an-ki, 'the house of the link between heaven and earth'. The most famous ziggurat, that at Babylon, was called E-temen-an-ki, 'the house of the foundations of heaven and earth'. There is a reference to this name in the text on a foundation stone of Nabopolassar, which reads: 'Marduk caused me to lay its foundations in the heart of the earth and to lift its pinnacle into the sky.' A text from Nippur addresses the temple tower in these words: 'Great mountain of Enlil, whose peak reaches the sky, whose foundations are laid in the resplendent depths.' These texts might almost be quoted as so many parallels to Genesis 11 : 4 and in support of the theory that the Biblical writer correctly states the concept of the ziggurat despite the hostile tone of his story.

But in addition to its purpose of joining heaven and earth, the tower's function as a symbol of a mountain is also stressed. This has already been seen from the Nippur text quoted above and is confirmed by the name of the ziggurat dedicated to Ashur and built in the city named after him – E-kur-ru-ki-shar-ra, 'the house of the mountain of the universe'. Nevertheless, it is not clear in this connection whether the mountain was thought of mainly as an abode of the gods, as many scholars have asserted.

The raised terrace was originally intended as a pedestal for a temple. That is why Andrae distinguished between *Hochtempel* and *Tieftempel*, the latter, according to him, being the *Erscheinungstempel*, or temple in which the deity manifested himself or herself daily upon earth. This classification is disputed, but it serves a purpose. In general the ziggurat was used as a pedestal for a temple. On the top of the ziggurat at Ur, which was built at the command of Ur-Nammu, there stood a small and simple but beautiful temple of blue glazed bricks which served as the bridal chamber of Nanna and Ningal. An assertion that this was the purpose of the shrine at the top is also found in Herodotus (*History*, i, 181ff.), who saw the ruins of E-temen-an-ki at Babylon about 460 B.C.

From the time of Ur-Nammu and Shulgi onwards the ziggurats developed into buildings of huge proportions. Originally comparable with the *bamoth* or high places which the Old Testament mentions as scenes of worship, they became gigantic, stylised mountains which by their massive shapes suggest frustrated attempts to reach the sky. The writer of the Scriptures could therefore see them as symbols of an arrogant undertaking foiled by divine wrath.

The temple towers of Ur-Nammu and his successors were massive monuments constructed of bricks which often bore seal impressions

Detail of a mural from Mari: the leader of a sacrificial rite.

stating the name and titles of the royal builder. They had to have drainage systems to protect them from destruction by rain water, while layers of reeds lent them a certain resilience. Yet they deteriorated and had to be restored regularly. The perishable nature of the materials is also the reason why we know so little about the constructional details. The best preserved tower so far known is the ziggurat at Choga-Zambil near Susa, on Persian territory, which the great Iranian archaeologist Roman Ghirshman has been investigating since 1951. The tower was built in the thirteenth century B.C. in honour of Inshushinak, the chief god in the Elamite pantheon. The tower, which must originally have been about 170 feet high, had five storeys. It was topped by a small temple reached by stairs and portals. The portal on the first storey was found to be surmounted by a well-preserved arch (see Pl. 281). The most surprising event, however, was the finding in the interior of the tower of rooms partly filled with hundreds of mushroom-shaped, hollow nails made of baked, glazed clay, as well as pottery and square terracotta plates. Ghirshman thinks that these provide the solution to the mystery of the *gegunu* mentioned in cuneiform literature in connection with the ziggurat, a word that can mean both 'burial vault' and 'shrine'. That is questionable; but at any rate we can look forward to some new light being shed on the riddle of the ziggurat by the finds at Choga-Zambil.

THE UNDERWORLD

The ziggurat raised men's thoughts up to the sky where the gods dwell. Heaven was conceived as consisting of seven separate vaults stretching one above the other across the earth; to each of these there was a separate access gate. The sky god Anu had his throne in the top vault. The earth itself was a disk surrounded by oceans which as 'waters of death' could not be traversed by any man. Under the earth lay the sweet water that fed rivers and fountains, the realm of Ea. Beneath that again lay the seven spheres of the kingdom of the dead, in which the goddess Eresh-ki-gal held sway. The ideas held regarding this 'house from which there is no return' have become familiar from a poem known by the title of *Ishtar's Descent into the Underworld*, of which both a Sumerian and an Assyrian version exist. The latter is

275. At Choga-Zambil, 19 miles southeast of Susa, the ruins of Dur Untashi, an Elamite city of the 13th century B.C. in ancient Khuzistan, were exposed. These bricks with cuneiform inscriptions were found there. **281.** The greatest surprise of this excavation was the ziggurat with its stairways and arches, some of which were found intact. Those that were missing have been drawn in. **276.** From the ruins of Erech the mysterious hill of Nefeji can be seen in the distance. **278.** This is not a ziggurat but a burial mound, as also is **280,** a hill near Samarra on the middle course of the Tigris. **277.** The ziggurat of Nimrud on the edge of a cotton plantation shows the same typical form that so forcibly struck its earliest visitors (see Pl. 21). **279.** Above the mound of Borsippa, south of Babylon, stand the incinerated remains of buildings which led travellers of earlier ages to believe this was the 'real' Tower of Babel.

282 283 284

285

282. This bronze lion with inlaid eyes of stone guarded the entrance to the temple of Dagan at Mari. Length 27¾ in. Date ca. 2000 B.C. **283.** Terracotta relief showing the demon Humbaba, who was defeated by Gilgamesh (7th-6th century B.C.). **284.** Demon's head of terracotta found near Babylon, also 7th-6th century B.C. **285.** Figure of a divine being, half man and half bull, wearing a horned crown. **286.** Bronze figurine (6 in. high) of the dreaded demon Pazuzu. He has claws on his hands and feet, eagle's wings, and a misshapen head. **287.** Detail of a religious ceremony from the time of Tiglath-pileser III. Note the third worshipper, who is shrouded in a terrifying lion's mask. **288.** Impression of a hematite cylinder seal, showing a deity seated on his throne beneath a crescent moon and holding a beaker in his hand. The worshipper is accompanied by a priestess or a patron goddess. The crescent of the moon god Sin and the star of Ishtar are ubiquitous symbols in Assyrian and Babylonian carvings (cf. Pls. 133, 156, 257-60).

286

287

288

Detail from a mural found in an inner court-yard of Zimri-Lim's palace at Mari. The upper panel shows the goddess Ishtar receiving homage from a king or other mortal in the presence of lower deities. The worshipper is touching the staff and ring of the goddess. Perhaps it illustrates how the king, in the course of the New Year festival, took the statue of Marduk by the hand and accompanied it. The lower panel depicts two goddesses, each of whom holds in her hands a vase from which a plant is sprouting. Streams of water are also pouring from the vases. A chapel in the palace contained a likeness of a goddess holding an incessantly flowing vase in her hand; both the water and the stylised plants are typical symbols of the goddess of fertility.

pessimistic and stresses the finality of death and the impossibility of gaining eternal life. Ishtar, it tells us, has amassed all her treasure to pay ransom for her beloved Tammuz, who is nevertheless kept captive in the Underworld. Ishtar's descent into the kingdom of the dead has meanwhile resulted in the cessation of all sexual commerce on earth: 'Since lady Ishtar went to the land from which there is no return, no bull has served a heifer and no ass covered its mare. No man has had intercourse with a maid in the alley. The man has slept in his room and the maid has lain alone.' The tale of Ishtar's journey to the Underworld is a fine literary effort, and the question naturally arises to what extent the poet's imagination is in tune with generally held conceptions. The popularity of the work and its relationship with views found in other sources regarding the land from which return was impossible seem to argue that it was deeply rooted in the tragic attitude to life of the Assyrians and Babylonians and their cheerless conception of death.

PERSONAL PIETY

The devout took part in the service at the temple by sacrifice and prayer. The gods needed the offerings of earthly mortals, while even the dead in the Underworld depended for their peace on the gifts of their near relatives. One gets the impression that offerings of food, perfumes, and drink were more important than bloody sacrifices. Another practice was solemn communion or *takultu*, which was believed to bring about a mystic union with the world of the gods by joint participation in a meal. As is to be expected, the stress in this religion was placed on the intermediary function of the priest, who by tradition was master of the gestures and words which gave access to the world of the gods.

Personal devotion finds its only expression in prayers and hymns.

Prayers ask for relief from sickness or other adversities, and the magic of exorcism is an important element in them. They are obliged to follow a certain sequence in their parts: invocation, description of the distress from which relief is sought, and panegyric. But there is nevertheless scope for the expression of pure religious feeling. The same applies in even greater measure to the hymns. For Ashurbanipal's library a number of these were collated in a sort of breviary with the title of 'Lamentations to quieten the heart', that is, the heart of the enraged deity. These songs to Marduk and Shamash date back to ancient times, although they are here available in more modern copies. Sometimes, however, the devout author spoke only of the 'deity' or the 'goddess' without mentioning any deity by name. His need to ascribe omnipotence to the god he revered conflicted with the multiplicity of gods acknowledged by Sumerian religion, but attachment to tradition prevented him from attaining a Biblical faith in God. Yet consciousness of sin against the holy world of the gods, and life as a result of forgiveness were concepts not unknown to him, as can be seen from the 'prayer for redemption from sin', which was found in Ashur and from which the following lines are taken:

What man is there who does not sin against his god?
What man exists who obeys his command always?
All men that live are conscious of their sin!
I, your slave, have sinned in every way once more....
I raised my hand to overthrow what was not overthrown,
Although unclean I walked in the temple time after time.
What you abhor I did and did again....
May your heart, my god, cease to be grieved by me!
The irate goddess, may her wrath be soon appeased....
If my sins are many, make my guilt as nought;
If my crimes are sevenfold, let your heart not grieve;
If my crimes are many, the greater your mercy be.

146

Mesopotamia as the Cradle of our Civilisation

BABEL AND THE BIBLE

It is beyond all doubt that European civilisation is connected with that of ancient Mesopotamia by an almost unbroken chain of tradition. Yet it seems dangerous to call this land the cradle of our culture, especially if we try to extend this dependence on Babylon to religion. The lectures on 'Babel and the Bible' delivered by Friedrich Delitzsch in Berlin in 1902 aroused much opposition because he called in question the independence and value of the Old Testament. The appearance in 1920 of the polemical work, *Die grosse Täuschung*, was a consequence of the ideas launched by Delitzsch at an earlier date; according to it, the Old Testament was entirely dependent on the achievements of the Mesopotamians and should therefore be regarded as a contemptible plagiarism. Nowadays there is no support for Delitzsch, for it has become quite obvious that there is no question of direct borrowings from Sumerian or Akkadian literature in the Old Testament. Even the Pan-Babylonism proposed by Hugo Winckler and integrated into an orthodox Protestant conception of life and the world by Alfred Jeremias is now virtually devoid of support. No serious Assyriologist or Biblical scholar now accepts that the Gilgamesh epic has influenced world literature to the extent suggested by Peter Jensen.

Nevertheless, the Old Testament is one of the channels by which themes from Assyro-Babylonian culture have reached us. This is about as far as we can go in any such statement, for the very parts of the Old Testament in which these themes are most clearly visible are characterised by the way in which they differ from the Mesopotamian myths of Creation and mortality, and offer an entirely new interpretation of the Deluge and the Tower of Babel.

The contribution that knowledge of Assyro-Babylonian civilisation has made to the understanding of the Old Testament is priceless. Israel has now taken its place in Eastern antiquity, a world with which it was linked by its entire way of thinking. New and unexpected light shed on certain texts, however, does not mean that there is any question of dependence with regard to religion or morals. On the contrary, now that comparison is possible, the Old Testament has been thrown into impressive relief by its utter difference from Babylonian concepts. While there is a considerable degree of agreement with regard to the pessimistic main theme between the story of the Garden of Eden in Genesis 2-3 on the one hand and the Adapa myths with the herb of life and the serpent on the other, the concept of responsibility breaks through forcibly in the Old Testament. Man is not subject to mortality as a result of a tragic combination of circumstances but by his disobedience to a clearly stated divine command. Comparison of Genesis 7-9 with the eleventh tablet of the Gilgamesh epic shows the contrast between the oneness of a creator moved by a sense of moral indignation and the diversity of a world of gods acting on whims and caprices. An increasing knowledge of the laws which regulated the human community in Babylonia from Ur-Nammu to Nabonidus has brought to light many analogies with the law of Moses, but these go no farther than the case law followed by the cadi at the gates of the town or, in the highest instance, by the king. Apodeictic pronouncements such as those contained in the Ten Commandments were completely without a parallel.

Thus the problem of 'Babel and the Bible' has been placed on a different and factual basis. The question of dependence is no longer relevant, because both systems of religion, science, and morals can be seen as closed circles, each with its own centre, from which all that is common to both should be understood. That customs of the patriarchs, such as the purchase of a burial place for Sarah as discussed by Abraham in Genesis 23, are made more comprehensible by legal documents from Nuzu can be readily accepted, but that fact has nothing to do with Pan-Babylonism. Generally speaking, we may say that Babylonian concepts are opposed rather than accepted by the Old Testament. Isaiah denounced the custom of planting 'pleasant gardens' in honour of the god who died and rose again every year (Isa. 17 : 10), an apparent reference to the Inanna-Dumuzi mysteries; Ezekiel opposed syncretism in the temple of Jerusalem to which even weeping for Tammuz had penetrated (Ezek. 8 : 14-15), and Jeremiah attacked customs honouring the queen of heaven (Jer. 44 : 15-25), which simply means he condemned the Ishtar cult. The main point of prophetic preaching was rejection of the Assyro-Babylonian encroachments which since the days of Tiglath-pileser III had threatened the faith of Israel with the undermining represented by syncretism.

The Israelite called his temple a *hekhal*, a word whose etymology is rooted in Sumerian. In Sumerian *e-gal* meant 'great house'; it became *egallu*, 'temple', and gave rise to the Hebrew *hekhal*. Etymology, however, does not determine the value attached to a word; only its use in time and environment does that. The same is also true of all concepts, just as it is for the texts of hymns and aphorisms whose resemblance to Mesopotamian sources is so striking. That is why the Old Testament could not be a vehicle for non-Israelite spiritual ideas. If, nevertheless, we are still in certain respects subject to the influence of Babylon, it is due to other channels of transmission. These channels by-passed the Bible and joined up, although often in a way that cannot be verified, with the classical world round the Mediterranean. There they were again picked up by the Christian religion and Christian culture. Thus it is possible to defend the thesis that ancient themes going back to the Sumerians and passed on by the Babylonians, Greeks, and Romans, live on in the adornments of churches and cathedrals. The tree of life, the battle with the dragon, the shepherd, fabulous animals, and beings half-man and half-bull are concepts which can be traced back to the motifs of the Inanna-Dumuzi mysteries.

ASTRONOMY AND MATHEMATICS

In one field where religion, philosophy, and science meet there is, however, no doubt about our dependence on ancient Mesopotamia, and that is astronomy motivated by astrology. Although the course of the stars was originally observed for the sole purpose of foretelling the future, observation in the schools of Erech, Sippar, Babylon, and Borsippa freed itself from this restriction and became scientific research in the modern sense. Their achievements were recognised, and their fame kept the name of Babylon in high honour during the rule of the Persians. One of the most celebrated astronomers was Kidinnu of Sippar, whom the Greeks called Kidenas. He knew the difference between the sidereal year, that is, the apparent period of revolution of the sun from the time it occupies a certain position in relation to a fixed star until it returns to that position, and the tropical year, which is the time elapsing between two successive transits of the earth through the first point of Aries. From this he discovered precession, which is the motion of the equinoxes on the ecliptic in a westward direction, that is, opposite to the sequence of the signs of the Zodiac. Furthermore, he was able to predict solar and lunar eclipses

289. Ruins of the palaces of the Persian kings in Persepolis. In the foreground the entrance to the audience hall of Darius I and Xerxes; in the background the palace of Darius. **290.** The reliefs on the walls were decorative rather than narrative, and thus differ in character from those of the Assyrians which could be examined at leisure on the walls. **291.** Although the same figures and motifs keep recurring, the sculptors succeeded in giving the reliefs liveliness by means of small variations, e.g. figures looking round, extending their hands, etc. **292.** By comparison with Assyrian reliefs, this procession of bringers of tribute is gentle in character. Accompanied by a Persian official, the nations offer a symbolic gift and their ambassadors retain their dignity. **293.** The mode of expression of the artists attracted to Susa and Persepolis from all parts of the empire of the Medes and Persians is marked by the spirit of their masters, the Achaemenians.

294
295

296

294. The mountain of Bisutun (also called Behistun) on the old caravan route between the highlands of Persia and the river plains of Mesopotamia has a flat face on its southern side. On his way eastward from Kermanshah the traveller sees this rock face rise steeply on his left. It was here that Darius had the inscription engraved which was later to provide the key to the decipherment of cuneiform writing. **295.** Extremely difficult of access as this site was, Rawlinson copied the inscriptions and the reliefs as best he could at the time. Professor Cameron of the University of Michigan repeated the daring climb and published a provisional report on his discoveries in the *Geographical Magazine* in 1950. **296.** The centre relief shows Darius with his foot on the defeated Gaumata. Above the king hovers the symbol of Ahuramazda, the winged solar disk. This photograph was taken during Professor Cameron's expedition.

accurately. Scientific astronomy, which first flourished in the time of the Greeks, was originally based on the results obtained in Mesopotamia by patient observation of celestial phenomena. Until then science had still not driven out pseudo-science, and it is certain that astrologers enjoyed greater popularity than astronomers. When the Bible (Dan. 2 : 2), Aristotle, and Cicero talk later of the Chaldaeans, they mean the priest-astrologers who roamed the countries round the Mediterranean as fortune-tellers. Thus a name which originally embraced the whole Aramaean peoples came to designate a small group which nevertheless presented one of the most typical and interesting aspects of Mesopotamia.

Like astronomy, mathematics in Mesopotamia proves to have been of a higher and more scientific level than was originally thought. The mathematical texts left behind are extremely difficult and demand a special knowledge of both Assyriology and mathematics such as few scholars possess in combination. It was mainly the French scholar François Thureau-Dangin who could and did explore this subject deeply. He drew attention to the 'problem texts' in which mathematical exercises were preserved. According to him, the Babylonians had made great advances in algebra thanks to a complicated method of reckoning. With regard to geometry it is certain that they could accurately calculate the volume of a truncated pyramid and that they knew at least approximately the value of π, which expresses the relation between the diameter and the circumference of a circle. They were able to calculate the area of triangles and trapeziums, which they called 'nail-heads' and 'ox-heads', showing that they drew these exactly the opposite way round to modern practice. It is striking that the reasoning which we employ in proofs was wholly absent; in every case they arrived at their results experimentally. The latter are nevertheless so astonishingly good that their achievements are being increasingly considered superior to those of the Greeks, whose fame is now on the wane by comparison with that of the Mesopotamians.

Like the Sumerians, the Babylonians used a sexagesimal system of counting. The number sixty was the smallest common multiple of the largest number of factors, and it was probably for this reason that the system was retained despite the many obvious advantages of the decimal system. That the sexagesimal system, once adopted, stubbornly resists displacement is very apparent from the fact that terms like dozen and gross are still very important in commercial language, not to mention the British system of weights and measures, which is still a source of trouble to foreigners. The units of time and angle handed down by the Babylonians have survived everywhere.

The use of the sexagesimal system was not entirely consistent. Even the Sumerians used ten as one of their basic digits, not unnaturally since the fingers of both hands constituted the first abacus. After ten the next basic number was sixty, so that in fact a mixture of the decimal and sexagesimal systems resulted. The division of the day as we know it is partly rooted in Sumerian practice, but is in fact due to Kidinnu, already mentioned above. To make his division of time independent of the constantly changing hour of sunrise, he made midnight the beginning of the day, which he then divided on the basis of the sexagesimal system, as we still do to this day. The months and their names were taken over from the Mesopotamians by Israel. The first month of spring was Nisannu, and this was followed by Aiaru, Simanu, Tammuz, Abu, Ululu, Tashritu, Arakhsamna, Kisilimu, Tebitu, Shabatu, and Addaru. These names differ little from those found on the modern Jewish calendar. As we have already seen, the New Year festival was celebrated in Nisannu, whereas the Old Testament situated the New Year in the autumn month of Tishri. It appears illogical to us nowadays that New Year's Day should fall on the first of the seventh month, but there are indications that even in Mesopotamia in ancient times a New Year festival was held in Tashritu, which corresponds to the month of Tishri in the Jewish calendar. As the twelve months accounted for a total of less than 360 days, a 'leap' month was inserted at certain times, as is still done in the Jewish calendar, in order to catch up with the solar year. A leap year thus comprised thirteen months, and the thirteenth occupied

the zodiacal sign of the Crow. The Zodiac is the 'belt' in the heavens along which the sun appears to move and within which the moon and planets actually orbit. It is divided into twelve 'houses', each extending over 30°, and these are named the Ram, the Bull, the Twins, the Crab, the Lion, the Virgin, the Scales, the Scorpion, the Archer, the Goat, the Water Carrier, the Fishes. For each of the signs there was a corresponding month. Not only this division of the Zodiac but also the beliefs that the crow is a bird of ill omen and the number thirteen unlucky are inherited from Babylonian thought, which could combine science and superstition in such a strange fashion. It is tempting to add other examples to those already adduced, but this is obviously a subject which offers much scope to the imagination. It is usually difficult to trace every link in the chain of tradition. If this is so in the case of pottery, where we have material to which sites and periods can be assigned, how much more forcibly does it apply to the routes by which primeval symbols reach us!

The sun, the moon, Venus, and the four other planets were very important. To each of the latter a quarter of the year was consecrated; they shared the power which the other three combined. There was thus a correspondence between Jupiter, Marduk, and spring, Mars, Ninib, and summer, Mercury, Nabu, and autumn, and Saturn, Nergal, and winter. One day was devoted to each of the 3 + 4 gods to whom the sun, moon, and five planets correspond, which gave a week of seven days. In general, however, a five-day week was observed, so that 72 weeks (a product of the sexagesimal system!) formed a year. Mars and Saturn then dropped out because they were both reputed to be unlucky, Saturn being the more dangerous of the two. As the planets followed their orbits they produced sounds whose pitch depended on the speed of the planets and which together formed the 'music of the spheres'. To what extent the ban on the seventh in medieval church music as the 'interval of the devil' was associated with the unlucky planet Saturn, to which Saturday was consecrated, is a debatable question. At any rate we cannot say that our custom of dividing the week into seven days is a typical Mesopotamian tradition.

EPILOGUE

When, after Alexander the Great's campaigns of conquest, the Greeks found themselves ruling territories whose language and culture they scarcely knew, the Ptolemies in Egypt and the Seleucids in Mesopotamia conceived a desire to know more about the history and religion of their subject peoples. In Egypt Manetho was found prepared to write an explanatory work. For Babylonia the task was undertaken by Berossus, a priest of the Marduk temple in Babylon, who dedicated a history written in Greek with the title of Babyloniaca to Antiochus I. In this he told the story of Mesopotamia from before the Deluge up to Alexander the Great. Only fragments have survived of this work by an author who, writing ca. 300 B.C., still had access to excellent source material. What we know of it we owe to quotations by Josephus, Eusebius, Alexander Polyhistor, and Syncellus. There was apparently no interest in his erudition when he wrote; not until centuries later did hard work lead to the right trail and we came to realise that the Greeks had built upon a civilisation which had reached full stature after thousands of eyars of growth.

In front of the Iraq Museum at Baghdad stands a bust of Gertrude Bell, to whose devoted work, uninterrupted by the heat of summer, the formation of this collection is due. The portrait of this remarkable English woman, who died in Baghdad in 1926 at the age of fifty-eight, is a symbol of all the strangers from the West who came to Mesopotamia to search for the past of their own civilisation and were so fascinated that they came to love this land and its people like another more mysterious and primeval mother-country. Gradually their enthusiasm for archaeological research communicated itself to scholars from Iraq itself, and these are contributing on an ever-increasing scale to the expansion of our knowledge. At the same time it is becoming more and more evident that Mesopotamia is a place of confluence of many streams whose sources must be sought on ever-receding horizons.

▲   Site of a ziggurat

A ziggurat or temple tower was a link in the contact between heaven and earth. As time went on, higher and higher towers were built, gigantic pedestals for shrines, the dwellings of the deity. In addition to the temple on top a second one was built at the base as the residence of the god on earth.

Four types of ziggurat are distinguished: 1. the rectangular type in the south (Ur, Erech, Nippur); 2. the square type in the north (Ashur, Calah, Dur Sharrukin, Kar-Tukulti-Ninurta); 3. the mixed type with square base (Babylon); 4. the shrine on a platform (the prototype of the ziggurat).

The ziggurat doubtless inspired the story of the Tower of Babel told in Genesis 11:1-9, where the Tower is located in 'Shinar' (probably Sumer and Akkad).

The ziggurat was built of brick and asphalt; the name means 'the tower rising into the sky', an idea repeated in the individual names of the ziggurats, e.g. E-temen-an-ki, 'house of the foundations of heaven and earth'.

Temple terrace dating from the late Jemdet Nasr period, 22.5 x 27 metres. The temple is called the 'Eye temple' because thousands of black and white alabaster figurines of gods with heads consisting solely of one or two pairs of eyes were found in the rubble.

Temple tower of Middle Babylonian period (1200-625). No staircase but a ramp round the four sides of the tower. Base 43.1 x 43.1 metres. Four storeys each 6.1 metres high. The tower probably contained seven storeys in all.

Temple tower of Middle Babylonian period (1200-625). No staircase but a ramp round the four sides of the tower. Base 51 x 51 metres. The ziggurat was probably originally 60 metres high; it still rises 42 metres above the plain.

Two temples probably stood at this ziggurat. From pottery found here it is thought that the tower was built at the beginning of the 2nd millennium B.C.

Ziggurat with square base 31x31 metres; not higher than 8 metres. The number of storeys cannot be established. No staircase but a ramp round the four sides of the tower. Dates from the Middle Babylonian period (1200-625).

Three temple towers of the Middle Babylonian period (1200-625).
Ashur: square base 60 x 60 metres. At the time of excavation only 20 metres high. Originally the ziggurat of Enlil, the city god, later of the god Ashur.
Name: E-kur-ru-ki-shar-ra ('house of the mountain of the universe')
Anu-Adad: two ziggurats, respectively 39 x 36 metres and 24 x 24 metres. These belonged to a double temple, the northern of Anu, the western of Adad.
This type of temple had no staircase but a ramp round the four sides of the tower.

Ziggurat 42 x 25 metres, rising 14.5 metres above the plain and 7 above the temple terrace. Nothing is left of the temple on the southern side. Ziggurat of a unique type; shows influence of four different styles of construction.

Shrine on oval terrace 72 x 104 metres, probably dedicated to the goddess Inanna. The temple terrace is about 6 metres high. Extensions have been added here four times.

Ziggurat with four storeys; the top floor was adorned with shining bronze horns (cf. Exod. 27:2 and 1 Kg. 1:50).

Parts of the temple terrace still rise 57 metres above the plain. A staircase is found up to 28 metres. Base 67 x 69 metres. Three temples stood at top of the ziggurat. Probably built in the reign of Kurigalzu II.

Oval terrace about 5 metres high. The shrine stands in a rectangle in the centre of the terrace. It is known for its wall paintings with decorative motifs and human and animal figures.

Ziggurat with square base 103 x 103 metres; five storeys high. With its height of 53 metres, this is the highest ever excavated. Originally three shrines stood here. The ziggurat probably dates from the 13th century. The whole was dedicated to Inshushinak, the supreme god in the Elamite pantheon.

Three ziggurats were found here. The first has a base 58 x 62 metres. North of it stood the temple of Zababa. The ziggurat rises 19.5 metres above the plain. The other two ziggurats were dedicated to Ingharra.

A ziggurat about 8 metres high with a base 40 x 40 metres stood on a terrace 5-8 metres high. The whole was enclosed in a 'temenos' 320 x 240 metres. The shrine was dedicated to the sun god Shamash.

Little-known ziggurat. Round in shape, with a diameter of 125 metres. Two storeys have been preserved.

Virtually nothing is known about this ziggurat. Its shape is not clear.

Seven storeys reaching a height of 91 metres. Base 91 x 91 metres. Strict uniformity of construction. Name: E-temen-an-ki ('house of the foundations of heaven and earth'). Closely related to the temple of Marduk (Esagila) in the same sacred area.

The existence of a ziggurat here is not definitely established. The small dimensions (about 6 x 8 metres) rather suggest a chapel. This is said to have stood in the centre of the temple of Ningursu, the city god. Known mainly from written sources.

Ziggurat with base 82 x 82 metres; 47 metres high. Seven storeys; the temple stood on the top floor. Dedicated to Nabu. Name: 'house of the seven leaders of heaven and earth'.

Ziggurat with base 57 x 38.4 metres; height about 21.5 metres. Dedicated to Enlil. Name: 'house of the mountain'.

Ziggurat with base 8 x 8 metres. Still only superficially investigated. Only the first storey, 1.5 metres high, remains. Dedicated to Ninhursag.

Ziggurat with base 30 x 30 metres. Still rises 15 metres above the plain. It has not yet been fully investigated.

On the temple terrace (107 x 78 metres) stands a ziggurat about 30 metres high. The kings Ur-Nammu and Shulgi (21th century) rebuilt and extended the shrine. At the time of Nabonidus the ziggurat had seven storeys. No strict uniformity of design as in the ziggurat at Babylon. The name of the shrine was 'house of the king, dispenser of justice'.

Ziggurats from various times were found here. The earliest temple terrace was about 9 metres high. Then the 'White Temple' was built on the ziggurat (23.3 x 17.5 metres). Dedicated to Anu, the sky god. Also a ziggurat of Eanna, with base 56 x 52.5 metres, which still rises 36.5 metres above the plain. The entire temple area covered 213 x 167.4 metres.

Ziggurat still rising 18 metres above the plain. It has only been superficially investigated. Name: 'house of the link between heaven and earth.' The kings of Larsa built various temples here in the reign of Hammurabi.

Oval terrace about 5 metres high, perhaps a natural hill, once an island, in the alluvial plain. In a rectangle 33.5 x 23 metres stands the temple of Ninhursag (18 x 11 metres).

On a terrace 180 x 110 metres rises a ziggurat with a base 50 x 50 metres. Vivid external architecture, entirely different from the closed character of later Babylonian temples. The numerous entrances also suggest this character of openness.

Map labels:
Tell Brak · Tell Irmah · Dur Sharrukin · Calah · Great Zab · Little Zab · Kar-Tukulti-Ninurta · Ashur · Tigris · Khabur · Euphrates · Mari · Tutub Khafaje · Dur Kurigalzu · Diyala · Sippar · Tell 'Uqair · Babylon · Kish · Borsippa · Nippur · Adab · Lagash · Nina · Urukug · Tell Hammam · Erech · Larsa · Tell el-Obeid · Ur · Eridu · Susa · Choga-Zambil

0   50   100   150 miles
0   50   100   200 km

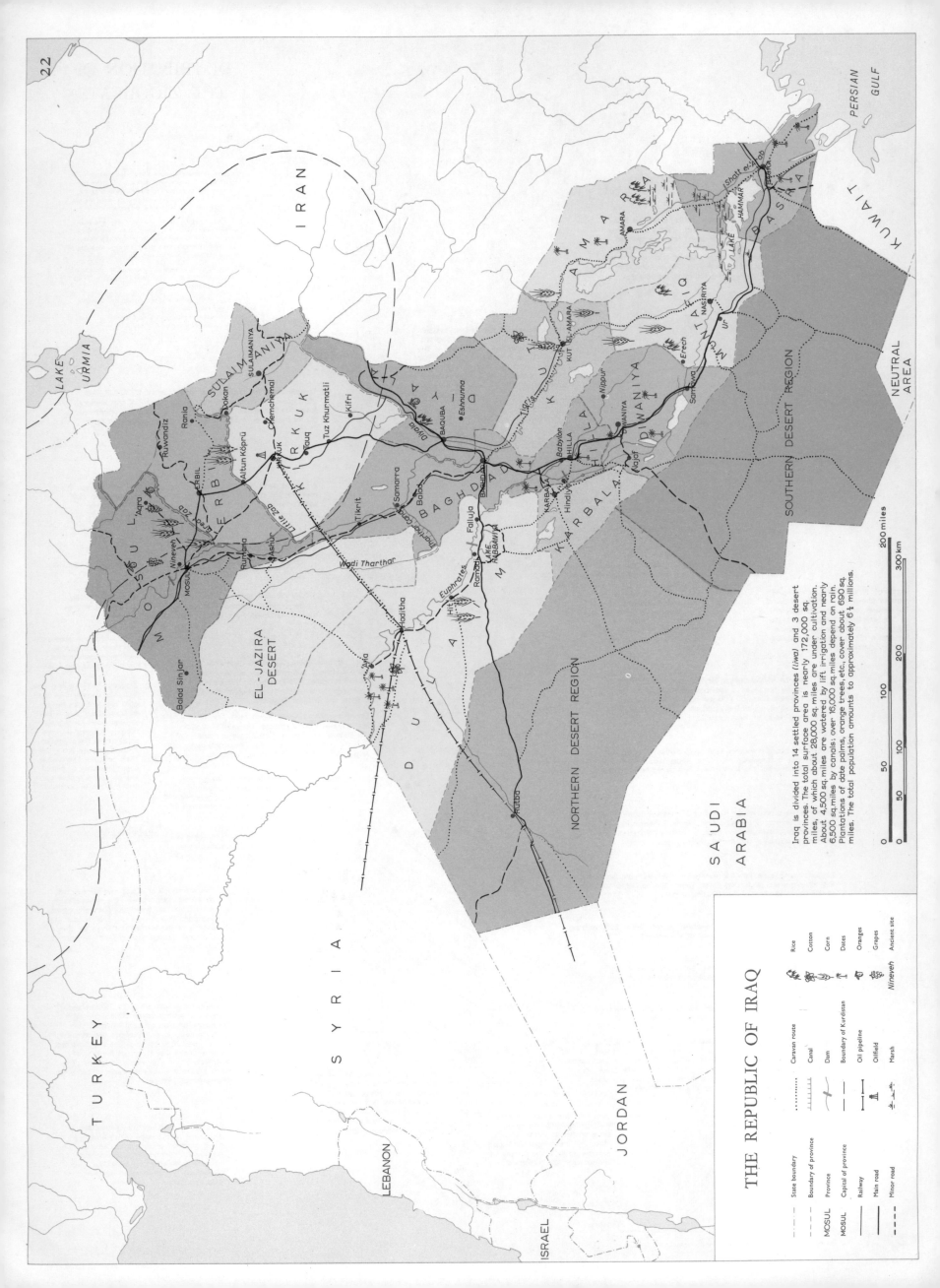

THE REPUBLIC OF IRAQ

State boundary	Caravan route		Rice
Boundary of province	Canal		Cotton
MOSUL Province	Dam		Corn
MOSUL Capital of province	Boundary of Kurdistan		Dates
Railway	Oil pipeline		Oranges
Main road	Oilfield		Grapes
Minor road	Marsh	*Nineveh*	Ancient site

Iraq is divided into 14 settled provinces (*liwa*) and 3 desert provinces. The total surface area is nearly 172,000 sq. miles, of which about 28,000 sq. miles are under cultivation. About 4,500 sq. miles are watered by lift irrigation and nearly 6,500 sq. miles by canals; over 16,000 sq. miles depend on rain. Plantations of date palms, orange trees, etc., cover about 690 sq. miles. The total population amounts to approximately 6¼ millions.

Scale: 0 50 100 200 miles
0 50 100 200 300 km

INDEX

The Index gives names of persons and places, Mesopotamian technical and quasi-technical terms, and some historical data. It covers all names of persons and places in the text and all names of places illustrated in the maps. References to names in the comments on the maps are given only when they are of special importance or interest and do not occur elsewhere, and with similar exceptions references to captions to the Plates are only to what is directly their subject or conspicuously shown in them.

Dates B.C. are specified as such only when equivocation might otherwise arise. Dates A.D. are always specified except where the context makes their character unquestionable, as in the case of archaeological campaigns. Dates in brackets when following immediately after a name are those of the subject's life, when following a title such as 'king of . . .' are those of a reign. Place-names in brackets following a head-word are the modern equivalents; these are also separately entered with a cross-reference to the ancient form.

ABBREVIATIONS

Akk.=Akkadian; Ass.=Assyrian; Bab.=Babylonian; Bib.=Biblical; Gr.=Greek; Lat.=Latin; Phoen.=Phoenician; Rom.=Roman; Sum.=Sumerian; fl.=flourished; loc.=locality

A

A-anni-padda, king of the 1st dynasty of Ur (2438–2399): p. 45

Abadan, centre of oil production on the border of Iraq, in Iran on the Persian Gulf: p. 12

'Abdi-Milkutti, king of Sidon, put to death by Esarhaddon: p. 110

Ab-i-diz, river in Elam: Map 8

Abi-eshu, king of the 1st dynasty of Babylon (1643–1616): p. 83

Abraham, forefather of the people of Judah and Israel; according to Biblical tradition originated from Ur and thence migrated to Haran in NW. Mesopotamia: pp. 9, 77, 90, 147

Abu, month in the Mesopotamian calendar: p. 150

Abu Habba; Map 1; see SIPPAR

Abu Khamis, tell in S. Iraq: Map 3

Abu Khatab; p. 29; Map 1; see KISURRA

Abu Maria, tell in NW. Iraq: Maps 3, 11

Abu Shahrain; Maps 1, 2, 3; see ERIDU

Abu Shbaicha, tell in SE. Iraq: Map 3

Abu Shujair, tell in S. Iraq: Map 3

Achaemenids, Persian dynasty named after its founder Achaemenes, to which Cyrus, Darius, and Xerxes belonged: p. 23

Adab (Bismaya), town in S. Mesopotamia; excavations here in 1903 and 1904 revealed a ziggurat and temples of Ishtar and Ninhursag and numerous tablets with cuneiform writing dating from the period before Sargon of Agade: Maps 1, 8, 21

Adad, *Bib.* Hadad, Babylonian and Assyrian god of thunder; took the place of the Sumerian Ishkur; worshipped at Babylon and other centres: pp. 13, 87, 90, 101, 120, 139

Adad-bela-ukin, governor of Ashur in the reign of Ashur-nirari V: p. 87

Adad Gate, gate in Babylon: Map 19

Adad-idri, king of Damascus in the 9th cent.: p. 98

Adad-nirari 1. II, king of Ashur (910–889): p. 98
2. **III,** king of Ashur (809–782): p. 101

Adam, in Bib. tradition the first man; paralleled by the Adapa of Mesopotamian mythology: p. 115

Adapa, in Mesopotamian tradition the ancestor of the human race, who incurred the curse of mortality; principal character in the myth named after him: pp. 115, 118, 138, 147

Adar, see ADDARU

Addaru, *Bib.* Adar, month in the Mesopotamian calendar: pp. 87, 150

'Adhaim, river in NE. Iraq: Maps 4, 11, 13

Adrammelech, son of Sennacherib, brother of Esarhaddon: p. 110

Adramyttium (Edremit), port on the coast of Mysia, in NW. Asia Minor: Map 9

Afghanistan, region from which lapis lazuli was imported to Babylonia from the earliest times: p. 86

Agade, city in central Mesopotamia whose precise location is unknown; the centre of the kingdom ruled by Sargon I (23rd cent.) and his successors: pp. 29, 39, 45, 46, 73, 76; Maps 1, 8, 10, 17, 18

Ahab, king of Israel (874–852); came into conflict with Shalmaneser III, by whom he was defeated at the battle of Qarqar: pp. 98, 101

Ahaz, king of Judah (735–716); called in the assistance of Tiglath-pileser III of Assyria against the allied forces of Israel and Aram: pp. 101, 108

Aiaru, month in the Mesopotamian calendar: p. 150

Akhenaton; p. 86; see AMENHOTEP IV

Akhetaton (Tell el-Amarna), town on the east bank of the Nile, residence of the Pharaohs Amenhotep III and Amenhotep IV (14th cent.); here were found the Amarna letters, some of which were sent by the Kassites of Babylon: p. 86

Akitu festival, New Year festival celebrated at Babylon by a ceremonial procession to Bit Akitu: p. 142

Akkad, district in N. Mesopotamia ruled by the dynasty of Sargon of Agade (23rd cent.): pp. 45, 51, 76, 90, 122, 123, 135; Maps 1, 8, 10, 17, 18

Akkadians, Semitic people inhabiting Akkad: p. 135

Akki, an irrigator, foster-father of Sargon of Agade: p. 73

Akshak (Tell 'Umair?), early centre of Sumerian civilisation, on the Tigris near Ctesiphon; the site of the excavations at Tell 'Umair in 1927 is tentatively identified with Akshak: Maps 1, 8, 18

Akurgal, Sumerian king of Lagash in the 'early-dynastic' period, son of Ur-Nina: Pl. 107

Akus, loc. near Babylon: Map 19

Alalakh ('Atshanah), loc. in N. Syria, on the Orontes; excavations in 1936–9 revealed among other things 150 tablets with cuneiform writing from the period of Hammurabi: p. 54; Map 9

Alashia, loc. in Cyprus: Map 9

Aleppo: pp. 77, 84; Maps 1, 9, 10, 17, 18; see KHALAB

Alexander the Great, king of Macedon (336–323); died in Babylon: pp. 16, 150

Alexander Polyhistor, Gr. historian (fl. ca. 70) whose works preserve quotations from the Babyloniaca of Berossus: p. 150

Alexandria, city founded by Alexander the Great at the delta of the Nile; centre of learning under the Ptolemies (3rd–1st cents.): pp. 9, 114

Ali-elatti, judge in the reign of Hammurabi: pp. 77, 80

Allatum, see ERESH-KI-GAL

Altun Köprü: Maps 1, 3, 11, 22; see ZABAN

'Amadia: Map 1; see AMAT

Amanus Mountains, SE. branch of the Taurus Mountains, dividing Syria from Cicilia and Cappadocia: pp. 51, 73; Maps 1, 10, 17, 18

Amara 1. loc. in SE. Iraq, on the Tigris: p. 12; Maps 4, 5, 22
2. province of the state of Iraq: Map 22

Amardos, see UZUN

amargi, Sumerian term for 'liberty', freedom from foreign oppression: pp. 46, 51

Amarsin: p. 54; see BUR-SIN

Amar-utu: p. 139; see MARDUK

Amat (Amadia), loc. in N. Mesopotamia: Maps 1, 3, 9, 11

Amenhotep 1. III, Pharaoh of Egypt (1409–1374)
2. **IV,** or **Akhenaton,** Pharaoh of Egypt (1373–1356). The Amarna letters contain their correspondence with the Kassites of Babylon: p. 86

'Amman, see RABBAH

Ammi-ditana, king of the 1st dynasty of Babylon (1615–1579): p. 83

Ammi-zaduga, king of the 1st dynasty of Babylon (1578–1558); to his reign belong the 'Venus tablets' important for the establishment of chronology: pp. 83, 87

Ammon, district east of the Jordan: Map 18

Amon, king of Judah (639–638): p. 109

Amorites, Semitic people who penetrated into Mesopotamia from the north in the course of the 2nd millennium: pp. 45, 77, 135; Map 1; Pl. 158

Amos, prophet in Israel in the time of Jeroboam II, shortly before the invasion of the Assyrians: p. 101

Amurru, ancient name for the district of the Amorites: pp. 29, 101, 123; Maps 10, 17

'Ana: p. 84; Maps 1, 22; see ANATU

'Ana ittishu' ('for information of . . .'), formulary for jurists, containing Semitic translations of Sumerian expressions used in contracts: p. 123

Anatolia, ancient name for Asia Minor: p. 76

Anatu or **Hana** ('Ana), loc. on the Euphrates: p. 84; Maps 1, 3, 10, 11, 18

Anbar: Map 1; see FAIRUZ SAPUR

Ancyra (Ankara), city in Galatia: Map 9

Ankara: Map 9; see ANCYRA

Anshan, Elamite district in SW. Persia: Map 8

Anshar, father of Anu; later identified with Ashur: p. 139

Antioch 1. town on the Orontes, important centre of Greek culture: p. 38
2. town in Pisidia, on one of the trade routes from Mesopotamia through Asia Minor: Map 9

Antiochus I, Seleucid king of Syria (223–187): p. 150

Antitaurus, mountain range in Asia Minor: Map 17

Antum, Mesopotamian goddess, wife of Marduk; identified with Hera: p. 138

Anu, Babylonian god of the sky; worshipped especially in Erech, later also in Ashur: pp. 46, 54, 62, 65, 73, 90, 114, 115, 120, 122, 123, 138, 139, 143

Anunnakki, originally the name for all the gods, later confined to those of the earth and water, as opposed to the Igigi, the gods of the sky: pp. 120, 123, 138

Apil-Sin, king of the 1st dynasty of Babylon (1762–1745): p. 83

Apsu, in the Mesopotamian cosmology, the primeval ocean, extending under the earth as fresh water: pp. 65, 123, 139 (illustration)

'Aqaba, Gulf of, eastern of the two northerly arms of the Red Sea: p. 101; Maps 17, 18

'Aqarquf: pp. 39, 84; Maps 1, 2, 3; see DUR KURI-GALZU

'Aqr: Map 1; see DER 2

'Aqra, loc. in N. Iraq: Maps 3, 11, 12, 22

Araban: Map 1; see SHADI KANI

Arabian Desert, district SW. of Mesopotamia: p. 132; Maps 1, 9, 17

Arabs, general name for the groups of Semitic peoples W. and SW. of Mesopotamia: p. 109; Pl. 208

Arakhsamna, month in the Mesopotamian calendar: p. 150

Arakhtu canal, name for the Euphrates within the city of Babylon: p. 10; Map 19

Aram 1. general name for the district occupied by the Aramaeans in N. Mesopotamia and Syria: p. 9
2. kingdom with Damascus as capital frequently at war with Israel: pp. 98, 101

Aramaeans, generic name of all the peoples dwelling to the E. of Palestine who overran the Near East in the 12th cent.: pp. 90, 98, 150; Maps 1, 17, 18

Aram Naharaim ('Aram of the two rivers'), Bib. name for a district probably on the upper course of the Euphrates, between the Balikh and the Khabur, described as the original home of the patriarchs; rendered as 'Mesopotamia' in the Greek translation of the Old Testament made in Alexandria and those derived from it: p. 9

Aras: Map 1; see ARAXES

Araxes (Aras), river in Armenia: Maps 1, 9, 17, 18

GUENNA—KALKHU

Guenna, district between the Tigris and Euphrates, subject of dispute between Umma and Lagash in the 24th cent.: Map 8

gufa, the modern name for the circular boat used in Mesopotamia from the earliest times down to the present day: Pl. 214

Gula ('the great'), one of the titles of the mother goddess; among the Babylonians goddess of healing: p. 139

Gunduk, prehistoric site in N. Iraq: Maps 3, 11

Gurgurri Gate, main gate of Ashur: Map 20

Gutians, inhabitants of the highlands E. of Mesopotamia: pp. 46, 51, 54, 76, 98; Maps 8, 10

H

Habbaniya, Lake, lake near the central course of the Euphrates, in the modern Iraq province of Dulaim: Map 22

Hadad; pp. 108, 139; see ADAD

Haditha, loc. on the Euphrates, in the modern Iraq province of Dulaim: Map 22

Haikal, tell in N. Iraq: Maps 3, 11

Hajji Muhammad, loc. in S. Iraq where pottery named after the near-by site of Erech was found: pp. 42, 43; Maps 2, 7

Halupe, tell in E. Syria: Map 3

Halwan Alaman (Sar-i-ful), loc. in Luristan in Persia: Maps 1, 3, 11

Halys (Kizil Irmak), the largest river in Asia Minor: Maps 1, 9, 18

Hamadan: Map 1; see ECBATANA

Hamath, town in Syria, on the Orontes; conquered by the Assyrians: pp. 98, 101, 108, 109; Maps 1, 9, 10, 17, 18

Hammar, Lake, lake in the S. of Iraq, in the provinces of Muntafiq and Basra: Map 22

Hammurabi, king of the first dynasty of Babylon (1724–1682), lawgiver and conqueror; made Babylon his royal residence and the centre of his empire: pp. 10, 29, 38, 77, 80, 83, 87, 135, 138, 139; Pls. 158, 159, 160

Hammurabi, Code of, code drawn up in the reign of Hammurabi, the most complete collection of the laws of ancient Mesopotamia yet discovered; found by French excavators in Susa during the campaign of 1901–2: pp. 26, 38, 51, 80, 83, 86, 138; Pl. 160

Hana: p. 84; see ANATU

Hanish, herald of Adad, the storm god: p. 120

Harada, tell in N. Iraq: Maps 3, 11

Haran, town in NW. Mesopotamia from which Abraham emigrated to Canaan: pp. 138, 139; Maps 1, 9, 10, 17, 18

Harappa, loc. in the area of the culture of the Indus valley which had trade relations with Mesopotamia: p. 76

Haridu, tell in W. Iraq: Map 3

Hassuna, site in N. Iraq, near the confluence of the Tigris and the Great Zab; here important discoveries were made of prehistoric pottery and indications of the beginnings of an agricultural community: pp. 39, 41, 42; Maps 2, 3, 6, 7, 11

Hatra (el-Hadhr), ruined town in N. Iraq, on the Wadi Tharthar, with numerous inscriptions in Aramaic dating from the 2nd cent. A.D.: p. 39; Maps 1, 3

Hattushash (Boghaz Köi), capital of the empire of the Hittites in Asia Minor: p. 114; Maps 1, 9

Hauran, district E. of the Jordan: Map 17

Havdian, prehistoric site in N. Mesopotamia: Map 6

Hazor, Canaanite royal city on the Jordan, captured by Tiglath-pileser: Map 1

Hera, sister and consort of the Gr. god Zeus; identified by the Seleucids with the Bab. goddess Antum: p. 138

Hermas (Jaghjagha), river in NE. Mesopotamia: p. 44

Hermon, mountain range in Palestine in which the Jordan rises: Maps 17, 18

Hermus, river in W. Asia Minor: Map 9

Herodotus (ca. 484–ca. 424), Gr. historian; visited Babylon and describes it and the two sieges of it by the Persians in his History: pp. 16, 109, 138

Hezekiah, king of Judah (715–686); in his reign occurred the siege of Jerusalem by Sennacherib (701): pp. 10, 108, 109

Hierapolis, town in Phrygia: Map 9

Hijiya, prehistoric site in N. Iraq: Map 6

Hilla 1. town in Iraq on the Euphrates below Babylon: pp. 19, 132; Maps 2, 4, 5, 22
2. province of the state of Iraq: Map 22

Hilla-Hindiya dam route, modern road from Hilla to the Hindiya dam: Map 16

Hindanu, tell in W. Iraq, on the Euphrates: Map 3

Hindiya, town in Iraq, on the Euphrates, where a famous dam has been constructed: Maps 4, 22

Hiram, king of Tyre at the time of Tiglath-pileser III: 101

Hit: pp. 16, 73; Maps 1, 3, 10, 17, 18, 22; see TUTUL

Hittites, *Bab.* **Khatti,** people who from Asia Minor ruled over an empire which temporarily extended as far as Babylon and was overthrown by the Sea People ca. 1200: pp. 76, 83, 84, 86, 98; Maps 1, 10, 17, 18; Pl. 172

Homs: Maps 1, 9; see EMESA

Hoshea, last king of Israel in Samaria (731–723); captured and led into exile by the Assyrians: pp. 101, 108

'house of tablets', the official school for scribes in the Sumerian civilisation: pp. 54, 62

Hubur, Bab. goddess personifying the sea: p. 123

Hulai, river in N. Mesopotamia: p. 98

Humbaba, giant who in the epic of Gilgamesh inhabited the Cedar Forest and was killed by Gilgamesh and Enkidu: pp. 114, 115; Pl. 283

Hurrians, people originating from Mitanni, centred on the district of the Khabur: p. 86; Maps 1, 10, 17

Huwaish, tell in N. Iraq: Maps 3, 11

Hystaspes, father of King Darius I of Persia: p. 23

I

Ibal-pi-el, representative of Zimri-Lim of Mari at the court of Hammurabi: p. 77

Ibi-Sin, last king of the third dynasty of Ur (ca. 1960–1936): pp. 45, 54

Ibrahim Bayis, tell in N. Iraq: Maps 3, 11

Ibzaikh, tell in S. Iraq: Map 3

Iconium (Konya), town in Asia Minor: Map 9

Idiklat: Map 1; see TIGRIS

idyah, the dust storm which churns up the desert and is a great obstruction to the operation of excavation: p. 12

Igigi, the gods of the sky, as opposed to the Anunakki, the gods of the earth and water: p. 138

Ilakabkabu, prince of Tirqa, father of Shamshi-Adad I: p. 90

ilku, land held in fee, granted by the Babylonian kings to their soldiers and commanders: p. 83

Iluma-ilum, founder in the reign of Samsu-iluna of the 'Sea-land dynasty' in S. Babylonia which as the Second Babylonian Dynasty controlled Babylonia in the 16th and 15th centuries: Map 10

Imgur Enlil (Balawat), town in Assyria, famous for the bronze gates of Shalmaneser III found in 1878: p. 98; Maps 1, 3, 11, 17

Imgur Enlil walls, walls in Babylon: Map 19

Inanna ('queen of heaven'), goddess of love, daughter of Anu, beloved of the god of spring Tammuz (Dumuzi); identified with Ishtar: pp. 38, 44, 46, 54, 65, 73, 84, 135, 138, 147

Indus valley, cultural area which from early times had relations with Mesopotamia, as appears from discoveries at Eshnunna, Mohenjo-Daro, and Harappa: pp. 39, 44, 76

Ingharra, goddess worshipped in Kish: Map 21

Inshushinak, chief god of the Elamite pantheon; a ziggurat was dedicated to him in Dur Untashi: p. 143

Iran: pp. 9, 45, 46, 87; Maps 2, 3, 6, 12, 22; see PERSIA

Iraq: pp. 9, 16, 22, 29, 38, 39, 45, 84, 142; Maps 12, 22

Irhuleni, king of Hamath, mentioned among the conquered on the bronze gates of Shalmaneser III at Balawat: p. 98

Irra, name of the god Nergal, especially in his capacity as the god of plague; the chief character in an Akkadian myth named after him: pp. 119, 122

Isaac, son of Abraham; belonged to one of the border tribes called Aramaeans which constantly harassed the Assyrian Empire: p. 90

Isaiah, prophet in Jerusalem at the time of Sennacherib; foretold the salvation of the city; advocated a policy of independence in respect of Egypt based upon a trustful neutrality: pp. 108, 109, 147

Isfahan, town in Iran: Map 9

Ishaku, Sum. title for a city governor: p. 46

Ishbi-Irra, king of the dynasty of Isin (1949–1917): p. 54

Ishchali: p. 38; Maps 1, 3, 8; see KABALATI

Ishkur, Sum. storm god, replaced by the Babylonian Adad: p. 139

Ishme-Dagan I, king of Assyria (1723–1693), during whose reign Assyria was conquered by Hammurabi: pp. 77, 83

Ishtar, *Bib.* **Ashtoreth,** *Phoen.* **Astarte,** daughter of Anu or Sin, goddess of love, identified with the Sum. Inanna; her symbol was the planet Venus; her worship was widespread: pp. 13, 73, 114, 115, 120, 122, 138, 143, 146, 147; Pl. 244

Ishtar Gate, the first gate at the entry to the processional way in Babylon; reconstructed in the Staatliche Museen in Berlin: pp. 29, 138; Map 19; Pl. 241

Ishum, god mentioned in the Akkadian epic of the plague god Irra: p. 122

Isin (Bahriyat), ancient town of Sumer, from which in conjunction with Larsa S. Mesopotamia was ruled from the 20th to the 18th cent., at the time of the 1st dynasty of Isin: pp. 51, 77, 86; Maps 1, 3, 8, 10

Iskhairi, tell in S. Iraq: Map 3

Israel 1. (in the Bible), the Northern Kingdom of the Ten tribes, led into captivity by the Assyrians in 722; the term is also applied to Judah and Israel together or Judah by itself: pp. 87, 98, 101, 108; Maps 17, 18
2. (modern state), Jewish republic in the Middle East: Map 22

Izmir, see SMYRNA

J

Jacob, son of Isaac; belonged to one of the border tribes called Aramaeans which constantly harassed the Assyrian empire: p. 90

Jaghjagha: p. 44; see HERMAS

Jarmo, site in NE. Iraq, famous for the excavations of 1950–1, in the course of which the earliest traces of an agricultural community in Mesopotamia were discovered: pp. 41, 42; Maps 2, 3, 6; Pl. 80

Jebeil, see BYBLOS

Jebel Hamrin, mountain range in NE. Iraq: Map 4

Jebelet el-Beda, site in NW. Iraq, in the neighbourhood of Tell Halaf: p. 29

Jehoahaz, king of Judah (609); attacked and deported to Egypt by the Pharaoh Neco after a reign of three months: p. 128

Jehoiachin, king of Judah (598–597), deported to Babylon by Nebuchadnezzar: pp. 128, 132

Jehoiakim, king of Judah (609–598), son of Josiah and brother of Jehoahaz, whom he replaced: p. 128

Jehu, king of Israel (841–814); his submission to Shalmaneser III of Assyria is commemorated on the Black Obelisk of Nimrud: pp. 98, 101; Pl. 180

Jemdet Nasr: pp. 29, 44, 76, 135; Maps 1, 2, 3, 7, 8; see KIDNUN

Jeremiah, prophet in Jerusalem at the time of Nebuchadnezzar's western campaigns; advocated a policy of independence from Egypt and a devout neutrality which against his will gained him the favour of the Babylonians: p. 147

Jeroboam II, king of Israel (781–753): p. 101

Jerusalem, capital of David's kingdom of Judah and Israel; withstood the siege of Sennacherib in 701, but was conquered and sacked by Nebuchadnezzar in 597 and 586: pp. 80, 101, 108, 109, 110, 128, 139; Maps 1, 9, 10, 17, 18

Jerwan, loc. in N. Iraq where Sennacherib had an aqueduct constructed and fortified with walls: Maps 3, 11

Job, character in the Bible, famous for his undeserved misfortunes; the Book attributed to him has marked resemblances to two Mesopotamian poems, 'I will praise the Lord of Wisdom' and 'Dialogue between two friends': pp. 118, 119

Jonathan, son of Saul and friend of David, whose lament for him shows marked resemblance to the lament of Gilgamesh for Enkidu in the Mesopotamian epic of Gilgamesh: p. 115

Jordan, 1. river in Palestine: Maps 1, 9, 10, 17, 18
2. modern Hashimite kingdom in the Middle East: Maps 2, 3, 22

Josephus (ca. A.D. 37–ca. A.D. 95), Jewish historian in whose works extracts from the Babyloniaca of Berossus are preserved: p. 150

Josiah, king of Judah (637–608); killed in the battle of Megiddo in attempting to arrest the expedition of the Pharaoh Neco to Mitanni against the Babylonians: pp. 110, 128

Judah, the southern of the two Palestinian kingdoms: pp. 101, 108, 109, 110, 128; Maps 17, 18

Jupiter, the chief god of the Roman mythology; identified with the Babylonian Marduk: p. 150

Jussa, loc. in Iraq W. of Mosul: Map 15

K

Kabalati (Ishchali), loc. on the Diyala near Baghdad; excavations in 1934–6 revealed a temple of Ishtar and a palace of the Amurru period; also conjecturally identified with Dur Rimush: Maps 1, 8

Kabti-ilani-Marduk, author of the epic of the plague god Irra: p. 119

Kadashman-Kharbe I, *or* **Kadashman-Enlil,** king of the Kassite dynasty (14th cent.); corresponded with the Pharaoh of Egypt: p. 86

Kadesh, loc. on the Orontes, scene of a battle between the Pharaoh Rameses II and the Hittites: Maps 1, 9, 18

Kaiwanian, prehistoric site in NE. Iraq: Map 6

Kaksu (Qasr Shamamok), town in Assyria; excavations in 1933 revealed ruins of Assyrian buildings and a Parthian necropolis: Maps 1, 3, 11

Kalkhu: p. 22; see CALAH

MEDITERRANEAN SEA—PADI

Babylon against attacks from the north: Map 18
Mediterranean Sea, *Akk.* **Tamtum Elitum,** inland sea surrounded by Europe, N. Africa, and W. Asia; the early civilisations of the West and Near East grew up largely around its periphery: pp. 42, 46, 73, 77, 90, 98, 114, 132, 147, 150; Maps 1, 9, 10, 17, 18
Megiddo, Canaanite royal city in Israel, on one of the routes between Egypt and Mesopotamia; here Josiah perished in 608 in battle against the Pharaoh Neco II: pp. 114, 128; Map 18
Meli-Shipak, Kassite king of Babylonia (1191–1176): Pl. 259
Melitene (Malatya), town in E. of Cappadocia, near the Euphrates: Map 9
Memphis, town in Egypt, on the Nile: p. 110; Maps 1, 9, 17, 18
Menahem, king of Israel (743–737) in whose reign began the Assyrian attacks upon Palestine: p. 101
Me-na-si-i: p. 110; see MANASSEH
Mercury, Rom. god of trade, identified with the Bab. Nabu: p. 150
Merodach: p. 139; see MARDUK
Merodach-baladan, *Bab.* **Marduk-apul-iddin III,** king of Babylon (720–709) who sent an embassy to Jerusalem in the reign of Hezekiah: pp. 10, 108, 109, 139
Mesannipadda, king of the first dynasty of Ur (2479–2439): p. 45
Mesilim, king of Kish (ca. 2600): p. 46
miktum, in the Code of Lipit-Ishtar, a citizen with certain established rights: p. 54
Mila Mergi, prehistoric site in NW. Iraq: Maps 3, 11
Miletus, trading port on the W. coast of Asia Minor: Map 9
Mitanni, district between Mesopotamia and Syria on the northwest; a Hurrian kingdom to which Assyria was originally subject: pp. 86, 90; Maps 1, 17
mithraeum, Rom. name for a temple of the Persian god Mithras; the discovery of a mithraeum (as for example at Erech) is evidence of the presence of the legions at the place where it was found: Pl. 57
Mitinti, king of Ashdod upon whom Sennacherib bestowed some of the lands which he had taken from Hezekiah: p. 109
Mlefaat, prehistoric site in NE. Iraq: Map 6
Moab, region E. of the Dead Sea, occupied by the Assyrians: pp. 101, 108; Maps 17, 18
Mohenjo-Daro, loc. in the Indus valley; excavations have revealed very early connections with Mesopotamia: pp. 39, 76
Moses, Bib. leader and legislator whose laws have certain similarities to, and also differences from, the Mesopotamian codes: pp. 73, 80, 83, 147
Mosul 1. town in NE. Iraq, on the W. bank of the Tigris, facing the ancient Nineveh: pp. 19, 39, 90, 114; Maps 1, 2, 5, 6, 11, 12, 22
2. province of the old empire of Turkey, now of the state of Iraq: p. 19; Map 22
Msejra, tell in central Iraq: Map 3
Muntafiq, province in the S. of Iraq in which numerous important tells have been found: Map 22
Murik Tidnim ('to keep Tidnim away'), wall built by the Sumerian king Shu-Sin along the middle course of the Euphrates to ward off the Bedouin of the western desert: p. 54; Map 8
Murshilish I, Hittite king (early 16th cent.) who brought the first dynasty of Babylon to an end: p. 84
mushkenum, in the Code of Hammurabi, a citizen of the second class, below the *awilum*: p. 83
Mycenaean culture, great civilisation of the Mediterranean area from ca. 500 to 1000, centred on Greece and the islands; resemblances to Mesopotamian culture have been discerned and relations conjectured: p. 43
Mylasa, town in Caria, near the SW. coast of Asia Minor: Map 9
Mysia, district in the NW. of Asia Minor: Map 9

N

Nabonidus, last king of Babylon (555–538); incurred the hostility of the priesthood of Babylon by impiety towards the god Marduk, and allowed his son Belshazzar to act as his deputy on the throne; pp. 13, 132, 138, 142, 147
Nabopolassar, *Bab.* **Nabu-apal-usur,** king of Babylon (625–605), founder of the Neo-Babylonian dynasty and father of Nebuchadnezzar II: pp. 110, 128, 143
Nabu, *Bib.* **Nebo,** god of wisdom, writing, and trade, patron of astrologers and scribes, son of Marduk, scribe and herald of the gods; especially worshipped in Borsippa and Nineveh: pp. 27, 111, 114, 128, 132, 139, 142, 150
Nabu-apal-usur: p. 128; see NABOPOLASSAR
Nabu-kudurri-usur, see NEBUCHADNEZZAR
Nacrasa, town in Asia Minor, in S. of Mysia: Map 9
Nahrawan canal, longest canal ever constructed, traces of whose bed can still be detected in many places E. of the Tigris between Samarra and Cuthah: p. 12
Nahr el-'Asi: Map 1; see ORONTES
Nahr el-Kelb, river in Lebanon, debouching into the Mediterranean N. of Beirut: p. 132
Nahum, prophet of the 7th cent. who foretold the fall of Nineveh: p. 110
Nairi, district NW. of Assyria against which the Assyrian kings directed their expeditions, especially in the 9th cent.: Map 17
Najaf, town in Iraq, in the province of Diwaniya; here is the tomb of Ali, fourth successor of Mohammed: Map 22
Namkhani, priest-king of Lagash (21st cent.), put to death by Ur-Nammu: p. 51
Nana, goddess worshipped in Erech, sometimes identified with Inanna-Ishtar: Pl. 259
Nanna, *Bab.* **Sin,** moon god worshipped in Ur; there was a remarkable revival of his cult in the last years of the Babylonian kingdom: pp. 46, 51, 54, 138
Nanshe, Sum. goddess of prophecy, interpreter of dreams, especially worshipped at Nina: p. 51
Naplanum, West Semite chieftan who occupied Larsa and reigned influentially because of its dominant commercial position in the marshland (1955–1935): p. 54
Naqqar, tell in central Iraq: Map 3
Naram-Sin, the last great king of the dynasty of Agade (2159–2123); campaigned against the Lullabians and Gutians: pp. 54, 76; Pls. 151, 152
Narru, primeval god mentioned in the 'Dialogue between two friends' as the creator of mankind; identified with Enlil by a cuneiform commentary: p. 119
naru literature, records inscribed on monuments, derived from historical tradition and concluding with a blessing or a curse: p. 73
Nasibina, see NISIBIS
Nasiriya, town in Iraq, capital of the province of Muntafiq, on the Euphrates not far from the site of Ur: Maps 2, 4, 5, 22; Pl. 10
Nebo: pp. 128, 139; see NABU
Nebi Yunus ('prophet Jonah'), loc. on the Tigris S. of Quyunjiq, built on part of the ruins of Nineveh; the name is due to the tomb of the prophet Jonah, which was on show in the mosque: p. 110
Nebuchadnezzar *Bab.* **Nabu-kudurri-usur** 1. **I,** Babylonian king of the second dynasty of Isin (ca. 1135); waged successful campaigns against Elam and for a while controlled Assyria: p. 90
2. **II,** Assyrian king of Babylon (604–562); built the Neo-Babylonian empire on the foundations laid by his father Nabopolassar; captured Jerusalem three times, and on the third occasion (586) deported its inhabitants to Babylon: pp. 19, 29, 80, 83, 84, 128, 132; Map 18
Neco II, Pharaoh of Egypt (609–594); attacked Assyria in 609, defeating Josiah of Judah at Megiddo on the way, but was defeated by Nebuchadnezzar at Carchemish in 605: p. 128
Nefeji, burial mound near Erech, of wide extent, with two smaller burial mounds: Pl. 276
Negub, loc. in Assyria, near the junction of the Great Zab with the Tigris; here Esarhaddon had a tunnel constructed for the purpose of water supply: Maps 3, 11
Nergal *or* **Erragal** ('lord of the wide dwelling-places'), Sum. god of the Underworld and later among the Babylonians also of light, the son of Enlil; especially worshipped at Cuthah: pp. 101, 120, 150
Nergal-shar-usur: p. 132; see NERIGLISSAR
Neribtum, loc. in the Diyala district: Map 8
Neriglissar, *Bab.* **Nergal-shar-usur,** officer of Nebuchadnezzar at the siege of Jerusalem in 586, later himself king of the Neo-Babylonian empire: p. 132
Nghara: Map 1; see KHURSAG KALAMA
'Nibmuwaria', name by which in the Tell el-Amarna letters the Kassite kings of Babylonia addressed the Pharaoh Amenhotep III: p. 86
Nibru, see NIPPUR
Nicaea, town in Bithynia in N. Asia Minor, to which a trade route ran from Mesopotamia: Map 9
Nile, great river in Egypt which contrasts favourably by the regularity of its flooding with the capriciousness of the Tigris and Euphrates: p. 86; Maps 1, 9, 17, 18
Nile delta, district of lowlands and lagoons where the Nile makes its way into the Mediterranean Sea by many mouths: Map 1
Nimit Ishtar (Tell'Afar), loc. in N. Mesopotamia: Maps 1, 3, 11
Nimrod: p. 90; see NINURTA
Nimrud: pp. 22, 27, 38, 108; Maps 1, 2, 10, 11, 12, 17, 18; Pls. 21, 70, 71, 277; see CALAH
Nina (Surghul), tell in S. Mesopotamia, S. of Urukug; excavations here in 1887 revealed burial grounds with traces of cremation: Maps 1, 3, 8, 21
Ninazu, see ERESH-KI-GAL
Nin-dada, wife of the victim in a case recorded in the Code of Lipit-Ishtar, regarded as a standard precedent in Sumerian jurisprudence: p. 54
Nineveh, *Bab.* **Ninua** (Quyunjiq), ancient city in N. Mesopotamia, on the E. bank of the Tigris opposite Mosul; capital of the Assyrian empire at the time of its widest extension; here in 1842–3 Botta made the first excavation of Mesopotamian tells; thereafter excavations have been carried on systematically down to the present day: pp. 10, 19, 39, 42, 98, 108, 109, 110, 111, 128, 138; Maps 1, 2, 3, 5, 6, 9, 10, 11, 17, 18, 22; Pl. 20
Ningal, Sum. goddess, mother of Inanna-Ishtar and wife of the moon god Nanna, with whom she was worshipped in Ur: pp. 46, 51, 54, 143
Ningirsu, city god of Lagash, patron of Gudea, who built the temple E-ninnu in his honour: pp. 13, 46, 51
Nin-gish-zi-da, Sum. god, in general a god of the earth, later also of the Underworld; patron of Gudea of Lagash: Pl. 134
Ninhursag ('lady of the mountains'), Sum. goddess, worshipped especially as the mother goddess: p. 45; Pl. 146
Ninib, Babylonian god, identified with the Roman Mars: p. 150
Ninkilim, Sumerian goddess, invoked for protection against vermin: p. 62
Nin-lil, Sumerian goddess, wife of Enlil, worshipped in Nippur; regarded by the Assyrians as the wife of Ashur: pp. 46, 84, 114, 138
Ninmakh, god to whom there was a temple in Babylon: Map 19
Ninos: p. 90; see TUKULTI-NINURTA I
Ninua, see NINEVEH
Ninurta, *Bib.* **Nimrod?** Sumerian god of life and nature, for the Assyrians the god of war and hunting, which perhaps associates him with the Bib. Nimrod; the son of Enlil; especially worshipped in Kish, Nippur, and Calah; an important figure in many myths: pp. 62, 84, 90, 115, 120, 138
Nippur, *Sum.* **Nibru** (Nuffar), town in the centre of Babylonia, originally the centre of Sumer; contained temples of Enlil; systematic excavations since 1889 have revealed among other things a temple library containing about 20,000 tablets: pp. 12, 22, 39, 46, 51, 54, 62, 65, 76, 84, 136, 139, 143; Maps 1, 2, 3, 4, 5, 8, 9, 10, 18, 21, 22
Nisan: pp. 87, 142; see NISANNU
Nisannu, *Bib.* **Nisan,** month in the Mesopotamian calendar: p, 150
Nisibis (Nasibina), loc. in NW. Mesopotamia, to the W. of the upper reaches of the Tigris, important trade centre and strategic point; here Esarhaddon defeated the army of the brothers leagued against his rule: p. 98; Maps 3, 10, 17, 18
Nisir, Mount, mountain where the human survivors came ashore in the Babylonian epic of the Flood: p. 120
Noah, the Biblical survivor of the Flood, paralleled by the Mesopotamian Utnapishtim: pp. 39, 115
Nuffar: Maps 1, 2, 3; see NIPPUR
Nukhar, suburb of Babylon: Map 19
Nusku, the son of Sin and minister of Enlil, and hence himself regarded as a god of light; especially worshipped in Haran: p. 139
Nuzu (Yorghan Tepe), town in central Mesopotamia, near Arrapkha; excavations 1925–31 have revealed clay tablets with contents of importance for the history of Mesopotamian law: pp. 39, 147; Maps 1, 2, 3, 10, 11, 17

O

Oizil, see UZUN
Oman, district in SE. Arabia; diorite was imported hence into Mesopotamia in the time of Gudea of Lagash: p. 51
Omri, king of Israel (885–874); mentioned several times of the records of the Assyrians, which speak of the kingdom of Israel as the 'house of Omri' and of the Israelites as the 'sons of Omri' long after the extinction of the dynasty which he founded: pp. 101, 108
Opis, loc. between the Tigris and Euphrates, thought to have been not far from the later Seleucia: p. 10
Orontes (Nahr el-Asi), river in Syria: p. 101; Maps 1, 9, 10, 17, 18
Osnappar: p. 110; see ASHURBANIPAL

P

Padi, king of Ekron upon whom Sennacherib bestowed some of the lands which he had taken from

Pls. 4, 6, 69, 173, 280

Tikrit, prehistoric site in central Iraq, on the Tigris N. of Samarra: Maps 3, 11, 18, 22

Til Barsib (Tell Ahmar), tell on the eastern border of Syria, on the Euphrates S. of Carchemish: p. 10; Maps 9, 17, 18

Tirhakah, Ethiopian king described in the Bible as being attacked by Sennacherib: pp. 109, 110

Tirqa (Tell Ashara), loc. on the Euphrates just below its junction with the Khabur; frequently mentioned as an important town in the Mari archives: p. 90; Maps 1, 3, 10, 17, 18

Tishri: pp. 87, 110, 150; see TASHRITU

Top Zawa, prehistoric site in NE. Iraq: Maps 3, 11

Tralles (Aydin), town in Lydia, in W. Asia Minor: Map 9

Trapezus, port in NE. Asia Minor, on the S. coast of the Black Sea: Map 9

Troy, famous ancient town in Troas in W. Asia Minor; discovered by Schliemann in 1868 near the modern Hissarlik: Maps 1, 9

Tuba, suburb of Babylon: Map 19

Tudmur, see TADMOR

Tukulti-Ninurta 1. I, *Gr.* **Ninos,** king of Assyria (1242–1206) and one of the first founders of its greatness; conquered S. Mesopotamia and destroyed Babylon; founded Kar-Tukulti-Ninurta and removed his residence there: p. 90; Pl. 263
2. **II,** king of Assyria (889–884): p. 98

tulul, see TELL

Tulul el-'Aqir: Maps 1, 11; see KAR-TUKULTI-NINURTA

Turkey, modern state in the Middle East of which Iraq formed a part until after the First World War; now lies NW. of Iraq: Maps 2, 3, 12, 22

Turnat: Map 1; see DIYALA

Tursaq, tell on the E. border of Iraq: Map 3

turtanu, title of the commander-in-chief of the Assyrian army: p. 108

Turukku, district in E. Mesopotamia, SW. of the Taurus Mountains: Map 10

Turushpa (Van), capital of the Aramaean Urartu, on Lake Van: Maps 1, 11, 17

Tushratta, king of Mitanni (14th cent.) whom the Tell el-Amarna archives show to have had friendly relations with Egypt: p. 86

Tutub (Khafaje), town on the Diyala above its junction with the Tigris: Maps 1, 2, 8, 17, 21

Tutul (Hit), loc. in W. Mesopotamia, on the central course of the Euphrates, with rich deposit of asphalt: p. 73; Maps 1, 3, 8, 10, 17, 18

Tuwaim, tell in N. Iraq, near the Tigris: Maps 3, 11

Tuz Khurmatli, town in E. Iraq, in the province of Kirkuk: Maps 3, 6, 22

Tyana, fortified town in Cappadocia, in E. Asia Minor: Map 9

Tyre, famous port and trade centre built on an island adjoining the coast of Phoenicia: pp. 10, 98, 101; Maps 1, 9, 10, 17, 18

U

Ubase, tell in N. Iraq, on the Tigris above Ashur: Maps 3, 11

Udug, *Bab.* **Utukku,** evil demon represented as having a lion's head: p. 65

Ugarit (Ras Shamra), port on the coast of Syria, mentioned in the Tell el-Amarna letters; inhabited by Semites from 2000; flourished especially after the 16th cent. and was destroyed ca. 1200; the tell was accidentally discovered in 1927 and has since been excavated; texts, some in alphabetic cuneiform, from the 13th cent. were found here: p. 26; Maps 1, 9, 10, 17, 18

Ukhaidir, tell in central Iraq, W. of the Euphrates: Map 3

Ululu, month in the Mesopotamian calendar: p. 150

Um el-'Aqarib, tell in S. Iraq: Map 3

Umma (Tell Jokha), town of E. Sumer, in S. Mesopotamia; the tell was excavated in 1902 and clay tablets were found: p. 46; Maps 1, 3, 8, 10, 18

umonia, title of the headmaster of the 'house of tablets': p. 62

Ur (el-Muqaiyar), famous town in S. Babylonia, with a temple of the moon god Nanna or Sin; excavations

in twelve campaigns between 1922 and 1934 made the sensational revelations of the Royal Tombs and the tomb of Shub-ad: pp. 9, 10, 12, 13, 29, 38, 83, 84, 138, 142; Maps 1, 2, 3, 4, 5, 8, 9, 10, 14, 17, 18, 21, 22; Pls. 64, 65, 273

Ura, town in Cilicia, in SE. Asia Minor; important trade centre: Map 9

Urartu, Ass. name for a state in the Armenian mountains near Lake Van: Maps 1, 17, 18

Urash Gate, gate in Babylon: Map 19

Urfa: Map 1; see EDESSA

Uri, Sumerian name for the region later known as Akkad: p. 45

Uriah, high priest in Jerusalem in the Assyrian period: p. 108

urigallu, title of the high priest in the Babylonian hierarchy: p. 139

Ur-lugal-edinna, the physician of Ur-ningursu of Lagash: p. 62

Urmia, Lake, lake in NW. Iran: Maps 1, 2, 3, 9, 10, 11, 17, 18, 22

Ur-Nammu, king of Sumer (ca. 2044–2027), founder of the third dynasty of Ur, lawgiver and builder: pp. 10, 45, 51, 108, 142, 143, 147

Ur-Nammu, Code of, earliest known Mesopotamian legal code, of which fragments have survived inscribed on bricks: p. 51

Ur-Nina, king of Lagash (25th cent.): p. 46; Pl. 107

Ur-Ningursu, king of Lagash (21st cent.): p. 62; Pls. 140, 142

Ur-Ninurta, 6th king of the dynasty of Isin (ca. 1853–1826), successor of Lipit-Ishtar: p. 54

Urshanabi, in the epic of Gilgamesh, the ferryman of Utnapishtim, who accompanied Gilgamesh on his return journey to Erech: p. 115

Ursu, loc. in NW. Mesopotamia, near the headwaters of the Euphrates: Map 10

Uruk, see ERECH

Urukagina, king of Lagash (24th cent.), reformer and upright administrator: pp. 13, 45, 46, 62

Urukug (el-Hibba), Sumerian town in S. Mesopotamia SE. of Lagash: Maps 1, 3, 21

Ur-Zababa, king of Kish of whom Sargon of Agade was the cup-bearer: p. 73

Usaila, tell in S. Iraq, near Ur: Map 3

Ush, city governor of Umma ca. 2600: p. 46

Utnapishtim, the chief character in the Babylonian and Assyrian tradition of the Flood, parallel to the Noah of the Bible: pp. 39, 115, 122

Utu: p. 138; see SHAMASH

Utu-hegal, king of the 5th dynasty of Erech (2028–2022) who liberated Sumer from the oppression of the Gutians: pp. 46, 76

Utukku, see UDUG

Uzun, *Gr.* **Amardos** (Oizil), river in Persia, flowing into the Caspian Sea: Maps 1, 9, 10, 18

V

Van: Maps 1, 17; see TURUSHPA

Van, Lake, lake in E. Turkey: pp. 41, 43; Maps 1, 9, 10, 11, 17, 18

'Venus tablets', astrological texts from the time of Ammi-zaduga grandson of Hammurabi, of great importance for the establishment of chronology: p. 87

W

Wadi Brissa, watercourse in Syria, known for the inscription of Nebuchadnezzar II carved on the rock face: p. 132

Wadi Tharthar, river in central Iraq, between the Tigris and Euphrates: Maps 1, 3, 11, 22

Wadi Tharthar Depression, low-lying district SW. of the Jebel Hamrin mountains, into which the superfluous waters of the Tigris have since some little while been drained by the Tharthar Canal: Map 4

Wannah-Was-Sadum: Map 1; see MARAD

wardum, the title for a slave in the code of Hammurabi, as distinct from the two higher classes of freemen: p. 83

Warka: Maps 1, 2, 3, 18; see ERECH

Warum, district in E. Mesopotamia, E. of the Diyala: Map 10

X

Xanthus 1. river in Lycia, in SW. Asia Minor: Map 1 2. town at the mouth of 1, in Lycia in SW. Asia Minor: Map 9

Xenophon (ca. 430–ca. 355), Gr. soldier and historian; travelled through Mesopotamia on the expedition of the Younger Cyrus and the return on which he led the Ten Thousand (401–400); the *Anabasis* in which he records his adventures casts some useful light on the region two centuries after the fall of the Assyrian empire: p. 110

Xerxes, king of Persia (485–465); Babylon was sacked early in his reign in consequence of a revolt: pp. 23, 132

Y

Yadnan: p. 10; see CYPRUS

Yamkhad, district in N. Syria, mentioned in the Mari archives, where Zimri-Lim of Mari took refuge after the capture of Mari by Shamsi-Adad I: Map 10

Yamutbal, district in central Mesopotamia, N. of Sumer, a dependency of Larsa; mentioned in the Mari archives: Map 10

Yarimja, tell in N. Iraq: Maps 3, 11

Yashmakh-Adad, son of Shamshi-Adad I of Assyria and by him placed on the throne of Mari at the end of the 18th cent.: pp. 83, 90

Yasin Tepe, tell in NE. Iraq: Maps 3, 11

Yeb: p. 109; see ELEPHANTINE

Yorghan Tepe: p. 39; Maps 1, 2, 10, 11; see NUZU

Yümük Tepe, tell in Cilicia, in SE. Asia Minor: Map 9

Z

Zab, Great, *earlier* **Zabu Shupalu,** river in NE. Iraq, tributary of the Tigris: p. 98; Maps 1, 3, 6, 7, 9, 10, 11, 12, 17, 18, 21, 22

Zab, Little, *earlier* **Zabu Elu,** river in NE. Iraq, tributary of the Tigris: p. 39; Maps 1, 3, 6, 9, 10, 11, 12, 17, 18, 21, 22; Pl. 2

Zababa, name sometimes given to the Sum. war god Ninurta, especially at Kish, where there was a temple to him: Map 21

Zababa Gate, gate in Babylon: Map 19

Zaban (Altun Köprü), ancient settlement in NE. Mesopotamia, on the Little Zab: Maps 1, 11

Zabum, king of the First Dynasty of Babylon (1776–1763): p. 83

Zagros Mountains, mountain range in W. Persia, frequently the entrance way to incursions into Mesopotamia from the east: pp. 12, 54, 76, 98; Maps 6, 8, 10, 17, 18

Zalmaku, district NW. of Mesopotamia, round the headwaters of the Balikh: Map 10

Zamua, district in the Zagros Mountains in E. Persia: Map 17

Zarzi, prehistoric site in NE. Iraq; excavations in 1928 and 1949 revealed traces of cave-dwellers of the Palaeolithic Age: p. 41; Maps 3, 6

Zephaniah, prophet in Judah under Josiah who foretold the fall of Ashur and Nineveh: p. 110

Zeus, supreme god of the Greek pantheon, identified with the Roman Jupiter and under the Seleucids with the Babylonian Anu: p. 138

Ziblayat, tell in S. Iraq: Map 3

ziggurat, name of the Mesopotamian temple tower: pp. 51, 84, 90, 142, 143; Map 21; Pls. 64, 174, 269, 270, 271, 273, 277, 281, Colour Pl. facing p. 142

Zimri-Lim, king of Mari (1722–1690), conquered by Hammurabi; frequently mentioned in the Mari archives: pp. 77, 83

Zuhab, prehistoric site on the border of Iraq and Iran: Map 3

Zulummur, Bab. deity mentioned in the 'Dialogue between two friends' as taking part in the creation of mankind: p. 119

NAMES OF AUTHORS

BIBLICAL REFERENCES

NOTES ON THE PLATES

Further details of some of the objects illustrated, particularly relating to the materials used, the dimensions, where the objects were found and where they are now kept.

Abbreviations used: B.M. = British Museum; I.M. = Iraq Museum, Baghdad; L. = Louvre, Paris; S. M. = Staatliche Museen, Berlin

12 Silver boat from the Royal Tombs at Ur. Length 25¼ in., width 3¼ in., height of prow 7¼ in. I.M. **37** Stone tablet with building inscription of Nabu-apal-iddin. Middle of 9th century B.C. Width of relief 7 in. B.M. **38** Bronze lion. Height 4¼ in., width of white stone tablet 4¼ in. Akkadian period. L. The inscription reads: 'Tishari, the king of Urkish, built the temple of Pirigal. May the temple of this god be protected by Lubadaga. He who destroys it shall be doomed to ruin by Lubadaga: may Anu not hear his prayer, may Ninnagan, Sinuga, and Ishkur curse him who destroys it a thousand thousand times.' **39** Sandstone relief. Height 14½ in. From Babylon. B.M. **40** Found at Nineveh. 5 × 5½ in. B.M. **77** Photograph by Aviation Française de Levant, taken in April 1937 after four excavation campaigns; numerous buildings already visible. **89** Hard stone. Height approx. 5½ in., diameter approx. 2¾ in. I.M. **91** Silver, with walls 1/12 in. thick; height 3½ in., diameter 5 in. I.M. **92** Height after restoration 3 ft. 7¼ in. I.M. **93** Copper relief. Length 6 ft. 6¾ in.,

height 2 ft. 11½ in. B.M. **94, 95** Limestone figures on slate background. Length 3 ft. 9¼ in., height 8¾ in. I.M. **96** Reconstructed lyre. Shell, lapis lazuli, red limestone, gold, and wood. Height 3 ft. 11½ in. I.M. **97** Golden helmet. Length 10¼ in., height 9 in. I.M. **98, 99** Dagger. Length 14½ in. I.M. **100, 101** Mosaic panel. Shell, lapis lazuli, and red limestone. Length 8 in., width 18½ in. B.M. **102** Rein-ring. Gold. Height 6 in. B.M. **103** Gaming-board. Shell, bone, red limestone, and lapis lazuli. Length 10½ in., diameter of pieces ⅞ in. B.M. **104** Votive tablet from Nippur. Slate. Height 7½ in. Museum of the Ancient East, Istanbul. **107** White sandstone tablet. Height about 15¾ in. L. **108** Copper chariot and four. Height 2¾ in. I.M. **110** Statuette of black volcanic stone. Height 15¼ in. I.M. **112** Female statuette. Limestone. Height 5¾ in. I.M. **113** Copper candelabra. Height 18 in. Natural History Museum, Chicago. **114** Copper standard. Height 16¼ in. I.M. **115** Limestone tablet from Khafaje. Height 12½ in. I.M. **116** Limestone tablet from Tello. Height 6¾ in. L. **117** Limestone stele. Height of this fragment 2 ft. $5\frac{1}{2}$ in. L. **118** Black stone. Height $4\frac{1}{4}$ in. B.M. **119** Stone bowl. Height 2 in. I.M. **120** Small limestone relief from Khafaje. Height $5\frac{1}{4}$ in., length $9\frac{3}{4}$ in. I.M. **122** Bronze statuette from Khafaje. Height $4\frac{1}{4}$ in. I.M. **123** Alabaster relief. Height 9 in. L. **124** Silver vase. Height $13\frac{3}{4}$ in. L. **126** Shell. Height 3 in. B.M. **128** Bituminous material. Height 2 ft. $9\frac{1}{2}$ in. L. **129** Seal surface of marble. Height $2\frac{1}{8}$ in., diameter $1\frac{3}{4}$ in. S.M. **132** Seal surface of lapis lazuli, to which was fitted a bronze shaft ending in a silver calf. Height $1\frac{5}{8}$ in., diameter $1\frac{3}{8}$ in. S.M. **133** Jasper seal. Height $1\frac{1}{4}$ in., diameter $\frac{3}{4}$ in. Pierpont Morgan Library, New York. **134** Grey limestone relief. Height about 2 ft. $3\frac{1}{2}$ in. S.M. **135** Diorite statuette. Height 2 ft. $4\frac{3}{4}$ in. L. **136** Diorite statuette. Height 18 in. L. **137** Stone statuette. Length 4 in. L. **138** Limestone relief. Height 4 ft. $1\frac{1}{4}$ in., width 2 ft. $\frac{3}{4}$ in., thickness $8\frac{1}{4}$ in. L. **139** Dark-green steatite beaker. Height about 9 in., L. **140** Alabaster statuette. Height 18 in. L. **144** Alabaster stautette. Height $20\frac{3}{4}$ in. Found at Mari in 1934. L. **145** Gypsum head. Height $5\frac{3}{4}$ in. Found at Mari in 1935. L. **146** Gypsum head. Height $1\frac{3}{8}$ in. Found at Mari in 1952. L. **147** Mother-of-pearl. Height $3\frac{1}{4}$ in. Found at *Mari* in 1938. L. **148** Made of fragments of gypsum, lapis lazuli, and shell *stuck to*gether. Height $5\frac{1}{2}$ in. *F*ound at Mari in 1952. L. **149, 150** Made of shell *and ivory*. Respective heights 3 in. and $2\frac{1}{2}$ in. L. **151** Red sandstone stele. Height about 6 *ft.* $6\frac{3}{4}$ *in. L.* **153** Terracotta lion. Found at Tell Harmal. I.M. **154** Bronze mask. Height about $14\frac{1}{4}$ in I.M. **155** Found at Sippar. Dimensions $3\frac{1}{4}$ in. $\times$ $4\frac{1}{2}$ in. B.M. **156** Black serpentine seal. Height $1\frac{1}{4}$ in., diameter $\frac{3}{4}$ in. Pierpont Morgan Library, New York. **157** Seal. Height about $1\frac{3}{8}$ in. I.M. **158** Limestone relief. B.M. **159** Diorite head. Height $5\frac{7}{8}$ in. L. **160** Relief of the diorite stele containing the Code of *Hammurabi*. Total height of stele 7 ft. $4\frac{1}{2}$ in., height of relief approx. 2 ft. $1\frac{1}{2}$ *in.* L. **161** Diorite statue. Height 5 ft. 8 in. All but head in the Museum of the Ancient East, Istanbul. **162** Bronze statuette. Hands and face covered with gold leaf. Height $7\frac{3}{4}$ in. L. **163** Clay model. Height $5\frac{1}{4}$ in., width $3\frac{1}{4}$ in. B.M. **165, 166** Terracotta. Height $2\frac{3}{4}$ in. I.M. **167, 168** Terracotta. Height of lioness' head 2 in. I.M. **175** Sandstone statue. Height 3 ft. $4\frac{1}{2}$ in. Found at Nimrud. B.M. **176** Statuette. Total height $9\frac{1}{2}$ in. Museum of Fine Arts, Boston. **177** Limestone sculpture. Height 11 ft. $5\frac{3}{4}$ in. From Nimrud. B.M. **178** Alabaster relief. Height 3 ft. 8 in. From Nimrud. B.M. **179, 189** Black basalt obelisk. Height 6 ft. $7\frac{1}{2}$ in., width at base about 2 ft. B.M. **181-3** Thirteen of the bronze strips which adorned the gates of Shalmaneser III's palace at Balawat are in the B.M. Fragments found their way to the L., the Museum of the Ancient East in Istanbul, and the Walters Art Gallery in Baltimore. The strips were about 8 ft. long, 11 in. high, and only $\frac{1}{20}$ in. thick. The doors to which the strips were attached must have been over 19 ft. 8 in. high and 6 ft. wide. **184** Basalt relief. Height about 2 ft. $3\frac{1}{2}$ in. 9th century B.C. Found at Tell Halaf. S. M. **185** Limestone relief. Colours red and ochre. Height about 2 ft. $3\frac{1}{2}$ in. 9th century B.C. Found at Tell Halaf. Walters Art Gallery, Baltimore. **186** Gypsum relief. Height 3 ft. $7\frac{1}{4}$ in. Found at Nimrud. B.M. **187** Alabaster relief. Height 2 ft. 10 in. Found at Nimrud. B.M. **189** White limestone. Height 7 ft. $1\frac{3}{4}$ in. Found at Nimrud. B.M. **190** Gypsum relief. Height 3 ft. $5\frac{3}{4}$ in. Found at Nimrud. B.M. **191** Gypsum relief. Length 9 ft. $6\frac{1}{4}$ in. Found at Nimrud. B.M. **194** Black stone relief. Height 9 ft. $11\frac{3}{4}$ in. Found at Khorsabad. L. **196** Alabaster relief. Height 9 ft. $3\frac{1}{2}$ in. Found at Khorsabad. L. **197** Black stone relief. Length 5 ft. 10 in. Found at Khorsabad. B.M. **198** Sandstone. Length 2 ft. 11 in. Found at Khorsabad. Museo di Antichità, Turin. **200** Limestone statue. Height 14 ft. 6 in. Found at Khorsabad. B.M. **201** Detail of 194. **204** Basalt relief. Height 4 ft. $3\frac{1}{4}$ in. Found at Carchemish; now at Ankara. **205** Diorite. Height 3 ft. $1\frac{3}{4}$ in. Found at Zenjirli. 8th century B.C. Museum of the Ancient East, Istanbul. **206** Ivory. Found at Nimrud. B.M. **207** Alabaster. Height 20 in. Found at Nineveh. B.M. **210** Basalt stele. Height 10 ft. $6\frac{3}{4}$ in. Found at Zenjirli. S.M. **211** Limestone relief. Height about $19\frac{3}{4}$ in. Found at Ashur. S.M. **213** Gypsum. Height $19\frac{1}{2}$ in. Found at Nineveh. B.M. **214** Photograph taken in January 1956 between Babylon and Kish. **215** Fragment of relief from Sennacherib's palace at Nineveh. B.M. **216** Alabaster sculpture. Height 15 ft. 5 in. From Khorsabad. L. **218** Origin uncertain; now in Museum für Kunst und Gewerbe, Hamburg. **219** Alabaster relief. From Nineveh. B.M. **220** Alabaster relief. Height $15\frac{1}{4}$ in. From Nineveh. B.M. **222** Detail of 228. **223** Alabaster relief. Height 2 ft. 10 in. From Nineveh. B.M. **224** Alabaster relief. Height 1 ft. $8\frac{3}{4}$ in. From Nineveh. B.M. **226** Limestone relief. From Nineveh. B.M. **232** Lion of glazed tiles. Height about 3 ft. $3\frac{1}{4}$ in. From Babylon. Museum of Fine Arts, Chicago. **239** Weight of hard green stone. Height $3\frac{3}{4}$ in. Weight about 3 oz. **240** Reconstruction of Babylon as situated on both banks of the Euphrates in the time of Nebuchadnezzar, seen from the northwest bank. **241** Reconstruction of the Ishtar Gate at Babylon. Height about 49 ft. $2\frac{1}{2}$ in. S.M. **242, 243** Photographs taken in January 1956. **248** Reddish marble seal. Height $\frac{7}{8}$ in., diameter $\frac{5}{8}$ in. Pierpont Morgan Library, New York. **250** Black serpentine seal. Height $1\frac{5}{8}$ in., diameter $1\frac{1}{4}$ in. Pierpont Morgan Library, New York. **252** Cornelian seal. Height $1\frac{1}{2}$ in., diameter $\frac{5}{8}$ in. Pierpont Morgan Library, New York. **255** Gypsum statuette. Height 9 in. Found at Mari in 1937. Aleppo. **256** Kudurru stone. Black limestone. Height $19\frac{1}{2}$ in. Found at Susa. Ca. 1300 B.C. L. **257** Black limestone boundary stone. Height 2 ft. $2\frac{3}{4}$ in. Found at Susa. 12th century B.C. L. **258** Limestone boundary stone. Height 2 ft. $1\frac{1}{2}$ in. Found at Abu Habba. 12th century B.C. B.M. **259** Diorite kudurru stone. Height 2 ft. $11\frac{1}{2}$ in. Found at Susa. 12th century B.C. L. **260** Detail of 257. **261** Ivory. Height $2\frac{1}{4}$ in. From Nimrud. B.M. **262** Terracotta. De Liagre Böhl Collection, Near East Institute, Leiden. **263** Gypsum socle. Height 1 ft. $10\frac{3}{4}$ in. Found at Ashur. S.M. **264, 266** De Liagre Böhl Collection, Near East Institute, Leiden. **265** Found at Nineveh. $3\frac{1}{2}\times2\frac{3}{8}$ in. B.M. **267** Basalt. Height 2 ft. $2\frac{1}{2}$ in. Found at Susa. 18th century B.C. L. **268** Stele of baked bricks with coloured glaze. Height 1 ft. 10 in. 8th century B.C. Found at Ashur. S.M. **269-80** Photographs taken during winter of 1956. **282** Bronze with inlaid eyes of stone. Length 2 ft. $3\frac{1}{2}$ in. Found at Mari in 1937. **283** Terracotta relief. Height $2\frac{3}{4}$ in. B.M. **286** Bronze statuette. Height 6 in. L. **288** Relief. Height approx. 2 ft. $7\frac{1}{2}$ in. Duke of Bedford's Collection, Woburn Abbey.

SOURCES OF THE ILLUSTRATIONS

Ankara Museum, 169, 170, 171, 172 – Archaeological Museum, Istanbul, 104, 152, 161 – Archives Photographiques, Paris, 38, 105, 106, 107, 116, 117, 123, 124, 125, 128, 135, 136, 137, 138, 139, 140, 151, 159, 160, 162, 188, 192, 201, 212, 226, 227, 228, 229, 230, 244, 256, 258, 259, 260 – Beek, M. A., Amsterdam, 3, 5, 6, 10, 13, 16, 49, 50, 51, 54, 55, 56, 57, 58, 59, 60, 61, 62, 63, 68, 69, 70, 71, 72, 73, 74, 75, 76, 80, 173, 174, 214, 231, 233, 234, 235, 236, 242, 243, 269, 271, 272, 273, 274, 276, 278, 279, 280, 281, and all colour photographs – British Museum, London, 37, 39, 40, 93, 100, 101, 102, 103, 108, 109, 118, 126, 130, 150, 155, 158, 163, 175, 179, 180, 181, 182, 183, 186, 187, 189, 190, 191, 197, 207, 208, 213, 215, 219, 223, 225, 226, 239, 245, 246, 261, 265, 283, 284 – Buringh, P., 4, 7, 8, 9, 11, 14, 15, 66, 67, 237, 270 – Cameron, G., Michigan, 294, 295, 296 – Chicago Natural History Museum, 113 – De Liagre Böhl Collection, Leiden, 262, 264, 266 – Éditions des Musées Nationaux, Paris, 141, 195, 217, 285 – Editions 'Tel', Phot. A. Vigneau, Paris, 193, 194, 209, 216, 224 – Froe, A. de, 64 – Guennol Collection, Brooklyn Museum, 121 – Hendrikse, P., 240 – Heyden, A. A. M. van der, 24, 28, 29, 30, 31, 32, 33, 34, 35, 36 – Hove, P. ten, 275 – Iraq Museum, Baghdad, 12, 48, 52, 89, 92, 94, 95, 96, 97, 98, 99, 108, 110, 112, 114, 115, 119, 120, 122, 153, 154, 157, 164, 165, 166, 167, 168, 253 – Louvre, Paris, 38, 127, 200, 222, 273 – Metropolitan Museum of Art, New York, 111, 177, 178, 232 – Museum of Fine Arts, Boston, 176 – Museum für Kunst und Gewerbe, Hamburg, 218 – Pierpont Morgan Library, New York, 133, 156, 248, 252 – National Museum of Antiquities, Leiden, 142, 143, 238, 254 – Staatliche Museen, Berlin, 129, 131, 132, 134, 184, 210, 211, 220, 241, 263, 268 – Teheran Museum, Photo Rostamy, 289, 290, 291, 292, 293 – Veen, van der, Leiden, 203, 204 – Walters Art Gallery, Baltimore, 185.

PLATES REPRODUCED FROM BOOKS AND PERIODICALS

Botta, P. E., Monuments de Ninevé, mesurés et dessinés par E. Flandin (Paris, 1849–50; Tome I, Planche 1) 19 – Dapper, Olfert, Naukeurige beschrijving van Asië, behelsende de Gewesten van Mesopotamië, Babylonië, Assyrië, etc. (Amsterdam, 1680) 17, 18 – Falkenstein, A., Archaische Texte aus Uruk (Berlin, 1936) 22, 23, 25, 26, 27 – Heinrich, E., Kleinfunde aus den archaischen Tempelschichten in Uruk (Berlin, 1936) 81, 82, 83, 84, 85, 86, 87, 88, 89, 90, 91 – Mari, No. 1 of Collection des Ides Photographiques (Éditions Ides et Calendes, Neuchâtel et Paris, 1953) 77, 78, 79, 110, 144, 145, 146, 147, 148, 149, 150 – Illustrated London News 281 – Iraq Petroleum, Vol. 7 (2 Sept. 1957) 1 and 2; Vol. 5 (5 Dec. 1955) 5 (after a drawing by Dr G. Roux) 53 – Layard, A. H., The Monuments of Nineveh (London, 1849–53; Vol. I, Pl. 98) 21 (Vol. II, Pl. 70) 20 – Mallowan, M.E.L., Twenty-Five Years of Mesopotamian Discovery (London, 1958) 206 – Place, V., Ninivé et l'Assyrie (Paris, 1867) 41, 42, 43, 44, 45, 46, 47 – Wiseman, D. J., Cylinder Seals of Western Asia (London, 1959) 247, 249, 250, 288 – Woolley, C. L., Ur Excavations (Vol. II; 1934) 65.

SOURCES FROM WHICH SOME OF THE DRAWINGS WERE DERIVED

Page 11. Rawlinson, G., The Five Great Monarchies of the Ancient Eastern World (London, 1879), p. 76 – Page 13. Buringh, P., Soils and Soil Conditions in Iraq (Baghdad, 1960), pp. 306–7 – Page 26. Kramer, S. N., From the Tablets of Sumer (1956), p. XXI – Page 27. Iraq (Vol. XVII, 1955), p. 17, and Driver, G. R., Semitic Writing (revised ed. London, 1954), Pl. 24 – Page 42. Iraq Petroleum (Dr J. Roux, April 1954), and Journal of Near Eastern Studies (Vol. IV), p. 4 – Page 65. Jean, C. F., La Religion Sumérienne (Paris, 1931), Pl. XXI – Page 108. From a photograph of the original in the British Museum in Carl Bezold, Ninive und Babylon (Leipzig, 1926), p. 95 – Page 118. Wiseman, J. D., Cylinder Seals of Western Asia (London, 1959), Figs. 29, 31, 51, 78 – Page 119. idem, Figs. 67, 68, 69, 70 – Page 139 (Marduk), Koldewey, R., Das wiedererstehende Babylon, p. 217, Fig. 134; (sacrificial rite), Rawlinson, G., The Five Great Monarchies, Vol. II, Fig. p. 35; (procession), Gressmann, H., Altorientalische Bilder zum Alten Testament, Fig. 336; (Adad), Koldewey, R., op. cit., p. 217, Fig. 134 – Page 142. Der Turmbau zu Babel, ein Märchen? (Bonifacius-Druckerei, Paderborn, s.d.), pp. 23, 38, 39 – Page 143. Mari, No. 7 of Collection des Ides Photographiques (Éditions Ides et Calendes, Neuchâtel et Paris, 1953), Fig. 118 – Page 146. idem, Fig. 114.

SOURCES OF THE MAPS

In drawing up the maps the following were used in addition to the literature cited:
1 Near and Middle East: Ancient Sites (Handbook to the Nicholson Museum, University of Sydney, 2nd. ed. 1948). 2, 3, 11, 12, 16 Buringh, P., Soils and Soil Conditions in Iraq. 4 Iraq Petroleum, October 1956, p. 28, map by G. Roux. 5 Ancient Sites of Iraq, published by the Department of Antiquities, Baghdad. 6 Iraq Petroleum, November 1956, p. 34, map by G. Roux. 8 Jean, C.F., La Religion Sumérienne (Paris, 1931), map on p. XVI. 10 Bottéro, J., and Finet, André, Répertoire Analytique des Tomes I à V, Archives Royales de Mari (Paris, 1954), Noms Géographiques, pp. 120–38 and map at end. 17 Bezold, C., Ninive und Babylon (Leipzig, 1926), map at end. 19 Unger, E., Babylon die heilige Stadt, nach der Beschreibung der Babylonier (Berlin, 1931). 20 Andrae, W., Das wiedererstandene Assur (1938). 21 Lenzen, H. J., Die Entwicklung der Zikkurat von ihren Anfängen bis zur Zeit der III. Dynastie von Ur (Leipzig, 1941); Der Turmbau zu Babel, ein Märchen? (Bonifacius-Druckerei, Paderborn). 22 Sousa, Ahmed, Atlas of Iraq (Baghdad, 1953); A Graphic Summary of Agriculture in Iraq (Baghdad, 1956); Illustrated Map of Iraq for Development Projects, compiled by A. Karim Rifaat; Nikitine, Basile, Les Kurdes (Paris, 1956), map 11.

Printed in the Netherlands by Koch & Knuttel (Gouda),
Rotogravure (Leiden) and Senefelder (Amsterdam).